21·
RUSSIAN
SHORT PROSE
FROM AN
ODD
CENTURY

Cultural Syllabus

Series Editor:
Mark Lipovetsky (Columbia University)

21·
RUSSIAN
SHORT PROSE
FROM AN
ODD
CENTURY

The publication of this book is supported by
TRANSKRIPT: The Program for the Support of
Translation of Russian Fiction, Poetry, and
Non-fiction.

Library of Congress Cataloging-in-Publication Data

Names: Lipovetsky, M. N. (Mark Naumovich), editor, writer of introduction.
Title: 21 : Russian short prose from an odd century / edited and with an
  introduction by Mark Lipovetsky.
Other titles: Russian short prose from the odd century | Twenty one
Description: Boston : Academic Studies Press, 2019. | Series: Cultural
  syllabus
Identifiers: LCCN 2019008808 (print) | LCCN 2019018911 (ebook) | ISBN
  9781644690567 (ebook) | ISBN 9781644690550 (pbk.)
Subjects: LCSH: Russian prose literature--21st century. | LCGFT: Fiction.
Classification: LCC PG3266 (ebook) | LCC PG3266 .A15 2019 (print) | DDC
  891.73/010805--dc23
LC record available at https://lccn.loc.gov/2019008808

ISBN 978-1-64469-061-1 (hardcover)
ISBN 978-1-64469-056-7 (ebook)
ISBN 978-1-64469-055-0 (paper)

Book design by Lapiz Digital Services.
Cover design by Ivan Grave.

Published by Academic Studies Press.
1577 Beacon Street, Brookline, MA 02446 USA
press@academicstudiespress.com
www.academicstudiespress.com

Contents

Acknowledgements

I am sincerely grateful to all of the authors who, without hesitation, generously granted us the rights to translate their brilliant pieces. My gratitude goes to Galina Dursthoff's literary agency for the rights to translate and publish Vladimir Sorokin's short story. I am extremely thankful to John O'Brien and Veronika Lakotová for the right to republish Kirill Kobrin's "Amadeus" from his collection *Eleven Prague Corpses* (© Dalkey Archive Press, 2016); to Grove Atlantic Press and Nick Allen for the republication of Arkady Babchenko's "Argun" from his *One Soldier's War* (© Grove Atlantic Press, 2009); to Columbia University Press for Linor Goralik's texts from her *Found Life* (2018); as well as to Pantheon Books for the republication of Lara Vapnyar's "Salad Olivier" from her *Broccoli and Other Tales of Food and Love* (©Anchor Books, 2008).

This project could not have happened if not for the dedication and talents of Catherine Ciepiela, Jason Cieply, Bradley Gorski, Sofia Khagi, Simon Schuchat, Margarita Vaysman with Angus Balkham, and Maya Vinokour. Bradley Gorski, Simon Schuchat, and Eliot Borenstein skillfully edited translations, reconciling them with the natural idioms of contemporary English.

I am also grateful to Dimitry Kuz'min, Ilya Kukulin, Mikhail Pavlovets, Pavel Spivakovsky, and other friends who helped me with their advice on the selection of texts for this collection.

Certainly, I am most indebted to Academic Studies Press—to its wonderful leader Igor Nemirovsky and to its staff members, former and current: Kira Nemirovsky, Ekaterina Yanduganova, Oleh Kotsyuba, and Matthew Charlton.

The texts included in this collection, first appeared in the following publications:

Arkady Babchenko. "Argun," in *Novyi mir* 9 (2006).

Nikolai Baitov. "Fokus Solovieva," in N. Baitov. *Zver' dyshit*. Moscow: NLO, 2014; "Silentum," in N. Baitov. *Dumai, chto govorish*. Moscow: NLO, 2011.

Polina Barskova. "Listoder," in Polina Barskova, *Zhivye kartiny*. St. Petersburg: Ivan Limbakh Press, 2014.

Mariia Boteva. "Gde Pravda," in *Oktiabr'* 4 (2009).

Elena Dolgopiat. "Postradavshii," in *Novyi mir* 10 (2015).

Marianna Geide. "Ivan Grigoriev," in *Vavilon: Vestnik novoi literatury* 9 (2002); and *Oktiabr'* 12 (2002).

Linor Goralik. "A Little Stick," "1:38 A.M.," "No Such Thing, Come On," It's Funny, The Foundling," "We Can't Even Imagine Heights Like That," "The Cyst," in Linor Goralik, *Found Life: Poems, Stories, Comics, a Play and an Interview*, ed. by Ainsley Morse, Maria Vassileva, and Maya Vinokour. New York: Columbia University Press, 2018.

Aleksandr Ilichevsky. "Vorobei," in *Novyi mir* 7 (2005).

Margarita Khemlin. "Temnoe delo," in *Znamia* 10 (2005).

Kirill Kobrin. "Amadeus." Translated by Veronika Lakotová, in Kirill Kobrin, *Eleven Prague Corpses*. McLean, IL: Dalkey Archive Press, 2016.

Nikolai Kononov. "Genii Evgenii," in *TextOnly* 5 (April–June 2000).

Leonid Kostiukov. "Verkhovskii i syn," in *Druzhba narodov* 3 (2000).

Stanislav Lvovsky. "Rouming," in *Antologiia russkikh inorodnykh skazok*. Ed. by Maks Frai. St. Petersburg: Amfora, 2003.

Denis Osokin. "Utinoe gorlo," in *Oktiabr'* 10 (2013); "Novye botinki," in *Oktiabr'* 9 (2005).

Pavel Peppershtein. "Iazyk," in Pavel Peppershtein. *Voennye rasskazy*. Moscow: Ad Marginem, 2006.

Evgeny Shklovsky. "Ulitsa," *Novyi mir* 8 (2011).

Sergei Soloukh. "Obysk," in *Novyi mir* 9 (2006).

Vladimir Sorokin. "Smirnov," in Vladimir Sorokin. *Monoklon*. Moscow: Astrel', 2010.

Aleksey Tsvetkov Jr. "Tsenart," in *TextOnly* 29 (2009).

Lara Vapnyar. "Salad Olivier," from Lara Vapnyar, *Broccoli and Other Tales of Food and Love* © 2008 by Lara Vapnyar. Used by permission of Pantheon Books, an imprint of the Knopf Doubleday Publishing Group, a division of Penguin Random House LLC. All rights reserved.

Valery Votrin. "Alkonost," in *Zvezda Vostoka* 6 (2000).

Introduction

By Mark Lipovetsky

Although all twenty-one texts included in this collection were written in the twenty-first century, they are notably far more different than they are similar.

First of all, the texts in this book can be united by the label "short prose" only in the most abstract terms—in fact, they belong to numerous genres: traditional short stories, essays, absurdist parables, quasi-photographic snippets, fairy tales, and others. Some writers in this book are contemporary classics like Vladimir Sorokin, while others have published just one or two books and have never before been translated into English. The majority of these texts were written in Russian—but not all of them, which testifies to the global character of contemporary Russian literature. In this respect, the writers' places of residence—Russia, Ukraine, Latvia, Israel, UK, Germany, the United States—are quite telling too.

Furthermore, the writers represented in this collection belong to at least three different generations. Writers born in the 1950s—Nikolai Baitov (b. 1951), Evgeny Shklovsky (b. 1954), Vladimir Sorokin (b. 1955), Nikolai Kononov (b. 1958), Leonid Kostiukov (b. 1959) and Sergei Soloukh (b. 1959) had their dose of Soviet experience—some of them belonged to the underground, others sought to be published (typically in vain), but the bitter taste of cultural suffocation and political stagnation remained with them for decades. Which is probably why their prose is saturated with a *countercultural* energy that frequently manifests itself through innovative literary forms.

The next generation are those born in the 1960s, such as Margarita Khemlin (1960–2015), Elena Dolgopiat (b. 1963), Kirill Kobrin (b. 1964) and Pavel Peppershtein (b. 1964). These writers also caught the experience of the literary underground, including harassment from the authorities (like Kobrin, who wrote songs for a banned rock-group, or Peppershtein, well known as a nonconformist artist), but for them the formative moment coincided with Perestroika. This perhaps explains their sensitivity to *social* issues, which provide new storylines or suggest provocative rewritings of old plots (see, for example, Elena Dolgopiat's interactions with Gogol's "Overcoat" or Peppershtein's rewrite of *Lolita*).

The generation of writers born in the 1970s and early 1980s—Aleksandr Ilichevsky (b. 1970), Stanislav L'vovsky (b. 1972), Valery Votrin (b. 1974), Linor Goralik (b. 1975), Alexei Tsvetkov (b. 1975), Polina Barskova (b. 1976), Lara Vapnyar (b. 1976), Arkady Babchenko (b. 1977), Denis Osokin (b. 1977), Maria Boteva (b. 1980) and Marianna Geide (b. 1980)— gives voice to the first post-Soviet generation, whose youth and early maturity were defined by the fluid and dangerous environment of the 1990s. From adolescence, this generation has encountered war, poverty, sometimes emigration along with other major and minor catastrophes. At the same time, this is probably the most cosmopolitan generation in Russian literature since the 1920s. Almost each of these writers has experienced living in several countries and even writing their prose in languages other than Russian (like Lara Vapnyar, a representative of the circle of American writers of Russian/Jewish descent writing in English and living in and around New York). Cosmopolitanism expands these writers' worldview, but at the same time, paradoxically, pushes them to seek *existential*, rather than social, political, or cultural, paradoxes, dramas and comedies within diverse situations. Their texts balance on the edge of a parable or myth—even when their subjects are far from abstract, such as the war in the Caucasus (Babchenko), the Soviet historical past (Ilichevsky, Barskova), emigration (Vapnyar), national minorities in contemporary Russia (Osokin), or semi-criminal youth groups (Boteva, Geide).

In the twenty-first century, short prose, along with poetry, has taken over the traditional leader of literary process—the novel. Each of the texts included in this collection can easily be read as the outline of a novel— historical, epic, philosophical, non-fictional, fantastic, psychological, and so forth. However, the compression of such a novel to ten or fifteen pages not only intensifies the impact and eliminates everything secondary and superficial, it also offers a concentrated version of the very idea of literature or even culture. Certainly, each of these stories offers an algorithm or, at least, a contour of *its own* model of culture, with its own spectrum of real or imaginary discourses, symbols, and memories. Thus, today's short prose can be compared with a memory stick or with zipped files containing huge volumes of information—in this case aesthetic—in the most portable form. Why did this compression become necessary?

Probably, because the cultural monoliths that existed in Russia throughout the twentieth century—not only in official Soviet culture, but also in the different nonconformist cultures—either collapsed or transformed into something unrecognizable and amorphous. The atmosphere of disappointment in the political and social results of the anticommunist revolution of the late 1980s (known under the name of Perestroika) further aggravated this process, enhanced by a growing alienation from the cultural and political mainstream in Russia. Many of the writers in this collection came to interpret the Russian 2000s and especially 2010s as the steady course of the disintegration or marginalization of everything dear to them forced by the changing political climate. Simultaneously, the first decades of the twenty-first century witnessed the restoration of those dead forms of culture that seemed justly doomed to oblivion in the 1990s.

In this atmosphere, the writers included in this collection started feeling a very personal responsibility for the state of contemporary Russian culture. In her or his own way, each of them intends to preserve the seeds of *contemporaneity* as each of them understands it, following their predominantly modernist and postmodernist sensibilities. In a certain way, these attempts recall the strategies of the first generation of the Russian literary emigration—with Nabokov, Tsvetaeva, or Boris Poplavsky as examples. Another set of examples belongs to the history of late Soviet nonconformism, and, not surprisingly, the names of Venedikt Erofeev, Sasha Sokolov, Evgeny Kharitonov, or Andrei Sinyavsky mean a lot for many of the writers in this collection. Not only had these writers been creating vibrant experimental literature in the dark times, but eventually, they successfully formed a parallel contemporary culture, alternative to its official counterpart.

Certainly, it is too early to speculate whether the experiments of the short prose writers from the twenty-first century will thrive as their predecessors' had, but it is obvious that their texts need to be closely read and studied, since they present the finest example of what Russian literature can offer today, and make it possible to imagine what it will become tomorrow.

Nikolai Baitov (b. 1951)

Solovyov's Trick

1.

The train slowed down . . . then stopped entirely. Merch was in the bathroom. He suddenly became aware of the total silence all around. It was two in the morning. He pricked up his ears—no, it wasn't a station . . .

Gradually the silence became less total; the wind was murmuring outside. Someone was walking around inside the train car. A compartment door clicked nearby. A bottle landed in the trash—he heard the crunch of plastic . . . Whoever it was didn't jiggle the bathroom door handle, but stood near the bin across the way. He'd probably stuck his head out the window, trying to discern the glow of a distant traffic light . . . Suddenly, Merch heard the man reciting poetry, and fairly distinctly, too. But the voice was muffled and occasionally dissolved into muttering. The man was clearly talking to himself—there was no one else around. Merch struggled to make out the words.

> After the Moscow high-speed train <rumbled past> <. . .> the graveyard columns,
> No one there to hear how slowly
> the echo <faded> in the empty spaces of the skulls,
> Only a binge-drinking guitarist, out in the <cold and filthy> mire
> Heard the wind howl a quarter-tone lower <. . .>, and a sheet of music trembled. And he understood that everything's so much less simple than it seems, and that he needed to scrape together enough cash
> To move house further from the churchyard,
> And maybe even get a dog.[1]

---

1   This story features a poem by Igor Alekseyev.

The last stanza came out louder and sounded somewhat more confident. Merch quickly flushed the toilet, glanced in the mirror, opened the door, and stepped out.

"Excuse me," he said to the man's back. The man didn't respond, but when Merch touched his shoulder, he started and turned around—fearfully, Merch thought.

"Sorry about that," said Merch, trying to smile in a friendly and disarming way. "I was in the bathroom and inadvertently heard the poem you were reciting . . . You know, it . . . uh . . . just blew my mind . . . You know . . . uh . . . if you don't mind, I'd like to . . . um, I guess . . . make your acquaintance?"

"Make my acquaintance?" the man retorted listlessly (fear flickered in his eyes, then disappeared). "Well, why not. I'm Igor." He extended his palm.

"Really? What a coincidence: that's my name, too!" said Merch, shaking the man's hand. "But my friends prefer to call me Merch. It's my nickname. (Some people who don't know me call me 'Igor Merch,' so it even becomes a kind of last name . . .) But that's not the point . . . Tell you what, why don't we go to my compartment and drink some cognac? And maybe I can get you to recite that poem again—because I couldn't hear it too well, though I really wanted to . . . I think I want to learn it by heart."

The man looked at Merch without speaking for some time, apparently distracted. Merch was suddenly struck by his own fussiness. It wasn't like him at all. And what was with that tone he'd taken—so nagging and fretful? Merch felt ashamed . . . This man, Igor, was more or less his same age and build: a short, sturdy, healthy guy with a slightly puffy face, a buzz cut, and a small earring in his left ear.

"Your compartment?" the man drawled, sounding doubtful. "They're probably all asleep in there, we'd be disturbing them . . ."

"There's only one person there—my coworker. Really, though, he's my subordinate, my business manager. I reserved an entire compartment just for the two of us . . . He won't drink with me. He's being shy, acting all official. Not that I'm offering him any—I don't want to make him uncomfortable . . . Anyway, I doubt we'd be disturbing him at all."

"Well, in that case, it's fine." Igor smiled. "Not like I have anything better in mind: my own compartment's full, and everyone's asleep."

A minute later, they were sitting at a little table and Merch was pouring Dagestan cognac into plastic cups.

"I hate being on the train. It's always a struggle, I can't sleep, can't sit still. And the crowding, people everywhere . . . That's why I ponied up for a separate compartment, but it's not all that much better."

"You on your way to Petersburg?" asked Igor, sipping from his cup.

"Yeah, Petersburg. On business." With his pocketknife, Merch cut a wedge of lemon and handed it to Igor.

"What kind of name is . . . What was it, again? Merch? Where's that from?"

"Let's switch to the informal 'you,' OK? It's easier that way."

"Sure, let's. It kind of reminds me of the French *mort*, for 'dead man.' Is that where it comes from?" guessed Igor.

"Dead man? Jesus!" Had Merch been drinking alone when that thought came to him, he'd have crossed himself. But he felt too shy to do that now. Big mistake . . .

"No," he said seriously. "My handle comes from the word 'com-merce.' 'Merchant,' 'mercantile'—that's its meaning . . . By the way, the Latin name 'Mark' translates to 'merchant.' It's also related to the word 'market.'" Suddenly it dawned on him. "And by the way . . . there's also Mercury, god of commerce!"

"Maybe. But you wouldn't think it to look at you. You're 'marked,' all right, but it's more like a vague shimmering . . . I would never have guessed that you're in finance."

"Thanks a lot! No, I mean it. It's good to know I make that impression. I really didn't expect . . . But what about you—what do you do? And where does your journey end, so to speak?"

"I'm traveling with friends. We're going to Petersburg, for a festival."

"Are you a musician?"

"Why?" said Igor with surprise.

"Well, you were reciting a poem about a guitarist. I thought maybe you were talking about yourself."

"Eh, not really. I'm an artist."

"An artist? Did you write that poem yourself?"

"No."

"Who then?"

"I can't remember. I read it somewhere, or heard it . . . A good poet . . . I feel like he's from Samara . . ."

"You forgot his name, but you remember the text?"

Igor shrugged:

"Yeah, I guess so. Selective memory."

"Read it again," asked Merch, pouring out more cognac.

"Sure . . . and since you liked it so much, maybe you could write it down this time."

"Good idea. So I will." Merch reached into his travel bag for his notepad. Igor watched him, thinking slowly—it wasn't clear what about.

"Ah, I forgot. I wanted to . . . I need to charge my phone. It's on its last legs." He stuck his hand in his pocket, then reached into another pocket—in his jacket this time—to fish out the charger.

"Stick it in there," said Merch, pointing.

"Oh, I thought you could only do it back there, by the bathroom . . ."

"No, all the compartments in this car have outlets. 'First class,' you know . . . You don't have outlets in your car?"

"Dunno." Igor shrugged listlessly.

2.

After the Moscow high-speed train rumbled by
Past graveyard columns lusterless,
No one was there to hear how long it took the echo
To settle in the empty spaces of the skulls.
Only a binge-drinking guitarist,
Lying in a puddle of vile liquid, gave a sigh,
Sensed the wind's howling changing by a quartertone. A sheet of music lightly trembled.
And then he understood: it's not that simple;
I need to scrape together enough cash
And move house further from the churchyard,
And maybe even get a dog.

3.

After that, Merch talked for a long time. The train sped along, clattering. Merch was telling his life story. Igor listened, sighing or grunting once in a while. To a third party (like the business manager lying on the upper berth, politely faking sleep), these confidential revelations might have seemed completely inexplicable—were they really triggered by a completely random poem about a Moscow train, a graveyard, and a guitarist? But neither Merch himself, nor the sympathetic Igor (they had already finished the cognac, and Merch had extracted a fifth of vodka from his bag) found the connection between poetry and life at all strange. On the contrary, it seemed perfectly natural. Merch was now describing how, exactly, he'd gotten into finance: it's the early '90s. He's hitchhiking across Kazakhstan. (By that point, he'd already traveled around India, Tibet, and parts of China—the western part, where the Uighurs live . . .)

But OK, no need to reproduce his tale here: it's fairly uninteresting and rife with dubious details. But most importantly, it has nothing to do with the point of this story . . .

"Are you asleep, Igor?"

"No. Keep talking. I'm fascinated, I'm amazed."

"Are you being sarcastic? What's so fascinating?"

"I don't know. It all seems so normal, at first. Ordinary. But I'm amazed . . . You must be a talented storyteller, Merch . . . a shimmering one . . ."

"But actually you're falling asleep."

"Eh, no . . . But I am going to go . . . there's two hours left."

"Sure, go ahead. Which compartment are you in?"

"Number eight."

"Maybe we could meet up in Petersburg?"

"Stop by the festival, if you want."

"Where is it?"

Igor took a crumpled program from his pocket. Merch glanced at it: "At the Manege?"

"Yeah. Come around three. Or later . . . Three is when it starts . . ."

4.

Merch lay down on the lower berth, fully clothed, and listened to the ambient sounds, newly audible in the surrounding silence. The train was moving quickly making little noise and shaking even less. "That poem had the word 'rumbled' in it. That's the wrong word," thought Merch, glancing over at the table, where he'd left his notepad next to the empty bottles. The train could be described as "gliding rapidly." Merch even thought he could hear the passing stream of air murmuring behind the double-pane windows. "But maybe it sounds totally different on the other side . . ."

He started dozing off, only to wake amid incoherent snatches of thought. He tried to puzzle something out—and then, apparently, fell asleep for real . . . Not for long, it felt like ten or fifteen minutes—but the conductor was already walking through the train, knocking on compartment doors. Merch kept lying on his berth. His business manager shifted around, yawned, got up—"Must be getting close!"—and went off to the bathroom. Merch looked around in embarrassment: bottles everywhere. "I should've at least stuck them under the table . . . eh, whatever . . ." Finally, he got up and saw the cell phone Igor had forgotten. He went looking for him and ended up at our compartment.

"Uh . . . sorry . . . good morning . . . where's Igor?"

"Igor?" We were confused.

"Is this compartment number eight?"

"Yes, number eight."

"There's a guy traveling with you, an artist . . . he forgot his phone in my compartment. He was charging it and forgot . . . He's going to some festival . . . Is that where you're going?"

"Yes," we said, looking at each other. "We are. Look: there are three of us. Is someone else also going?"

Merch looked around the compartment in surprise (Sosna was still asleep).

"Who's in the fourth seat?"

"No one. That seat's been empty since Moscow. Maybe you've got the wrong compartment. Did he say he was traveling in this one?"

"Yes, number eight."

"Weird," I said. "Who could it have been? . . . And he said he knew us?"

"Yeah, I think so . . ."

Sveta took the phone from Merch and looked through the contacts.

"Look," she said, showing me the phone. "Here we are! And Elmar . . . and lots of other people, too . . ."

"Hm, interesting! What did he look like?"

Merch gave a brief description.

Sveta looked over at me.

"Sounds like Solovyov . . ." she said quietly.

"Who's this Solovyov?" asked Merch, sensing something amiss.

"An artist," I said with a sigh. "Our friend. Except there's no way he could be here. He died a year ago."

Sveta put the phone down on the table and got out her own. She found Solovyov's number and dialed. The phone on the table started ringing.

Translated by Maya Vinokour

Silentium

The purser said to start the sauerkraut. Mishka and Fedka went down to the village and loaded up the cart, but on the way back they broke an axle. The back of the cart sank to the ground. Cabbages started sliding off and rolling away. Cursing, the men began unloading the rest. Suddenly, they realized they didn't have an axe. There was no way to fix the axle.

"The prosphora baker borrowed it."

"Why didn't you say something?"

"Forgot."

"Oh, Lord, what a trial!"

Some young peasant matrons were passing by, on their way back from market.

"Hi there, dearies! You don't perchance have an axe, do you?"

"Ha ha ha! No axe here, just a barrel of beer!"

"It's not too heavy, is it? We're happy to help."

"Thanks, we're feeling all right."

"I bet we could make you feel even better."

"Ha ha ha! Like you'd be any good—I can see your tonsure from here!"

"I'm not tonsured everywhere—why don't you come on over and see?"

"Oh, so your parts haven't gone sour, you cabbagy oaf?"

Fedka answered with an even raunchier joke, which only made the women laugh harder. They sat down on a hillock overgrown with wild strawberries and started drinking.

Presently a wanderer appeared at the edge of the woods.

Though he'd downed a fair amount of beer, Mishka hadn't forgotten their task.

"Hey, man of God, you got an axe?"

The wanderer paused near the cart, glancing dully and humbly up at the women sitting with the monks.

"Axe," he said.

Mishka was confused.

"See, look, our axle broke, we need a new one."

"New one."

"That's what I'm saying. You got an axe?"

"Got."

"Give it."

"Give it," said the wanderer, not moving.

Mishka had jumped down from the hillock. Fedka stood up, too.

"Give it, where've you got it?"

"You got it," said the wanderer, staring so hard into Mishka's eyes that Mishka winced and looked abruptly over his shoulder. Behind him was only sandy road.

"What do I have?" said Mishka, perplexed.

"I have," said the wanderer, his gaze steady.

Mishka shuddered.

"Are you playing with me, man?" he blurted out menacingly.

"Playing," said the wanderer.

"Oh, so you're playing? How'd you like a punch in the face?"

"In the face."

"Here you go, then!" shouted Mishka and slugged the man in the ear. The wanderer rocked backward, but stayed upright, not even lifting a hand to protect himself. He simply repeated, "Here you go," in the same even, expressionless tone.

Fedka, who was milling around nearby, burst out laughing, and Mishka too felt himself released from fear.

"Ugh! God forgive me! A ploy of Satan, that was!"

"He's not right in the head!" the women remembered, belatedly. "They were talkin' about him at the market. He can't really talk, just repeats things."

"Not right in the head! He can understand right enough . . ." grumbled Mishka. "He's no fool—see how he looks at me . . . What're you looking at me for, man?"

"Looking."

"Yeah, 'looking.' You scared me . . ."

"Me . . ."

"What a trial! But what can you do," said Mishka, turning to Fedka. "Listen, give him a coin and let him be on his way."

Fedka searched his pockets.

"Here, man of God, forgive us . . ."

"Us."

"Go with God."

"With God," said the wanderer and stayed where he was.

"We shouldn't have hit you . . ."

"You."

"All right, enough," Fedka waved him off and started back toward the women. Mishka lingered for a while longer, cringing and hiding his face awkwardly. Then he began shuffling back over to Fedka.

The wanderer still stood in the road, as though guarding the fallen heads of cabbage.

The carefree little feast had now lost its charm. The matrons tensed up, pulled long faces, and, after a brief while, gathered their things and set off. Mishka couldn't bring himself to stay any longer, either, and soon went off to the village to get help.

Fedka didn't care, he wasn't afraid of the wanderer. Making the sign of the cross, he clambered onto the cart and dozed off.

Soon, however, the Hegumen's carriage came into view. He was returning to the monastery. Fedka thought nothing of it, felt no surprise at how lucky it was that the wanderer had appeared and the women had gone—though something to that effect did run vaguely through his mind.

"Stop!" the Hegumen shouted at the coachman as they rode up to the pile of cabbages. "Fedor! What on earth happened here?"

"Well, the axle broke, Father."

"So fix it . . ."

"We have no axe, Father," said Fedka, scratching himself in embarrassment. "Mikhail's run to the village . . ."

"Oh, so Mikhail is with you? And who is this?" said the Hegumen, looking at the wanderer.

"Some simpleton, been pestering us. Doesn't say anything, just repeats your words . . . And stands there, stock-still."

The Hegumen examined the wanderer.

"I know this man," he said to his companion, Nikolai Petrovich, a pious pilgrim from the nobility. "Hey, you, want to come up to the monastery with me?"

"To the monastery."

"Yes, to the monastery. Come sit up next to the coachman."

"Next to the coachman," said the wanderer and climbed up, readily enough.

The coachman slapped the reins. The carriage rolled slowly into the woods.

"Quite an autumn we're having this year," Nikolai Petrovich was saying. "So dry, it's such a blessing! There's been years when you could hardly take this road at all."

"Ten years ago, in Hegumen Pavel's time, he came to the monastery," said the Hegumen. "Lived among us for a while, then disappeared. I remember this man and wish to speak with him."

"What news of Father Zakhar? Is he well? Is he saved?" Nikolai Petrovich wanted to know.

"They say he's well. As for being saved—I know not: he does not attend services," the Hegumen answered with displeasure. "He has his repast brought to the woods. The people visit him also . . ."

"I will assuredly need to pay him a call . . ."

The Hegumen sighed.

"Let us hope you will find it instructive."

"Of course! Of course! Instructive, certainly!"

"Let us place our hope in the Lord, that He may help us understand everything in the correct way!" the Hegumen insisted, combatively and with mounting irritation. But Nikolai Petrovich had turned deaf as an infant or a grouse. The Hegumen realized that, in this case, hope wasn't in the cards.

By the time they drove up to the monastery, the vesper bells were ringing. Nikolai Petrovich made his way straight to the church. The Hegumen asked that the wanderer be fed in the kitchen and then sent to his cell. This was done.

The Hegumen was very preoccupied. He frowned, lost in thought.

"Sit," he said to the wanderer.

"Sit," said the man, and remained standing.

The Hegumen thought some more.

"I don't know what you keep your silence for. Is it for Christ?"

"For Christ."

"Or no?"

"No."

"There, you see . . ."

"See."

Suddenly, in his mind's eye, the Hegumen saw the multitude of people the wanderer must have encountered in his life. There were surely jokers among them, people who laughed and uttered curses . . . The Hegumen could not bring himself to imagine even a single one of those curses, so repulsive did he find them . . . but the wanderer repeated them all . . . There was probably blasphemy, too . . .

"I never once saw you cross yourself. Do it."

"Do it."

The Hegumen turned toward the icons and slowly crossed himself. Then he looked back at the wanderer, who stood there, motionless.

"We allow ourselves to imagine too much, and yet there are things we fear to imagine . . ."

"Imagine."

"But if we renounced all imaginings, could we love God? Answer!"

"Answer."

"I pray. And, of course, He to whom I pray exists. That is beyond doubt. The prayer itself is evidence. But where does the rest of it come from? Is He the one who answers?"

"Answers."

"I don't know. What if it is all my invention? What if others invented it?"

"Invented it."

"And if my prayer is vain and there is no answer, what should I do—cease to pray?" the Hegumen probed.

"Pray."

"You see . . ."

"You see."

"And what of strength?"

"Strength."

"Strength has its limits. Anyone might despair . . ."

"Despair."

"It is wrong to despair . . . Take Father Zakhar . . . It's a sin to speak ill of him, of course—he has descended into second childhood. But he prays to God, and moreover believes in many other entities: demons, angels, heaven, hell, in the miraculous power of relics and icons . . . He lives as if in a fog . . . But should this fog dissipate and he stand as though naked, will he not lose God? That's what I'm afraid of . . ."

"Afraid."

"Afraid?" frowned the Hegumen. "Don't be afraid!"

"Don't be afraid."

"That's right. Think for yourself."

"Think."

"That's what I'm doing. But answer me this—what of the Kingdom of Heaven?"

"Heaven."

"Does it exist?"

"Exist."

"Does it exist, or no?"

"No."

"So it's all the same to you?"

"To you."

The Hegumen nodded.

"Then it's not in the name of the Kingdom."

"Not in the name."

"And will we die?"

"We die."

"And if . . . there's nothing?"

"Nothing."

"And—it's all the same?"

"The same."

The Hegumen fell silent for a long time. A measureless fatigue spread suddenly through his whole body. He sat down on his cot. After a moment, he began to pray silently, but the words floated away and tangled together. He began to doze.

A short while later, he shuddered, sensing movement in his cell, and returned to himself.

The wanderer was standing in front of the lectern and writing something in a big book. At his feet lay a meager bindle.

"That's where he got the book from," thought the Hegumen. "He carries it with him."

He stood up to see what the wanderer was writing. He took a step—and realized he was still sitting on the cot. Horror boiled up within him. He jerked his body as hard as he could and this time stood up for real. He walked over to the wanderer and looked over his shoulder. Before him lay a thick heap of pages sewn through with coarse string. An inkwell, which the wanderer evidently carried with him as well, stood on the lectern. He dipped the quill into it and wrote in crooked, enormous letters, scratching the paper at every stroke.

AGAFYONA

IVAN

PROKHOR

MARYA

NIKOLAI

PYOTR

IVAN
MAVRA
MIRON
PYOTR
VASILISA
LUKERYA
PELAGEIA
PANTELEY
IVAN
EFIM

"A commemoration book?" thought the Hegumen, then guessed: "Ah, those are all the people who gave him alms and asked him to pray for them, and now he's writing them down . . . They probably said their names to him one by one so he'd repeat them . . ." But suddenly the words changed:

AXE
NEW
IS
GIVE
YOU HAVE
I HAVE
PLAYING
FACE
AT
LOOKING
ME
US
WITH GOD
YOU
TO THE MONASTERY
COACHMAN

Here the Hegumen recalled something and guessed the answer once more: "He's writing down *all the words he said!*" The Hegumen contemplated the huge number of filled-up leaves with dismay. "Is that in all his years of silence? From the very beginning?"

The wanderer kept on writing, then turned the page. The Hegumen saw that it was the last one in the book; all that remained was the nail-studded board to which the string that held the leaves was attached . . . As he approached the bottom of the page, the wanderer wrote more and more slowly, in larger and larger letters:

SIT CHRIST
NO
SEE
CROSS YOURSELF
IMAGINE
ANSWER
ANSWERS
INVENTED
PRAY
SEE
STRENGTH
DESPAIR
AFRAID
DON'T BE AFRAID
THINK
GOD'S
EXISTS
NO
FOR YOU
NOT
DIE
NOTHING
ALL THE SAME

The Hegumen leaned forward as far as he could, looking over the wanderer's shoulder . . . Suddenly, he said and thought at the same time:

"Would you give this to me to read? All of it. From the very beginning."

"No," said the wanderer and, without turning around, closed the book.

Translated by Maya Vinokour

Evgeny Shklovsky (b. 1954)

The Street

We often spent time on that main street. It was, of course, the most of everything. The most beautiful, the most enigmatic, the most enticing . . .

From time to time, toward evening or even a little later, after a few drinks or with nothing better to do, we'd get on a bus and make our way across the entire city. Some sort of incomprehensible force drew us there. By that time, the tall street lamps would already be lit, window displays with all sorts of exotic commodities would light up behind slightly dusty glass, neon advertisements would radiate forth . . . A lilac-colored twilight would spread over all of this grandeur, and through it the approaching night peeked carefully out into our eyes.

We immersed ourselves in this radiance as you would immerse yourself in the depths of the night sea, illuminated from within by little mysterious, trembling lights. We moved along the edge of this chasm, of these possibilities—indistinct but perceptible to every cell of our bodies—as along the edge of an abyss, experiencing the sweet and restless sensation of its proximity—all it would take is one step! We were ready . . .

But apart from this general atmosphere there was something (or, to be more precise, someone) in particular, which drew us there.

Women, naturally.

We knew that *those ones* were always on this street . . .

The older, more experienced guys said that there are plenty of them there, so many you couldn't even choose. Some of them do it for money and some just for fun (if they like it). They're just waiting for someone to call to them, and some of them offer themselves, practically grab you by the hand.

We understood that this wasn't in our cards—for them to grab us by the hand—we weren't old enough, but the thought that a woman could take you by the hand and lead you to a pre-determined destination, this thought would turn us into zombies.

God only knows how many kilometers we trekked along that rather long street. We loitered there on the lookout for hours on end but we never discovered the sort that our mentors told us about. Sure, we came across women, on the old side and on the young side, even plain old girls—in flocks, in pairs, and alone (this was rarer), but how were we to figure out if they were *those ones* or not?

No, really, there were plenty of them, plenty of people in general, in the evening on that street—some rushing somewhere with a fixed goal, some just walking, and some just out, *flâneurs*, like us, gawking about to the right and left, not hurrying anywhere. We came across ones standing around with or without ice cream or a bottle of beer—alone, in pairs, or, as I said, in flocks—discussing something amongst themselves or, it seemed, expecting something . . . But were these *those ones*—who could tell for sure? Neither their clothes nor anything else gave us any clues.

Just try and figure it out . . .

But we really wanted to figure it out.

Of course, the word "w . . ." is a curse word and was used most often precisely as a curse word. However, at times something sleek, supple, almost magical suddenly rang through its icy sonority. There was a summons in it, at times quiet like the rustling of leaves at night, but at others deafening like a roll of thunder, seizing you with a strange, uncontrollable shudder . . .

We stopped next to some kind of window display that reflected the portion of the street that interested us (where the individual or group that caught our attention was standing about) and, pretending to be immersed in the contemplation of the clothes, shoes, bottles, or electronics on display, looked on intently.

It was captivating: a girl might stroll by, thoughtfully smoking or impatiently glancing at her watch, her face at times obscured by shadows, at others lit up distinctly, her body hunched over wearily or taking on, as it seemed to us, an enticing pose (one leg held forward or a little to the side) . . . In each of what were, perhaps, her entirely accidental, involuntary gestures we discerned that special, enticing something . . .

Anyway, each time the fruits of our observations turned out to be entirely insignificant: alas, there was still no certainty that we had not been mistaken, that we had at last found her. More often than not the girl finally found her suitor, joyously ran to meet him, and walked away with him to a café or somewhere else, who knows where (maybe the theater or the movies), and there was nothing to attest to the fact that she was . . . precisely that . . .

It often happened that one of us would suddenly cry out (like Archimedes in a textbook: "Eureka!"): right there, right there, that's her . . . . And, once again, we'd act out a scene from a spy movie or something like that. We'd line up next to the display window and, in this mirror world, greedily examine our sought-after object.

Sometimes, getting carried away, we'd lose our sense of time and space, we'd forget that we were looking at the reflection in the glass, at the world turned imperceptibly inside out, and then we'd no longer be here. We'd be *there*, among the shimmering little lights of *that* street, in the restless dance of shadows and specks of light, among *those* women, who would then mysteriously disappear, leaving us only with the slightly bitter dregs of deceit. After all, it was us, not someone else, walking up to them, or them walking up to us, and then we'd walk somewhere together in order to immerse ourselves in the depths of this mirror world.

This mystery haunted us.

Once we were sitting late in the evening in a little square, not on that street but near our courtyard. It was deserted, nobody there except a solitary couple fifty meters away from us on a bench covered by a big, overgrown lilac bush, which reached out to us with its sweet, intoxicating aroma. We were smoking, growing more adult with every puff and gazing into darkness before us, where the couple was either hugging or something else . . . And at that moment one of us said: "She's a w . . ., for sure, I know her. She lives in the next courtyard over, and she's always with different men. Maybe she even takes money."

The couple, almost invisible behind the lilac, suddenly took on a degree of distinctness. A tension hung in the air.

There was something else happening between them, some kind of stirring.

But all the same we distinctly heard (together with a gust of light, warm air): "Some little boys are watching . . ."

The bushes trembled. The man who stepped out from behind the bushes made a step in our direction—it wasn't hard to guess his intention. "Don't," resounded out after him, no longer a whisper but a full voice, and the panic that pierced through it rang out like an alarm.

We got up, not waiting for him to reach us. We weren't looking to get into anything with anyone; we didn't need that. The woman's face grew pale in the darkness through the dull glimmering of the street lamp, and in that paleness there was a sort of sickliness.

After that incident we would occasionally run into her in our court-yard, alone or with someone else, and we'd follow her with our steadfast gazes until she disappeared from sight.

However, the mystery nevertheless remained a mystery, and what we wanted to read was encrypted far more artfully than the codes that we had deciphered. The collection of signs included: a thick layer of powder, brightly painted eyes and lips slightly resembling a mask, a short skirt, black pantyhose, a low-cut top. All this was very circumstantial (where did it come from?) and didn't prove anything.

The street, the street . . .

At some point we suddenly noticed that, wherever we found ourselves, one and the same gentleman—thin, on the short side, in a navy raincoat—would be milling around us. He kept appearing from somewhere.

At first we didn't ascribe any special meaning to this: so he's standing there, it could be anything . . . Maybe he's waiting for someone, maybe he's observing someone, just like we do. It wasn't out of the question that he was observing the very same girls. What if he had the same interest in them as we did (all the more so if they were *those ones*)? We didn't even give him a second glance (he wasn't reflected in the display window, but we could see him from the side), until it became clear: this person wasn't exactly here by chance . . . He kept glancing at us in a sort of strange way, too attentively for us not to catch on.

This started to ruin our mood. As soon as we'd appear on this street, he'd turn up right along side us, and not just when we'd stop, but also when we were just walking along the street. He'd follow us, taking up a position somewhere nearby and pretending that he was just going for a stroll or examining some display windows. It was clear he was spying on us.

But why?

We knew that *those* girls sometimes had bodyguards or whatever they're called. But he didn't look like a bodyguard: he was unattractive with a narrow, thin face and a small, black mustache and a cap pushed down over his eyes. No, there was nothing special about him, but the more time passed, the more a feeling of alarm took root in our hearts. If he wanted something from us, why didn't he approach us? And what good did it do him to spy on us, especially if we weren't doing anything in particular? Or was he waiting for something to happen?

He annoyed us. It's very unpleasant when someone's spying on you, especially in such a strange and, most importantly, meddlesome way.

It was like an apparition: all we had to do was turn onto that street, and in every woman we started to see . . .

How many times did it seem like someone was watching us in an inviting way? We'd glance back and we really would notice some woman nearby, catch her sudden, grasping gaze. But nevertheless nothing else ever happened.

We already knew a lot about relations between men and women, mostly, to be honest, from the stories of the older guys who had already figured everything out. But there was something unreal about it, something more like fiction than truth. The street held the promise of truth for us, and we pursued it like moths pursue a flame, sought it in the flickering of lights, in display windows, in the flashing of different faces and in the noise of passing cars.

We sought but didn't find it.

But every time, as soon as we got in the bus, which crawled along intolerably slowly through the enormous city, our hope was revived. In any case, the mystery had to reveal itself to us, too, who knew how, but it had to. We just had to build up enough patience. The spaces we inhabited—the courtyard, the school, the neighboring alleys and back streets—all these were different from that street. All this was just like it was for anybody else—day-to-day life, schoolwork, yelling, quarrels, fights, games—but it wasn't like it was on that street.

There it was a holiday.

All we had to do was get out of the bus, walk a few blocks and turn left, and immediately we saw the glistening of the lit-up display windows, the headlights of automobiles swimming by, the advertisements radiating forth, people scurrying back and forth . . . All this meant that it was in store for us, too, but when and how, nobody knew.

So that was the game: look for a woman.

Or, to be more precise, determine—if it was *her* or not. All it took was for a hint to slip past and we'd put on the brakes and start to peer. The mirror world of the display windows served as our trusty aid, but if there wasn't a display window (the woman might be standing under the poorly lit arch of an entryway or at the corner of a building or somewhere else), then we'd have to look for other ways to observe her. We'd hide behind a newspaper stand or a ticket booth or contort our bodies into various poses, one of us with his back to her, the other half-turned, as if we were just standing there, without any special purpose.

We couldn't figure out where he kept appearing from.

Suddenly, as if he was waiting especially for us . . . Maybe he lived here, or maybe he worked here, who the heck knows. But he appeared almost immediately, as soon as we stepped on the pavement of that street. Now we had no doubt that he was spying on us, even though he was pretending that he was just doing his own thing. Since he didn't ever do anything, that was always the extent of it. But he killed the entire buzz for our game. Constantly feeling someone's steady gaze on you doesn't bring you much joy, especially if you don't know what's behind it.

At first we thought he'd eventually get tired of it: he'd walk and walk and then leave us alone, because what could be the sense in dragging himself along after us. No sense at all. We were behaving completely modestly: we weren't breaking bottles or harassing passersby. The only thing we did was bum the occasional cigarette. We didn't have any money, if that was what interested him.

But he kept tailing us.

We stop and he stops somewhere nearby. His cap pushed low over his eyes, he stares as if at something else, but without fail his gaze catches us, too, we could feel it. We didn't like that severe, almost mocking gaze. It was as if he knew that we were onto him, as if he knew why we were here. And this was the most alarming thing, some sort of unknown danger in store for us.

Everyone has probably had multiple instances in their lives when it seemed like someone was watching them, precisely when they'd prefer not to be watched. When they're ashamed. For instance, when you get into the fridge when nobody else is in the kitchen and take something that's been prepared for a holiday without asking. Or when you're digging around in your father's archive. Or examining your mother's bead necklace. Or when you're peeping at your curvy neighbor at the summerhouse when she's tanning in her bathing suit right in the middle of her yard. You're peeping at someone, and someone seems to be peeping at you, and you feel uneasy, because someone sees you engaged in this unseemly activity.

Although you can confront this unknown person who's watching you. You can say—hey you, go to hell!—and continue to do what you were doing:

smoothing off the marks on the cake that's been reduced to two-thirds of its size, longing for your neighbor with your dull gaze as she bakes in the sun, or something like that. You can spit on the whole thing and pretend it's only an illusion, that no one is really watching you.

The question is: who's watching you?

Some believe that it's your guardian angel (everyone is assigned their own). Some have more vigilant ones than others, and then you almost always feel their presence, especially if you're about to do something unseemly. Some have angels who aren't too sharp, and these people can ruin their lives pretty badly, and it's their own fault, all because their angel didn't look after them in time, because they didn't catch themselves with an admonishing gaze. Who knows what peeping at your neighbor—at first glance a totally innocent activity—could lead to if your angel takes a *laissez-faire* approach to his responsibilities. Or digging around in other people's things, even if they belong to your own parents?

But maybe he's not angel at all, let alone your guardian, but a terrible and righteous Judge. And he's not just spying on you but collecting all of your misdeeds and faults in a separate folder, filing one after the other so as to present you with your unpaid bill when all's said and done.

Or maybe it's someone else?

With an incomprehensible purpose.

One day this person in the cap ended up right next to us, really close, so close that we could see the blue bags underneath his eyes, his thin, sneering lips, and the pink birthmark on his chin.

We were standing next to the display window of a sporting goods store, pretending to be admiring some imported sporting gear: all sorts of balls, rackets, fitness machines (we really did admire them). But in reality, as usual, we were spying on two babes, who were hanging around near the newspaper stand with its bright, glossy journal covers. And suddenly we saw . . .

Yes, suddenly we saw him through the glass, right in front of us. He was looking right at us from inside the store, from behind those very same balls and rackets, which were reflected in the reflection of the two in short skirts and black pantyhose behind our backs . . . All this formed a sort of triple exposure: he was superimposed on us and them, they on us and him, and so on. It was like when you're telling fortunes by candlelight and a long, long corridor appears in the mirror and, from the murky depths, someone comes foggily into view.

Whether it was because his face appeared so suddenly and so startlingly close to us, or because he was looking us right in the face, barely hiding the fact, or because their was something unusual in his expression, in his sharp and fleeting sneer, we were overcome by an fleeting shudder, as if we had been caught at the scene of a crime (but really, we hadn't even . . .).

This was all too much. It seemed as if he really was expecting something from us, some sort of decision or action, he was beckoning us somewhere, dragging us into his game, the meaning and rules of which we didn't know.

Now, in this triple reflection, we felt like those girls in short skirts and black pantyhose next to the newspaper stand. They, too, it was entirely possible, may have caught onto the fact that somebody was observing them—with an incomprehensible intention—and for this very reason were glancing around.

Suddenly something connected us, as if we were threaded us onto the same, invisible axis, joined together for a single moment. But that was enough for us to get an uneasy feeling. At that instant, three more figures, male ones, also reflected in the glass of the display window, grew out from behind our backs, which we had turned away from the newspaper stand, and covered everything else.

They stood their behind us, strapping, strong, one in a jean jacket, another in a blazer, the third in a baseball cap, obscuring the girls next to the newspaper stand with their torsos and cutting us off from the street, which, none the wiser, continued living its bustling life. Meanwhile, the guy, the one with the mustache, just kept watching us and the shadow-figures (or, more likely, we were now their shadows) behind our backs, as if closing the circuit that had formed.

"So, kids, enough playing around. It's time to get down to business," one of the three said in a nasal voice, and they took us firmly by the hand (you won't get away). "Let's take a walk?"

Translated by Jason Cieply

Vladimir Sorokin (b. 1955)

Smirnov

For Boris Sokolov

Ivan Petrovich Smirnov—a stocky, undersized, eighty-four-year-old man with disproportionately long arms—was standing in his tiny, cramped, overstuffed kitchen, noisily slurping his tea and constantly glancing out the window, when the doorbell rang twice.

"Already?!" he exclaimed, shaking his large, thick-lensed glasses. Nearly throwing the half-empty cup, which was missing its handle, onto the tiny table, he hurried into the foyer.

He opened the door.

A well-dressed, smiling young man stood on the threshold.

"I've come to pick you up, Ivan Petrovich."

"How'd you manage to drive up?! I completely missed it! What a bird-brain, right?"

"We're parked on the street."

"On the street?! Sure! No way to get through around here! They've put all sorts of crap in the way! And here I am just staring out the window like a dummy!"

Ivan Petrovich jerked the keys out of the lock. He spoke sharply, loudly, abruptly, almost shouting, as though constantly arguing with an invisible but mighty foe.

The young man, smiling, walked up to the elevator and pressed the cigarette-scarred call button. The elevator arrived, and the young man held open the scratched-up, graffiti-covered door with his foot.

Ivan Petrovich locked his door, stuck his keys into his pocket, and buttoned his light-gray suit jacket, which was covered in medals. He walked briskly toward the stairs.

"The elevator, Ivan Petrovich," prompted the young man.

"Oh, no! No elevator for me!" shouted Ivan Petrovich, waving a long arm. "I'm stepping my way to heart health! Elevators are for the handicapped!"

He began to stomp down the grimy steps.

"No kidding," smirked the young man and stepped into the elevator.

Ivan Petrovich walked down the stairs, counting down the floors, medals clinking in time with his movements. When he reached the ground floor, he grabbed some junk mail out of his box, looked through the letters, balled them up, and lobbed them into the bin:

"How do you like that!"

He exited the building and began walking resolutely along the court-yard wall. No one was around at this late-morning hour except a woman with a stroller whom Ivan Petrovich didn't know, plus three sleeping stray dogs. Ivan Petrovich swung his arms as he strode, looking all around, like always. Now and again, he would peep into people's windows. His thick head, with its vestiges of short-cropped gray hair, sat snugly on his wide shoulders. He had almost no neck, his nose was as big as a potato, his chin small but stubborn, and his ears large, with heavy white lobes. His thick old glasses twinkled cheerfully in the warm August sun.

Rounding his five-story building, he saw a steamship-sized white bus with tinted windows. To Ivan Petrovich, the bus looked almost bigger than the building. Near the open door of the bus stood the young man, smoking.

"Like a battleship, right?" said Ivan Petrovich, walking up to him.

"Ready to sail around the world," said the smiling young man, exhaling smoke. "Please join us on the upper deck."

Ivan Petrovich climbed the bus steps, which were covered with a pleasant gray rubber.

Inside sat several veterans, their bodies sinking into the complicated-looking seats. Ivan Petrovich knew or had seen almost all of them before.

"Good day, comrades!" he cried, raising his hand in greeting.

A dissonant chorus answered.

He sat in the first available seat, next to a bearded old man in a light-colored hat. The man's blazer was also spangled with medals. He reached out a bony hand:

"All the best to Petrovich."

"Howyadoin, Kuzmich!"

"How you feeling?"

"Battle-ready!"

Smirnov and the old man laughed. The young man got on the bus. The door closed behind him. He picked up a microphone.

"Comrade veterans, we're all here and ready to go. Anyone have any questions, or is everything clear?"

"Clear! We got it! We read everything! We know!"

Ivan Petrovich also shouted:

"Everything's clear!"

And as proof, he took a little pamphlet out of his breast pocket and waved it around. On the cover was a photo of a man with a serious face and a chinstrap beard. A red bull's-eye had been superimposed onto his face.

A hand went up. "I have a question!"

"Go ahead," said the young man into the microphone.

"Is he in there for sure?"

"One hundred percent."

"Are you sure?"

"Absolutely. He's been in his apartment for four straight days."

"He hasn't been out?"

"Not even once. He's ashamed," smirked the young man.

"Those people have no shame," someone muttered.

"Oh, I assumed he wasn't there!" The quavering voice kept on.

"You know what they say about assumptions!" said Ivan Petrovich, shifting around in his seat. "They said so yesterday—he's there all right, the bastard!"

"Oh, yes, he's there," Ivan Petrovich's bearded neighbor nodded seriously and spread his hands. "Otherwise, why go?"

Voices sounded all around: "He's there, he's there."

"Case closed," smiled the young man. "Let's go!"

"Let's go!" answered the veterans.

The bus rumbled, started softly, and began driving down the streets of the little town. From his cozy seat, Ivan Petrovich studied his native town with pleasure.

"Five Tigers," said his neighbor, shaking his head. "And on our side, a hundred ninety-three!"

Ivan Petrovich laughed out loud:

"Five Tigers! Well, why not one, then?! Why not one?"

He poked his bearded neighbor in the ribs.

"That's right. Why not just one?" the man replied, holding on to his hat.

"Because they paid him!" said Ivan Petrovich, raising a short, thick index finger.

"They sure did," nodded the bearded man.

"They pay those bastards!"

"They sure do."

"You bet they do!" agreed someone in the back.

"And they'll keep on paying them!" Ivan Petrovich said, pounding the armrest with his fist.

"They sure will," agreed his neighbor.

"Sure will . . . sure will . . ." said someone in back.

"As long as there's a Russia—they'll keep on paying!"

"They sure will. And why not?"

"But when Russia is no more," said Ivan Petrovich, shaking his head menacingly, "that's when they'll fiiiinally stop!"

"That's when they'll stop."

"And then what?"

"They've got it all figured out."

"They pay when it makes sense to. When there's a political agenda."

"A specific one! A specific one!"

"Well, naturally, a specific one. It's all specific to them: how much, to whom, and to what end . . ."

"Here's what they're thinking," said the bearded veteran, grabbing his knees. "They are thinking, 'We'll aim at Stalin, but hit Russia.'"

"That's right! Good aim's the name of the game!"

"It's all about the money!"

"They'll pay all right, they'll pay through the nose . . ."

"They're all paid up already," said a singsong voice in back.

"Money doesn't stink!" Ivan Petrovich shouted.

"But not everything's for sale," nodded the bearded man and poked himself in the chest so hard his metals clanked. "This ain't for sale!"

"It sure isn't!" Ivan Petrovich shook his head, hard, and immediately straightened his glasses.

The trip to Moscow took almost an hour and a half. Ivan Petrovich's neighbor even managed an open-mouthed doze. Ivan Petrovich himself was wide awake, busily examining his surroundings. By the time the bus got to Profsoyuznaya Street, it was already past noon.

The bus turned onto Kedrov Street, drove a little further, and stopped.

The young man again picked up the microphone:

"We're here. It's a five-minute walk to Tkach's building. We can't drive right up—everything has to look natural, so to speak. You'll be relieving a group of veterans that's been there since early morning; they'll all go home. We'll be there for exactly two hours, comrades. If you feel ill, there's an ambulance on call around the corner. We'll be providing you with some picket signs . . . oh, right, I almost forgot! I asked you to think of some chants—any luck?"

"We thought of some! I did . . . I've got one . . ."

"Tkach is a crook!" shouted one of the veterans.

"That one we've got, but good start," said the young man approvingly. "Any others?"

"Tkach, your pants are on fire!"

"Great! We'll take it."

Everyone applauded.

"What about 'Tkach is a murderer'?!" Ivan Petrovich shouted.

"He's not a murderer," said the young man, making a serious face. "He falsifies the history of the Great Patriotic War. We must be precise in our definitions."

"That's right! We shouldn't exaggerate," said the bearded man.

"Yeah, we don't want him suing for defamation!" shouted someone from the back.

Everyone laughed.

"Any other chants, comrades?" the young man looked around the cabin.

"Hands off the GPW!"

"Sure . . . OK."

"Snotty Tkach!"

"That one I don't really get. It's not a crime to have a cold. Anything else?"

A tall old man with a long, gloomy face stood up and declaimed in a low, muted voice:

> Tkach, you bastard, listen up:
> We've had just about enough.
> Now it's time for us to say
> "Go back to the USA!"

Everyone applauded.

"Super!" said the young man, clapping his delicate hands.

"That's Potapov, he's a poet, you know, a famous poet," said the bearded man, shifting around in his seat.

"Well done, Potapov! Right on target!" said Ivan Petrovich, clapping harshly and loudly.

"You hit the nail right on the head!" someone shouted.

"Excellent, comrades," said the young man, raising a fist and giving the driver a sign.

The bus doors opened.

"Onward!" commanded the young man, and exited first.

The veterans began getting off the bus. Ivan Petrovich came out directly behind the organizer. After waiting for everyone else to come out, the young man nodded, pointing the way, and began walking.

The veterans set off, moving slowly through alleyways and backyards. The young man kept looking over his shoulder to make sure no one had been left behind. Then someone called his cell phone, and the young man began explaining something in tense, angry tones, bending forward slightly and jabbing himself in the chest with a skinny finger.

When they reached the right block, they saw a group of elderly people much like themselves, with medals and protest signs, standing in front of an eight-story brick building. The young man was immediately approached by two other young men, who said a few quick words. He nodded. One of the other young men gestured toward the group of veterans standing near the building. They immediately put down their signs and followed him around the corner. The young man who had arrived by bus led his group up to the building's entryway.

"Comrades, grab some signs," he said, pointing at some picket signs propped up against a bench.

The veterans distributed the signs among themselves. A couple of them featured the same face with the chinstrap beard, superimposed with red letters reading "Shame on you, GPW falsifier!" Others said simply, "Arseny Tkach is a falsifier of the GPW!" "Hands off our history!" "Shame on the falsifiers!"

One of the young men gave the veterans a megaphone. After conferring briefly, they gave it to frontline poet Potapov, who repeated his poem. After that, they all began shouting at once, looking up at the sixth-floor windows where Tkach's apartment was supposed to be. The windows were heavily curtained.

"Shame on Tkach! Shame!" shouted Ivan Petrovich, waving his fist.

"Get out of here! Go back to America!" chanted the bearded man.

They took turns shouting into the megaphone. Two young men stood nearby, handing out pamphlets to the odd passerby. The pamphlets briefly explained how military historian Arseny Tkach, PhD, had falsified the history of the Battle of Kursk.

Over an hour passed in this way.

Passersby repeatedly stopped and struck up conversations with the veterans, who in turn clarified the purpose of their protest. An old man wearing glasses and the uniform of an artillery major gave a detailed explanation to two women—one young, the other older:

"On July 12, 1943, a great tank battle took place near the village of Prokhorovka. As a result, our tankmen halted the German offensive on the southern edge of the Kursk Bulge, which affected the entire course of the Battle of Kursk, the greatest battle in the history of mankind, a decisive battle, as they say, in which the Germans sought to make up for their defeat at Stalingrad. After that battle, Soviet forces launched a counter-offensive, defeated thirty German divisions and liberated the cities of Oryol, Belgorod, and Kharkov. Stalingrad and the Battle of Kursk broke the Germans' back, as they say, once and for all. But the man living up there, where those windows are," and here the old man pointed to the sixth-floor windows, "insists that during the Prokhorovka battle, the Germans lost only five tanks, whereas we lost one hundred ninety-three! Thirty-eight times more than the Germans!"

"Five tanks . . ." the women looked at each other. "Isn't that too few?"

"Too few!" the old man smiled, revealing gold teeth. "We veterans also think it's too few. But not historian Arseny Tkach, PhD. He's written several articles on the subject, he speaks at international conferences, he travels all around the world and just lies, lies, lies. Now, how many people do you think were killed in the Great Patriotic War?"

The women looked at each other.

"Like, twenty million?" the younger woman asked the elder.

"Yeah, like, twenty," she nodded.

"No, my dear ladies!" said the old man, shaking his head. "Forty-three million! How's that for a number?"

"Forty-three? Isn't that too many?" smirked the older woman.

"Not according to Tkach!"

"But why is he doing all this?"

"That's what we're trying to find out!"

One young man with a bicycle couldn't for the life of him understand what was happening. He kept repeating:

"But, like, what'd he do that was so bad?"

Ivan Petrovich elbowed his way to the young man and raised a short finger:

"He shat all over the GPW! Yes indeed, and he'll keep on shitting all over it unless we stop him! Get it?"

"Got it," nodded the young man and rode away.

Some of the veterans began to grow tired and took turns resting on two benches. But Ivan Petrovich didn't feel tired. On the contrary, he was invigorated: he shouted, spoke energetically to the other veterans, gave explanations to passerby, and paraded around like he owned the place.

Suddenly Tkach's balcony door opened, and Tkach himself emerged. The veterans perked up and began shouting, jeering, and gesturing with their signs.

"Couldn't take it, the bastard!" said Ivan Petrovich with an angry, victorious laugh. He took a deep breath, filling his lungs, and, clenching his fists, gave a thunderous shout.

"Shaaaaaame!"

"Shame!" fitfully chanted the old major, who was standing nearby.

"Shaaaaaaaaame!" Smirnov shouted with all his strength.

"Shame!"

"Shaaaaaaaaame!"

"Shame!"

"Shaaaaaaaaame!"

A flat, rectangular object appeared in Tkach's hands. He turned it, catching the light: it was a mirror, which Tkach aimed at the crowd of veterans below. A large spot of sunlight started creeping over the group. The veterans turned away, covering their faces with their arms and picket signs. The frontline poet grabbed the megaphone and began speaking into it with his muted voice:

"Get out of our country, Mr. Tkach! There's no place for you here! You defecated into the holy spring of our Victory! Get out of here, go to your foreign masters!"

"Get out! Out! Double-dealer! Scoundrel!" the veterans shouted.

Ivan Petrovich walked to the front of the crowd and shouted out, louder than everyone else:

"Scoundreeeeeeeell!"

Tkach aimed the sunspot at him. A dazzling light blazed in Smirnov's thick lenses, flooding his eyes. But he didn't cover his face, didn't turn away.

"Keep shining! Keep shining, you bastard! Keep it up!"

Sunlight filled Smirnov's eyes. He opened them even wider, as though trying to suck in all of the sun's energy:

"Keep it up! Keep shining, you coward! Keep shining, you traitor!"

Tkach kept aiming the light into his face. This duel continued for a few long minutes. Then Tkach lowered his mirror and left the balcony to the sound of shouts and jeering.

Ivan Petrovich stood his ground, repeating:

"Keep it up! Keep it up, you bastard! Keep it up!"

He couldn't see anything; red spots floated in his vision. Two young men took him by the elbows.

"Are you all right?"

"I'm fine! Just great!"

Ivan Petrovich took a step forward but stumbled, seeing nothing. His feet in their old shoes scraped the pavement.

"One sec, guys, one sec . . ."

The young men brought him over to a bench and sat him down. He began to squirm, shaking his head and bulging his unseeing eyes, then suddenly went limp and fell over onto his neighbor, another veteran. An ambulance immediately drove up and Ivan Petrovich was carried inside. The ambulance drove away.

"He's fainted from overstimulation," explained the doctor to the young men after examining Ivan Petrovich. "His heart is all right. He'll be fine after a good lie-down."

And indeed, Ivan Petrovich soon came to. They gave him a couple of shots and drove him to the bus. He made it up the stairs by himself and sat down in the empty cabin. The driver was dozing in his seat.

Ivan Petrovich sat for a while, looking out the window. After about fifteen minutes, he stood up, got off the bus, and started down Kedrov Street. Then he turned and began walking through the alleyways, past some new buildings, past garages and a playground. He swung his arms as he walked, like always, and kept an eye on his surroundings. He paused to watch a rusty Volga with a shattered windshield and four flat tires being dragged onto a flatbed truck.

A pigeon landed on a low concrete wall near some trash bins.

"How do you like that!" Ivan Petrovich winked at the pigeon, indicating the Volga with his chin.

The pigeon cooed softly.

Ivan Petrovich moved on, avoiding the alleyways. He crossed the street and came out onto a spacious square with a large, new supermarket, to the right of which some Tajik workers were laying asphalt.

Ivan Petrovich stared at the supermarket. Its entrance was decorated with a garland of blue and red balloons. Underneath were the words "NOW OPEN!"

"Now open!" Ivan Petrovich nodded in agreement.

He stood there for a moment, then walked toward the supermarket. The glass doors slid open in front of him. He stepped inside. The supermarket's interior was spacious, well lit, and filled with the smell of newness. Solitary shoppers wandered with carts down long aisles filled with goods.

Ivan Petrovich took a cart and rolled it along the clean new floor.

He passed the produce section and paused for a moment near the juices, reading the names on the packages. He kept going, past a shelf of dry goods and pasta, then stopped near a long shelf of canned goods.

"Baltic Gold," he read off a can of sprats. "How do you like that!"

He nodded approvingly and kept going. He caught sight of the meat display and walked over.

"Hello," said a tall saleslady, smiling.

"Hello!" said Ivan Petrovich, shaking his glasses.

"How can I help you?"

Ivan Petrovich examined the meat, moving along the case. He read out: "Kebobs . . . steak . . . ground lamb . . ."

"We also have ground beef, pork, and chicken," the saleslady was moving parallel to Ivan Petrovich, eyes on his medals.

"How do you like that!" said Smirnov, shaking his head approvingly.

Next to the meat section was the deli.

"Salami!" said Ivan Petrovich, stopping.

"Salami," said the saleslady with a smile, also stopping.

"Oh," sighed Smirnov and straightened his glasses. "And sausages."

"And sausages. What kind of sausage do you like?"

"The white kind."

"There they are, right in front of you."

"How much?"

"Three hundred and sixty rubles a kilo."

"How do you like that!" nodded Ivan Petrovich.

"How much would you like?"

"Me? I'd like . . ." he paused, thinking.

"Half a kilo?"

"No," he shook his head. "Give me one hundred and ninety-three sausages."

"One hundred and ninety-three?"

"One hundred and ninety-three!" he nodded.

"Whatever you say," said the saleslady, smiling even wider.

She got out a pile of sausages and began to count. Ivan Petrovich stood there, staring hard at the display case. It turned out that the pile wasn't big enough, so the saleslady went behind a white door with a round window.

"Braunschweiger," said Ivan Petrovich, wrinkling his forehead. "How do you like that!"

The saleslady returned with another pile of sausages and resumed counting.

"Braunschweiger," said Ivan Petrovich, shaking his head. He gave a low whistle. "Yeee-up . . ."

"One hundred ninety-three exactly," said the saleslady, finishing up. "That's eight kilos and four hundred twenty grams. Would you like it all in one bag, or is two better?"

"You can . . ." muttered Ivan Petrovich, gazing intently at the deli case.

"I'll split it into two bags so it's more convenient."

He didn't answer.

The saleslady packed up the sausages and handed him two hefty bags. He took them and placed them in the cart.

"Anything else?" asked the saleslady.

"Also . . . some of that . . . Braunschweiger."

"How much?"

"Five whole ones."

She silently got out five Braunschweiger sausages, weighed each one separately, stickered them, and passed them over to Smirnov. He placed the sausages into the cart neatly, side by side.

"Anything else?"

"Um . . . nothing . . ." he shook his glasses and pushed the cart onward.

He passed the dairy section, turned and ended up in a blind aisle. On the wall was a large poster depicting a dog and cat eating out of the same bowl. The shelves in the aisle were filled with pet food. A young woman in a white coat was transferring bags of kibble from a cart onto a shelf. Surveying the shelves, Ivan Petrovich approached the woman. She turned around to look at him and immediately turned back, continuing her work. She bent over, stuffing bags onto the lowest shelf.

Ivan Petrovich took a Braunschweiger sausage and hit the young woman on the neck with all his strength. She collapsed on the floor.

"How do you like that . . ." muttered Ivan Petrovich, looking at the motionless woman. "How *do* you like it."

He stood still for a few seconds, chewing his lips ruminatively. Then he straightened his glasses, bent down and carefully placed the sausage onto the young woman's back. He took four more Braunschweiger sausages out of his cart and placed them on the young woman's back next to the first one, in a neat row.

He turned around and rolled the cart out of the aisle, then headed toward the checkout. The cashier scanned one bag of sausages, then the other, and said:

"Three thousand twenty-four rubles, forty-four cents."

"You like that?" Ivan Petrovich said and stuck his middle finger right into the cashier's face.

She stared at it in bewilderment, then turned her gaze onto Smirnov and his medals.

Smirnov grabbed his bags of sausages and walked toward the exit. The cashier simply stood there, mouth agape. Two security guards at the entrance were engaged in a lively, laughing conversation; one of them was showing the other something with his fingers. The crestfallen cashier shook her head, sighed, brought her palm to her face and doubled over. A small grayish-brown egg fell from her mouth onto her palm.

"I can't make it crack just like that!" said the cashier tearfully, shaking her head.

One of the security guards, a tough-looking redhead, suddenly began to flail around and whisper, his head jerking. He grabbed a penknife out of his pocket and slashed his left hand, still whispering. Another guard covered his face with his hands and emitted a harsh, deep, guttural sound.

Smirnov walked toward the guards. His movements slowed. He put one foot in front of the other as though walking through molten glass. His old shoes detached themselves from the floor with the greatest difficulty, floating like the air cushions of an obsolete landing-craft.

All around the supermarket, shoppers began leaping into the air, remaining aloft for a long time after each jump. A portly woman in a bright dress hovered in the air, tearing apart a loaf of wheat bread and joyfully, solemnly pelting other shoppers with the pieces. Those below didn't dodge; tears of joy streamed down their enraptured faces, spreading through the store like a slow rain.

Smirnov walked toward the guards.

A balding man with a mustache clung tightly to the back of a ten-year-old boy. Holding the boy aloft, he leapt into the air and, growling and crying, rammed him headfirst into a fridge of non-alcoholic beverages, slowly but with terrible force. The boy's head shattered the glass and began crushing the multicolored bottles, whose contents spurted out in energetic streams. The boy's blood and brains mingled with these streams.

Smirnov walked toward the guards.

In the fish department, a shortish saleslady solemnly lifted her colleague up over her head in outstretched arms, and, with a series of long screams, crashed her down onto the fish display. The colleague, frozen with delight, crossed her arms over her chest in slow motion, gratefully closing her eyes. Tearing off the woman's coat, pants, and panties, the saleslady grabbed a live sturgeon and began stuffing it into her colleague's vagina with incredible strength and tenderness.

Smirnov walked toward the guards.

Pushing powerfully off the floor with her cane, an old woman slowly and deliberately launched herself over the dry goods and pasta aisle and paused in the air over the meat section. There, a shorthaired saleslady was already awaiting her with two long knives and a solemn, wordless song. Prudently placing the cane between her teeth, the old woman descended and offered her back to the saleslady. With a joyful cry, the saleslady plunged the knives into the old woman's back and pushed her toward the wine aisle with all her might. Moaning patiently, the old woman floated across the store with the intense menace of physical potential, gathering energy along the way. The old woman's impact with the rows of bottles was spectacular: dark-red explosions sent sprays of liquid into the air, producing a constellation of droplets and shards.

Smirnov walked toward the guards.

A young man in glasses, jumping all the way up to the ceiling, kissed his own palms with furious intensity. His distant relative, genuflecting, sang and prayed as she hurled jars of eggplant caviar at him. Miraculously, the jars missed the young man and slowly crashed into the ceiling, showering the praying woman with their contents. The young man, paying no attention to this, kissed his palms passionately, whispering to them secret, vital words that came straight from the heart.

Smirnov walked toward the guards.

A swarthy, dark-haired cleaning woman, having torn off her clothes, solemnly placed a blue plastic bucket on her head and began vaulting through the store in long, catlike leaps. Threatening, triumphant howls issued from beneath the bucket. As if to propel herself forward, she broke wind in time with her wide, daring jumps. A gray-haired but youthful shopper chased after her, trying in vain to daub her with a piece of raw beef. In his delight and confusion, he ground his teeth with such force that they began to crumble. The shards fell onto the fresh meat, sticking to its surface.

Smirnov walked toward the guards.

Two female stockers, singing rapturously, departed the stockroom, bringing along a large slab of bacon and a radiator they had torn from the wall. One of them took a running start and slid across the floor, using the bacon as padding. The other jumped onto her back, brandishing the radiator. Steering with the help of their bodies' momentum and the bacon's slipperiness, the stockers glided along the floor in the direction of the checkout. On the way, the top stocker hurled the radiator at a shopper standing on his knees. The radiator sheared off half of his head, spraying brains onto the back of the cashier holding the egg.

Smirnov walked toward the guards.

Paying no attention to the shopper's brains dripping down her back, the cashier, grayish-brown egg still in her palm, removed a brass bobby pin from her hair and poked gingerly at the egg, sobbing and muttering:

"A crack . . . a crack . . . a fast crack . . . the crack we all need . . ."

But the egg showed no sign of cracking.

Smirnov reached the guards.

The supermarket rang with roars and screams of delight. The redheaded guard waved his lacerated left hand in a theatrical gesture. Some of his blood landed on Smirnov's face.

"You like that?" said Smirnov without stopping, nodding approvingly with his bespectacled head.

"A crack, a crack, a fast crack, a good crack . . ." muttered the weeping cashier.

The redheaded guard continued gesticulating theatrically with his bloodied hand, whispering something or other in delight. His colleague, still squatting down with his face in his hands, was making harsh, fitful sounds with his throat. The supermarket resounded with songs, prayers, and the sound of crying.

Two bags of sausages in hand, Smirnov exited the supermarket.

Translated by Maya Vinokour

Nikolai Kononov (b. 1958)

Evgenia's Genius

So.

The most important thing.

That you must remember while reading.

This is not a funny story.

1.

Although laughter, glassy splashes of merriment, choked giggling, masculine chortles, delightful squeaks, groans and a stiff, short general hubbub, blazing like a torch, will be the curious background of this serious narrative.

After all, these sounds, alternating, brazenly crawling over each other, flashed and swayed on the theatrical backdrop that was the corner of our small courtyard. It was like several chaotic radio dramas playing simultaneously over the invisible black plates of loudspeakers.

A hollow zinc bucket lit up with the screw-shaped ringing of a stream of water.

A shaggy steel-frame bed moaned and creaked like a carnation metronome.

Human guts moaned.

Tartar leather flip-flops shuffled on a path.

A knife scratched across frying pan, scraping off leftovers.

An empty bottle rolled onto nowhere.

A lid fell from a pot, like an apotheosis.

And, finally, a sagging door thumped a shaky slap in the face of sluggish sleepy time.

All of these multicolored, sumptuous screens of confusion, from which the joyful Evgenia emerged as a sleepy figurine, I can summon up as a trembling pneuma of hallucination.

At the very edge of my faultlessly distant, present perspective.

When I get a little distance from all of this, I can sort through it like golden onion peels.

Grind them to dust.

Disperse them.

And now the mirage, bounded by her laughter or singing, flows down to the utopian past, where, it seems, I too ought to have been happy to remain.

Forever.

. . . Her fully sounded life was encircled by only useless and somewhat painful non-aggressive accessories. After all, she herself was amenable, simple and absolutely transparent to the sight and hearing of strangers. But only the first, cursory and superficial glance.

After all, strangers could never in any way wound, infect or spoil her. Not a beautiful young woman, but an indestructible educational still life in the art studio of the nearest cultural center, or a skit played in the pensioners' drama club in our housing cooperative. Through its simplicity and completeness. What else can you add? Just a few instructive stories.

To begin with, her pragmatic mother, at least, considered her mature and fully developed by the age of twelve, so she sold her on May Day for a new six-button "fuck me" coat to a legless invalid on the ground floor. Strong and evil. Like an animated stump of ash lying in our yard. So Zhenya's[1] mom, like a decent woman, could walk out the gates of number seven on Glebucheva Street in a proper plush jacket that did not fully do her justice, which was given the indecent, but apt word, cited above.

But I, of course, did not catch those moments, because all the events belonged to a foggy post-war past, when invalids, like trolls or hobbits, piled up like a dam at the sources of meager rivers of commodities. And along the streets the wind was dressed in leaves of devalued money and piles of meaningless but beautiful bonds.

I was not yet in that pale world.

And only the tarnished shadows of that unwritten, sad mythology of irrecoverable price tags and unused ration coupons reached me.

---

1   Zhenya is a short form for Evgenia.

Folk memories of the era of ration coupons, cards, line records, and postcards surrounded the bitter past with the trail of a healing fairy tale.

Bond certificates were given to children, so that they got used to money, they were glued to the walls under the wallpaper, and the cleverest begged them for nothing—just packs of beautiful papers from stupid neighbors.

The final re-division of inexpressibly beautiful trophy crystal glasses and furs was over, which, however, did not enrich or ennoble anyone—neither the softest warmth nor the diamond soprano of cut glass.

They decayed, were used up by moths. They were just broken, they were not divided into six.

So, did Zhenya's encounter with a passionate invalid mean a moral catastrophe, a mockery of all her confused thoughts and foolish dreams?

Of course not.

A legless Priap, a splendid Xerxes in a garage-shed, where a blue, well-maintained two-wheel carriage glistened, with all sorts of small bins and boxes useful for home improvement on the shelves, tactfully and knowledgably performed on a low mattress behind the homemade altar that, within a month or two, with hasty rudeness, would have happened without him taking part, but went absolutely uncompensated for the miserable, fatherless family.

So it was not a fatal moment or a change in the whole being of a girl, but a simple dull fact in the life of normal people's springtime routine.

Whether it was good or bad is not for us to judge.

However, as they whispered later, this "fuck me" coat turned out badly in quite a literal way. Three years later, she fell ill and died of cancer. Long tormented, and tormenting a growing daughter by her agony. The daughter crawled, half defenseless, like an overgrown snail, from the house to the idiotic school.

No, all the same, there was no sin, because, as became clear, sin did not stick to her at all.

A winter scene.

The girl eats a mandarin, given by the invalid, and says dreamily, turning to the petticoat-shaped orange peel, before tossing it in a fresh snow-bank:

"So, why isn't the mandarin long, like a sausage . . . I would eat it for a long time."

All other scenes are exclusively from summer

. . . Having closed two doors at the entrance to the kitchen, she blocked the way to the toilet for about twenty minutes, which savagely plagued ten neighboring families. Suddenly everyone became impatient. They were nearly, violently, unable to hold it any longer.

A couple of buckets of hot water are steaming on the gas stove.

On the floor stands a small zinc trough, like the wingless fuselage of a glider.

The chemical smell of strawberry rises from the pink remnant of soap on the saucer.

Rainwater glistens in the big jar.

. . . Bathed, Zhenya went back to her room, illuminating the courtyard with a white glow of untrammeled cleanliness and extravagant freshness.

From the first basement floor angry Granya, in her hole, stopped chewing her holiday chicken wing, to look at white Zhenya on parade.

I remembered her appearances into the light from the stuffy, damp kitchen.

With hastily washed floorboards.

After the bath.

As if she had nothing secret and she existed only on her surface—in the swaying of her flesh, purring, in a chuckled "oh, I'll catch cold," in some amazing smoothness and totality of her voluptuous carriage with a towel on her head and soft rounded movements.

It was as though she was and was not simultaneously.

It was as though air streams were taking her to the place where she would become invisible or not exist at all.

Her white body was her only asset, with which she could pay, because her jobs were stupid and frequently changing. She worked as a conductor on regional trains, which barely crept along and consisted only of the smelly low-class cars. Then as a cleaner in the metalwork shop at the hardware factory. Drunks and rude people frightened her, like arrogant fauns, startling the lost but still unattainable nymph. After the night shift, she appeared in the kitchen as a pale spirit. Sometimes she appeared somewhere else, too—in the full twilight and deep silence of the unknown.

The height of her career was selling fresh bread in a blue stall on Neglinnaya Street. But how hard it was to pass the qualifying exam. She stared stupidly at other people's notes, sitting on the bench in the courtyard. How much anxiety before seeing the medical commission.

"And if I'm at all sick, what then . . ." she muttered like an offended child for days, before going to the departmental polyclinic, where the highest committee of demanding doctors sat.

Only her body helped out.

They fell in love with her, they took care of her as best they could.

Below her window, they trampled the fallen leaves of the elm in the deep evenings, rolled crackling snowballs, and shuffled through the summer dust. They sighed, deeply and hopelessly. Excited, they blew up her name in the darkness, like a soft big soap bubble:

"Zhenya, Zhenya, please . . ."

"What's this 'please,' wanker, I know your 'please,'" she would answer the wankers.

"Come on out, huh, Zhenya . . ."

And so on.

Sleepless Granya began to hiss in the darkness from the basement window.

There were always cigarette butts at Zhenya's door and beneath her window, the signs of failed visits.

Incidentally, she had a husband and a single offspring, who resembled like a drop of water the blond-haired handsome dad, and this, as is well known, is not good.

The history of the marriage was not lengthy. Long Anatoly turned out to be, as she said in the kitchen, fearfully, "just totally psycho." The evidently quiet life with white-haired Zhenya so affected him that by the end of the first year of living in close quarters he found himself in a serious psychiatric hospital. And a flock of white-feathered angels descended onto him from the hospital ceiling in the sparks of electric shock.

He talked about this, sitting on the bench, piercing the glassy gaze of his interlocutor.

She somehow and quite easily distanced herself from him.

"And what if he suddenly gets it into his head to burn me with his little boy or something else," the divorcee thought aloud in alarm, as she turned to a frying pan of burning potatoes.

It should be noted that, for all her bodily airiness and lightness, she always overcooked the food, brought it to a "golden crust," to "heat and fervor," fried it, as they say, "sweet and black." And all the neighbors were notified by the scent of burnt lard or vegetable oil about her latest culinary somersaults. The only thing worse than her black anthracite blanchings were her brown ceramic minnows. It seemed that the kitchen was drowning in explosions of applause and burning ovations without end.

—Well, and off it went! Well, Zhenya, straight out of the witches' garage!—That wicked wise Granya, a professional chauffeur all her life, waved away the smell of smoke.

The lenses of Granya's glasses were tied with an elastic band to the gray bun on the crown of her head. She always broke off the handles, explaining: "They rub at my hearing."

Like an amphibian, she first sniffed squeamishly, then with hatred enlarged a hundred times by the lenses, she stared fixedly.

"Is that how you cook a carp, you idiot?! Look, it's still dancing on the fire!

So, Zhenya lived with her little tot.

More precisely, the tot lived first in a nursery for infants, then in a regional kindergarten, then in a rural boarding school for troubled youth, and then in other such institutions of tender state oversight.

From there he brought home lovely juvenile prison crafts.

A tiny guillotine for green sap flies.

A skillful net to catch kitchen wastewater mice.

A large slingshot for furious dogs, and a trap with a tin catch for rabid cats.

All inlaid with a homey surface—covered in checks, stars, crosses, and oblique-pitted tick marks . . .

The whole courtyard was touched, in an exaggerated, ingratiating manner by these marks of his arrest.

The residents seemed to understand that one day they too would be executed. So, at least it should be with beautiful weapons.

They felt and stroked them, like strange letters from the blind, squeezed out and punctured in the curious tattoo of Braille.

The kindly neighbors obsequiously, almost bowing, gave the kid tools and shamed me with the example of this skillful butcher. After all, I could not cut up anything so well, saw or moreover, burn anything. Our little dog Tobik, that senseless barker, and old mangy Muska, just in case, were lured home with something delicious.

But Tobik's owner, my grandfather, a short while later, bitterly mourned the fate of beloved marvelous telescope goldfish. Granya shook their eyeless, scorned bodies with stars carved on their sides by something very sharp, as she crouched over the frightened cat. Although under no circumstances would the pagan Muska drag them off to such a cruel ritualistic killing.

The ritual murder was hushed up. After all, no one was caught red-handed, right?

And the first shock came down to our courtyard that gentle evening.

In fact, I must admit that if it were not for Zhenya's son, then my oedipal history would be much more complicated.

During his short weekend visits to his mother Zhenya, he had a lot of time to teach me.

After all, we were friends then. And this friendship brought about great envy for my parents.

But the story is not at all about that.

It is mainly about the simple preparation of overcooked holiday food and the uncomplicated style of carefully kept vulgar clothing, about simple techniques of straightforward courtship and even more obvious ways of love and passion.

The fact is that the staircase to Zhenya's seven-square-meter nest on the second floor ended in a very small veranda, just like a perch, cut with maxi from overlapping thin boards, and I learned a lot, crouching against the cracks of this pitiful refuge where the officer's bed was stuck, listening with an ear, then an eye, then a nose.

The landing, all twigs and rushes, came out onto the roof of a low shed.

It was not difficult to climb the shed at all.

And this is what will be discussed next.

It is easy to imagine a musty evening's jelly atmosphere filling the whole room. Musty, because the inhabitants happily urinate right there into an empty tin bucket of the most responsive kind. Without quieting the muffled singing or simple purring.

I could see only the soft shoulders of a woman, the veneer of a light, beautiful dress, a head in curlers under a gauze scarf, a few escaped tresses.

I hear a knife scraping the frying pan, tearing away the burnt mounds of food. What is there? Pasta? Buckwheat? Potato? Noodles?

I was entirely indifferent to her expression at that moment, I did not want to see it.

I never suspected her of gluttony, slovenliness, hoarding, or other minor domestic sins. Overall, I conceived of her as the pure image of some sort of physical generosity. An image, as natural as light and healthy unblemished existence. Everything dark stretched somewhere out there, beyond the boundaries of my vision and, consequently, of my understanding.

With a basin full of various, soiled dishes, piled high with a ringing sound after a night's banquet, Zhenya walks through the whole courtyard.

As if bearing gifts to perform a ritual sacrifice.

She is charming, because she does not know she is being watched.

How did she share the enclosure of a tiny room, when that scoundrel child was there on weekends and holidays, that little saber-toothed predator, who taught me this sweet childish voyeurism through a delicate little sliver of light, through the trick in the wood? This is totally incomprehensible.

He whispered loudly, smiling, incisors smoothly grinning like an advertisement, looking at me, describing how "everyone" slept there on one cot as if camping

Who's "everyone"?

What do you mean, "as if camping"?

This is when he himself—at the wall with his nose buried in the rug, so as not to look, his mamma in the middle, and third the philanderer all completely covered with hair, at the cot's edge, so as to smoke freely or in case of the necessity to get up at midnight. An officer, you understand! During the warm season, the sleeping place on the veranda was usually also occupied. By Zhenya's girlfriend or someone else.

"Bastards bother me with their fucking fucking!"—he complained, bestial eyes flashing.

But most of all I liked it when Zhenya simply stood alone, taking up most of my visual field, bounded by the knot in the wood. Almost without moving, in the limp evening light. Like an amazing vision, equal to the timid light that nurtured her.

She seemed to ascend through its weakening strength, almost translucent.

I saw something through her. As if she were worn out, but not like a piece of clothing, but like a season, a time of year, like a ritual, repeated countless times, and therefore already able to let light pass through her.

As if I had managed to follow the course of her vague and equally transparent, unpretentious life. I did not find anything there, because there was nothing to witness.

I saw through to her feminine essence, because she did not hold my gaze at all.

The illusion of presence and evidence of impossibility . . .

I felt like a little squirrel, looking at the images of a dangerous world from the cozy oval of a tiny hollow.

In the lively, luscious fairytale forest, where everything ends well.

It's like I lived by her transparency.

Her girlfriend, who would often drop by, elegantly dressed, vulgarly painted. With one, or less frequently, with two guys. A totally flawed, crooked chicken-legged beanstalk next to her. Like an unearthed knobbly root.

At any time of the year, she and Zhenya, in thin, lightly smelling robes, would run to the main toilet with Zhenya, in thin, barely odorous gowns, several times an evening, passing through the whole courtyard. Embarrassed, sort of choking with laughter, gaggling, blundering with some nurses' accessories in a children's tin sand bucket. Like girls playing doctor, who were driven out of the sandbox by watchful adults.

Quickly and swiftly, like the wicked nymphs in the second act of *Giselle*.

I also saw and heard through the microscopic eyehole their hot exercises with a mighty naked knight. On a nail hung a tunic, a leather jacket or overalls, and I counted the stars on the epaulets or buttons. But Zhenya always shone not so much by her innocence, but rather by her guiltlessness. She seemed to have been forced to be involved in all these games. Tricked, when there was nowhere to retreat. It was as if she succumbed only because she could not refuse to receive her guests with kindness. It was as if it was essential to the plot of a story. After all, she could not leave her room to spend the night in the courtyard, or on the street.

"Quiet! Quiet!" She murmured invisibly from under a collapsed and gasping masculine mountain.

In general, they seemed to me characters from another distant world. Like germs. And, not seeing them, I could hardly restrain my agitated breathing, afraid to catch some special incurable pestilence, traveling through air from them to me. I didn't want to be in their place, I wanted nobody to stop me from watching, and to swim in the murky air around them like a sour fly.

In fact, Zhenya was most like a black-and-white photo of a bride. Especially a bride who is not yet a wife, but already a widow, somehow simultaneously. She seemed to have been caught in proud loneliness. Standing tall, leaning on the high back of an empty office chair. As leaning on the past, which in some incomprehensible way stiffened into the shape of a chair. Against a backdrop of the romantic folds of the vulgar gauze curtains. In a certain magic workshop.

I only now realized her special marital status.

I just now realized, to what she was married.

She was married to emptiness.

Since she needed no one.

Ever.

And, in fact, she nurtured the void.

Her offspring grew up, came into his own, became fiercely handsome and prepared for more serious challenges than those offered by the simple life of an ordinary student.

He stole with pleasure, turning various goods requisitioned from the neighbors into small sums of money. Maybe he was right to do so, because even in my mind, that of an educated, patient "good" boy, the neighbors had a definite oversupply of all sorts of knick-knacks, stuff, and things.

As it turned out much later under tragic and wild circumstances, the widow of his invalid father helped him, and even directed his activities. She used to go out to the junk markets in her late husband's two-wheeled cart, which she had never returned to the rotten state.

She wiped away tears of remorse, snot mixed with a baboon's makeup, bitterly lamenting, desperately shrieking an operatic recitative how she fiercely, oh how fiercely, her whole life, she hated this Zhenya. And she would not be forgiven for this inhuman, ferocious hatred. She hated this successful young bitch, this wench, whore, a rival, twelve-year-old odalisque, lying on the bed of her truncated, limitlessly loved beautiful emperor, czar, ruler, a Xerxes. And he was such a man, such a husband, when he was whole, when he had arms and legs. He could have been any-thing, and everyone knew that. And he was good. Oh how good he was! Oh!

And that is why she quietly developed in Zhenya's son the most laud-able qualities.

It was her revenge, cruel ruthless female revenge, stretched out over so many years, full of vengeful sweets and a comfort inexpressible in words!

But repentance came to the widow too late.

When everything smelled of frying.

So that is what Zhenya paid for the plush little "fuck me" coat—with credit, long-term and at a high rate.

When the beautiful blond adolescent returned from boarding school on vacation, the neighbors, in dull anguish before the inevitable, counted and tagged their better things.

But this time, the scratched and marked kitchen items remained intact, but a foreign tie with a monkey design, much beloved, unique not just outside, but also in the city, and—in fact, in the entire country.

Or even worse, and even more outlandish—a still decent, although once refurbished, German war-trophy gabardine jacket, and a not very old, also imported, rubberized raincoat.

They did not have scratch marks to indicate which room and which apartment they came from, and were not signed with blunt pointed initials, like the bucket, kettle, double boiler, or pot.

I myself saw how a wonderful raincoat, blue as the sea, was shamelessly taken off its nail and carried away, and how when it was handed off to some foul dealer close to our gate, its dry sleeves, as if in anguish, came free and with a crackling of their paper stuffing, strove to unroll themselves, like an epileptic.

To this day I can see that dramatic scene. So dramatic, that I don't know if I actually saw it.

The bills, which passed into the hands of the handsome boy, were smoothed, folded, and buried in the tight pocket of his stylish bell-bottoms. In the wildest, most natural gesture. Squeezed between two fingers. Between the middle and index.

To people's allegations, angry shouts and loud desperate threats Zhenya peaceably responded with unsatisfactory nonsense, not meeting the furious eyes of the crowd as it spewed curses. She sadly turned her face toward a dark corner of the filthy kitchen. There was a blue tin box, wherein dwelt an electric meter like a little god, monitoring the use of energy in our most stupid lives.

"O Lord, is there anything that doesn't happen in the wide white world?"

It was not in vain she said "white" because she had probably already imagined in her cloudy mind a world of an entirely different color.

"Such things don't happen in the white world!!!" Granya yelled at her, mumbling and ancient as fate, as the ecstasy of punishment, rolling half a wheel forward like the leader of an ancient chorus. She violently swallowed the vowels in verb endings, as it is done in the southern, the sun-scorched regions.

"They don't happen! Don't happen! Don't happen . . ." chanted the discordant amphitheater of dishonored, slightly better-educated neighbors.

The guy started frothing at the mouth.

A low smoke of dark rumors crawled out.

Like a dumpster fire one street over.

But the question was, did he wash the dried spot of blood from the sharp blade of his big knife?

And where did he wash it off?

Under the nozzle of the copper faucet in our kitchen.

The invalid's widow, she saw it herself.

And whose dried blood was so red?

An innocent victim, of course.

Or here's another question, more terrible than the first: in the courtyard, did not Zhenya use a rag on the raggedy cuffs and lapels of his Beatles jacket to clean off the sticky brain matter of those innocently felled by bat or sledge hammer? A good mother is capable of more than that for her child. All alone she scrubbed-washed-scraped so that not-a-thing was found. And they left with nothing.

Actually, it was unlikely—the neighbors reasoned. Our handsome boy doesn't look like a cold-blooded killer. They are completely different, an absolutely bestial breed. And he visits his mother from time to time. Brings her this or that.

But after all, a lovely dagger, the pride and charm of a man, that was good for everyone, ever since the previous war, and an iron ax, which is probably three hundred years old, sharpened and indestructible, and an absolutely indispensable sledgehammer—they all vanished.

In just a moment.

Here—only yesterday they were in the middle drawer of the cupboard in the corner of the shed, in the toolbox.

And now, search all you want—not there . . .

But was there vodka with faded ink stamp from some cheap bar or other, or just a little bit of damp sugar, such little lumps, bagged in newspaper, about a kilo each, as it happened, that Zhenya offered to her good neighbors.

And who among normal people would say no to such a good, inexpensive product?

After all, sugar, even slightly wet, is sugar, and vodka is still vodka.

And soon, in the middle of the freezing winter, when frost whitened the top latch of the front door, that strapping handsome blond guy, who never wore a hat, dropped out of sight for two and a half years.

The lives of our house's residents once again flowed in the usual way. From weekend to weekend. From winter to summer.

The residents even collected compassionate care packages from the entire kitchen. Cigarettes, cakes, underwear, a plastic comb, a book to read, tea, of course. It was too bad, after all. He was still a person.

They gave Zhenya a plywood box full of the goods.

Allegedly she used to send it all off to the cold, correctional distance.

But the collected donations sometimes returned.

After all, often people do not realize that all their sacrifices are pointless. In the long run.

But who thinks of the long run?

The stuff was not returned through the mail, of course. But in a completely different way, when those things that were donated had been forgotten. Like a vision—that distinctive green comb in the hands of another of Zhenya's boyfriends. A man's underwear, washed, hanging on Zhenya's clothesline. Granya suddenly recognized the origin of the underwear, their home port, so to speak, and she snatched the blue satin flag off its pins and brought it home.

Zhenya, sitting on the bench nibbling pumpkin seeds, did not say a single word.

It was as if nothing had happened. She didn't even stop nibbling.

2.

Exactly at the end of his sentence in the middle of the summer, he returned.

No longer as a person, but a blond, if darkened genius, with an undercurrent of violence.

He was full of an irrepressible force, like a spring wound a hundred times inside a child's tin toy.

But somehow it was obvious that inside he was quite dark, maybe even black.

That he was about to break apart. Because, despite his beautiful appearance, he was worn out inside.

Whirling like a dervish, faster and faster.

In the twilight of the kitchen, when he occasionally stopped in, he gave off faint, barely visible rays, which slowly trickled down into slippery stippled sparks.

Granny slipped, carrying a frying pan with a sizzling egg, as she moved around him on the completely flat, though not very clean floor.

"Ay, son of a bitch! Ay, go fuck yourself!" she hissed into the phone, which she had picked up to answer a call. It wasn't addressed to whoever called, though, but to the whiskers of a cockroach, that crawled out of the splattered black lattice of heavy pipe. "We don't have him, no, there's no Amphibian Man here . . ." she softly muttered a spell no longer into the phone, but into the oily darkness of the short hallway. Her eyes blazed behind the 150X strength eyeglasses, burned through the wardrobes in the corridor.

The young man's handsome face and elegant figure resembled those of the young movie star Korenev.[2] Only the actor is a brunette, and this one, ours, is blond. A wet and slicked back coiffure, whiskers shaved at an oblique angle, the depraved dull eyes of the touched without pupils, a lazy, but purposeful step to his rosy, light feline stride, and so on.

He never really let his cigarette leave his bent and painted mouth, curved like a snorkel. As if he could no longer breathe any other way in our despicable, poisonous misery, which was totally alien to him.

All the neighbors fell silent, stopped quarreling and snitching on each other.

It was as if they could sense with some secret gland, which is deep inside every person, but which lies dormant until needed, that he did not have long to live in the human environment.

That his term was over.

And that was needed was a special day and hour, for it all to come together, or multiply.

So that he would finally move to that other environment, unimaginable to an ordinary, limited human mind.

In the meantime, they just had to tolerate him.

He was still out there, vaguely inhabiting some place, appearing before his mother a few evenings, allegedly only to spend time with her as a good son, a night like before, in their cramped quarters. And in order to let everybody know that, for the most part, nothing had changed, and the end was in sight.

Later that evening I went to the kitchen to put the kettle on the stove.

---

2 The actor Vladimir Korenev's famous roles include that of the Amphibian Man mentioned above.

"If that's a woman, wait, let me rinse off," his body pronounced, turning to the sound of the opened door.

I went into the kitchen.

He was bathing, his thick legs spread wide, his white shiny butt sticking out, bending his lean waist, so as to somehow get under the stream of icy water flowing from the tap. A puddle of soapy water spread shamelessly all over the floor. Standing with his back to me, he dried himself slowly with a white waffle-weave towel. It was a flag one could use to surrender. Smoothly he combed back his curly hair. He dressed.

"Zhenya will clean it up,"—he said in disgust, stepping over the wetness. After another moment, finding the second sock, he corrected himself: "Mother will wipe it up."

"Mother, I said," he croaked somehow strangely, as though not to me, but to himself.

He was already not speaking to me, he would only say hi. Proudly offering a skinny, lazy, unmanly hand, always saying the same thing: "*Ziama*, gimme five." I became a *ziama*, a kike.

His smoky, almost blurry tattoos visible in the cut of his stylish "liberty" shirt, shone with a dim, alluring light.

It was impossible not to look at this catalogue of stars streaking his smooth, faintly shining skin.

One wanted to touch his skin.

Like one wants to touch a hot iron, spitting on one's finger and immediately pulling one's hand back from the hissing, sort of a not-fleshy body.

When he came by, or more precisely, made himself known out of someplace like a reproach to all living things, Zhenya turned quiet, waiting, like they sing in a restless Russian song, for something. And her awful silence spilled like a dark, unexpressed threat.

Those days she left behind her heavy, invisible traces, while her ordinary existence I saw as absolutely without any trace.

She struggled through the day.

She got caught in it, like a bee in molasses.

"My God, if I knew, if I only knew"—passing through the kitchen fumes, I heard a scrap of her dark mumbling.

She couldn't even wait for the kettle to boil,—the water inside did not even want to hum.

Oppressive silence dripped from their window on the second floor down to the yard, which turned to felt in the silence. And the silence trampled down everything, like a flock of dumb sheep.

It seemed that the day, which was barely reaching evening, would never end. Since everyone had already lived through it at one point, either in a dream, or in waking, like coming to in horror and cold sweat. They lived through it, but they left no traces of their lives in it. When and how? Why? God knows.

What happened during the nighttime, can't be described, it dwells in the shadow of nightmarish, absurd speculation; random incidents from the lives of others, absolute strangers, whom I have never seen near me.

What I heard with my own ears belongs to the category of sabotage and travesty of the foundations of life.

After that something happens.

At least all the leaves should have fallen from the elm that extended its powerful old branches to them through the window.

I went out to walk our dog. In his old age the once-agile Tobik had became a fat, wheezing, moody mutt with a bent tail. In addition, he had a weak bladder. But most important—he was very sad.

Here's a simple dialogue, signifying next to nothing.

It flowed like a dark sludge from their wide-open, single window into the yard, right on little Toby, who was disdainfully sniffing the miserable grass, and me standing next to the old Toby.

In total darkness, she asked him to do something.

Sleepy or languid, he quietly replied something or other.

She spoke more loudly, more irritable, demanding, inexorable, hotter.

"Yeah here, Zhenya, I'm fed up, I've fucking had it with you . . . you won't let me doze. What did you have me for? Answer me, you bitch, for what? For fucking? So, for fucking . . .?"

"What do you want from me? Well what? Well one more time . . ."

The ensuing sounds left no doubt as to what was happening between them.

Who they were to each other.

And how could they be anything other than what they were.

And how else could they come together into a single whole.

And my mind, as opposed to my heart, does not blame them, nor condemn their union, which took place where neither sins, nor nightmares, nor horror can reach.

3.

Big and wrapped in a pink and blue flannel bathrobe, frying pan in hand, leather slippers on her bare feet, she sneaks through the hushed courtyard, looking morosely in front of her.

Behind her, chewing on a cigarette in tight pants and a loud shirt, unbuttoned to expose the tattoo on his chest, a pan in his hands, he follows.

Narrowing his eyes, he looks around the courtyard.

Like a watchman.

Like a beautiful exorbitant price she has paid for an unknown something.

Both are beautiful, but quite different.

She is like a silent model who has left the sculptor's workshop, where she had just been formed. Like a bitter replica of herself from the past, full of sound, laughter. Like a hole, which nothing can fill.

He is just pure flesh, the substance of the body, that inexplicably may contain anything in itself: passion, suffering, happenstance, threat, but very little of the foundations of life, as if something had been removed from it. Or from him. He is like a piece of paper, tightly rolled, able to burst into flames on its own.

He comes out of the kitchen and sits down on the bench. A cigarette smolders in the corner of his mouth.

No one can confirm or deny what happened next—there were no witnesses.

I only saw a box of matches, a not-so-big burned spot on the bench, and some soil dirtied by something incomprehensible.

In short, she burned him up.

Burned him alive.

A one-liter can of gasoline was enough.

(Pause)

A funny, excessive tableau.

It takes place in the dirty kitchen downstairs, again almost without witnesses.

A stupid forty-five-watt greasy lamp is always on in the kitchen.

So it doesn't matter what time of day it is.

The length of the tableau is measured by unneeded words and is the width of one fierce unjustified action, repeated twice.

At the end of the same day.

Granya, surprisingly clearly, says to the whistling stove:

"Well, I guess he guess he caught fire all by himself."

The widow quietly and caustically hisses to the washbasin faucet:

"If I were Zhenya, I'd kill myself with my own two hands right away."

The widow and Granya each take a half-circle turn and uninterruptedly devour each other with their eyes.

Thirty-three years pass.

But going backwards.

"You've already done it, oh and it's done! Oh how long will you burn!"

Finally, chest full of burning air, the beautiful young Agrippina, who has magically gotten younger, spits in the nightmarishly painted ugly face of the fiend, like she wants to put out her fire, or stoke the flames even more.

The distance between the stove and the sink—usually less than two and a half meters—can no longer be measured in the ordinary metric system in this world.

Translated by Simon Schuchat

Leonid Kostyukov (b. 1959)

Verkhovsky and Son

For Nikolai

1.

State Counsellor Andrei Petrovich Verkhovsky was seeing his son off to the army.

He stood in a smallish crowd of people much like himself, enjoying the day without meaning to. The weather was autumnal, windy, and somehow merciless, with an uneven gray sky liberally sprinkled with crows. The ceremony was taking place near an old church, cracked and missing numerous bricks. Hideous birch saplings sprouted from its fissures. Andrei Petrovich, holding nothing back, inhaled through his open mouth and felt a sharp cold tearing at the back of his throat. These were the colors of the surrounding scenery: dirty white, gray, brown, black.

Verkhovsky's state was such that everything human felt false. The quiet, motionless sorrow of the older woman standing next to him might have been touching yesterday, but today it seemed like an artfully contrived mask of sorrow, well rehearsed in front of a mirror. All at once, Verkhovsky realized that he probably looked some such way himself—and felt ashamed.

His eyes sought out his son among those like him, and a long, cold needle gently touched his heart, as though testing it. He thought about how he had always been embarrassed to express his love for his son, which was little better than not loving him at all.

Verkhovsky, you see, believed that the boy had his mother, his grandma, and Aglaia for that sort of slobbery tenderness. His paternal mission, as he saw it, consisted in strictness (that is, in a single motion of the eyebrows) and sagacity (that is, in the unbearable repetition of platitudes). Now the hillock was filled with people seeing off their loved ones, and Verkhovsky thought he could see the crown of his son's head: his son, standing at ease, had taken off his cap and was spinning it on a fingertip.

Why had he not noticed this crown before? Tenderness and love, until now rigorously confined, gushed forth in a torrent, breaking through barriers, locks, vessels. The State Counsellor's eyes and nose began to run; he grabbed his handkerchief and blew his nose with a loud, unpleasant sound.

In that moment, he fully understood that he was seeing his son for the last time. Trying to ground this feeling in logic, Andrei Petrovich related it to the precariousness of peace in Europe. He juxtaposed the ambitions of the great powers with their capacities. He realized, with bitterness, that at any time some part of this rotting body could become inflamed and begin to bleed. (Yet even in this moment of oddly lucid intuition, the thought of world war did not occur to him.)

The sun was rising toward its zenith. The ambient light grew brighter, but for some reason the air did not warm up. Angry, truncated commands began ringing out. The splotch-like crowd of young men tensed, then transformed into a well-defined rectangle. The newly minted protectors of the fatherland were now almost indistinguishable from one another. In another minute, his son would be unrecognizable. Andrei Petrovich, his mind a blank, rushed down from the hillock, stumbling awkwardly and nearly falling at every step. Breaking the ranks, he embraced his son, pressed himself against his body, not kissing him, but only touching his cheek with his own, lightly. Two long seconds passed in this way. Then the elder Verkhovsky began looking for his son's commander so he could apologize and explain about the impending, ineluctable war. But the commander was waiting coldly, demanding no explanations. And so Verkhovsky gained one more precious second.

He was already walking away—not toward the crowd or the church, but in a third, vacant direction—when a well-rehearsed chorus of mothers began keening behind him, only to be drowned out by an overenthusiastic military band. He was walking away, promising himself he would not turn around. And so he didn't.

Glumly climbing into the carriage, he closed the curtain and found himself in such solitude that he nearly screamed. He jerked the curtain back right away. Hats, coats, and storefronts began to flash slowly by. His cheek burned slightly, as if remembering his son's touch.

Verkhovsky imagined telling his wife about what happened—but had anything actually happened, besides what had been known and promised long before? Verkhovsky recalled that he loved his wife. True, they hadn't spoken much over the past few years, probably because they had little left to say. Verkhovsky felt a desolate sucking or pulling inside his chest. He arrived at home, but his wife wasn't there. Aglaia served him a tasty dinner; he ate little, and with disgust. It felt like a rose was preparing to bloom inside his chest. He lay down, still wearing his best suit. There were approximately a hundred objects of various kinds around him in the large, well-lighted room, but right now he had no use for any of them.

Then, with a gentle burst, the rose opened slightly. He realized what it *was* and felt happy, because it meant his intuition had nothing to do with his son or the war.

He died rather serenely after three days, being of sound mind and memory, in his own room and his own bed. He spoke very little, but always about his son, Dmitry—how they should welcome him home, who might be good for him to marry. He recalled a toy sword that Dmitry had asked for as a child. He regretted never buying it for him. Now it was too late.

2.

Dmitry met the news of his father's sudden death with relative calm, having neither the time nor the freedom to respond more actively. He was merely an appendage to the body of the army, a body composed of senseless, but well-organized drills and a particular way of relating to peers and commanders. Dmitry, a pensive and bookish boy, grasped his new life with difficulty, and only intellectually. He struggled if not to understand, then at least to remember all those minute, innumerable rules and sub-rules. Meanwhile, his thicker-skulled comrades slotted themselves into military life as easily as cows find their place in a cowshed—a fact he observed with a certain envy. The experience of grief, and therefore grief itself, would have to wait until later. When "later" failed to arrive within a reasonable time-frame, his grief dried up and hardened according to the higher laws of time, which do not distinguish between body and soul.

As if in parallel to the young soldiers' maturation, the great European conflagration continued apace, in a manner so astonishing that certain of its characteristics passed by unremarked. Hearing the reports, glancing at the odd newspaper, Dmitry Verkhovsky felt neither fear nor sorrow. Over time, even his astonishment dulled, replaced by a torpor resembling the pupal stage in insects.

Dmitry's unit was deployed like a chess figure, all at once and to a distant location—in a way that evidently violated the rules of the game, since postal communications immediately broke down. A new, otherworldly life began, which could be reduced, in essence, to the alternation of day and night. Dmitry's body followed commands perfectly. His role in the war largely consisted in occasional exposure to so-called "enemy fire." Three times he and those like him were ordered into bayonet attacks, but not once did his blade meet living flesh. The war was being fought neither for God, nor for Tsar, nor for Fatherland. In the morning, it would always take Dmitry a moment to remember where he was, exactly, and to recall the month—both of the year, and of this ridiculous war.

It was in the very eye of this mad storm that he became a man, obeying with deft exactitude the unwritten law of the frontline soldier. He seduced a young Polish girl driven insane by the surrounding chaos. Verkhovsky won her over by giving his last name, which happened to be Polish. His unit changed its disposition practically that same night. His memory preserved the girl's frightened eyes, shining in the half-light of an enormous shed, at the other end of which a different soldier was making brutal love to a girl half-crushed by war.

Parsing the leaden language of the newspapers, Dmitry began to comprehend the law underpinning the current war. Strictly speaking, the existing language was inadequate. Words like *Italy* or *howitzer* were best discarded as trash. What mattered was that a kind of madness, or a global evil, had taken root and was now unfurling itself. Coldly, almost academically, Dmitry imagined new ways of eradicating human beings—and soon enough, he would read news of gas attacks. He predicted that people would exterminate their own kind in the general turmoil, that there would be pogroms, cannibalism, and systematic fratricide. Which is exactly what happened, shattering the traditional logic of war as easily as the average war shatters the logic of the world, occupying a realm beyond the laws of patriotism, ordinary human greed, even the law of money. It felt like pure evil, like a monstrous Mr. Hyde stripping off his one remaining disguise and trampling even this with fervid intensity, to say nothing of truth and beauty. Dmitry got used to lice. Even more quickly, he got used to losing his comrades. To be fair, he wasn't close with any of them; they were no more important to him than fellow train passengers. Besides his mild sorrow over the fallen, the younger Verkhovsky felt a touch of gambler's zeal, as though he were participating in a parlor game or a long-distance race. He moved himself forward day after day like a game piece, always outplaying his rivals.

He didn't think about who he would become after war's end: he didn't consider the future at all. But if we dissected and deciphered his brain, we would find a vision of madness and evil expanding steadily into realms inaccessible to reason. That, and a polite interest in the impending end of days.

For his authentic fearlessness, Verkhovsky was gradually promoted to the rank of lieutenant. He learned to drink and carouse while thinking of something else in the meantime . . . or rather, while avoiding thought entirely. One morning, it occurred to him that the external world was a pure formality.

This insight suggested a possibility for the continued survival of humankind. Awakening in a stranger's hut, in a country with an arbitrary name, a baffled Verkhovsky stepped outside and ascertained that, yes, it was cold. The dawn was mercilessly bright, the yard thickly overgrown with weeds, and a chicken was picking its way skittishly toward him. He understood that all this was normal and *absolute*, that only humans were afflicted with madness. We might say that Dmitry perceived a divine arbitrariness in the chicken, the thistles, and the wild mint, though he couldn't have named any specific plants. In that very moment, Lieutenant Verkhovsky tore off his epaulets, abandoned his weapon in the hut, and deserted.

He walked the road in uncomfortable military boots, vowing to trade them for regular shoes in the nearest town. He made his way northeast-ward: that was where Russia lay.

That night he fell asleep near the roadside and was overtaken by yet another advancing unit. When interrogated, he told the truth, expecting immediate execution for desertion and a subsequent meeting with the Author of the ongoing comedy. But the dead-tired officers, who were much like himself, evidently misunderstood him, concluding that he was exactly where he was supposed to be, or that his unit had been entirely destroyed. Perhaps they had themselves been swept up in the madness engulfing the world. In any case, they simply nodded at his answers, then saw to it that he was fed, given a weapon, and returned to the ranks. Out of politeness and gratitude to his inadvertent saviors, Verkhovsky played along with them for one battle: he ran where he was supposed to, crawled where he was supposed to, shouted incoherently, sent several soldiers to their deaths, and was praised for *bravery*. The very next night, he deserted again and began walking due northeast.

3.

In time, he managed to trade his uniform for worse-quality, but civilian, clothing, and became indistinguishable from the legions of superfluous members of his species. It wasn't that he couldn't be arrested or put to death, but he was now in no more danger than any of his fellow travelers in time and space. His face grew over with unkempt stubble. He bathed fully clothed in gray, alien rivers.

All that remained was to eat once in a while; luckily, the reigning condition was chaos, not famine. Verkhovsky would walk into abandoned houses and, without fail, find food that was touched with rot and degeneration, vile to the taste—but which nonetheless gave him strength to keep moving due north-east. Almost without thinking about it, he would throw into his bag one or two things that had been left behind in a panic: a copper coffee pot, a tarnished bronze pocket-watch case with no watch inside, a set of fussy sugar tongs.

At yet another half-dead market, a young woman rushed toward him. He did not immediately recognize the same Polish girl he'd sinned with in an enormous shed however many miles ago. Dmitry embraced her mechanically. Then he held her at arm's length and gazed into her face: the beauty of this woman, who was called Stasia, was blooming in the midst of war, the way grass bursts through the cracks of a brick wall.

From then on, they traveled together, even more slowly and without a clear sense of direction. They slept pressed against one another; rarely, and always suddenly, their touch crossed over into lovemaking. Both of them learned: she, Russian, and he, Polish—trading one word for another.

Dmitry didn't tell Stasia about his theory of global madness, but he did notice his companion's attentiveness to those norms that had not yet washed away. Stasia gathered little bunches of flowers and could distinguish more tolerable food from complete trash. She traded some of her valuables for a bottle of kerosene and used it to eradicate both Dmitry's lice and her own. Sometimes it seemed like they were finally approaching the outer limits of this inflamed territory, like they might spend a while pleading with some border official, and, paying him off with their meager treasures, return to the world of regular unfriendly folk as its most destitute and disenfranchised members. Such was their mirage of happiness.

Gradually, two names surfaced from the murk: Łódź—where Stasia's mother might be—and Voronezh—where Dmitry's mother possibly still lived.

4.

In some coastal town or other, Dmitry Verkhovsky was arrested by the local militia and subjected to a long but non-violent interrogation. He was questioned in English, which the counterintelligence officer hardly spoke and which the former Russian lieutenant had almost entirely forgotten. Verkhovsky felt comfortable and good because he couldn't tell which side the officer's countrymen were fighting on. Every one of Verkhovsky's deeds, every one of his words could be interpreted in several ways, which meant he could afford to tell the truth. When they had sated their appetite for conversation and all but exhausted their meager vocabularies, the officer took a drag of his stale cigarette and fixed avid eyes on Verkhovsky. And Verkhovsky saw with perfect clarity that moderate penal measures were in catastrophically short supply here. There was no place, and no reason, to keep prisoners; there wasn't even a need for forced labor.

Therefore, he would either be shot or released.

Three things occurred to Verkhovsky in the space of a single second: first, that he felt neither fear nor a desire to live; second, that he didn't want to prevent the officer from making the decision on his own—he even looked away. The third thought was a bit strange: the officer's hesitation, he reasoned, could never resolve itself completely. Even if he, Dmitry Verkhovsky, came out of this alive, in future he would always be a tiny bit dead; and were he to die, his death would not be total.

The officer released him.

Verkhovsky walked out into bright daylight. A carriage driver called roughly to his horse; sunlight blazed in a shop window across the street. The house next door was in ruins, brick debris arrayed in a fractured arc on the ground nearby. Inside the hollow building, a group of children were playing at war. Dmitry choked—it all seemed so normal to him. He headed home, to Stasia. On the way, he passed two of his comrades in minor marauding and nighttime bonfires. Verkhovsky greeted them, and they answered with dignified nods.

Stasia wasn't there. Through hand gestures and broken German, the aged Jewess next door explained that she had been taken away almost simultaneously with Dmitry. Where to? The old woman pointed southward.

Verkhovsky spent a month waiting for Stasia. During that time, the wooden house where he squatted was stripped for firewood. Whole groups of talkative people would show up and, paying no attention to Dmitry, tear out beams, planks, doorframes. Had Dmitry objected, they would have killed him, due to fatigue and lack of time. Dmitry took the overcoats from two corpses and was almost warm enough. In spite of the raging madness all around and the loss of Stasia, he felt *normal.* Moreover, he began to think that perhaps the tide of madness was slowly receding. In one ruined house, he encountered a library of Byzantine proportions and carefully picked out all the Russian books. In another, he found a sack full of various grains, all mixed together for some reason. At the market, Verkhovsky traded a pretty amber brooch for a capacious pot and could now regularly cook a mixed, tasteless porridge or simply boil water. The problem of nourishment was solved; moreover, an old man and a cat, both equally terrified, had now attached themselves to him. Verkhovsky spent his spare time reading and greedily absorbing: the history of Spanish theater, culinary wisdom, the confessions of an aging prostitute, the ravings of Tolstoy in his dotage, and the slow poison of Chekhov.

When he tired of this monotony, he left half a bag of mixed grains to the old man and the cat and started southward in search of Stasia.

5.

When he next shook off his mental fog, it was 1925, and he was a petty clerk in a dingy Soviet office in Tambov: a union member in good standing, a regular reader of the newspaper *Train Whistle,* husband to a medical orderly, and father to two little girls. Memory mercifully reshuffled all that had befallen him over the last eleven years, so that this bald, smiling man couldn't distinguish his actual past from the stories and myths swirling around him. Whether it was he who killed, or was to be killed—it all "stuck together," as the poet Sergei Yesenin so aptly put it, in one big, superfluous wad. The deeply normal worker Dmitry Verkhovsky, if we really did dissect and examine his brain, would be inclined to assume that it was he who had been insane in the past, not the world. But one good interrogation would be enough to send him spinning, to force him to divulge, through torrents of bloody snot, his abominable theory of global evil.

Global evil hadn't disappeared. It had merely switched disguises, discarding the mask of chaos and adopting a mask of order. And the sturdier and surer this new order became, the more attentive grew the sensitive beast dwelling inside this unremarkable man.

He was so unremarkable that it was unclear what his wife saw in him, and for what reason his antediluvian mother sent him packages from Voronezh, and why his two lovely blonde daughters stretched their little arms toward him. Smiling with his mouth closed (because his teeth were partly knocked out, partly decayed—in short, they weren't nice to look at), he would lavish children, both his own and not, with cheap candies made of poor-quality sugar. The children would accept them—some with sincere joy, others out of politeness, since food was no longer hard to come by.

Once, when he was absentmindedly making his way through the stalls at a lackluster Tambov market, Dmitry saw a woman who resembled Stasia. He looked at the woman, and the woman, lost in her own thoughts, stood motionless and looked back at Verkhovsky. In his new life, Verkhovsky was rather emptily gregarious—he walked up to the woman to explain his lingering gaze and tell her about the young Polish girl that she didn't even resemble all that much, in the end. Now they were face to face. "Hello, Dmitry," said Stasia. They sat down in the nearest canteen and compared trajectories. They could have met twice: in Krakow and in Lviv. Dmitry invited Stasia to his home and introduced her to his wife and daughters. His wife was in a hurry to get to work at the hospital and therefore inattentive. His daughters cozied up reflexively to the guest, for no human being had ever done them harm.

Not that Stasia wished them any. She felt peaceful and good among these people, like a seed inside the earth. They began to meet up frequently, almost daily. Stasia lived with her son, a tall, quiet boy bearing the Polish name *Mariusz*.

Stasia never did get around to mentioning that she wasn't in Tambov by chance—that she'd been searching for Dmitry and had finally found him.

6.

Dmitry Verkhovsky, waste processor for a new political order, was no fool. He knew that, more likely than not, Mariusz was his son. The best way to put it is that sometimes, he would have small, groundless doubts on this point.

Verkhovsky found an amazing, almost ingenious solution to this rather delicate problem: he treated the boy the way a good father would treat his son, or the way a transcendently kind person might treat the pleasant child of a stranger. We might say that they became father and son without calling each other "father" or "son." Verkhovsky felt no attraction to Stasia, though her beauty was now even more deeply rooted, in the style of the new state of order. He felt no attraction to his own wife, either, dispatching his spousal duty officially and seldom. Through the surrounding silence, he could hear a dull roar. That was what held his attention.

And when the first arrests began cropping up in a life that was increasingly orderly, and therefore better for Russia, Dmitry felt oddly relieved, because he had been anticipating something of the kind, and nothing is worse than anticipation.

The sensitive animal that had crossed Europe inside his skin during the First World War stirred within him. In this new, deadly game, there was nowhere to run; it was dangerous even to show signs of life. An invisible master of ceremonies pointed his finger at anyone who made a false move. Moving only his eyes, the cornered animal searched for a power capable of withstanding global evil, but found it neither in the world nor within himself. Verkhovsky struggled to keep himself from making the sign of the cross near the former church with its severed onion dome, where they were now storing potatoes. Storing them badly: they were constantly rotting.

It was probably Aglaia who had taught little Dmitry to cross himself near churches, but a strange aberration of memory cast his father in the role. Dmitry pictured him old, flabby, clumsy, as he had never actually seen him—not even that last time, when he'd suddenly started down the slope. At the time, Dmitry thought the State Counsellor had forgotten to tell him something important. On two subsequent occasions, he would wake up in field barracks with the feeling that his father had, in fact, told him this *important thing*—but it was already sliding away into the murky chasm of sleep, the way a cherry pit slides down your throat.

Balding, wispy-haired, slumped, he stood in front of the potato warehouse. Himself a father three times over, he thought about his own father, about a love that neither speaks nor hears, about the fact that, most likely, God didn't exist. The bell tower of the former church was fully perforated, wind blowing through enormous holes in its walls. A hunchbacked birch tree displayed its green leaves shamelessly from what had once been the building's second story. The animal plucked gently at Dmitry's sleeve. It was time to go, to float on a current of people like himself.

7.

The workdays began to grow longer, like daylight hours in summer. Neither decrees nor bosses, it seemed, were ultimately responsible for this change. It was a spontaneous phenomenon, as though the supreme god's insomnia meant that nature, too, would be afforded no rest. Only the stupid sun, which stubborn human reason had not yet been able to duplicate, kept creeping below the city's broken horizon. In those days, Verkhovsky returned home at night and departed at night, in the darkness around his building and the darkness of his family's two rooms in the communal apartment. He rarely changed his shirt or socks, not wanting to wake anyone by rummaging around.

But today there was light in his windows. The animal understood everything at once. The man dashed homeward—to protect his wife and daughters, if only ritually, to shield them from offense or humiliation—but the animal stopped him, gently. At this point he was the disease, the danger. In his absence, the family risked nothing.

Verkhovsky stepped silently into the shadows and left, himself more a shadow than a man. He walked quickly. His back was straight and his feet light, just like twenty years earlier.

He found himself in Stasia's neighborhood. He desperately wanted to enter his son's room, wake him, and press his lips to the lightly scented hair, to kneel for a moment near his bed. But this was a bad idea.

A terrible fatigue overwhelmed the former imperial army lieutenant. He nearly turned back, but stopped when it occurred to him, rather bizarrely, that his nighttime guests wouldn't let him sleep anyway.

Like a bare handful of others in those extraordinary times, he had the strength, brains, and courage to escape. He hitched a ride to the next town, where he wandered for three days like a soul after death, briefly joining little flocks of people, trying to become like them, spending his change on bread and beer, sleeping rough in the interiors of town parks. His guide was less the animal within him than the droplet of death infused into his blood by the foreign officer who had once held his life in the palm of his hand.

And when Dmitry Verkhovsky returned, he learned that the local NKVD branch had, all this time, been composed entirely of enemies of the people—which was God's honest truth—and had therefore been liquidated. Here was the frenzied mischief-making of global evil so familiar to Dmitry.

His terrible nervous tension resolved itself in a long sleep lasting more than a day, during which he was visited by: a union delegation from work, Stasia and Mariusz, and Kornetsov, a chess-loving neighbor from the next block. He was awakened by sunlight lashing his eyes. Bright, beautiful, woodwind-heavy music wafted from the radio speaker. The sky was a soft blue; everyone—his wife, Stasia, even Aglaia, rendered colorless by time and fear—everyone was still alive, he could press his cheek against any one of them . . .

8.

As a boy, Mariusz was quiet and cold, at least on the surface. When receiving gifts, he did not rejoice noisily, but expressed a dignified gratitude; never went wild for a delicious dish, but waited calmly to be offered seconds. Once in a while, the younger of the two Verkhovsky sisters (*the younger of the two*, the boy would repeat under his breath, savoring the ambivalent, unfinished phrase)—anyway, the younger of the Verkhovsky girls would sometimes succeed, with her simple-minded tricks and exaggeratedly feminine antics, in riling him up, and Mariusz would be transported into artless, childish playfulness. His thin cheeks would turn red as he laughed and squealed, whereupon Stasia and Dmitry, without conferring, would give him the exact same look.

Mariusz never asked his mother who Uncle Dima really was to him, because he knew: Dmitry was his father. He loved his father so much that there was sometimes too little Mariusz left for anything else. Love overtook him like toothache. With an involuntary, painful grimace, the boy would recall Verkhovsky's face, his hands, his gestures, the sound of his voice. Or he would strain his ears, listening for sounds in the echo-filled stairwell: wasn't that his father coming? He was always waiting, his heart skipping beats, for Dmitry to call him *son*, though Dmitry never even called his daughters *daughter*, but simply used their names. Mariusz dreamed of calling Verkhovsky *Dad* as if by accident, then watching him carefully for the next few seconds. He put off fulfilling his dream not from fear or shyness, but simply because no particular moment ever seemed quite right. The time ahead seemed endless to him.

It was love that enabled him to parse and articulate the era's defining trait: children's fathers were disappearing. Whispered discussions of *guilt* and *error* held no interest for Mariusz. Were he even three years older, he would have become an avowed enemy of the regime, of the exact type that the whole enormous country was then vainly seeking. But at seventeen, he could not yet distinguish the structure of world from that structure's flaws. This was unsurprising: even people much older, smarter, and more experienced than Mariusz were tragically confused about what was happening to them. Mariusz didn't grow to hate the world; he simply distanced himself from it. He became a consummate observer—and observers always appear cold to the objects of their observation.

Mariusz practiced losing his father. He would try to imagine *what*, exactly, would remain: his own memories, a couple of bad photos, three journals—although they didn't contain much about his father at all—no, the main thing would be his memories, and also, love itself. Maybe Natalya Fedorovna, who knew exactly who Mariusz was to her husband, would let him have one of his father's two suit jackets to press his cheek against. Returning from work at the school where—in an ironic twist of fate—she taught Russian language and literature, Stasia would often find her son red-eyed from crying, but her careful questions yielded nothing.

One morning, Mariusz awoke feeling oddly calm. As he puzzled out the origins of this state, he stumbled across the idea of the immortality of the soul. He plunged into faith instantaneously, lucidly, and so deeply that he needed no traditional religious supports. His didn't even think about God; he simply felt that there was a world beyond the limits of visibility, the way the wall of a building keeps going around the corner. He shared his discovery with his friend, a dreamy, sensitive, pudgy C-student. The friend responded very earnestly; and so, the space of Mariusz's imagination expanded to incredible proportions.

9.

There was a time when Mariusz's faculty for observation looked like sluggishness. He seemed to lag behind reality. But later, to his own retroactive surprise, the boy noticed that he far surpassed his peers in terms of reaction time. He didn't get swept up in waves of emotion; thanks to his long habit of avid observation, he could instantly grasp the essence of a situation. Mariusz knew exactly what to do and always had an extra second in reserve, whether it was a matter of answering a teacher's question or landing a counterpunch in a truncated schoolyard fight. At the age of fifteen, Mariusz dedicated himself to strengthening his muscles and excelled in this endeavor. He was not on friendly terms with the world. He earned only its cold respect, but that was all he needed.

By the time the war broke out, he was a strapping man, a Candidate of Science, and a junior lieutenant in reserve. By war's victorious end, he was already a colonel and soon became the director of a large scientific institute. As for the war itself, Mariusz didn't like to talk about it. He was wounded twice. His medals, he often said, were unit awards, not personal decorations. An *observer* who felt no fear and always had an extra second in reserve, he fought so perfectly that he may as well have been made of tin, with a living human brain. In his presence, people felt serene and detached from ongoing events, as though separated from the terror of destruction by a sturdy, transparent screen. Eventually, though, the screen would tear like the thin film of a soap bubble. People would break into a sweat or shiver uncontrollably, releasing tension by screaming, drinking vodka, or falling into the torpor of fatigue. But the big blond lug with the chiseled features never went to that place. Only once did the gaze of the army cook accidentally catch him crying: Mariusz's mother, Stasia, had just died from some seemingly harmless illness in a Tashkent hospital.

Most of those fighting alongside Mariusz believed in victory to a somewhat hysterical degree. Fully articulated, their credo was *victory or death*, which could be reduced to the impossibility of imagining defeat. Mariusz, by contrast, knew from the beginning that the USSR would beat Germany—through breadth of land and population size alone, through its refusal to surrender. Death was each man's personal business, but victory was the nation's destiny. Mariusz followed the Germans' advance with near cynicism: they were obviously *drowning* in the enormous country. The further they went, the thinner the air around them became. As for the dead, Mariusz kept in mind that their condition was temporary. Even the loss of his mother was merely a separation; the painful thing about it was its length, since Mariusz foresaw for himself a long and successful life. When a professionally rude surgeon told him he would likely lose a leg and looked inquisitively into the wounded major's eyes, Mariusz shrugged dispassionately. The doctor ascribed this cold indifference to shock and preserved the leg with lapidary precision—either on a bet, or simply to keep up the count of military livestock. Soon Mariusz was once again issuing orders, running, crawling, lying in wait—all of this in ideal quantities and with perfect timing, preserving a crystal-clear, devilishly beautiful snapshot of events on the transparent surface of his spare second.

Moving through Europe in a southwesterly direction, he inadvertently found himself near the locations of his conception and birth. Twice, he sorrowfully remembered his mother. Curiously enough, the thought of Dmitry Verkhovsky barely entered Mariusz's mind. Liza, *one of the sisters*, wrote the letters he received at the front; his father confined himself to falsely cheery marginalia. Were time to double back on itself by mistake, were the stern-faced colonel to encounter the philosophical deserter on the roads of Europe, he'd never understand him—or perhaps he'd simply shoot him dead.

10.

You're going to laugh when you hear how I got here. First, I got on the bus, for no reason at all. I wasn't even tired, I just had a sudden urge to get on, the way you sometimes desperately want things as a kid. The bus was a special treat for me—so pleasant, so cozy, with that familiar smell. You know how much smell means to us? It stirs our memories, stirs them right up . . .

Did I tell you I was your father? No, of course I remember telling you that, but you get so comically angry every single time. But still, just in case, have I told you that before, son?

Right, the bus. I got so comfortable in my seat that I fell into a stupor and missed my stop. It's not that I forgot, or got distracted by what I saw through the window; I understood perfectly well that it was time to get up and go, but I didn't have the strength, the same way you sometimes don't have the strength to wake up. I would try to stand up, and each time I'd feel dizzy—an intense fever would rise in my brain and my legs would ache. Fine. At that point, it would have made sense to ride all the way to the furniture store. I've been wanting to go in and have a look. But I didn't make it to the furniture store, because I felt an urgent need to get off the bus. No, it's not what you think, I just suddenly felt disgusted. I could hardly wait for it to stop. And when I got off, I nearly choked on the wind, it was such a clean wind, I thought it smelled a little bit like acorns. I love that air so much, son.

There on the hill stood a church. I started making my way to it, carefully. Carefully, because the sticky mud is so treacherous, and it's not just because I'm old—the same goes for you. You're no spring chicken yourself, son. I can't seem to remember, are you retired yet or not?

I walked along carefully, and a mother and child began to pass me, slowly, and the child was whining that it was cold, and wet, and windy, and I was thinking of the magical advantages of old age: for example, I didn't feel any of those things. But of course, I do wrap my scarf very tightly. The only problem was that it was slippery.

I recognized the area, there used to be a potato warehouse there. What a ridiculous custom—to set up churches in former potato warehouses . . .

I've been alive for a very long time, and my memory can sometimes get hazy. It's not that I don't remember things; no, it's the opposite, I remember too much, and things start to get confused, like tangled threads. I can't separate . . . actually, I don't know what exactly I can't separate. My mind works perfectly. I can easily multiply two-digit numbers in my head and rarely make mistakes.

And that's when it hit me. That hillock, those dirty yellow leaves underfoot. I was inducted into the Young Pioneers here, or maybe it was the imperial Page Corps, although, if we think logically, neither the one nor the other could have applied to me. The sound of trumpets, a drumroll . . . In some place just like that, I once shot at some people or other, or maybe they were the ones shooting at me.

The scene started to blur, the church began to change shape, so I leaned against that blotchy kind of tree . . . a birch, yes, a birch . . . so as not to fall, because it's very difficult for me to get up afterward, and I didn't want to bother anyone.

Liza is in Spain for the year. That means I have to live for one more year. And then something else will happen. You know, I'm a very lucky man, because I made it through the First World War without a scratch and was never behind bars for more than a day. Just try and find another person like me in my generation. I'm a regular champion, son.

They say my voice has changed from a man's to an old woman's—a strange metamorphosis. If I call somewhere where they don't know me, that is, some number other than yours, they always say: *Grandma's calling.* What a long life!

Yesterday—no, this morning—I remembered my father when he was young. He had just gotten some prestigious job, he was laughing, he sat me absentmindedly on his knee and bounced me up and down a couple of times, then put me down. You should go visit his grave, I can't make it out there anymore. I love staring up at the sky, the gray autumn sky, at the huge gray sky just starting to darken around the edges.

Translated by Maya Vinokour

Sergei Soloukh (b. 1959)

A Search

It was all gone. The shield was gone, as was the sword. A regular black-and-white photo was glued onto faded lines of the Russian flag. Just that. The rank, though, did not change. Remained the same.

"Senior Lieutenant Tagirov," Pavel read. No computers. Loopy. Handwritten. That particular skill is definitely not going anywhere. Obviously. And enough ink to last for an age.

"How can I help you, Comrade Senior Lieutenant?"

"Pavel Petrovich, are you aware that our department is currently investigating a criminal case of illegal entrepreneurial activity of the firm StarNet?"

"And how does this concern us, the ComServis company?"

"We have received investigative reports that in your office, located at the address of number 12 on the Prospect of Heroes . . . It is number 12, isn't it?"

"Yes," Pavel confirmed, "exactly. Prospect of Heroes, number 12."

". . . Here there are located documents and some computing equipment that belong to StarNet. Do you know anything about that?"

The lieutenant turned every statement he made into a question. A tail with a full stop. As if, you know, he was full of doubt. Contemplating out loud. Meanwhile, this is a completely different type of story. Comrade is looking straight into your eyes. No blinking. And there is no shadow of doubt in his black, investigative-service pupils. Well, maybe doubting Pavel Petrovich Valentinov's moral fiber.

"No, I am not aware of anything," Pavel replied with conviction. The temperature of the two pieces of black ice in front of him remained the same, below zero, this means it's OK, since Pavel's own eyes were not expressing anything aside from slight fatigue. Late-afternoon haze. The pewter of 4 pm. Good.

"OK," said Senior Lieutenant, "in that case, let's proceed into one of your vacant offices; do you happen to have any of those?"

"Yes, we do—a conference room on the second floor . . ."

"The investigator will show you the warrant, and we will start the search of the premises of your office."

"A search!" thought Pavel. "That's news! An unexpected turn of events. Before, they used to inquire exclusively about your soul, in a clean, hands-free way, with hints and allusions, and now they go straight to the business at hand. Give us your stuff. All of it. Show me. It seemed that they have changed not only the colors of their flag but also their status. On the other hand, could have been the change in my own status rather than theirs. We'll see."

A black jacket of a John Lennon–cut was flowing over Senior Lieutenant Tagirov's body. It had a stiff upright collar instead of regular lapels but was made, for some reason, out of shiny fabric and with ranks of biggish gypsy buttons. The Investigator and bearer of a wonderful surname, Mokrov, on the other hand, was dressed without any aspirations. Casual. The most worn-out fleece Wrangler shirt and grayish jeans with the same label. The only thing that linked those two co-workers were their boots. Shoes that were polished to a mirror perfection. Two Cinderellas.

"Pavel Petrovich, are you aware that our department is investigating a criminal case of illegal entrepreneurial activity of the firm StarNet?"

"Your colleague has just informed me five minutes ago."

"Very good. In that case, please, familiarize yourself with this warrant," said Mokrov and put a piece of paper on the table. Greenish. "Sit down, sit down," he added, as if the host here was not Pavel, not Nikitin, but he, Investigator Mokrov. Andrei Vitalyevich.

He was, though, quite possibly. They come in without knocking, with, so to say, their own keys. From Moscow to the farthest ends of the country.

"Thank you," said Pavel and pulled the insignificant-looking piece of paper toward him.

At least some kind of technology, some progress in their investigative file-keeping. This time, the document was printed on a laser printer. The important bit listed all of the sins of Leshka's company.

". . . illegal use of the main microwave transmission line . . . twenty-four illegal unregistered base stations . . . illegal profit . . . damage to the state . . . on a massive scale . . . fifty-four million rubles . . ."

"Twenty-four unregistered stations," Pavel thought, that's not too many for a common cell service provider. About a fourth, probably. I have about the same percentage, but not on cell service. About four stations without permits. Yes, exactly four. The papers have been circulating for about four years now. Walking about. Reorganizing the ministry. Governmental thinking. Yep: some of them are setting up traps while the others are waiting in the bushes with the bat. Lying in wait for the game. Calculating the inflicted damages. Inflicted on their nets and mousetraps.

"Pavel Petrovich," someone said above Valentinov's head. "Do you know anything about the documents and the computing equipment belonging to StarNet, and located in your office here in this building on the Prospect of Heroes, number 12? If you would straightaway point out where they are kept, it would save time for us and for you."

"It is, after all, the end of the day, on a Friday," added the friendly, approachable Investigator Mokrov, looking at Pavel in a tender, friendly way.

The bathhouse at the countryside dacha has not been warmed up yet—that was the obvious reason.—Well, well . . . The meat for the barbeque is spoiling in the pot . . . pork chops . . . Pavel decided for himself. Well, no matter—on the other hand, your beer in the city flat's fridge will have more time to chill, Comrade Investigator . . .

"I do not know anything about any documents or computing equipment belonging to StarNet."

A shadow of slight disappointment flickered over the investigator's eyes. A change of the shade of blue. Good. That meant Pavel's own eyes were still doing well. His green eyes. The same matte non-transparency of a man who works a lot, day after day.

"Tell me," he asked Investigator Mokrov. "Why is this statement signed by yourself rather than a prosecutor?"

"We don't need a prosecutor's signature, in this case," replied the bearer of the gloomy surname, in an unexpectedly cheerful way. "Here's the criminal code, article 182; here, you can have a look."

The book was opened on the required page. But Pavel did not read it. He understood, anyway, that they did not need it, in this case. He asked without any obvious goal. Just by the by. As a reflex. Silly, really.

"Where should I sign?"

"Here."

Another man with perfect shoes looked into the room. Pavel had noticed him already on the way here. He was going back and forth along the corridor. He could almost be mistaken for a visitor who came after hours. Looking out for something. For an energetic manager in the far corner of the office, or for a cleaner in the stairwell. Nope. He was just keeping watch.

"No hurry," said the new guest quietly but articulately to the investigating officer Tagirov. "All quiet . . ."

And then after a pause:

"The witnesses are waiting at the reception."

"OK, then."

And it turned out he was indeed looking out for the cleaner. They led in a fat girl with a mottled face, wearing a blue working robe, and some guy from the third floor. Probably the ski instructor from the tourist agency. In trainers. Both smiling incongruously. Well, why wouldn't they. Like they're in a movie!

Mokrov quickly filled in the forms with the surnames and job titles of all present. They signed again. Pavel managed to read: "Before the search (confiscation) commenced those taking part were given explanations of their rights, responsibilities, as well as the order of the process of the search (confiscation)."

"We will start from the right-hand side and will go through all the offices clockwise," Tagirov suggested.

No one disputed his suggestion. The hand of the clock pointed first to the only door that was locked.

"What do you have here?" asked the second officer. The other one, the one who was everywhere at once. Pavel learned his name from the report, too. A common one. Vaschilov. It's, like, OK. Kinda. Will do.

"The server room."

"Open up."

"I don't have a key. I need to call someone."

"In our presence, please," said the lovely Mokrov. A complete opposite to the fake Beatles fan Tagirov.

"Yes, yes, of course." Pavel took out his cell phone. "Artyom, could you please come up here with the server room key."

"Who is this Artyom?" Tagirov inquired.

"Our systems administrator."

It took Kutepov one or two minutes to come up. With a cigarette break, probably. As usual, for him. All of this time Mokrov was humming something to himself. Tagirov was studying Pavel, and Vaschilov warmed up his muscles by walking from one end of the corridor to the other. Looked into open doors, while all the others stood in front of the closed one. Did reconnaissance.

Meanwhile, Artyom showed up, the little devil. He came unhurriedly from the far stairwell and his face did not express anything. You might think someone comes in to inspect the company's hardware every day. Just like in the Tretyakov gallery. Or the Hermitage.

"Who has access to the server room?" asked Tagirov.

"All of the systems administrators and the engineers on duty."

"Who has access to the server room?" Tagirov repeated his question, this time addressing Kutepov. He had finally made it over. And was standing there, squinting quietly.

Artyom shrugged.

"Well, as usual . . . Those on duty . . . sysadmins . . ."

Harmony, thought Pavel, that's nice. I wish it was always like that.

The lock clicked in Artyom's hands. The air-conditioned semi-darkness of the server room opened up. A blinking of green lights and a rhythmic buzz of fans.

"Must be here," said Vaschilov with confidence and was the first one to dive into the *sanctum sanctorum*.

"If you could manage to not disrupt our client service," Pavel said as a follow up. Expressed natural anxiety. The technical director, after all. His duty.

"We can," Mokrov promised to him, sweetly. What a nice man.

"Thank you."

Meanwhile, StarNet's server was standing a floor below them. A big one. Right in the middle of the systems administrators' room. New and black. Among white tables. It was precisely Artyom who installed it and carved out a hole in the firewall for Leshka's accounts. Two weeks ago. Does Artyom understand why these people are here? It feels like he does. His lips and eyebrows seem to have changed their position on his face. Moved.

Only a little, though, and Kutepov's face did not express anything in particular. Even considering the small changes in its geometry. Going, going, stopped. Scratched his head. With his not particularly clean hair, bless him. What about his eyes, though? Today, Pavel Valentinov was interested in the optics. In breaking and reflecting the light. He wanted to make sure that the harmony of the five minutes ago was not a coincidence.

Because sometimes it just happens—singing in tune. Singing or snoring. Maybe, on a day. Or the day of the tricolor.

Well, it wasn't really important. The color of this Friday will be established later. After the negative's fixed. For the last time. For now, he just wanted to meet Artyom's eyes. For a moment. But alas. Officer Tagirov was getting ready to catch just such a moment, a synchronized second. He was waiting for it. Definitely. No doubt. And Pavel Petrovich simply turned away. His duty as technical director was to observe Vaschilov's movements in the semi-darkness of the server room. So, that was what he did. Just that.

"Are you the systems administrator?" Mokrov the investigator asked Artyom.

"Yes," confirmed Tyoma.

"In that case, please, come here and explain something to us . . . Is all of the equipment here property of your company?"

"Yes, all of it."

"And why is there no dust on this unit?"

"This is our developers' server," said Kutepov. "Two weeks ago, we took it from their office and moved it in here. For a guaranteed electricity supply."

"Connect the monitor," ordered computer-literate Vaschilov.

Even Tagirov was distracted. He really wanted to see what kind of invitation would light up on the black-and-white face. Pavel knew very well what kind, so his gaze slid indifferently along the walls of the corridor. Nikitin's secretary looked out from the reception room. Natalia. She was holding a cordless phone in her hand and looking at Pavel. She was trying to communicate something to him. Pavel immediately understood what it was and who was on the line.

Aha, this means that Nikitin has received an update. So he knows. And is waiting for the final report. Well, excuse us, Roman Andreevich . . . Excuse us . . .

Not losing an extra second. As if he saw neither the secretary, nor the cordless phone in her hand. Pavel once again looked into the depths of the server room.

"What is this?"

"Linux."

"That's not what we want," confirmed Vaschilov the professional.

"Just a minute, miss," Pavel heard someone saying behind his back. "Remain where you are."

Senior Lieutenant Tagirov paced the corridor with long strides. Natalia's face merged with her white blouse. Only her eyes flickered. Alive.

"Who did you just talk to?"

"To our director, Nikitin Roman Andreevich."

"What about?"

"About a meeting, scheduled for tomorrow morning . . ."

Meanwhile, Tagirov was already standing under the sign 'Reception.' Proprietorially, he took the phone from Natalia's hands and put it close to his own ear. Judging by the right angle of the senior lieutenant's cheek-bones, the plastic emanated only the sounds of someone having hung up on the other end, and no other information.

OK, said Pavel Petrovich Valentinov to himself. The electricity is on our side, for now. And miss Natalia. This is good.

He thought that and then turned away, indifferently. Facial muscles need to be relaxed. Like dough. That, he remembered. Of course he did.

From the depths of the server room, from its furthest corner, officer Vaschilov was dragging out a box. Dragging it on the floor. Like a pig, dragged by the ear, by the badly glued-on upper flap. The box was far from fresh. All covered in a dull velvet of dust, family silver. Just a wide line of duct-tape was shining as if it were new. Devil knows why. Dielectric static of the synthetic rainbow. Probably.

"What do you have here?"

"Old tape archives," said Kutepov, "we should have thrown them out ages ago."

"Open them."

Artyom ripped off the cheerful band of the duct-tape. Indeed, old tapes. Digital cartridges. The old format of the old company. They had not been used for about three years.

Vaschilov removed the first row. Just like from a jar of sardines. Underneath it was the second row. The labels, written in a red felt tip pen on the white background on the backside of the tapes, were immediately con-spicuous. StarNet Archives 2000. StarNet Archives 2001. StarNet Archives 2002.

"Pavel Petrovich, is this yours?" Mokrov asked. With the nicest of smiles. Just inquired, out of interest.

"Yes, it is ours." As usual, Tyoma had barged into the conversation without asking. Pavel did not correct him. But he had noted, just for him-self, how the fat girl in the working robe reacted. She was standing there, her dead eyes downcast. Cleaning the toilets was, it seemed, more agreeable to her than carrying out her civic duty. Even if it was an honor. The ski instructor, professional athlete, was looking at the ceiling. Plus and minus. Equal. The pair of unhappy witnesses reminded him of a battery that had lost its charge.

"Ours," Tyoma confirmed, "for a couple of years, they have been testing their internet through our pipes . . . stealing and stealing megabytes off our network, and now they can't make up their minds . . . Whereas Siberian Cell had signed up with us straight away."

Indeed. Next to the suspicious labels there were others, in the same row. SibCell. Archives 2000. SibCell 2001. Vaschilov and Mokrov exchanged glances. Material evidence?

"To be confiscated," Tagirov stated, shortly and distinctly. And it became finally apparent, who was really in charge here. Comrade Ringo. Lieutenant Starr. All of the cartridges were put into the box and taken to the conference room. Tyoma carried them. He put the box on the table, unloaded and asked a question. Lazily and with total indifference. He was done. An hour before the bell. Typical paid employee.

"Would you be needing me anymore?"

"No," Mokrov answered.

Kutepov left. Looking the same. Without energy. Just as the pair of witnesses. You can't put a light into a government-issue torch. Can't light it up.

It would be good if he did light up, just for his own sake, thought Pavel. Behind the door. Even better, downstairs, on the first floor. In the room where StarNet's black server is chewing through, chewing up the quarterly report . . . it's about time for him, for the big guy, to have a cigarette break somewhere in the cupboard . . . to break in pieces for an hour. All separately: the hard drive, the motherboard, the black tower unit—as an empty box, a home for hamsters . . . Petting zoo.

In any case, Pavel Petrovich Valentinov wanted to know. Just to know. For general knowledge. Where did Kutepov go? Systems administrator. And with what goal? Officer Vaschilov, it seemed, was interested in the same thing. What a champ. He slithered out of the room right after Tyoma. But he came back after a minute.

"He did not go into any offices," he said quietly to Tagirov.

No, this trio had picked up the scent. And they were not ashamed of it.

It was the other officer who was ashamed. Or he was only pretending to be a bit embarrassed.

Because of his shoes, maybe? They have definitely not known any government-issue shoe polish. Never even met any. On the other hand, the government was different back then. As was the fashion. Nineteen eighty-five, a long time ago . . .

It was a pretty regular call. From the office of graduate studies. They had asked him to pop in. Pavel left the lab building and took a little path, the short cut, and made his way to the main building under the paws of the university's maples. A smell of mignonette in the air. A happy August.

To his surprise there was no one in the Department of Graduate Studies when he got there. Not even young Alla, who gave Pavel a call five minutes ago. Just some stranger. By the window. Wearing a jacket, but no tie. He thought it was a part-time student, maybe, just visiting. Everyone needs a degree. Never too late for an education.

"Pavel Valentinov? Pavel Petrovich?"

The tone was of a statement rather than a question, though. A chance visitor, a gray pseudo-student had peeled himself away from the window-sill, opened the door to the office next door, the connected room of the dissertation council's secretary, and invited Pavel in, like it was his very own office.

"Do come in."

It was there in the office, where he showed Pavel his little book with the shield and the sword. And his photo right next to it. In the uniform with epaulettes. And only a year or so after did Pavel understand what actually happened. He, Pasha Valentinov, had got a referral from his countryman. Who thought to help him, in his own way, of course. Made a mistake. Took Pavel for someone else. But the government offices do not acknowledge mistakes. No fishing about. If you are not one of us yet, you will be soon. Small fry, dab, whitebait. Come here.

There was one problem, though. Pavel did not want to come. No connection was made.

Not at the first meeting, not at the second one, and as for the third one, he missed it altogether. He found a good excuse—he had to take his supervisor's manuscript to the publishing house. The man in a gray student-style turtleneck did not think it was a good enough reason.

"You should not do anything like that in the future, Pavel Petrovich. I gave you my phone number. I gave it to you specifically for situations like this one."

So he told Pavel off. And then started pressuring him. He talked about Pavel's upcoming dissertation defense, a job in the lab, a possibility of getting a residence permit in Moscow. He hinted that a life can be ruined, almost by accident, or the opposite of that—lived to the full, so that there are no regrets. Ever. Just say a word.

"It is a bit strange, of course, Pavel, that you are not close to your housemates in the student accommodation. You barely socialize with them. And then there are very interesting things happening right under your nose, interesting things requiring close attention. We know, for example, that your next-door neighbor Oleg Buchkin keeps a copy of *The Gulag Archipelago* in his room and sometimes, in the evenings, retypes certain chapters in the lab, pretending that he is working on one of his articles. You could drop by, ask to borrow the book. As neighbors do. Check out the mood. And help us to stop your friend, while there is still time."

And it turned out, it was not just Buka who needed help. Semka Gorenfeld, and Lekha Makarov, and even Lenka Vysheslavtseva, who for some reason chatted with foreign guests at various exhibitions in Sokolniki Park and at the Exhibition of the Achievements of the National Economy. Pavel was the only one whom the officer did not have any leads to work on. Just a reference from Valera Filipov. A countryman. Looking out for him. Did not mention Pavel in his reports. As it turned out, Filipov was preparing a substitute for himself. While he was away for two years at Doughty. In the United Kingdom. Eh, it would have been better if he had collected some information on Pavel. But not a single line, alas.

That's why this fake graduate student was embarrassed. Of course. A little bit. There was a small sparkle in his eye, though. Sometimes. A needle of excitement surfaced, at times. Lighting up, going out. A sharp point. Of course. It's not every day you get to work with pure psychology. Like Professor Freud. Neither pliers, nor a vice. Using exclusively analysis and higher math. Indeed.

And Pavel Valentinov kept silent. Like a girl at a date in a café. Although, why like a girl? Wasn't it in the old second-hand bookshop, that the kindest and nicest of salesmen had once invited him to come over? Young Pashka. Over to his house. To have some wine and to look at some books? And a year after, on a train, on the way to Perm for a conference, Assistant Professor Korzun was talking him into going to the toilet, to take a leak, together, as one. In a cramped train toilet. All kinds of things happened. Even a knock on the door of his student accommodation, in the middle of the night, like a shameful weak leak from a drunkard's open fly. Dima Potapov, on a business trip from Petersburg: "Pavlik, open up . . . I've brought fish and some beer . . . Pavlik, Pashen'ka . . ."

All of this had happened. The only thing that did not happen was a deflowering. And Pavel Valentinov's consent. As to the bookshop, he stopped going there. The assistant professor got a punch in the ear. And he never opened that door to Potapov. But there was no way out of the office of graduate studies. Even through the door. Even outside, onto the street. The state is a somber fiancé. It does not take no for an answer. Does not accept it. Looks are not everything. First comes marriage, love comes next. Folk wisdom is not for nothing, it's your turn now, you are an adult, and it's time for you to join the rest of the people, to become a small but inalienable part of it. The time has come. With Mendelssohn's wedding march. Spread your legs and think of communism. It has chosen you.

"You know what, Pavel, let's try this again. Your colleague, Sergei Zhirkov, regularly visits a church at the Voevodskaya station. And you, I happen to know, are very interested in ancient architecture. So you can take a ride together with your friend. Chat about faith and science. Ask some questions about the church's parish. Yeah . . . And admire the sights while you're there. A building made entirely of wood. Like the church in Kizhi, almost. But in our own, in the suburbs of Moscow. How about that?"

When Pavel, for the very first time, was late and did not manage to pick up his mother, arriving on a plane from South Siberia, from the airport, he, upset as he was, told her everything. The whole truth. Confessed. She did not cry. She just held his hand silently and for a long time. By the granite railings at the Lenin Hills. And then she said: "Oh God, does this mean it is your turn now?"

And then, as usual, she started talking about something else. About something big and grand. About his grandfathers. Who died not at the war. About his grandmother, who learned to milk a cow and harvest potatoes while in exile. She was thinking about her own life. And Pavel was thinking about his. And, as strange as it was, as surprising, they were thinking about the same thing. A rare, atypical case of mutual understanding in a family. A shared understanding of what is important. It was Pavel's turn, another Valentinov's turn, to come in and never to come out. Once and for all.

There was a row of buildings behind the Moscow river. The windows, stars and spires were shining. But there was no glimpse of the Canadian border.[1] You could not see it. Or the Old Square[2]—you could not see it either. But it was there that something happened. It happened, and they stopped summoning Pavel to the office of the university board's secretary. They never asked, sternly, where his report about the beauty of his homeland and the subversive power of enlightened obscurantism was. Why he neglected his report. Again. Why he did not get his things together and never went to Voevodskaya. To see the wooden church.

Something that by definition had no end in sight, suddenly was no more. An endless, light-less day was followed by a light summer night. And the day again had twenty-four hours. Pashka defended his dissertation. Stayed for a job in the lab. And then, at the dawn of capitalism, he left science behind and went back home to make money. Back to Siberia. And just got stuck there. Remained. Married and respectable.

"Pavel Valentinovich, are you waiting for someone?" the poster-man, Senior Lieutenant Tagirov asked, suddenly. Harrison-McCartney. Black-and-white copy.

"Excuse me, I didn't catch that?"

"Well, I see you are very drawn to the window for some reason . . ."

He noticed. A professional. He came over and looked over Pavel's shoulder.

"No," Pavel replied calmly and evenly. "I am standing here waiting for you to finish putting together your report. That's all."

And on the other side of window there was Kutepov, smoking. Laurel without Hardy. Pavel noticed him just now. Amazing. A little figure by the parking lot. Across the street. About ten paces away. Pavel noticed him and was now wondering if Artyom had been stuck there, pacing, all fifteen minutes while investigator Mokrov measured, wrote down, found the most fitting expressions. Chatting with the drivers from all of the local firms at once. Without a care in the world. It seemed so.

"Pavel Petrovich," Tagirov continued with his investigation, as if by magic catching the drift of Pavel's thoughts and the direction of his

---

1   A reference to the finale of O'Henry's short story "The Ransom of Red Chief": "How long can you hold him?" asks Bill. "I'm not as strong as I used to be," says old Dorset, "but I think I can promise you ten minutes." "Enough," says Bill. "In ten minutes I shall cross the Central, Southern and Middle Western States, and be legging it trippingly for the Canadian border."

2   The location of the Central Committee of the Communist Party in Soviet Moscow.

observation, "could you tell us if you have any other equipment in the rooms on the ground floor, where all the administrators are based?"

"Yes," Pavel said simply, "of course we do."

The two officers exchanged glances. Vaschilov and Tagirov. Indeed, this time they had something on him. Without a doubt. Fingerprints. Biological, definite material. And somewhere nearby. They just needed one small thing. To find it. Without being too delicate. To touch it. To expose it. To make sure.

"Got it . . ." Vaschilov, good boy, nodded, quickly. "Just a sec . . ."

And left.

Mokrov put a full stop on the document and started to read it out loud, line by line. No hurry.

"In the process of a search in office number seventeen, in the corner on the right, by the window, there has been found a cardboard box, taped shut with dark-color duct-tape . . ."

Pavel pulled up a chair and sat down. He had nothing to lose. He just had to mind his own eyes and face. As usual. So as to not lose face when Vaschilov would burst into the room triumphantly: "It's there . . . I have found it . . ."

Or maybe Vaschilov would call. On a mobile. Call his commanding officer Tagirov. And the phone in its dark case would play Ob-la-di, Ob-la-da. To the right and slightly lower than the officer's spleen. His digital appendix.

But the phone was silent, the door remained closed and the investigator kept trying to make sense of his garbled handwriting with all possible thoroughness.

"In the second row, on the top, were found magnetic tape cartridges . . . Is that the right term to use for these, Pavel Petrovich?"

"Yes, that is correct."

". . . with sticky labels attached to them and inscriptions, accordingly, StarNet Archives 2000 on the first, and then on the second . . ."

Pavel thought they would try to shame him, at first. And then would start talking about state security, although now it would probably include a discussion not of the sunny socialist society but of economics. Based on private property and initiative.

Interesting, what kind of church would they suggest I should visit, what community should I infiltrate? Although, no. Probably, they would just want me to give them information about Lekha and his whole business,

StarNet. All his communication channels. Left and right. Blood, sweat, and tears. The Russian Lefty[3], who is always running ahead of the steam-train of history and, most importantly, ahead of its laws. It is, of course, our favorite national pastime: to hunt for mushrooms, not to play football. That's why we cannot play within the lines, we do not know how. And what's the point of that anyway, if today the lines are drawn here, and then tomorrow they are already behind your back. Or, more likely, all around you. Like a circle. So you either die from petrification, or you cross the line. Not the England–Germany one. Your own lines. Yes. At home. That's why now, Pavel Petrovich, it is your duty to help us, you cannot refuse. Mistakes should be corrected, not made worse. Would you agree?

Because you, sir, have spent too much time as an old maid. Still a wall-flower at forty-two, like you were when you were twenty-two. No, it's almost a joke by now, isn't it? You don't have any choice, though, anyway, so what's the problem. It's all safe now, no way for you to be sorry. Open up. Come with us. We already have a special office set up. Diligence is the mother of success. Just relax and enjoy the journey. Love knows no age.

"Afterwards, all the cartridges were packed, as they were, back into the box that was sealed with three paper ribbons marked 'For Departmental Use,'" Mokrov kept reading, steadily, informing, when the door to the office opened and Vaschilov appeared on the threshold. He was not, for some reason, alight with happiness. He did not carry his luck in front of him like a light bulb.

"There is nothing there, downstairs," he said to his commanding officer. John Winston Tagirov.

"Are you sure?"

"I have gone through all the rooms and sat down with the systems administrators, listened to what they were saying, chatted to them."

In this moment Senior Lieutenant Tagirov was not looking at his colleague, the all-purpose Vaschilov, but at Pavel. Pavel Petrovich Valentinov. Sent a short-wave signal. But Pavel did not even flinch. The light was coming through his eyelids. It seemed pink. But no other changes. Temperature, humidity, pressure, all normal.

"Pavel Petrovich," Mokrov clearly decided to be straight and approach Pavel directly, "would you like to add anything or explain anything in

---

3   A reference to Nikolay Leskov's story "The Lefty" (1881), which is about an artful Russian craftsmen who managed to put horseshoes on the feet of a microscopic mechanical flea.

relation to archival materials that have been found on the confiscated magnetic memory tapes?"

Think about it, my friend . . . better we do it now rather than ruin another Friday night by questioning you in the big green house at the square, you know, as a result of the data we will find . . .

"No," Pavel replied, with no changes in his posture or facial expression. Like a potato. In a jacket. Excuse me.

"So? Are we done here?" asked Investigator Mokrov then. Meaning, of course, his own hand-written document. The report about the search and the confiscation. Asked his colleagues. It seemed.

But they all turned to look at Pavel. All of them at once. Actors. Directors, cameramen. Mosfilm.

The three officers were looking at him, as if they were checking their own movements in the reflection on Pavel Petrovich Valentinov's face. To see if his features would distort, would move. Tagirov was scowling, and Mokrov was looking at him with his usual kindly half-smile.

What country house? This and that. Barbeque? Ha-ha. This is a completely different, real fishing trip . . . Here and now, thought Pavel. Although, it seems, there is no bite, no bite at all . . . God knows why.

"No," Tagirov said quickly and confidently, as if drawing the line under their entire conversation, "let's go on through to the end. Finish this as we should. By the way, Pavel Petrovich, you must have some storage space. Would you have some equipment there, too?"

"We would," said Pavel very calmly. Because you can't die more than once. And one death he can manage. He is not a cat, after all. He walks on his own two legs.

But there was no server. Quick Vaschilov did not miss the machine. Did not miss out. He has done his job well. The machine had indeed disappeared. Without a trace. Dissolved. In any case, there was an innocent ray of sunlight instead of a big black box on the floor in the giant room where the systems administrators were sitting. Half past five. We are done here.

No, no way. The guests would not believe it. They wanted to finish the meeting on an appropriately high note. On the white keys. That is why, for some reason, they kept switching on the old equipment in the storage room, the dead, ruined machines. All of them, one after the other. But there was nothing they could drag out from the depths of the old half-dead machines. Turns out, there was no computing equipment in the building at the Prospect of Heroes, number 12. In the office of the ComServis company.

Just some electronic documents. So their informant must have been wrong. Made a stupid mistake. Wishful thinking. The only thing they could find were the magnetic tapes, which would need to be taken apart. Decoded. Before they can rejoice or bemoan. Before they can start their chat with Pavel Valentinov, Pavel Petrovich. Another chat. A serious, fundamental one about unrequited love. Of the state for him. Of the big, sweaty and insatiable state. His omnivorous motherland.

There was, by now, not just a little ray of light, but a yellow ball on the second floor, in the conference room. Ninety percent fat. All of the sun at once. Indeed, it was Friday. The light—reflected by the dark varnish of the bookshelf with leaflets, brochures and other promotional rubbish—fell onto the backs of Mokrov's and Tagirov's heads.

Little Red Riding Hoods. Could not lead the wolf to his rightful end. Again. For some reason, it did not work out this time around. He is leaving. The clock strikes twelve.

"I'm finishing this, then?" The tone of the question was more that of a statement, again.

"Finish," Tagirov said definitively, this time. The commanding officer.

"Could I ask everyone to sign," Mokrov offered with his unchanging civility. "Let's start with you," he said and offered his pen to the patient cleaner, the girl in the blue robe.

After that the professional athlete and ski instructor had put his signature on the document. That's it. Witness number two.

"And now you, Pavel Petrovich."

'Then, during the rest of the search nothing was confiscated.' After that, across the remaining school-notebook lines on the paper of the government-issued writing pads, there was, crossing everything, the last letter of the potential enemy's alphabet. Z. Be alert, comrades. The fight is not over.

No, excuse me, Pavel thought. Excuse me. I, personally, am putting an end to this. This time, at least.

So he signed, standing up, quickly and somewhat clumsily, even.

For some reason this had made Mokrov, the cheerful investigator, really quite happy. As if he had noticed something. Checked, saw something he was really looking for behind the gray color of a face. Behind the wind-beaten plaster. Caught Pavel Valentinov. A man with compliant nerves and trained muscles. A desire to part company. That's what the Investigator felt. Immediately. Once and for all.

And then Mokrov unzipped a lock on some little pocket on his slight folder, a student-style envelope with a flap, and took out a little rectangle of paper.

"If you do remember anything, Pavel Petrovich, you know, some information. If, you know, if anything comes up. You know how it is. There are two phone numbers here. The office and cell. Give us a call. Don't be shy about it."

A business card. Gray like the stones on the Red Square. With the stately two-headed eagle, frozen above the small print of the name and surname. Hanging over. A real handwritten spell, a mark, a secret—private, straight from the hot and clammy hands. Keep this and remember. You are ours. The chosen one. You were, you are and you will be. Progress. Some progress at least! A colossal step forward. A leap. A revolution in science and technology. Or a cultural revolution?

For some time Pavel stood on his own in the middle of the empty conference room. Suddenly, the phone rang. An inquiry from the security guard on duty, the bodybuilder from the ground floor. To ask if Pavel authorized for the cardboard box to be taken out of the building.

"I authorized it," Pavel replied.

"Should I put this under your name, then?" the shaved-head would not let this rest. Keeping watch.

"Yes, under my name," Pavel confirmed, hung up and went downstairs.

The systems administrators' room looked the same. Aside from the ray of sunlight that had now moved closer to Kutepov's desk.

"Where is it?" the technical director asked his systems administrator, simply and concisely.

"Right next to you," Kutepov nodded his head lazily, without taking his eyes off his monitor.

"Where?" Pavel did not really understand.

"In a box behind your back."

Pavel turned around. Next to the desk of Zhenia Zhukov, who had left to inspect a station at Kiselevsk this morning, there were two boxes. And not just one, as there was just yesterday night. One had some new Microsoft leaflets on top of it, some fresh-looking envelopes with some drivers, a mouse with a curled up, not yet straightened little tail. This one even looked unopened. Untouched corner. Future web-server of a future client in some industrial or commercial company. Brought here on Wednesday, the day before yesterday, untouched until now. Aha! And there, right next to it, in a cardboard box that looked identical, an object lusted for during the two-hour search was innocently hugging Zhukov's desk. The black server with all of StarNet's accounts. So simple it was almost funny.

"Nicely packed," said Pavel. "Where did you find the second box?"

"In the storage room—it's the box the developer's machine came in. Exactly the same. All standard boxes." Kutepov took his eyes off the monitor and glanced at Pavel. He was squinting. As if. Even happiness was expressed on his face sparingly. With two strokes of the small lines close to his lips and nose.

"We took this box and put it up vertically. It even had the original packing tape on it. That guy believed it at once. Even commiserated that we have so much work to do. Two servers at once. So much work, we don't have enough time to unpack the boxes."

That was, obviously, the indefatigable Vaschilov. The junior officer. Here, there, everywhere.

"And where was he?"

"He was sitting at Zhenka's desk. Right next to the boxes," Tyoma answered. And then stared again into his screen. Cybernetic individual. Silicon character. And then he kept silent. And just his immobile ears were emitting a reflected blue light of today's lucky achievement.

"And what did he do?"

"Nothing, really, he was listening to us reading jokes out loud from a website. Then he asked what weather was forecast on the web. And how much we earn."

It was fishing, then, thought Pavel. Tomorrow morning, early on. Hooks and flies.

"But you realized, didn't you, you were aware that they would take StarNet's machine if they found it?"

"Sure," Kutepov answered quickly; he raised his head and Pavel, for the first time today, saw his very alive, very human eyes. "Sure they would have taken it away. And I have just downloaded four pirated films on it yesterday. 'Cause there is so much free space on it. So I just put them there. And did not have enough time to transfer them to my own DVDs . . ."

Four films! About five gigabytes. Normally, this would be something to be punished for, to be summoned to explain yourself in front of the rest of the crew, something to lose your bonus over . . .

"Your charger is plugged in," he said to his systems administrator in a quiet and calm voice. "Take it offline, please. It will fry . . ."

And so their conversation came to its natural end. Because a little bird went live in Pavel Valentinov's pocket. His mobile phone started feeding on seeds, vibrating enticingly.

"Where are you?" As usual, Nikitin omitted all the non-functional forewords and afterwords.

"Downstairs, with the boys."

"Come up. I'm in my office."

He came, then. About fifteen minutes late. Too late to receive the honored guests. Too late to see them off.

"What happened?"

Pavel explained.

"Were they looking for the server with the accounts?" Nikitin asked not without malice. "They know what they are doing, then. If StarNet does not submit their quarterly tax report in time, that's the end of them. But why did they come to us?" the CEO's train of thought made a sudden turn. "Was that your friend Lekha Lobov's work? First, he kept using our network for free, and then he decided to set us up?"

Pavel realized that it would not be appropriate to relate the details of this story at the moment. But he knew it straight away anyway. He did not doubt it for a second. There was no love lost. Between Roman Andreyich Nikitin and the CEO of StarNet, Ivan Bogachev. He would just need to stop by at Lekha's tonight and explain everything. The job has been botched. Take your beauty of a machine away early tomorrow morning, before they get back. Before they find some more leads. Some more info. You can let it do the rest of the computing somewhere at your place over the weekend. And finish your quarterly report at the same office. That was a good idea, by the way.

"So, why are you not saying anything? Are you everyone's friend, everyone's brother? A colleague?"

"No." Pavel suddenly realized what he needed to say and how and where to direct this useless conversation. "I don't know why they came to us. They probably come to everyone who worked with StarNet. What I really don't understand is why the FSB is working on this, rather than the Economic Police, for example?"

"Well, even a fool would understand that," Nikitin became livelier again, more cheerful, he started smiling. "StarNet is the only one of the private providers who did not want to pay into the regional fund for communications development. Voluntary donation. They have explained it to

Vania ten times, they have explained it to his master Gusarov five times. But they don't understand. They are dumb. This means, it's time to replace them. Both the management and the owner. It's time. This is their dialectics. Look and learn. Study 'Eugene Onegin.'"

Nothing improved the CEO's mood as much as his own jokes.

"OK," Nikitin waved Pavel off when he finished laughing. "Go. You are free for tonight. The suspect. Every cloud has a silver lining. At least they have cleaned your server room up. Took out the trash. It has been taking you ages. Yeah, and don't forget," that, to Pavel's back, "We have a meeting tomorrow at ten-thirty. About development strategies. Don't miss it. Because we will cut your budget down if you are not there. Also about time."

"Pavel Petrovich." Natalia took over the baton of information in the reception room. The secretary. "There is a meeting tomorrow at ten thirty. In Roman Alexeevich's office. About development strategies."

"Yes, yes, thank you," said Pavel, already walking out of the office. "I know already."

Well, another person of whom he thought too highly. But most importantly, electricity. Electricity. His own, his favorite. Tame.

At the exit he ran into Kutepov. He was going out with an unlit cigarette in his teeth. With a light step. No night duty this weekend. Lovely.

"Look," Pavel stopped him. "Before I forget. There is something I wanted to ask you. Who came up with the idea to put a new duct-tape on the old box in the server room?"

Kutepov shrugged. "Who? Well, Zhukov of course. Kazakov bought this tape roller for the storage room, remember? Like a laser gun. Well, Zhukov was running around with it for two days. Just putting scotch on everything he could find. Jedi."

"I see." Pavel turned around and—he did not know why, or what for—again went into the systems administrators' room.

Everyone had left by now. Only the engineer on duty was sitting in the furthest corner. With a screen in front of his eyes and a hands-free phone set on his head. All in good order. As it should be. And still it felt weird. Among the white walls and desks.

The girl. Straightening her back. The blue robe. The same girl. With a rag in her hands. A red bucket on the floor.

"Good day." Surprised, Pavel spoke totally incongruously.

"Good day," the cleaner replied.

"You have already cleaned today," Pavel Valentinov was still struggling to pull his thoughts together. "I remember. Yes. This morning. As usual."

"I did, yes," the girl confirmed, "but then all kinds of people came, touched everything, left everything dirty . . ."

She had regular blue eyes. Round ones. Not clever and not stupid. Not sad and not happy. Just her own. The eyes of an older sister. They looked straight at Pavel. Without approval or judgment, but with faith. With faith. Complete and absolute. As you would, in a family.

They kept looking. Insistently and directly, so Pavel smiled in reply. It just happened. Widely and cheerfully. Because someone understood him. Someone, the only one who could and should be able to understand him. Big, clumsy, unmarried girl, keeping herself clean. Herself and the world around her.

"Thank you."

Translated by Margarita Vaysman and Angus Balkham

Margarita Khemlin (b. 1960)

Shady Business

Bella Levin had left Kiev for Israel many years ago, even before they'd started privatizing real estate. In Israel, she was tormented by nostalgia. After her husband died and her children moved to America, Bella started writing relatives and friends, asking them to take her in.

Her missives always ended the same way: "I am totally alone here, like the fickle finger of fate."

People responded sympathetically, but no one was about to invite her to move in.

Bella returned to Ukraine anyway.

She arrived in winter, which everyone said was deliberate: who would be so hard-hearted as to send an old woman into the winter chill?

It's more likely, though, that Bella just didn't think about the winter, having forgotten all about the cold during her time in Israel.

Anyway, for about three months she split her time among a couple of different relatives.

Everyone was nice to her, but hinted that it was high time to figure out a longer-term living situation.

Bella had a little money of her own; plus, someone called up her kids in America, and then the Kiev relatives pitched in. And this turned out to be enough for a small one-bedroom apartment in the 'burbs—in the little town of Brovary.

They donated some of the furniture they'd set aside for the dacha and even fixed up the wallpaper in all the excitement. Then they deposited Bella in Brovary and wished her the best.

Bella settled into her new life. She didn't pester anyone with phone calls, didn't ask for help. She made contact only rarely and with a great deal of tact. Her children regularly sent her money from America, so she didn't lack for anything. Cheese, salami, whatever—no problem. There was even enough for medication.

Everyone breathed a sigh of relief.

A year and a half passed.

Out of the blue, Bella informed her relatives that she wished to change residences once again. She wanted to settle in her hometown, the tiny village of Ostyor. Three generations of her family were buried there (we're talking before 1941). Those of her relatives who didn't manage to escape in time in '41—including her grandfather, grandmother, and lots of other relations—were also there, in a mass grave. What it came down to—and this is oversimplifying things a bit—was that Bella's best bet was to move straight to the cemetery, so ardent was her wish to reside near the dead.

To sell an apartment in Brovary and buy a house in Ostyor was no problem in itself. But Ostyor wasn't what it used to be. It was a backwater. Water from a well, an outhouse instead of a normal toilet. No stores to speak of. Just village, as far as the eye could see.

They pointed this out to Bella, but she wouldn't listen:

"It's an hour's drive from Kiev. Hardly a backwater! You think the toilet situation scares me? Ha! Nowadays they have all kinds of wiring, and any kind of service—all you need's a little cash. I'm not asking anyone for help. I'm telling you what's going to happen."

Bella called her children in America and said she intended to make her way to Ostyor, and that as soon as she was settled, she'd tell them her new address.

After agreeing, for appearances' sake, to wait for the new address, Bella's children rushed to phone up the family in Kiev, asking if their mother had lost her mind. The Kiev relatives answered: unclear. On the one hand, you know, she's eighty years old. On the other, she's an energetic lady and all her parts are in pretty good working order.

After a couple of serious conversations, Bella's resolve appeared to weaken. She relented.

Her relatives breathed a sigh of relief.

Then she didn't call for a month. They went to see her in Brovary. Rang the bell, knocked on the door: silence. They broke in—the apartment's in perfect order, newspapers stacked in a neat little pile, two-week-old TV guide marked up in color-coded highlighter. They looked in her closet: her clothes and suitcases were gone. On top of the pile of linens where Bella used to hide her money, they found a note:

"Don't worry about me! I decided to go. Bella. 5 June 2004."

They called the police: a woman is missing, blah blah blah.

The police didn't want to take the report due to the missing person's advanced age. She's probably in bad health on top of it. She said she was going back to her hometown? Yeah, that's all the rage for old ladies, they just go back and forth, back and forth. You should've kept an eye on her instead of wasting our time.

In the end, the cops took the report—obviously, just to get rid of them.

One of the relatives was sent to Ostyor. Where could Bella be? He paced the streets, looking for her. After a long while, he met an old man in a hat, aged about ninety; he seemed like he might be a Jew. The relative started asking about the Grobmans (Bella's maiden name); the old man knew exactly who he meant and offered to show him their old house, from before the war.

"But what do you want with the Grobmans? Hardly any left," the old man grumbled.

"Well, not here. But Bella Grobman is alive. You haven't seen her around, have you?"

The old man looked at the visitor in surprise, but didn't respond to the news about Bella.

"That's their old house. Pretty nice, right? I bet it'll still be standing a hundred years from now. During the war it was the German HQ. They damaged it during the retreat, but only a little. Bielke's great-grandpa built it. But in the end it was her father's undoing. He didn't want to leave it. They say that's where the Germans killed him. Right there on the porch. You could say that's Gotlib's claim to fame—the first Jew in Ostyor to be killed . . . And then about three days later, they shot the rest, one after the other . . . Near the Desna River, in the ravine . . . Old Gotlib used to say: first of all, they're a cultured nation, and second, Leyb'll get me out in some prisoner exchange, like in the First World War. Leyb was his son, Bielke's older brother—he volunteered for the army as soon as war broke out. Bielke stayed home with her father. Her mother had died back in '36, real young. Gotlib had a bad limp. Got real weak right before the war—his leg stopped working. That's why he and Bielke stayed here alone . . . Eh, why talk about it! War is war, am I right?"

"Wait, so she was here through the whole war—Bella was? How's that? Did she join a partisan unit?"

"Who's she to you?" asked the old man, suddenly suspicious.

"I'm her relative. Look . . . Bella Gotlibovna's disappeared. She was living in Israel, then came back home . . . And now she's disappeared. We thought she might be here—in her hometown, as it were. Now I'm looking for her."

"You got ID?" asked the old man.

"Sure, of course! We have different last names, though; my wife is her second cousin once removed."

The old man gingerly picked up the passport with the trident on the cover and thumbed through the bluish-yellow pages.

"Eh, who can say if you're her relative or not. Not that it matters . . . Seems like you might be thinking of a different Bella. This one"—he nodded in the direction of the Grobman house—"met her maker long ago."

"How can that be? Bella Gotlibovna Grobman, born 1925. Her family lived here, three generations, she said so herself. Her father was a shoemaker, he played the tambourine. Her grandfather Yankel was a blacksmith who played the violin, at weddings. And her uncle—I think his name was Meir—could down a cup of vodka and then crush the cup in his hand."

"That's right. Except it wasn't a cup, it was a glass. He'd drink and then take a bite out of the glass. Sure. Yes. And Bielke was their youngest. She died, I'm telling you." Without saying goodbye, the old man turned around and walked away as fast as his legs could carry him.

Bella's relative stood in the middle of the road, not knowing where to go or what to do. It just didn't make sense that Bella, assuming she made it to Ostyor, wouldn't go see her own house. He knocked on the door.

A woman with a baby in her arms answered.

"Excuse me, an elderly woman didn't happen to stop by here recently, did she? Her name is Bella Gotlibovna. Not bad looking, her hair's dyed a dark brown, kind of plump, glasses."

"No, no one stopped by," said the woman in dialect. "Who're you? And who is she?" she asked with interest. "Come on in. You from Kiev? I can always tell when someone's from Kiev. Come in, come in, I'll pour you some kvass."

The relative went in.

Over kvass, he got to talking with the woman, told her about Bella, about her moves, and about the old man he had met on the street.

"Oh, that's our Chaim. He's a little . . . not right in the head. Gets everything twisted. Told you a bunch of nonsense, I bet, and now you're upset."

"Yeah . . . could you please tell me where the old Jewish cemetery is?"

The woman explained how to get there.

"Not like there's a new one. Only the old one. Not many Jews left around here. Just Chaim, plus another couple old folks."

"Oh, it doesn't matter. I just wanted to have a look, since I'm already here."

The relative walked the cemetery from end to end, reading the names off the gravestones and rotting wooden plaques, searching for the Grobmans—but found nothing. He sat down on a bench to rest.

"There you are—I was watchin' you go behind the fence, but where you went after, I couldn't see. Hi there, I'm the caretaker. Would you like to make a donation to the local Jewish community? Just a couple of hryvnias, if you would. I'm the caretaker here. I look after this place. Like, instead of retiring. The name's Ilya Moiseevich Kamsky," said the caretaker, holding out his hat like a beggar.

The relative put three hryvnias and change into the hat. The caretaker scraped out the coins, dropped them into his breast pocket, and gave the visitor a probing, businesslike look.

"Who you lookin' for?" he said, straightening his jacket lapel, which sagged under the weight of numerous medals.

"The Grobmans."

"Ah, the Grobmans . . . I'll take you there. You a relation?"

"Yes, a relation."

"Lots of Grobmans around here. From before the war, and others besides. Wanna see all of them?"

"All of them," exhaled the relative. They walked all around the cemetery. Growing tired, they sat down on a large bench under a weeping willow.

"Well, that's about it—I showed you everything, kind of like a tour. Whaddaya think?"

"It's great, thank you. Say, you haven't seen Bella Grobman around here have you? Gotlib Grobman's youngest?"

The caretaker hesitated.

"You sure she's still kicking?"

The relative nodded.

"Well, well, well. Bielke wouldn't dare show her face here. Not while me'n Chaim'n Sunka Ovrutsky are still alive. When the last of us dies—she might come around then."

"Chaim told me about Bella, but I didn't really get it . . . He was sure that Bella died right after the war. But she's alive. What was she doing during the war? Was she a partisan?"

"A partisan . . . Sure, maybe she was a partisan. The people who were still here during the war were scared out of their minds—not a lot of information we were getting, you understand. All kinds of things they said . . . But what a beauty she was! Good Grobman stock—pretty as a picture!" The caretaker glanced quickly at the relative: "You're not from abroad, are ya? You writin' a book? Makin' a movie?"

"What movie! I'm looking for Bella, the woman's vanished!" The relative once again recited the story of Bella's various moves. The caretaker didn't seem surprised.

"Uh-huh. Yeah, that one always had a high opinion of herself . . . Not so long ago—about ten years—they came all the way from America to make a movie about the Jews, and they talked to all of us. Really grilled us, although they did pay. You know, before the war, Ostyor was quite a place! A big Jewish town! Something like seventy percent Jewish. By the way, we didn't say word one about Bielke to the Americans," the caretaker said, looking at him pointedly. "I'll tell you, though, since you're a relation. You interested?"

The relative nodded.

"When the occupation started, there were still lots of Jews in Ostyor— not like anyone warned us to leave, weren't no informational campaign. Before the Germans came, refugees from the East would say that they were shooting all the Jews they could get their hands on. We didn't believe 'em. We thought the Germans were shooting everyone—Jew, Ukrainian, Russian . . . we didn't think they were coming after the Jews specifically, no sir! Didn't believe it. All of us had a little something, a few coins or a shack. And some people had nice houses, furniture—how could they leave all that? That's why Gotlib stayed, and Bielke didn't want to ditch him. We young men all went to the front right away, like model Komsomols. We went away, and while we were gone . . . They shot all the Jews that stayed behind, every last one of them. My people and everyone else's—in the ravine near the Desna. After liberation, they re-buried 'em in a mass grave. We all thought Bielke was in there, too. And when we started comin' back from the front—me, Chaim, Sunka Ovrutsky, other people—we gathered together a Jewish community. At that time, people were rollin' in from wherever they'd evacuated to; no one was demobilized yet, but a few wounded came back. And plenty of other people, Ukrainians, who'd been in Ostyor under the Germans. We talked about the occupation's outcome. But what outcome? Half of Ostyor was collaborators, but there they were, sittin' right next to us. And everyone knows who's who. Then the local authorities start comin' out, saying they condemn individual cases and all that, but we're one big family, blah blah blah. Comrades, they say, if you know about any collaborators, just say it straight out, you have nothing to fear now.

"Well, the ones who actually pulled the trigger, the women had already pointed 'em out to us, and we'd executed 'em right away—soon as we re-took the territory. Martial law, you know. So by that point there weren't any like that around anymore. But the ones who'd helped in other ways—they were still there, sittin' with us in the former synagogue, which by then was a workers' club.

"Bielke'd shown up shortly before that. Not one word about where she'd been or how she'd stayed alive. 'Same as everyone else,' was her answer. Other people'd practically shriveled up in the war, but not her. She was real skinny in the body, but her face looked fine, just like before.

"And so she stands up, in all her glory—used to public speakin' from all those Komsomol meetings, she was. I can see it like it was yesterday. And here's what she said, word for word: 'All of us here've suffered a great tragedy. Those German bastards killed my father, and my brother died a hero on the battlefield. Not to mention what I went through. Everyone here lost a loved one just because they was a Jew. And the Ukrainian people suffered, too, though they weren't shot on the spot. I'm talkin' about the so-called collaborationists. True, no one ever saw a Jewish collaboration-ist—but that's because they'd shoot Jews on the spot, they didn't give them a choice. But the Ukrainians all had children, they wanted to live. You can't raise the dead.'

"She says this and sits back down. Say what? In whose name? What for? How could she open her mouth to say those things? People were outraged! Oy gevalt! Sunka Ovrutsky, who was there on crutches, he was an officer, just started shootin' off his gun, shoutin':

'Lemme at that Nazi-lover, she's worse than Fanny Kaplan!'

"Bielke started to answer, but the whole mob rushed her and just started whalin' on her. You bet! The authorities had to pull people off her. The police came. Bielke's lyin' on the floor, all bloody. They poured some water on her; she stands up, and off she goes. No one followed her. No one."

The caretaker fell silent.

After a long pause, he asked:

"How do you like them apples?"

"Yeah . . ."

"Yeah what? Do you like them or not."

The relative said nothing.

"And after all that you tell me she's comin' here . . . We thought she took her own life that very day, hopped into the Desna. No one's seen her since . . . But she's alive! Got nine lives, that scum!"

The caretaker jumped up and began counting on his fingers, starting with the thumb:

"Chaim's alive. I'm alive. Sunka Ovrutsky's alive, just barely. We're the Jewish community around here. We won't stand for her coming back!" The caretaker sat back down, his fingers still bent like he was preparing to make an obscene gesture.

"It's been so many years . . . how can you still . . ."

"How can I still? They shot every single Jew in Ostyor, but not her. What do you know, she's still alive. You say maybe she was a partisan—but they wiped out all the partisans, and she lived to say all that garbage!" The caretaker wouldn't look at the relative, shouting into empty space. "What did we fight for at the front? What did they shoot all our people for back home? For us to talk like Bielke did after?"

"Try to calm down, please," said the relative.

"I'm not sayin' it 'cause I'm mad. I'm sayin' it 'cause I know what's right," said the caretaker, straightening his medals and drawing himself up to his full height.

"What about Gotlib Grobman, where's he buried? I didn't see him on the tour," said the relative, craning his neck to look up into the old man's face.

"Gotlib? His neighbor Khomchikha buried him. The same night they shot him. Buried him in her own cemetery, the Orthodox one—she was afraid to bring him over here. Buried him respectful, she said, wrapped him in cloth, some clean burlap. I couldn't find him there now. As for Khomchikha, she died long ago. Didn't seem right to move him while she was still alive—she did her best, after all. Risked a lot. And then, after she died, everyone was still real mad about Bielke. So Gotlib's at the Orthodox cemetery to this day."

The caretaker straightened his jacket and started walking the relative to the exit:

"Some wise-ass from the city tried to do without my help in here. Got turned around, started shouting 'Help, help!' Like he was lost in the woods or something!"

The relative returned to Kiev empty-handed. The city police sent several inquiries to Ostyor, but heard nothing comforting back. No, she hadn't turned up. No one had seen her. If Bella isn't found within seven years, she'll be declared dead in absentia.

Translated by Maya Vinokour

Elena Dolgopyat (b. 1963)

The Victim

"It was a successful debut. But all the same, the winners (not to mention the losers) still needs to put in a lot of persistent work if they want to reach a top-notch level and grasp all of the subtleties of this most interesting of games . . ."

The officer on duty was reading an analysis of the game. He heard the door opening and lifted his eyes from the newspaper page. A scrawny man, shorter than average height, walked into the station. Without a coat. He approached the window and looked at the officer. The man's lips were shaking. The officer guessed that he would burst into tears if he tried to speak.

"What is it?" the officer asked. "Did they take your coat?"

The man nodded his head.

"A nice coat?"

The man nodded.

"With a fur collar?"

The man shook his head to say no. The reflection of the lamp swung across the wide bald spot on his head.

"They've lost all shame." The officer laid a piece of paper and a pen out on the counter. "Just the other day they robbed a woman, yanked her hat off, tore her purse from her hands, and her house keys were in there; it was the wife of some high-up man, really high up, you probably haven't even seen such a man, but I had the honor. He came here himself, yelled a bit, of course, until he saw our chief, but as soon as he saw him he hugged him on the spot; they served together on the front, broke through the encirclement together at the beginning of the war. Did you serve?"

The man nodded. He looked tensely at the talkative officer, and, it seemed, didn't really make out the meaning of the story, but the officer's soft, rounded drawl calmed him down.

"Ah, you see, maybe you know the chief, too. As for me, I never had the chance to serve, I was catching bandits here." With these words the officer placed an inkwell on the counter and told the man: "Better get writing."

The man raised his bewildered eyes to the officer. They were light blue with thin, reddish eyelids. It occurred to the officer that the victim's eyes were bird-like. But did birds have blue eyes?

"You need to write a report about the theft. I'll file it, and you'll go home. Do you live far? It's a real cold one out there. It's the beginning of March, and it's so cold out there. I didn't even think about it, you must be frozen stiff. I'll get you some tea. I've got a special tea. I won't tell you the secret, so don't even ask. In the meantime, you write."

The officer went over to the stool where, against all the rules, he kept an alcohol burner, lit it, and placed a little bronze teapot on the flame. The victim bent down close to the piece of paper, stared at it for a long time, and, finally, carefully putting the pen to the paper (as if stepping onto the ice with one foot to see if it was strong enough or if he would instantly go crashing through into the dark river water together with the ice), began to write. He wrote and sniffled through his sharp little nose.

"Just like a mouse," darted through the officer's head.

The water in the teapot started to boil, the officer tossed a small amount of dry, gray herbs into a mug, poured the boiling water over it, and a sweet aroma spread through the air and reached the sharp little nose of the victim. The victim raised his unseeing eyes and immediately looked back down at the page. He was writing carefully, line after line, in neat, even handwriting.

"He's writing an awful lot," thought the officer. But he decided not to interrupt him.

The victim was a retoucher at a photo shop. He sat in his corner and colored skies blue and cheeks pink. His favorite job was to color prints. He also corrected negatives. He had a box with a little glass window for this task: he'd place the negative on the window, turn the electricity on in the box, cover himself with a black cloth, and use ink to darken shadows on the illuminated negative for contrast; or he'd use an eraser to remove black dots from faces. He lost his vision doing this work, but they took him into the volunteer corps during the war. Of course he didn't tell them about his vision: the Germans were approaching Moscow. He returned from the war in August of '45, without earning any awards or medals. He lived in the Mary's Grove District, in his own room (in a two-story, wooden house with a courtyard and a garden out front) on the second floor. He'd climb up the stairs in the evening, and the stairs would respond with a groan.

The retoucher lived alone. He'd unlock his room and walk into the darkness, then turn on the light. He'd put the teapot on in the shared kitchen. He'd look out the window and see the men sawing firewood. The neighbors dried the laundry on clotheslines, and when it was cold outside it would turn into something like thin cardboard. Children would run around, throw snowballs. He'd eat bread and cold potatoes. He'd wipe the table with a clean rag, spread a newspaper out on it, get his paints and brushes out, pour some water into a special glass, and sit down to work. He'd always take some picture home with him so he could color in some black-and-white shot in the isolation of his own room. Usually it was portraits; people wanted to bring their faces to life—their own and those of their loved ones—with color.

With tenderness he'd put his slender brush to children's cheeks. He loved coloring eyes and always wondered what color they should be. He loved coloring pioneers' ties red, flags, too. After work he'd wash his brushes under the faucet in the kitchen. Usually by this time the whole house would be asleep, and only the legless Nikolai would be there smoking at the window, his back to the radiator. The retoucher would say, "Hello, Nikolai," when he walked in and, as he left, would always wish him a good night; Nikolai would always answer: "Same to you."

The retoucher would return to his room and place his brushes in a glass that stood on the shelf he had mounted above his desk. He'd put his brushes and pens in the glass, push his box of paints and ink jar toward the glass, and pull the little curtain down. He had a special shelf with a curtain that his neighbor Vasilii Ivanovich had cut for him out of a scrap of lavishly colored chintz before the war. The design had tender tea roses, and the retoucher admired them as he ate his breakfast of tea and bread with sugar sprinkled on it or his dinner of tea and potatoes. Vasilii Ivanovich worked in a sewing workshop and brought work home, and the whirring of his sewing machine was a customary and even necessary sound to the retoucher's ears.

A photographic portrait of a woman used to hang between the shelf and the window, behind the glass of a thin, brown frame. Its history is simple.

It was a long time before the war. One bright July evening in 1935, a woman came into the shop. She sat down on a chair with a high back in front of tightly drawn white sheet. The photographer stood up in front of the tripod and asked the woman to straighten her back and refrain from blinking. Meanwhile, the retoucher was hunched over in his corner. The woman stood in front of him as if on a brightly lit stage. He looked over her round face, small button nose, firmly pressed lips, and dark-gray eyes beneath a low forehead, creased in a frown. She was an unattractive woman. Tired. She got her picture taken, left the money, and never came back for the photograph.

In the fall, when the trees were already barren, they decided to throw some photographs away so that they wouldn't take up space. There wasn't much of it in the shop. The retoucher took one picture for himself: the woman in the picture caught his fancy. She didn't look much like the living prototype; the eyes in the picture seemed bigger and the forehead higher. At home, the retoucher brought the lips to life with a soft pink color (it would be more appropriate here to speak of light, rather than color), he gave the face a warm, golden tint; the eyes began to glisten against the washed-out background and seemed to come to life. He fell in love with the image and tucked it behind glass in a frame. He didn't know anything about this woman. About these women. He didn't know anything about them and didn't make anything up about them. He'd move on to admiring a second one and forget the first.

In 1940, just before the war, a man of about forty came into the shop with his six-year-old daughter. He said that he had found a receipt for a photo among the papers of his deceased wife. He explained:

"Not long before her death she came to get her picture taken. She died suddenly. In a minute. It was an easy death."

The man held his daughter by the hand as he spoke. The retoucher's coworkers let him off work, and he brought the father and daughter to his house and took the photograph off the wall.

"That's what she was like," the man said, "your mother."

And he gave the girl the heavy, framed picture to hold.

"She's pretty," the girl whispered.

"Yep," the man said. And he added: "You look a lot like her."

The retoucher wrapped the framed picture up in newspaper for them.

After the war he went around in his infantry greatcoat without epaulets from early fall until late spring. In the summer, he aired the coat out in the dry shade and then hid it in an ancient dresser; his parents had brought this enormously heavy dresser from the village.

They moved to Moscow in 1920. The factory gave them a room on the second floor with a window facing the courtyard, and the first thing he remembered was the quiet of the fall morning, the quiet, scattered sunshine. Some little boys stood down below: he could hear their conversation, the sun lit up their faces, and they turned away from the sun. He was eight years old. He was shy and afraid to go out into the courtyard, but his mother said: "Come on, you're getting in the way." She was washing the floors and walls and wanted to the wash the windows. So he walked down the long corridor, went down the creaking steps, and stepped out of the dark opening into the light.

An old man was sitting on a bench near the entrance, and the boy settled himself down on the edge of the bench. A cat came up and jumped up onto the old man's lap. He picked up his bony hand and started to pet the cat. And they sat there like that: the old man, the cat, and the boy. The sun went down behind the house, and the wind blew and brought with it the yellow leaves of a birch tree.

His mother used to tell people:

"I got frightened when I was pregnant with him, and so he was born speechless. Some think that he can't speak at all; how such a quiet boy is going to live I can't imagine."

They'd ask her:

"And what was it that frightened you, Nina?"

And she'd eagerly tell them about how she was walking along the path from the barn one winter day, carrying firewood.

". . . and suddenly there was a black dog standing there in front of me and looking at me. There was nowhere for me to go, the path was narrow, and there was so much snow piled up that if you stepped off the path you'd be up to your head in snow. The dog was enormous and calm. And suddenly it came at me, and I just sat down in the path, and the firewood fell out of the basket. I'm sitting there, and it's breathing into my face. It breathed for a bit and left, and that's why my boy came into the world so shy. And so what, there are all sort of people, aren't there? That means that's how it's supposed to be."

The victim set aside the piece of paper covered in neat, tiny writing. The mug was steaming, untouched. The officer asked:

"Did you sign and date it?"

The victim nodded, and the officer took the sheet of paper.

"I'll read it, and you drink, it helps for colds."

The report was lengthy, but the officer didn't make any remarks and decided not to say that it would have to be rewritten and compressed, leaving only the gist of the matter. It was no big deal, he could accept it as it was, or so he decided. Though he expected that he would get scolded by his superiors.

He read the following, verbatim:

"A report.

On February 1st of this year, 1955, I discovered that my army great coat had been worn thin in the back in the course of careful use. I gave it to my neighbor, Vasilii Ivanovich in the hope that he would patch it. Vasilii Ivanovich is a professional tailor and doesn't ask any money from me for minor repairs, just as I don't ask anything of him for my work as a retoucher, if he ever needs that sort of thing. Vasilii Ivanovich held my coat up the light, took a close look, and said that he wouldn't even try to mend it. He showed me the holes in the armpits, showed me that the lining had already started to decompose and was holding together only by some sort of misunderstanding. He said that he was willing to sew me a nice warm coat for half the price. I was taken aback, since I had made it through the entire war in that coat, it had become a part of me, it had become like a girlfriend to me, it protected and watched over me, and there was even an incident when a bullet got stuck in the top button. I preserve that crippled button. They mended my coat up nicely then so that even Vasilii Ivanovich couldn't find the location of the wound. And everything on me healed completely, too. Be that as it may, ten years after the war, my faithful girlfriend had grown old and could no longer warm me up. I would have switched to my father's coat, I wore it before the war, but it didn't wait for me to return from the war; I think someone stole it, just like my mother's down shawl, which they wrapped me in when I was a baby. They also wrapped the pot with buckwheat porridge in it, covering the pot in newspaper first so as not to burn the shawl; mother explained to me that this was the best way to finish cooking the porridge; mother wore the shawl in the winter; I too wrapped the shawl around my waist after my parents left for the better world; and it was the loss of the shawl that I regretted most of all; although I did regret losing my brushes and paints more. I had the coat sewn on credit, and I haven't paid it off to this day. Vasilii Ivanovich doesn't hurry me. He sewed me a nice coat that went all the way to my ankles, so that no drafts would get to my bad back, no matter how bad the wind, and I hoped that I would wear this coat until the end of days. It was a black coat with a strap in the back; the collar was English, but you could snap it completely shut: everything had been thought through in advance to guarantee warmth."

(For clarity, the victim drew his coat with the sleeves spread wide from two angles: from the front and from the side; the drawing was smallish and didn't take up much space; but, despite its small size, he managed to fit all of the details: the buttons, the loops, the pockets, the lapels, and the stitching).

"Today, March 1st, 1955, I put the coat on for the first time," the victim continued his confession. "I never paid so much attention to myself as today. Or, to put it more precisely, the coat paid attention to me. Vasilii Ivanovich really outdid himself, and it sat so well on me that I myself would stop, if I happened to see a mirror, to look. At our photo shop they asked me to try the coat on for every colleague that would come in, and everyone was surprised by how I had been transformed. After work they wouldn't let me go and said that we had to celebrate the new coat. I wasn't against it. They collected money, each one contributing what they could. I gave thirty rubles and fifty kopecks, everything I had. Grisha Altufiev ran to the kiosk and brought back two bottles of wine, some bread, some candy, and a can of stewed meat. He also brought a bottle of vodka and some partially frozen pickles. He told me that I owed him three hundred rubles now. I don't know if he was joking or not, I can't always tell the difference. At first everyone paid a lot of attention to me, they interrogated me about how much wool it took to make the coat, whether the tailor squeezed a lot of money out of me for it, and how I could make it through the entire war and ten more years after in a single great coat. I grew weak from all this attention and questioning and, once they started talking about scientific experiments with flying apparatuses, quietly got dressed behind the wardrobe and left. The metro was already closed, and I headed off on foot, taking a short cut. In the alley I heard some quick footsteps behind my back, someone caught up to me, and I didn't have time to turn around: they hit me in the head from behind. The bump on the back of my head hurts badly. I woke up in a snowdrift without my coat. My hat was lying there next to me. After realizing what had happened, I started to cry. I didn't feel the cold. I picked up my hat and walked to the nearest militia station.

March 1st, 1955. A. S. Andreev."

The officer finished reading the report and looked at the clock. It showed one o'clock in the morning.

"What to do?" the officer said.

The victim looked at him as if lost.

"I'll take your report," the officer continued, "but how will you make it home in only a sweater? Is your house far from here?"

The victim thought for a moment and answered:

"I could run home in twenty minutes."

"So this is what we're going to do, Comrade Andreev. I'm going to write your address in a special journal, you'll sign your name in a special column. I'll issue you a quilted jacket. It's old, of course, and the stuffing sticks out in a few places, and it will be too big for you, of course, but it'll protect you a bit from the cold. You'll wear until you get to warmth and then return it."

And the officer pulled out a tattered, gray quilted jacket from somewhere beneath the counter. At night he used it to warm his frozen feet.

The victim, not fully understanding, it would seem, what was happening, obediently donned the quilted jacket.

"Button up," the officer commanded.

And the victim buttoned up the two remaining buttons.

"Not bad," the officer said. "It's okay. It'll do. If you find something else to keep you warm, return it right away. Put your hat on. Goodbye."

The victim put his hat on but didn't leave.

The officer repeated:

"Goodbye."

The victim stood there submissively looking at him with his bird-like eyes.

"Go on home, you have to go to work tomorrow."

"I. Yes. Wanted to ask. About the coat. Will they find it?"

"That's not for me to know, I don't want to get your hopes up. We know about these night robberies. We're taking measures. But there have been no results yet. They sell the stuff, and it's hard to track them down. To be frank, it's a lost cause."

"But you . . ."

"We'll try. Go on home, Comrade Andreev, it's late."

The victim finally put on his hat and quietly made for the door without saying goodbye. When the door closed after him, the officer set himself down at on the chair behind the window. He took the mug with the now-cool infusion and finished it.

The next day after work the victim came to the militia station.

Vasilii Ivanovich still hadn't mended his quilted jacket. He'll mend it by this Sunday: put neat patches on it, sew on the missing buttons. In the meantime, Andreev the victim had a rather wild look about him. People looked askance at him, a woman in the bus pressed her purse to herself with her palm spread wide, never taking her eyes off him. What was more, the victim was coughing, sniffling, and hiding his sore, red eyes.

At work they took pity on him and offered to let him go back home and sleep it off. But he didn't take them up on the offer. He crammed himself into his corner, hid himself under the black fabric, and turned on the light in the box.

There were lots of people depicted on the negatives, standing and sitting, and throughout the entire workday the retoucher peered into their faces, accentuating the shadows, whiting out the specks. And after work, he unhunched his back with difficulty, put on the tattered rags that the officer had given him, and set off for the militia station. The snow crunched loudly beneath his feet, the streetlights shown brightly and blinded his work-weary eyes.

The previous officer wasn't there, there was someone else sitting behind the window. He gave a stern look, checked the notes in the journal, and said that an investigator had been assigned to the case and was undertaking investigative measures. The victim expressed his desire to meet with the investigator. The new officer on duty asked about the purpose of his inquiry.

"I recalled some new details," the victim exclaimed meekly.

He sat in front of the investigator's door for an hour, and then they invited him to come in.

The investigator read his report and got out his cigarettes. The victim said that he didn't smoke and coughed into his fist. The investigator lit one up.

"It's difficult to undertake any concrete action in your case."

The victim kept silent and looked at the investigator. He was sitting on the edge of his chair, pressing his knees together and crushing his fur hat. A puddle was spreading from the galoshes he had on over his felt boots.

"You told the on-duty officer that you recalled some details."

"Yes. What I mean is. I had handkerchief in the right pocket of my coat. A fresh one. A nice, thin handkerchief. Chinese. They gave it to me on my last birthday. People from the shop. A white handkerchief. And a dark-blue hem."

(He said this as if the hem was separate from the handkerchief, like they came as a set.)

The victim sniffled, and the investigator wrote something down on a piece of paper and politely said:

"Okay. Thank you. Goodbye."

The victim kept sitting as before and looking with his bird-like eyes.

"I wrote everything down."

"Will it be of any help?"

"It's possible."

"If I remember anything else, I'll come back."

"Of course."

The victim got up and, with his back hunched over, wandered toward the door. He reached his hand out to the doorknob and looked back over his shoulder. The investigator was writing something down. When the door had closed behind the victim, the investigator set his pencil aside. He finished smoking his cigarette, got up, rubbed the small of his back, opened a safe, and pulled out two cases files on instances of theft from the winter of 1954–1955.

The next day after work the victim showed up at the station again, but he didn't find the investigator there.

"He left to interrogate a suspect at a crime scene," they explained to him.

"Related to my case?" the victim brightened up.

"No."

Just in case, he waited at the door. The cleaning lady came and chased him off the bench. He watched for a while as she washed the floor with an enormous mop and turned out the light in the hallway, and then he wandered toward the exit.

He tracked down the investigator the next week, on Monday. He went into the office, only this time his quilted jacket had been patched up and almost looked respectable, and, standing in the doorway, he informed the investigator that he had recalled some new details. The investigator invited him to come in, and the victim shuffled his way over to the chair and sat down on the edge, pressing his knees together. The temperature had risen, and the smell of melting snow drifted in through the open ventilation window.

"The third button from the top on my coat," the victim informed him in his high voice, "was sewn on a little more tightly than the others. The thread stem (if you sew a button according to the rules there should be a little stem left between it and the coat), came out a little bit short, and the button ended up almost flush to the fabric, it was hard to button, and I thought about telling Vasilii Ivanovich."

And he fell silent. The investigator looked calmly at him. A yellow circle of light was lying in front of him on the table.

"Okay," the investigator said, "I got it."

The victim remained silent for a bit and asked:

"Aren't you going to write it down?"

"What? Yes, of course." The investigator picked up a pencil and a sheet of paper from a thin stack, and he neatly wrote something down with the pencil. And he reassured the victim: "I'll include this in the case."

The victim still wasn't getting up to leave, and the investigator decided to explain the situation:

"To be frank with you, your case is complicated. How can we find your thief (or thieves)? We've got nothing in our hands, just air." And he showed the victim his empty palms and wiggled his fingers. After showing him he continued, "We have no intention of closing our eyes to this case. This winter in our district there were thirty-four thefts. The very same (or different?) people (or person?) carried out these attacks. And it's not like they (he?) only went after nice things. There were cases when they literally tore rags off people, things not unlike what you're wearing today."

"This isn't a rag anymore," the victim uttered. "Vasilii Ivanovich patched it up it."

"I see that. Very good. Your jacket was a rag until it was patched up, I agree. Be that as it may, they went after used things even worse than that. And it's not like poor people regretted their losses less than the rich. It's hard to say who cried more bitterly."

The investigator fell silent. The victim looked at him attentively. His lips were clamped tightly shut. Sorrowful creases ran outward from the corners of his mouth.

"Here's what I recommend that you do," the investigator continued in an even voice, "you head on home and try to forget about what happened for the time being. Don't torment yourself. As far as we're concerned, we'll do everything that we can." He peered at the motionless figure. "Do you hear me? Do you understand what I'm saying?"

The victim got up without a sound and, hunched over, wandered to the door. When it closed after him, the investigator broke his pencil in half, flung the broken pieces on the floor, and uttered an energetic profanity.

The desk lamp was shining, and Vasilii Ivanovich was mending the quilted jacket, which had come apart at the seams again, and mourning the coat. After all, the fabric was pretty nice in comparison to the quilted jacket, and Vasilii Ivanovich had cut two whole pieces out of it and hid them in the dresser. He was thinking of sewing a little coat out of the scraps for his grandson. Vasilii Ivanovich worked, and the needle flashed in the yellow light. The tailor's wife Tamara set herself up at the other side of the table, poured some millet onto a plate, and set about picking through it, fishing out blackened grains or tiny stones, and throwing them into a mug.

"Thieves can get away with anything these days," she said, "They do whatever they want, the militia themselves are afraid of them, and there's no protection for ordinary people."

"Did you hear about the professor's wife?" Vasilii Ivanovich asked.

"I heard something."

"And you?"

"Me?" The victim didn't realize at first that Vasilii Ivanovich was addressing him. "No."

"I'll tell you. They took the coat off her back, too. An Austrian one. With a silver fox collar. She was coming home from the theater. She and her husband got into an argument during the intermission, she got her coat and left. She didn't have any money on her, so she had to go by foot. Well, and in the alley, when she was just about home, a thief pounced on her, a really tall man, a giant. She didn't get a good look at his face. His faced was covered with a beard."

"A fake one," Tamara observed.

"We don't know that. He pointed the knife at her, ordered her to take off her coat. She obeyed. She ran home, called the militia, they have a phone at home, of course."

"Her husband's an award-winning professor."

"I don't know about that. The fact is, that they have a phone and go to the theater."

"And wear silver foxes."

"You can say that again."

"And they have a five-room apartment."

"People gossip too much," the tailor observed sternly.

"Aniuta was there."

"Don't believe Aniuta. The fact is, they're wealthy people."

"That's a fact."

"They're not exactly in need. She had a real fright, of course, but she wasn't exactly left naked. She had another fur coat hanging in the wardrobe, and not just one. And there was a top coat, too, an austere one, with an Astrakhan collar."

"Like you saw it," Tamara snickered.

"Just listen. She called the militia, they told her to come to the station in the morning and write a report. She didn't wait for morning, put on her fur coat, took her housemaid with her, and went right to the station. At the station, they took a look at her fur coat, didn't say anything, took her report, and assured her that they were already looking for the thief and would find him soon."

"They were having a laugh at her."

"She didn't really believe them either, and in a couple of days she called and asked what measures were being taken, but they didn't tell her anything of any significance. Her husband explained to her that it was a lost cause, that they wouldn't find it, and that they wouldn't even try."

"They had already made up." Tamara nodded and threw a tiny stone into the mug; it was dirty millet.

"Her husband is a smart person, and she's no fool, she understood that it was unlikely that they would find it. But she regretted losing the coat."

"What's the coat have to do with it? She was upset."

"So she went to Tishinskii Market."

"To Minaevskii Market."

"Don't argue with me. Gavrilov told me, he works as a cobbler outside of Tishinsky Square, he saw the whole thing."

"Well Maria told me. She sells milk at Minaevskii."

"Maria's a blabbermouth, and she doesn't fill the milk up to the top. And the way she looks at you your blood could turn sour, not to mention the milk. You buy it, and it seems fresh enough, but when you take a closer look, it's sour. Her milk is only good for making buttermilk."

"Well I don't buy from her."

"Good for you. And you should spend less time listening to her, too. So the professor's wife showed up at Tishinskii, took a look at what people were selling, asked about her coat, and, maybe it was then or another time, she saw her coat, a lady was selling it. The lady sensed her interest and went about praising it, talking about how wonderful the wool was, and how nice the silver fox was, fit for a queen. The professor's wife inspected the coat, found some little spot on the lining, some kind of identifying feature, and that meant it was definitely her coat. She tried it on, and the lady began to cluck: "Ah, it sits so nicely on you, just like it was sewn for you." "Alright," the professor's wife said, "I'll take the coat, but bring the price down." They haggled, the lady brought the price down. She wrapped the coat up in paper, tied it up with twine, and the professor's wife took the bundle and left. But on the next day she showed up again."

"What was it that drew her back there?"

"Boredom."

"She could have gone to the movies."

"The movies are all make-believe."

"Did she have any kids?"

"Nobody ever told me anything about any kids. You're interrupting me, Tamara."

"I'm not saying anything."

"She walked up to that saleswoman, you know, like she decided to show off her coat. The saleswoman said, 'Yep, that coat sits wonderfully on you, just like it was sewn for you.' The professor's wife answers: 'I'm really grateful to you, maybe you have a men's coat? It's hard to pick things for my husband, he's short, my husband, and round. Something mustard-colored and made from wool would suit him.' 'And what kind of collar?' the lady inquired. 'The collar should be black. Astrakhan. And a hat just like it. Round.' While they were discussing the coat, a little boy ran up to the counter and shouted: 'Mama, give me the keys.' The saleswoman asked: 'What keys? Why aren't you in school?' 'The gym teacher got sick. They cancelled class.' 'And what about math?' 'The teacher didn't call me to the board.' 'You're lying' 'I'm not lying.' She gave him the keys and said: 'Watch yourself.' 'I am watching myself.' He ran off, and the saleswoman sighed. And she told the professor's wife about her troubles: 'The little guy had his own keys, but he lost them. He doesn't go to school. He's getting a D in math.' The professor's wife suddenly says: 'I can work on math with him. Do you want me to? I can explain it really well.' The saleswoman was surprised. 'So you're a teacher?' she asks, 'that can't be.' The professor's wife responded that, no, she wasn't a teacher and didn't work anywhere. Her husband worked, he was a scientist. 'But I can explain it,' the professor's wife says. 'You can be sure of it.' 'But what's in it for you?' 'Out of gratitude. And for the future.

I don't want to lose touch with you. Who knows what I might need.' The saleswoman said: 'No, thank you.' She flat out refused. The professor's wife left. And just then a man walked up to the counter, a lanky, sinewy guy with dark eyes. He quietly asked the saleswoman what the woman was doing hovering around there. The saleswoman answered, and the man said: 'Well, next time you invite her home.' And he looked at the saleswoman. Just like that." And Vasilii Ivanovich looked solemnly at his wife.

She snickered:

"Ooh, I'm really scared."

"You listen."

"I am listening."

The retoucher was silent throughout the entire story. And he kept silent afterwards, too.

In the meantime, Vasilii Ivanovich told about how the professor's wife showed up at the saleswoman's house, in the Sokolniki, and about how the dark-eyed man met her there, let her into the house, and locked the door, and about how there was nobody else in the building except him. The professor's wife wasn't afraid. She looked at him cheerfully. She told the dark-eyed man that she recognized him even without his beard, that she even recognized him back at the market. That is, not only did he recognize her, but she recognized him, too. And she told him that she wanted to work with him, get in on the business. The dark-eyed man couldn't believe it, but he kept silent. She said that she would tip him off. Tell him about the apartments of rich Muscovites, what they have there and when and how it would be best to break in. "I don't do apartments," the dark-eyed man said. She didn't believe him and smiled. She said, "If you decide to start doing them, give me a call." She left her phone number. She also said: "I understand that you don't believe me. But if I was an agent, I wouldn't go taking any risks, I would be careful. Anyway, it's up to you, there's only one thing that I can't help but tell you: there's nobody looking after the apartment of my friend the pilot, a war hero, and I know who has the keys and can make copies. Think about it." And with this, she left.

"She's a reckless one," was all Tamara said. She had already forgotten about picking through the millet. She was looking at Vasilii Ivanovich with her mouth open, as if she didn't already know what he was going to say.

"The dark-eyed man was reckless, too, he took the risk, got the keys, did the apartment, and things went so well for them, it was really a sight to see. The professor's wife went on living just like she did before, she went to the theater with her husband, to concerts, she scolded the housemaid if the coffee happened to be cold. Everything was as before, only sometimes she would suddenly start laughing without any reason. For example, she and her husband would be sitting at breakfast and she would suddenly go, ha ha ha. The professor looks at her, doesn't understand, but the professor's wife just waves her hand, it's nothing, she says, no reason. Her health got stronger. She started loving her professor even more sweetly. Their life became pure joy."

"But other people's lives became woe."

"She only sent him to wealthy people's apartments, the loss didn't really hurt them."

"And did she love the dark-eyed man just as sweetly?" Tamara asked, as if she didn't know the answer.

"People say no. She didn't let him get close to her. He fell in love with her, but she didn't; I'm married, that's what she said. She kept her defenses up."

"Well done."

"The dark-eyed man did well, too. He didn't give her an inch."

"You can't force someone to love you."

"He didn't use force. He behaved very respectfully toward her. As if she was the tsaritsa."

"Did he share the money with her?"

"He tried. She didn't accept anything, money or gifts."

"You see."

"But he prepared a gift for her that she couldn't refuse. A mustard-colored men's coat for her short-legged husband. With a collar made of Astrakhan. And a round hat. It was all arranged, just as she asked. She couldn't refuse such a present. He wrapped it up in paper and said: "It's yours." She carried the bundle home, her legs could barely move. Her husband wore this very coat and hat, God only knows why she described precisely this coat with this hat to the saleswoman."

"It was the first thing that came into her head." Tamara whispered.

Vasilii Ivanovich didn't even glance at his wife. He kept on telling his story in a stern voice:

"She, of course, figured out that he had taken the coat and hat off her professor. She didn't even want to take them into the house, so she threw them into the alley, but when she got home her housemaid met her and began to wail: they killed your husband, the professor, they robbed him and killed him. And on that same day the professor's wife poisoned herself."

After this story, on the very next day, the retoucher went to the Tishinskii Market and to Minaevskii. He pushed his way through the crowd for a long time, hoping to see his coat somewhere on the counter, but he never saw it. And Vasilii Ivanovich later told him that he was lucky he didn't.

The investigator working on the retoucher's case was new at the station. People treated him with caution. For nine and a half years he had worked as an investigator on especially important cases at the public prosecutor's office, and people in the know said that he was an ace. Why they transferred him to their backwoods station to work on trifles, nobody knew. He had gotten in trouble for something, but what? He was calm and polite with the victims as well as the suspects. He kept the paperwork on all his various cases in impeccable order. He wrote up the documentation competently, in great detail, and in neat handwriting. He sewed it into the folders, numbered them, marked the date and even the time. He kept getting insignificant cases, run-of-the-mill things. He investigated them with ease, since he was a meticulous person and didn't let any minor details pass him by. People thought he wouldn't stay with them for long, that the duration of his punishment would pass, they would forgive him and take him back at the prosecutor's office. It was a sin to keep such a person penned up, like keeping a whale in a washbasin. It was irrational. But the investigator knew that nobody would ever transfer him back from this station.

At six o'clock in the evening he came back to the station from a call, a worker had beaten his wife half to death. Their neighbors at the communal apartment called the militia, but by the time they got there, the wife had come to and refused to write a report, so it turned out that they had rushed over in vain. There were a few people waiting to be seen in the hallway by his office. The investigator saw the retoucher among the people waiting there, stopped in front of him, and asked with irritation:

"You? What are you doing here?"

The retoucher got up and babbled something unintelligibly.

"What?!" the investigator yelled, "I already told you! What are you doing here? Don't you have anything else to do? What? We're working on the investigation! Leave the building! Huh?!"

"I came about the ticket," the retoucher uttered.

"What?"

"A detail. A new one. A ticket. A bus ticket, in the right pocket. That day I happened to take the bus to work, in the morning."

The investigator didn't let him finish. He roared:

"Out!!!"

People started to peek out of their offices. The officer on duty, who had once warmed the retoucher up, ran up, unbuttoning his holster on the way. The retoucher stepped back out of the way and collapsed. His head hit the floor. People rushed toward him and yelled out: "Call an ambulance!" But he had already stopped breathing.

The doctor wrote down his conclusion, the officer on duty wrote up a report, and then they took the retoucher's body away to the morgue. The investigator left to go to the restroom. There he washed his hands for a long time and splashed water in his face.

The people waiting to be seen went home. The investigator told them that no one would be admitted.

He sat in his office and smoked. The officer on duty stepped in and asked, would Igor Petrovich like some herbal tea. That's what they called the investigator, Igor Petrovich. The investigator politely declined, and shortly thereafter got his things together and left. The officer on duty noted that he looked calm, as usual. The officer suspected that the investigator had been demoted from the prosecutor's office on account of a fit of rage; these sorts of things happen with people with good self-control, an outburst out of nowhere. "Maybe he shouted at his superiors," the officer decided for himself.

The investigator made his way to the Leningrad train station. Walking calmed him down. Suddenly, in a dark alley, he heard a child crying, a child groaning: mma! He froze and turned toward the voice. It was coming from the garden, just beside him: mma! A cat leaned over the picket fence then jumped on him from the bushes. He staggered back. He stood there for a minute in the quiet of the garden and then started onward.

An hour later he approached his country house.

He was unpleasantly surprised by music. It wound itself around their usually quiet house like a cocoon. The windows were glowing, voices rustled in the garden, the glow of a cigarette smoldered through the dark curtain of the night. Igor Petrovich wasn't expecting guests. He made up his mind to return to the train station, head off to Moscow on the last commuter train, and spend the night alone in his apartment. But he didn't carry out his intention. Someone called his name. Igor Petrovich turned around. His brother caught up with him.

His brother was in high spirits; he was talking excitedly about a meeting at the institute, and apologized for being late. He had barely entered the house when he announced that had brought some salted fish. The room was full of cigarette smoke and booming voices.

"What is this, Natasha?" Igor Petrovich asked his wife. "Why are these people here?"

"Did you forget, Igor? Today's Lialia's birthday." Lialia was their daughter.

Igor Petrovich responded dryly that he had worn himself out today, that God forbid someone else should have such a day.

"Don't worry about it," his wife said, "it happens. Come to the table, I fried you some cutlets."

Igor Petrovich drank to his daughter's health, told a funny story from the world of criminal investigations, ate, and went out into the garden to have a smoke.

He went deep into the garden to get away from the couple whispering on the porch, lit a match, and saw an awkward figure in a patched-up quilted jacket on the path behind the gate. He tried to get a look at the face but could only make out a pale spot in the twilight. He cried out and threw away the match, which had burnt his fingers. He pulled the cigarette out of his mouth and approached the fence. The victim stood behind the fence and looked at him.

"My apologies," he uttered in a weak, limpid voice, "I didn't finish telling you earlier today."

The investigator was silent and didn't take his eyes off the retoucher.

"It's about the ticket. It was in my right pocket. And there was the change from the ticket, a kopeck, in there. It's another detail. Who knows, it might help."

He looked at the investigator with a nearsighted, vacant stare, as if there was a wall of dark water between them, rather than air.

"My apologies."

"It's nothing," the investigator whispered.

"I'll go now."

The victim turned and started walking away from the house. The investigator watched him as he left. He stepped away from the gate. He shuddered at the snap of a branch beneath his foot as if it was a gunshot.

He remembered the cigarette. He got out his matches and managed to get a flame with his trembling hand. He smoked and went home. He looked at the guests and his family quietly, foggily, as if from afar.

The next day, the investigator headed to the morgue and asked to be shown the body. They pulled the body out of the refrigerator and showed him. They showed him his clothes: his patched-up quilted jacket, his felt boots in galoshes, his grease-smeared pants, his ancient undergarments, his worn-out military shirt, his black jacket with elbows so worn-out that they were transparent, his army hat with a dent from the little star. The coroner said that the victim died instantly.

The investigator went to the apartment of the deceased and talked to his neighbors. They had never heard about the victim having any brothers.

"He was all alone," the tailor's wife Tamara indicated. "We were the only ones who cried when he died."

The tailor Vasilii Ivanovich told him about how he had sewn the ill-fated coat, about how excellent the quality of the wool had been.

"And the lining was like silk."

The investigator listened patiently and almost attentively. Once he heard what they had to say he went back to work.

A few days later he was a little late to work: he had been finishing up some paperwork relating to some murders on suburban trains. Someone knocked on the door and, quietly, without lifting his head from the paperwork, he said:

"Yes."

The door creaked and he saw the victim meekly stepping through the doorway. All the buttons on the patched-up jacket were buttoned. His thin, bird-like neck was sticking out of his wide collar. He was crushing his hat between his hands.

The investigator found the strength to say, "I'm listening."

"My apologies," the victim said, "You're getting tired of me. But I remembered that there was an old woman looking out the window when I was walking down the alley. There was a little wooden house in the alley. And the old woman was sitting at the window. Well she probably saw the thief when he was walking after me. What do you think?"

"I'll find out."

"Thank you."

"Have a nice evening."

"You too."

The victim left. The investigator wiped his sweaty palms on his pants. Outside in the dark a spring rain was pouring.

That same evening Igor Petrovich set off for the alley indicated by the victim and found a shortish building with a black roof. He made out the pale blot of a face in an unlit window. It floated behind the glass like a fish lit up in an aquarium; it moved toward the glass border between the two worlds and froze, lacking the strength to pull its flat, round eyes away. He knocked on the window frame, and the old woman disappeared. He stood there waiting for a long time but she never appeared. He knocked on the door, but nobody approached from the other side. Igor Petrovich set off for home.

The victim was waiting for him at the entrance to his building. The investigator greeted him politely. Offered him a cigarette. The victim thanked him and declined the offer.

"Have you remembered some more details?" Igor Petrovich asked.

"It's a really remote detail," the victim responded sadly, "A plane was flying westward at the time, and I saw its lights. Who knows, maybe it will help."

"Yes," the investigator said, "very good, and it's a good thing you came by. I have some news on your case. Come with me, and I'll show you something."

And then he led the victim through various courtyards and back alleys, farther and farther away from his house, through some backyards to an abandoned foundation pit. They were planning on building something there before the war, but then they forgot altogether. The investigator led the retoucher to the edge of the pit and shot him in the back of the head with his service gun.

The next day a message came about a corpse that was found in the foundation pit. They called Igor Petrovich so that he could see the resemblance between the person who was shot and the victim with his own eyes. What was most astonishing to everyone was how closely the most minute details of their clothing corresponded.

"Someone's playing a joke on you," the coroner told the investigator. "Why on earth would someone get dressed up in felt boots and a quilted jacket in the middle of summer?"

The investigator gave orders for the fingerprints of both of the deceased to be compared. In an hour he was informed that the fingerprints were identical.

There was an envelope glowing white in the mailbox. His wife had sent a letter.

"We went swimming."

"We took the boat out."

"They're feeding us well."

"We've been buying fruit."

"Lialia's tan like chocolate."

He read the letter, took a pen, filled it with ink, and wrote his response on a piece of stationary.

"Everything's going well with me. I've been listening to concerts on the radio. I'm eating okay. I miss you."

He thought a bit and added:

"It's been raining here."

He addressed the envelope, put the letter in, and sealed it. He put the teapot on the stove. Someone rang the doorbell. He was not surprised at all to see the victim in his doorway.

"Hello, come on in. I just put the teapot on. Take off your quilted jacket. Don't worry, it's not going anywhere, I'll latch the door. Take off your felt boots, let your legs have a rest. Here are some slippers for you. They're women's, but what does it matter, they'll fit you just right."

The victim didn't say no to the tea. He drank two cups with sugar. And he ate a sandwich with cheese and butter. He wiped his sweat with a well-worn handkerchief.

Over tea the investigator told him in his quietest voice, a tired voice lacking the strength to get any louder, that he was once the best investigator at the prosecutor's office. He took on the most convoluted cases and solved all of them. There wasn't a single exception.

"That lasted a long time, until last spring. In the spring I always feel a little bit worse. I am tormented by headaches, as if my head is encircled in a blockade and gives birth to weak thoughts, feeble and sluggish thoughts, and each one poisons my brain, and there's no possibility at all of actually thinking. In the spring I always check into the clinic. They do some procedures there, I let go of my cares, and I return to my normal state. This all started after the war, after the shell shock. But that spring my head didn't hurt at all, I was happy at first, but not for long. It may not have hurt, but it also didn't think. It was as if I couldn't see the entire picture, could only grasp at little pieces, but they didn't fit together into a whole. I became forgetful. I myself asked to be transferred to a simpler job. But it's hard for me here, too. My wife takes pity on me. My daughter doesn't know about it yet. She hasn't noticed. She's engrossed in herself, and thank God. The longer it goes on, the worse it gets. Eventually I'll leave my house, start wandering across the Russian land, forget myself."

He went on talking like this, and the victim listened.

"You know what I learned at my new job? That a very simple case is the most complicated kind. You can't solve a simple case. Like yours, for example. It's impossible to come up with a way to track down your coat. That is, you can come up with one, but you can't carry it out. It's impossible. There are no people, no time. You'd need an entire army. And an entire eternity."

They parted on friendly terms.

That summer they talked a lot. More often than not, the retoucher waited for the investigator after work, in the alley. And they walked without hurrying. The investigator spoke freely. Sometimes about cases, sometimes about his health, sometimes about the war, sometimes about his daughter. The retoucher was usually silent, but sometimes he talked. Usually about his childhood, about the time when his mother and father were still alive. From his stories it became clear that this was a heavenly time; the sun would shine or would hide behind a storm cloud, the fire would roar in the fireplace, they would rake up the old leaves, a cat would go walking, and its shadow would stretch out behind it. It wasn't as wonderful as it was in his stories. Or maybe it was. Who am I to judge?

In the beginning of the fall they caught a gang in the Khamovniki District. The investigator shot the leader like an animal as he was trying to run away. He walked up to the dead man and noticed that he was dressed in a coat very similar to the retoucher's description of his own. In the pocket of the dead man, in his pants, he found a white handkerchief with blue trim. And there was a bus ticket lying in his pocket. The investigator checked the numbers: it was from the same bus ride that the retoucher mentioned. The investigator impounded the coat and took it to Vasilii Ivanovich. Tamara got the stains out, and the tailor patched up the bullet hole. The investigator carefully wrapped the coat in paper and took it back to his house (by this time other people were living in the retoucher's room). Igor Petrovich hoped to present the victim with the coat the next time he saw him. But the retoucher never returned.

For a long time people scared little children with stories about the professor's wife and the retoucher, until the seventies, until they tore down the old Mary's Grove District: the houses, gardens, vegetation, and benches. And all of the former people left these places. Both the people and the ghosts.

Translated by Jason Cieply

Kirill Kobrin (b. 1964)

Amadeus

This is the picture: snowy courtyard of a former bishop's palace, currently used as a museum. Actually, not a courtyard, just an enclosed garden, and thanks to baroque masters' vainglorious endeavors, it's full of big-butted sculptures, paths, various plants, and even a small stream, with a chubby stone boy in the middle, spouting water from his little weenie. He pees here in the spring, summer, and at the beginning of autumn; but now it's winter in the courtyard, there are no leaves, no fountain, and no visitors, there's nobody to enjoy the sight of the half-frozen stream, with the grayish ice floating in the black water. But there are people here, or, rather, there were, quite recently: somebody walked there and back, from the massive curved door opening onto the main alley of the courtyard to the furthest wall, embellished by a gallery that used to be draped with plush, but all that remains now is a skinny wooden frame, interwoven with dry, thin plush tentacles, unpleasant to look at. Through all that a wall can be seen, yellow and covered in wet spots; cracks and peeled-off plaster constitute its main decoration. Footprints lead straight to the gallery and then back to the door; they're printed clearly in the snow, untouched since last night, nobody comes here at this time of year, nobody drops in. Their appearance itself is strange but what's even stranger and more incomprehensible, is something else: in the middle of the courtyard the two pairs of feet going together turn into one pair that serenely heads for the gallery, turns around and, as if nothing happened, comes back. The other pair is suddenly cut off on the way there, without a reason or even an excuse, just so: here's somebody walking next to the person number one, maybe they went in silence or maybe they were talking, calmly or heatedly, we don't know that, and suddenly—the person is no more. Strange thing, strange and unfathomable.

* * *

The courtyard looked desolate from the museum window as is proper at a place which great style has left, abandoning all its material paraphernalia, and those now continue to live on in a wholly different world—shabby and worn down, but still heavily protected, which adds a particularly hopeless air to the loneliness of the stone and iron, twisted, wrought, united into strange constructions for the glory of ideas that the descendants won't understand. There were a lot of footprints in the snow, they were roaming around without crossing the main line: the chain of four parallel footprints, later of two, leading there and back. Turning away from the window, I asked the first and most important question: "So, did you tell them?" Sergey Morvid merrily nodded his big head, his eyes cheerful, lively, and frightened. The police had only just left him alone, they were now wandering around the museum, which was closed for this reason, its staff were questioned and then sent home, the entrance was barred with a striped band and by a sluggish giant wearing a uniform, with a big handgun stuck in too small a holster (how did he manage to fit it in? Or is all of it together, the gun and the leather case, a model, a toy, a scarecrow for the nervous Prague pickpockets and grim junkies, destroyed by cheap crap?). Neither my level of insolence nor my beastly Czech would've been adequate for me to enter into an interesting conversation with a policeman about big handguns and small holsters (something almost divine rings in this word, doesn't it: *holster*, a rhyme for *apostle*), I should be glad he let me in at all—me, a foreigner and journalist, and therefore doubly dangerous and suspicious. Saying, Mr. Morvid doesn't have a lawyer, so he asked a friend to come and offer him both moral support and advice in this strange situation he cannot begin to understand. Had there been a real offense, robbery, rape, murder, nobody would've let in such a villain as me but here . . . What's there to investigate when there's nothing: just the footprints and fables of a museum guy, who's certainly nuts, about how he was walking in the courtyard with a crazy guest from Russia and how, halfway through an unhurried discussion about divine retribution and its falling upon the heads of sinners, one of the participants suddenly disappeared, dissolved in the damp air of the Prague Castle—or was by the wave of the Lord's hand instantly taken away in an unknown direction, hell or heaven, it's impossible to say which. "So was it heaven or hell? What do you think?" Morvid scratched his chin with his miniature monkey-like hand and blurted out: "Heaven!" "Why so, my dear Sergey? He was . . . I mean he *is* . . . either way, he's a blasphemer?" "Apophatically, Andrei, apophatically. These days you don't have many people who'd think about God. I don't mean take His name in vain or in times of need, but *think*. Be it in an ill way, without any preparation or skill for it, but *think*. Laika thought." "In the past tense?" "Of course, my dearest Andrei! He doesn't think now, he *sees*." It was difficult to object to this exaltation, born of a long habit of homemade sweet-and-sour theologizing mixed with a quiet hysterics caused by the fantastic event. Go to Lourdes and try to give the ill a scientific lecture on remission.

"So what, did he disappear?" "He did!" shouted Morvid in raptures, his eyes glistening, his hands playing with the museum leaflets. A fidgety police specialist with a gigantic bag is wandering around the courtyard. He stops. Takes a camera out of the bag. Snaps. Puts the camera back in. Wanders around again. "Did you tell them everything?" "Of course! Everything they wanted to know." "As in, not everything?" "Andrei, tell me, why would the police need to know about the concept of awakened God?" "What God?" "Awakened. Woken up from a sleep. Disturbed. Emerged from a coma."

This was how Morvid described the whole thing. Laika, having arrived in Prague on an early train, immediately went to the museum, as he'd agreed with Sergey, who on this special occasion crept to work at seven thirty in the morning. The idea was that they'd spend the whole day together in a theological dispute, after which the artist would take the Moscow-bound train late at night and go back home. Morvid would go home, too, but much closer, into his small apartment not far from the Strahov Monastery, about half-an-hour's walk from the former bishop's palace. Sergey was counting down the years left to his retirement so that he could ride on the tram free of charge; for now, the modest salary made him exercise his legs and heart on the magnificent cobblestones of the Hradčany district every working day. Once, at the height of the January black ice, he slipped and fell down so badly that he then spent ages in hospitals, where his broken legs were being put together, glued together, and grown back together. Then it took Morvid a long time to learn how to walk anew; the doctors advised him to use ski poles, so that's how he was moving about Hradčany now—a skier without skis, a shoe-nonmaker with huge boots that the doctors had prescribed him because of the heavy damage to his legs, the poles moving back and forth, knocking on the pavement. A look to make saints laugh—but Sergey would never let those be offended. Some time before we knew each other, that is before I moved to Prague, he even wrote up something of a treatise about the Czech saints. Didn't manage to have it published but I got a home-printed copy of this masterpiece at our first meeting in autumn 2001—that precisely was how Morvid advised me to start my studies of the local life. Not from the dumplings, beer, foreigners' police department, and discussions about President Havel's second marriage, but from the saints of the Czech lands (and of Moravia alike). I didn't conquer his work but I did have a look: the author was basing it on a concept, created by himself, of a special gently malicious type of the Slavic holiness; all of his heroes possessed, as the author put it, "kind cunning," which was the result of the transitional position of the Czech nation between the warlike eastern Slavs and no less cruel and rough Germans. None of my arguments about, as it seemed to me, true personal characteristics of the local inhabitants were having any influence on Morvid; he took it so far as to believe the Czechs played ice hockey in a gentle and cunning way. To discuss the kind cunning of Jaromír Jágr was more than I was capable of.

And so, here I am, sitting in his office like hundreds of times before; by the entrance door stand the legendary ski poles, on the rug stand the equally legendary boots four sizes larger than Morvid's feet. It's them that are printed out there, in the snow, next to the mystically vanishing footprints of the blasphemous Russian artist who'd been punished (or rewarded) by the Lord Himself. "And how did you get that idea at all? What theological disputes? Or even duels—that's what you called it . . ." "Andrei, and how else do you imagine a discussion about God's wrath and retribution? What's it supposed to look like? Filthy posts in Livejournal?" Morvid moved here immediately after the notorious shelling of the White House in Moscow, learned the local language perfectly, but still, strangely, kept using his Russian. That is, not even kept; he jumped, fluttered, galloped, emptied himself, reproduced himself by division with his mother tongue that had fallen in a perfectly whorish position in the modern world, offering itself to everybody right and left: the merry American, the gold-toothed Mongolian, the distilled auditor, and even the Tajik caretaker. We've been enjoying the fruits of lexical fornication for about twenty years and together with us—the emigrant of theology, Czechophile, and connoisseur of saints, Sergey Morvid.

"Yes, Livejournal . . . But, Sergey, wasn't that where you bumped into Laika for the first time?" "Andrei, dear, I beg you, what nonsense is this now? Are you saying that if you meet an interesting partner for discussion in a dirty alehouse, you shouldn't go beyond its pissed boundaries for anything in the world?" I liked the "pissed boundaries"; there was something Jesuit, Latin, Mercatorian about it. Isn't he a Catholic, by the way? Hardly.

The more so that the ascended (descended) Laika, they say, was friends with the author of the work that caused an outcry in its time, *Obossany pistolet* [Pissed Handgun], which Morvid knew well—it was him who let me read this work of the cheeky artistic genius, who'd defaced Kazimir Malevich's colorful squares. A year in a Dutch prison he got for it . . . Some time ago, in the half-starved Russian years, it would've seemed to me that's not exactly a punishment . . . As for Laika, he didn't write books. Or paint pictures, God be praised. First he barked, and he did it so credibly that dogs were gathering when he did and started a yapping shootout with him. How Boris Mitrich-Korovin—who only later received his sweet doggy nickname—did this, is hard to understand. Cynologists shrugged their shoulders, specialists babbled something or other about certain wavelengths with which Laika's voice resonated, but nobody was able to find out for sure. One way or another, Laika kicked off his career with real zeal, standing on his hind legs and with his head proudly tilted back: as soon as a year later he was touring around with a pack of dogs performing the anthem of the Soviet Union and "God Save the Tsar." The dog-and-bitch band was desperately out of tune, but the look of it was unforgettable. The main role in the success of the Dog Anthem performance was played by Communists and monarchists who put up wild protests, creating open letters demanding an exemplary punishment. Laika also got beaten up in a Moscow passageway but not too much, which gave the audience a reason to doubt the authenticity of the incident. The artist beat himself up, right. The doubts made sense: the thing was that nobody ever saw Laika. At the performances, he was always wearing an overalls made of dog skins, and a mask depicting a werewolf; his voice wasn't heard either because the artist didn't speak, he barked. In Austria, Laika was known as X-Mongrel, the British named him Russian Banksy. Anyway, the doggy music show became boring pretty quickly; furthermore, anybody could tear the dog skin from his trembling body or shout: "Laika, take off the mask!" To make a long story short, he disappeared.

Not altogether, of course. All Laika did was simply move, having made for himself an online kennel. There he began the main project of his life, called *Dear God, Punish Me!* Laika was exercising in blasphemy, posting various nasty pictures that would've been punishable not only by thunder and heavenly fire but also very simply in accordance with the criminal law. Pedophilia, little jokes about the victims of the Holocaust and the GULAG, appeals to overthrow the authorities—all this mixed with juicy anticlericalism and dishonoring of Him above. Laika's blog was attacked by Orthodox and liberal hackers, it was shut down by the grim prosecutors of Saransk and Magnitogorsk (and Moscow prosecutors issued an arrest warrant straight away), all in vain; the Kennel (as he called his internet bunker) kept coming back to life all the time in various places; the diligent warrior with the World Order and the Divine Order was regularly posting documents proving how he, wretched and unloved, was being pursued by everybody around; then he again took up the atrocities. The public were in turns mocking him, taking offense, and applauding—anything but forgetting the son of a bitch. And he was enjoying the power over people's minds and imaginations, and once a month he sent to God a detailed electronic list of his heroic deeds, always adding at the end: "Well, dear God, punish me!" And now my friend Morvid here was persuading me that He had punished him. Or at least taken notice.

Normally quiet Sergey immediately got pulled into the whole story. At first he was honestly writing comments to Laika's offensive posts, and later created a special blog, where he entered into a theological dispute with the artist. Oh, no, he didn't subject the blasphemer's opinions to rough moral judgment, didn't argue with him about humanism or even common sense, didn't persuade, didn't curse, didn't yap. No. Morvid came as an interpreter, translator of God—only not of the Word of God, but the absence of the Word. Why the Highest One is silent when He—and His people—are ridiculed by a half-illiterate, primitive, stupid, cynical swine, stinking ugly bitch Laika? Sergey calmly and logically offered him an explanation; everything was as it should be: the jester's raging, the tsar's smiling into his beard and not saying anything. The more hysterical the clown's frenzy, the more reasonable the theologian's argumentation. Finally Laika, beside himself with fury, announced that he'd beat Morvid black and blue. Sergey's reaction to this proposal was perfectly cordial: come to Prague, we'll meet, we'll talk. And so they did.

Having drunk some tea and more or less calmed Sergey down, I set out for editorial—to put together the material about what had happened. The local expat English-language newspaper had no business dealing with Dostoyevskian contentions of former Russians, but the story about the footprints in the snow was eagerly accepted. So, two plots were created. One, Baskervillian, about the disappearance of the other pair of feet. The other one, Leskovian, about a psychopathic blasphemer and a calm saint. I alone knew about the third one, the Chestertonian, about the theology duel with the violent (volant?) outcome.

The issue was swept under the carpet rather quickly; or, it swept *itself* based on the fact that the injured party (or, the disappeared party—we don't know whether Laika was *injured* in the process of vanishing) was never seen by anybody. The border control confirmed that a citizen of the Russian Federation of the surname "Mitrich-Korovin" did enter the territory of the Czech Republic on a train the night preceding the fatal discussion. He did not leave the country. Nobody missed Laika in Russia, understandably, and the internet mockers, certain that the artist went into hiding while working on another prank, refocused on some scandalous lexicographer and his cohort. Timur the self-appointed linguist was producing one after another dictionaries, dedicated to the culinary vocabulary of the Russian language, and his retinue were attacking the customers of famous Moscow restaurants, tying them up, and sticking into the mouths of the bourgeoisie pages torn out of the immortal works of their black-bearded guru. The project was called *Quail the Gourmet*. One of the victims didn't survive the mockery and died on the spot in the hands of the art-revolutionaries. The lexicographic war ended in trials, hurried escapes abroad, warrants from Interpol, and a large-scale international discussion about how far contemporary art is allowed to go. As usual, no conclusion was arrived at. Who'd remember some poor blasphemous dog? As for the Czech police, for them, of course, the absence of a person meant there was no problem to solve. And who ever saw this guy? Who looked for him?

Morvid did look for him. He kept sending letters to the police directorate, went on audiences to the deputy minister of the interior, and made his journalistic acquaintances write articles about the strange, incomprehensible disappearance of the insolent blasphemer. All in vain. In the end, the authorities hinted that should Mr. Morvid stubbornly persist in his actions, they should be forced to question the state of his mind as well as examine the issue of whether such an exalted (although very knowledgeable, cultured, and professional) person should be working at a position which requires him daily to deal with the treasures of Czech painting. Maybe he shouldn't. Sergey fell silent, withdrew, almost stopped calling. He didn't believe that anybody believed his version of the story of Laika's disappearance; to tell the truth, I didn't quite believe that I believed it myself.

A year passed. It was winter again, and there was snow—a thing not all that frequent in this region, but almost obligatory in recent years, global warming, cooling, devil knows them. I was making my way through the wondrously slippery square between the Loreta cloister and the ministry of foreign affairs; the tourists around were staggering, falling, guffawing (Italians), swearing (Russians). It was fun and it was dreadful to move one's feet carefully from one cobblestone covered in ice to another, especially on the sloping pavement; to cut a long story short, when I fell down and was on all fours, musing about which hand was supposed to come off the ground first, Sergey's gigantic boots suddenly entered my vision and stopped. He was standing above me, with ski poles in his hands, a kind and awkward smile on his lips, above his head was a strangely blue sky, embellished by allegorical, curly clouds. "I'm sorry for not giving you a hand—but I'd fall myself!" "No worries," I was back on my two feet by now, shaking the snow off, fixing the backpack on my back, greeting my good friend, "I can do it. Haven't seen you for ages! What's your news?"

There was a lot of news, a lot—almost five hundred pages of the second Morvid treatise—this time not about the Czech saints but about the source of all holiness, about God. Sergey had settled the score with the story of Laika's disappearance, and with Laika himself, who now couldn't respond to anything. And there was a lot to tell him, a lot to bark out! Not content with banal judgments about the apophatic proof of God's existence, Morvid suggested a wholly unimaginable treatment of the issue: he called the blasphemer "saint," who was with his insults attempting to "awaken God from His sleep." "You wouldn't start telling off a hoodlum who slapped an old man lying in coma, if the man magically woke up as a result? Quite the contrary. Endless will be the gratefulness. The artist Laika set as his goal to wake up God, who had stopped granting attention to this world. And he succeeded. God woke up and took Laika, like He took the saints when their lives, full of work, ended." All this I read later, in the evening and during the following several evenings; and then we sat down together in a tearoom in Neruda Street, with a certificate hanging behind Morvid's back about how here, in this building, Miloš Forman had shot some scene or other of *Amadeus*. I was sipping tepid gyokuro, Sergey was fighting his way through some complicated ayurvedic drink, a group of cheerful Russians fell into the café, with cameras, small bags, guides, all wrapped in carefully tied "casual" scarves of bright colors, three girls, two boys. One of the boys immediately went to search for a bathroom, made a mistake, instead of the bathroom opened a door into some staff room, awkwardly excused himself, snagged on a chair, dropped something . . . "Borya, have you gone mad!"

shouted one of the ladies with rosy cheeks, her black eyes like olives, unruly curls falling out from under a knitted Tibetan cap. Morvid sighed. "I don't want to rush you but I'd really appreciate it if you could read that book I gave you. You understand, after what happened a year ago, I can't return to my previous life. I'm lonely. As if I'd lost myself." I had my doubts regarding the sincerity of his words, but upon noticing the serious, almost martyred look of him, I realized he wasn't exaggerating.

The treatise was dedicated to "B. M.-K." and was Morvid's masterpiece. About four hundred years ago, in the baroque Prague, it would have been examined, reprinted, passed from hand to hand, from library to library, extolled and reviled. Nobody needed it now, myself included. I don't know about the Highest One, but the God of the theology genre wasn't sleeping—he'd long been lying in his grave, giving no hints of resurrection. But I couldn't get out of my mind this Laika story; and crucial was not the question *where* the blasphemer had disappeared and not even *whether* he'd disappeared at all, but something completely different: has the main and only witness of the event, Sergey, taken leave of his senses? In my mind, I was analyzing that discussion we'd had together, when I rushed to his office immediately after he asked me to, how I was questioning him, who was taken aback, frightened and exalted, how he was staring at the courtyard, at the chains of footprints in the snow, how he turned his look at the room, the writing desk with an old-fashioned computer, the ski poles and the boots in the corner, next to them a black bag, darkened with dampness, a funny coffee table from the "normalization" era of the seventies, two cups, a teapot, carefully wrapped in a perfectly vintage towel with an embroidery, almost an ancient Slavic ritual cloth, a very Soviet sandwich with butter and cheese, which the nervous theologian is offering to share with me, excuse me Andrei, I never expect anybody, always bring food only for myself alone but it's too much for me, too much, I actually don't feel like eating . . . God, what nonsense.

Unlike in 2001, I couldn't avoid discussing Morvid's opus this time; even the treatise itself was of a wholly different type and quality, let alone the conditions and motives of its writing. I had to meet with Sergey; as soon as I understood that, I started the preparations: knowing the museum-ish, bibliographic character of my friend, I had to be fully armed—to speak persuasively, to have all the facts and versions in my hands, to interpret seriously, logically, and, after all, irrefutably. I did my best. After (and often instead of) my work I browsed Russian forums and blogs and studied the

infamous biography of Boris Mitrich-Korovin aka Laika, his howling, barking, and teeth-grinding, his despicable provocateurship, his heavy schizo-
phrenia, which, I'm sure, had determined his destiny from its start, covered
in Soviet fog, to the uncomely end. Finally, I was ready. Called him. Agreed
to meet in the same tearoom as before. It's strange they haven't named the
place Amadeus.

Ayurvedic tea. Gyokuro. Everything exactly like two weeks ago, only
there are no Russian tourists this time, nobody takes the staff room for
the lavatory. "Boris . . ." Morvid tore his eyes away from the cloudy cinna-
mon-like liquid in his cup and gave me a strange look. "What?"

"You remember, how the last time there were Russians here, shouting
loudly . . ."

"Oh, yes. So, the book? Do you like it?"

"Wonderful, Sergey, wonderful. You, how they'd say nowadays in
Russia, closed the issue. There's nothing more to say. The truth's there, dis-
closed in all its light. Black light."

"Why black? You aren't accusing me of Gnosticism, are you?"

"No, how could I . . . Although there is something Gnostic about this
whole story . . . No. It's not Gnosticism but immeasurable, monstrous,
unchained vanity."

" . . . ?"

"So, yes, of course, vanity, and what else? A quiet life during the last
breath of the socialist regime, wretchedness of a provincial associate professor in Gaidar's Russia, what else? . . . Escape to the pitiful Czech land, to
the museum, strangers around, strange books, all strange, cold, making no
sense. All that's left is to weave together fairytales about the Czech holiness
. . . More tea?"

"No-no, I still have some, thank you! So, what else?"

"Yes . . . And then suddenly, thanks be to you, God of Silicon Valley,
some internet appears there, Russian drivel, forums, blogs . . . Gives unlim-
ited possibilities to preach, create, make up things . . . You begged somebody there in Russia to act the dog?"

"Andrei, you're a skeptic, and such are not to understand the whole
greatness and power of the Lord, be it a regional and silicone one. Who
ever saw my Laika in person? And his dogs? Nobody. His performances
were written about, true; even some video appeared but, you understand
yourself, to find a few minutes of doggy video on the internet and add a
different sound to it . . . Well, I mean . . ."

"Damn, you're even smarter . . . And I naively thought about collaborators, accomplices, assistants . . . But it doesn't matter anymore. Then your Laika got listed as a blasphemer and villain. What for?"

"Andrei, you read my book! Or didn't read it again? No? Yes?"

"All right, got it. To awaken God from His sleep. More precisely, to awaken the most esteemed public from its sleep with regards to God. A beautiful and most noble goal . . ."

"And what is it that you don't like about it?"

"The lies, dear Morvid, the lies. The sophisticated, hysterical, creative lies. No, not theology—the lies of a schizophrenic. It was all for the sake of power, and not for God, was it? You made up a son of a bitch, then silenced him, in the same way silencing the Highest One, and then wrote a treatise about it, didn't you?" Morvid was silent. He wasn't disturbed. Or upset. He was rejoicing.

"Well, and then you reached the finale, a true Chestertonian finale, theology together with the disappearance of a person in the middle of a city—that's typical Gilbert Keith. Your other passport came handy, the one in your real name?"

"First, Andrei, my first passport."

"Well yes, Boris. That's what I mean. The first. Just don't tremble at the sound of this name. Aren't there enough Borises?"

"Andrei, my dear, I knew I'd be caught on this."

"And the other, the wet pair of boots in the bag? And only one sandwich for two people, for yourself and—don't get upset—Boris, you were meeting him at the station? Wouldn't you feed the blasphemer?"

"Mea culpa. Several blunders. But the plan was carried out! It all succeeded!" Cunning flamed up again in his look, but this time it was heavy, evil, hopeless, nothing besides it, except the wish to lie, just for the sake of it, to mystify everything, his own life, another life, life in general, theology, criminalistics, everything. There's nothing except the lie, that endless winking at oneself in the mirror that reflects in the mirror opposite, and so on, until everything in this world becomes an eternal, evil, cunning sneer, hopeless smirk of the specter of Communism, Hirst's grinning skull, covered in gritted brilliants. "Well, in fact, Gnosticism, yes."

"You think so?" I heard a bashful hope in his voice, no, don't give any hints on the fulfilling of wishes, plans, etc., none, or else cunning again, that holiness for the wretched. "I'll pay for it. The tea."

"You're very kind, Andrei . . ."

"You think so?"

We were slowly making our way up the Neruda Street, that is, I was making my way, and Morvid was crawling along, swinging his poles. People were backing away awkwardly, only children were giggling, but from afar, at a safe distance. "If you dress your poles in those shoes, there'll be three of us, not two. Did you practice for a long time? The footprints looked very real."

"I'm a serious person, Andrei. Of course. A few months. Traveled to Russia. Bought two pairs. Threw away one of them later, they were falling off the pole baskets. Sprinkled sand on the floor at home, learned, studied the prints. I'd say I was successful!"

"It was splendid, just splendid. And further, the way I imagine it? You came to the museum before anybody else, put the boots on the poles, walked with them halfway through the courtyard, then took the poles into one hand, shoes into the other, to the wall, then back, and no more Laika? Dissolved in thin air? Gone with the wind?" Morvid cut a nice look: flushed, either from the walk or from the satisfaction, or from God knows what. No, not nice, of course not, strange, just strange; it was joy but joy that had no relationship whatsoever to me, to the others, to the human race. It was as if he were giving thanks to a God unknown to me, and I was present somewhat awkwardly, a stranger to his joys and games . . . And anyway, I'm tired and it's time to go home. We came out to the square, in the middle of it stands a plague column, behind us and on the left is a church, turned into a hotel, kiosks selling trifles, a café for idlers. A gray, rag-like sky. Freezing, freezing to the bone. "Well anyway, I've got to go. Thank you, Andrei, for reading my book to the end. You understood almost everything truthfully, bravo." He took both the poles in one hand and held the other out to me. Oh my God, of course! "Listen, you don't need those!"

"What don't I need?"

"The poles. Ski poles."

"Well, no, I don't. So what?"

"So why have you been dragging them along for ten years? Who do you want to fool?"

"No, Andrei, I shouldn't have praised you. You haven't understood anything. Goodbye."

He hardly ever changed them during all the years, those ski poles. Their points had worn down against the Prague cobblestones. The baskets were all damaged and badly scratched. The handgrips were disfigured, the straps had long gone nobody knows where. I took a close look at them while I was waiting for the investigator the next day, in the little courtyard of the former bishop's palace, in the shallow, thawing snow. The scared museum workers were crowding behind a huge glass door, I could see their vague, limp gestures, gray faces, soundless sentences. Two chains of footprints were leading from the door; in the middle of the courtyard the two pairs of feet turn into one pair that serenely heads for the gallery, turns around and, as if nothing happened, comes back. The other pair is suddenly cut off on the way there, without a reason or even an excuse, just so: here's somebody walking next to the person number one, maybe they went in silence or maybe they were talking, calmly or heatedly, we don't know that, and suddenly—the person is no more. Strange thing, strange and unfathomable. But there's something else, even stranger. Next to the door, next to the trashcan, lies a pair of ski poles. Next to them, leaning on the wall, sits their owner, Sergey Morvid, he's mort, excuse me, he's dead. Rigor mortis has set in. His head is drooping in an ugly way with the unnaturally extended neck, from which hangs a piece of a cord. Another piece is tied to the gorgeous, baroque-style, copper door handle. Morvid's legs are stretched out. If you wish, you can compare the pattern of the soles of his huge boots with the footprints in the snow, those that walked there and back. As for the other pair, it's lying, hurriedly stuck into the wet black bag, in the trashcan. I know it, but won't tell anybody.

Translated by Veronika Lakotová

Pavel Peppershtein (b. 1966)

Tongue

In 2008, a certain rebel detachment was retreating under attack by government forces in the jungles of Latin America. The detachment was large, Marxist, with a long history and considerable fame: the story of their struggle had already stretched over thirty-five years. Since the seventies of the last century, they'd fought in the forests, at times took cities, at other times the detachment was shattered and completely destroyed, but inevitably it was resurrected and once again undertook the struggle. Sometimes it joined with other rebel armies, sometimes the commanders of the detachment entered the government, but that never lasted long, and they once again disappeared into the forest, accompanied by loyal friends and automatic weapons.

Since 2004, the detachment had been led by a woman—legendary in that country—named Aureliana Toledo, but better known as Comandante Aura. She was a thirty-five-year-old half-native woman—not tall, dark-skinned, with black hair and a beautiful, decisive face. That face—in a Che Guevara beret with a small red flag pin on it—could be seen throughout the country on illegal posters and leaflets. At one point, she had studied at some university in North America, then she became a popular journalist, headed up the Central Committee of the Freedom Front, for a year she even served as Minister of Labor. But after the military putsch of 2002, she took up arms and went into the forest.

From that moment, the name "Comandante Aura" became a symbol of the resistance—songs were sung about her, indigenous legends were retold about her online on popular rebel websites. In 2007, Aura's detachment supported an attempted coup d'état undertaken by the so-called "Red Majors," but the coup failed and the group of officer-conspirators was shot, and government forces then turned to the most decisive and severe measures in their fight against Aura's detachment.

After innumerable battles and skirmishes with military units, her detachment had lost more than half of its people and had retreated farther into the forest. Government forces had followed on their heels.

In the last few days the military had begun to surround and "seal" the detachment into a tight and swampy piece of jungle that would deprive them of the freedom of movement and doom them to a slow extinction in the pathogenic miasma of the swamps. They needed to break the enemy line.

Comandante Aura sat in her tent staring at the screen of a small computer. Suddenly she shut the computer case and ran a tired hand across her face. In half an hour she was supposed to go out to her fighters and say a few words before launching the attack. Such things always came easily to her—she knew how to inspire her people, to find the necessary "magic" words that would breathe strength into the weary, chase away doubt, awaken courage, make them believe that death was nothing but a scarcely noticeable blemish on the body of the struggle.

Into the tent came Juan Callo, her loyal assistant and lover, her "subcomandante," a former ethnographer and now—for many years already—among the most intelligent and experienced of her commanders.

"Everything is ready," he said, looking at her with his dark, very attentive eyes. "Everything is ready for battle."

They both understood the meaning of those words.

Aura pulled him toward her, and in a rough motion she tore at the buckle of his old Soviet belt, emblazoned with a five-pointed star, and unzipped his camouflage pants. She took out his dark, indigenous member and with quick motions of her tongue made him hard. Despite the harsh rebel life, she was a sophisticated and passionate lover. Love became an indispensable part of her struggle, and when the fighting allowed she gave herself over to love with an ecstatic art. She was fluent in a "dance of the tongue" that made her lovers moan in ecstasy as if in pain and made them see waking dreams. With the motions of her tongue she reproduced, it seemed to her, the heated rhythms of those dances that men and women since the ancients had danced in her region. A native music sounded in her head as her tongue danced and simultaneously words came to her—words of the Spanish tongue interspersed with indigenous words and turns of phrase. Those words that she would say to her fighters.

She went out to the fighters, the taste of her lover's sperm still on her tongue—that taste for her hid the rivers and secret pathways of the country, for whose freedom she was fighting. With that taste on her tongue, she knew her speech would not be fruitless: it would reach their hearts.

She stood before her fighters and pronounced:

Soldiers of the Revolution!

Do you remember what the natives call "*valluzo*"? It is a sickness that even today can be found in our villages—a person looks just like everyone else, he does his daily work, lives his life, but he no longer feels that he is living. It is with this disease that Capital is trying to infect us all. Living corpses are attacking us with their warfare—Capital has bought not only their conscience, but their entire existence. There is a pale impotence in the power with which Capital has entangled the entire world. Its spider web becomes ever thicker, infiltrating every crack. Capitalism has changed—before, it gave at least some measure of an evil joy. Now it brings joy to no one, and so it strives to destroy those who still know the taste of joy. Mighty Capital is permeated by its envy of us, the dispossessed but unvanquished, the last to retain the joy of the struggle. Capital made the word "poetry" indecent, it made the word "happiness" into a name for its transactions, it made the word "life" into a synonym for "profit." It destroyed the meaning of the word "dignity." We fight not only for the oppressed and the deceived, we fight for the cry of birds and the words of poets, we are led by the Spanish tongue itself, and it demands that we return meaning to its words.

We struggle against suffocation, against *valluzo*, against a world of sleek robots! I dedicate this battle to the red flag, just as poets dedicate verses to their beloved. It is said that no little evil has been committed under this flag or in its name, but who can count how much evil has been done in the name of love? This flag, like Venus, who became virginal after every copulation— every act of love with her spills blood. Flag of love, you won't be left to rot in the swamp! You cannot be bought! You are the living flame of our hearts. Our war is not like that of the coyotes of profits. It is a war of life, a war to break through the web of suffocation! Long live war! To battle, children of the poor!

The people of the detachment threw their weapons in the air and cried: VIVA LA GUERRA! VIVA AURA!

Many of them were natives and poorly understood the words of the speech, others—old fighters—had heard similar speeches many times, but none of that mattered—the magic of the Spanish words, Aura's low, mysterious voice, her flashing, narrow, black eyes, her impassive face—all this had an intoxicating effect. Fear and fatigue disappeared. The confusion of thought and torpidity of action brought on by the jungle dissipated. The battle began.

They broke through. They counterattacked with breakneck speed and desperation, they tossed aside government forces and pushed out of the marshy area of the jungle onto a plateau where the forests were clearer and drier and where there were many villages sympathetic to the red guerillas.

The next morning Aura awoke in one such village in the gymnasium of a Catholic school, which they had made their temporary headquarters. She immediately realized something had happened to her. She was lying on a leather mat, above her head hung rings for gymnastic exercises, next to her slept Juan Callo. Everything was quiet, but she knew something terrible had happened. At first she thought she had contracted one of the diseases of the jungle, but no—she felt perfectly healthy and full of strength. She quietly got up and went to the open window. And suddenly she realized— she had no tongue. She went numb. She got out a mirror and looked at the reflection of her open mouth. Her tongue was gone. She saw no wound or blood or anything of the sort. She did not feel the slightest pain. Her tongue simply disappeared as if it had never been there at all.

She quickly got out a flask of rum and took a drink. The alcohol lightly burned in her throat but she didn't sense any taste. Then she lit a cigarette— it was extremely strange to inhale the smoke without a tongue. Without that sensitive pathway against which the smoke curls.

She fell into thought.

She asked herself what happened and her consciousness answered with one single word:

"Llaba."

It was an indigenous word: that's what they called it in those places where she was born. This word, extraordinarily important in those parts, meant sorcery. What happened could have only one explanation—llaba. She was the victim of a curse.

Aura was an ardent Marxist, but not a benighted Marxist. She was educated and intelligent and fully understood that magic was real. Her native roots informed her of this and she did not see the least contradiction between magic and Marxism.

Even in her youth, while studying at the university, she copied down in her notebook passages she liked from the book of the Soviet scholar Propp who studied fairy tales and ancient rituals:

"Frazer writes that physical strength was the decisive quality during the ritual athletic competitions on the ancestors' graves. But Frazer is a bourgeois scholar and his view on such things is limited by the framework of his class-consciousness. We, as Marxist scholars, clearly understand that it was not physical strength but magical power that played the decisive role during such competitions."

Aura sat on her haunches on the floor in the small school kitchen. She took one more drink of rum—she tasted nothing but she felt more at ease. She lit another cigarette. She thought intently about her situation. What was to be done?

First, without delay she would need to give over command of the detachment to Juan Callo or Major Tajo, two people she fully trusted.

Second: no one in the detachment was to know what happened to her. A rumor about how Comandante Aura was the victim of *llaba* and had lost her tongue could demoralize the unit. None of the fighters should even see her. As soon as possible one of her closest allies (Juan Callo) should take her away somewhere to another place, and she should not return to the detachment until the curse had been lifted. The fighters were to be told that she had gone to the neighboring country for talks with its government: that quarter might be able to offer support.

Third: as quickly as possible they would have to find a *llaba-chocho*, a breaker of curses. It would be best if he (or she) was from her own region, though those lands were not nearby.

Having made this plan, she wrote a note to Juan Callo, woke him, and handed him the piece of paper. He read the following:

"I cannot talk. Don't ask questions. It's *llaba*. Get a car and take me to town."

Juan Callo wasted no time on empty astonishment. In the dark of the night they walked through the school building where exhausted soldiers slept in hammocks and on the floor. Then they woke Major Tajo, explained that they were leaving for several days, gave him the necessary instructions, got into a small truck, and left the village. In the next settlement they altered their appearances and took on false identities. Aura had to continue in men's clothing—her hair was cut short: she transformed into a small mestizo with the somewhat gloomy appearance of a *pájaro*, or homosexual.

In the pocket of her black suit were identification documents under the name Raul Jurgens, an employee of a large commercial company based in the capital—the company did actually exist and had long supported the red guerillas. Throughout the trip, she wrote notes of instructions to Juan Callo. And then lit those notes aflame and tossed them out the window—they flew apart into burning scraps behind the truck. In each settlement, they were greeted and quickly offered anything they needed: they changed vehicles, appearances, papers. But Aura always remained a man. As if having lost her tongue, she lost her right to her sex.

Several days later their car stopped in front of a house in the dirty outskirts of the capital. The neighborhood had a bad reputation. A sign glowed with red and blue lights that announced "Strip Bar Suaveseco." The name could be translated as "Gently," or "Slower," or even "Slow Down." And indeed many cars slowed down in front of this place. Two men in black got out of the car and went into the place: one strong, about forty years old, the other a skinny, slightly effeminate mestizo. At the entrance, the older one told the guard simply, "Don Guino."

Don Guino met them in his office, the owner's office. He was a bald, sweaty man in a red silk shirt with the face and mustache of an inveterate lowlife, made of, it seemed, nothing but sperm and money. Very few knew that he was a confirmed supporter of the revolution.

He recognized Callo immediately, but not Aura. The office was thick with the smell of cigars and alcohol. Guino was ready to offer his services. Callo briefly described the situation without unnecessary details. The word *llaba* explained everything.

"I knew one *llaba-chocho*," Guino said thoughtfully. "She lived in Corte Siesta. I don't know if she's still alive. Go downstairs, watch the striptease. I'll make some calls to find out about the old *llaba-chocho*. For now enjoy watching our girls. It's a beautiful garden we have. Our establishment is the best around; you won't find anything like it downtown. If anyone doubted that before, our competitors have been biting their elbows over the last couple days. A few days ago an unbelievable beauty appeared, a dazzling orchid. The way she dances, it takes your breath away. The customers come non-stop. Over the last couple of days we've gotten rich like Bill Gates. She's eclipsed everyone. Her name is Giralda, the weathercock. The way she swings around that pole kicks up a breeze to blow the head off your beer. Go downstairs. You'll see her soon." And he reached for his phone.

Callo and Aura went down to the club, which really was packed. They squeezed through a group of men, drunk and sober, with cigars and without. Aura felt that all these people saw that she was a woman dressed as a man and looked at her mockingly, but in reality no one paid them any attention. The clientele here was diverse. Some came from the gold mines, lips black from *chimo*, paying for their drinks with gold dust; others were lowlifes from the capital, eyes flashing from cocaine, drunk military types, gringos, people in expensive suits who came with bodyguards. Everyone here mixed together, and the faces of the men appeared and melted away in the blue reflections of thick tobacco smoke.

The girls came out one after another onto the illuminated platform, danced around the pole, undressed while they danced, the audience applauded, threw money on stage. Sometimes they went out into the crowd, danced at one table or another, men tucked bills into the threads of their nominal underwear. They did the Dance of Liana around one client or another, then returned to the pole on stage and finished their performance. To Aura it seemed that this whole smoke-filled and crowded place, the whole "Suaveseco" establishment was like a mechanical carousel: colorful tin ponies running in a circle, neighing and ringing bells, while everything inexorably revolved around the shining metallic axis held under the pressure of an invisible hand—around the pole.

Some of the girls were pretty, but everyone here was waiting for Giralda, and at times they took to shouting her name. And then, from behind the red velvet curtain appeared a long beautiful leg in a red heel, and then across the velvet slid a tender hand with thin fingers, and then Giralda herself appeared in front of everyone in a close-fitting red dress sparkling with gold. Everyone clapped and raised their voices in exultation. She traced the contours of the room with a lethargic, moist, absentminded gaze and for a second her languid and strangely moist eyes paused on Aura's face. She seemed to smile and immediately began her dance. Aura had seen many women dance but this was something new. There was something unusual and almost inhuman in her movements—their absolute fluidity combined with a constantly changing pace, as if it happened on its own—the lick of a flame, the flow of a waterfall, the furl of a flag . . . At times it seemed that this body—moist, hot, flowing, sparkling with gold—balanced on the edge of disappearance. Whole cascades of movements, it seemed, slipped from view but left a strange trace on the soul. Clothing also disappeared imperceptibly from this body as if on its own. The red dress all of a sudden hung over a picture frame, covering a dark Venus. One shoe topped a vase in the back corner of the room and the other found itself in the hands of a young officer. Barefoot and naked, Giralda continued her dance, not the least thread of clothing left, not even a necklace or a ring on her finger, only the golden sparkles and the strange moistness covering her whole body. Perfect nakedness was completely natural to her body, and if nudity signaled the end of the performance for some dancers, Giralda threw off her clothes at the very beginning. Her bends and headlong flights around the pole (for which, apparently, she got the name Giralda, which means weathercock) inspired enthusiastic cries from the crowd, countless thirsty and awestruck men's eyes drank in the movements of the dance, but Comandante Aura stared most intently of all, because no matter the thirst with which a man looks at a woman, a woman always looks at another woman much more intently.

Aura noticed that even her companion Juan Callo was staring at Giralda just like everyone else—with a face gone dumb from delight. The comandante considered jealousy (along with envy) to be the worst of the bourgeois passions that animated the slippery mechanisms of Capital, but nevertheless she felt a strange light pain in her heart. She herself was enchanted by the dancer—not by her dazzling beauty, but by a feeling of recognition. She knew for sure that she had never seen the girl before, but nevertheless Aura recognized everything about her. She knew her. She foresaw each of her movements the moment before they happened. The whole dance resonated in the depths of her body in streams of anticipatory convulsions. All at once, Giralda was next to her. She was all contorted and looked Aura directly in the face. Aura heard her voice, thick and tender. Giralda said:

"I know you. You're a woman."

There was something swampy and hot in that voice, in that slightly lisping, as if unpracticed, pronunciation. Something of the wet jungle where Aura's detachment had nearly perished.

Aura nodded. She wanted to say something but could not. She had no tongue.

Giralda turned to Juan Callo, who was staring directly at her, laughed, and drew a hand across his cheek. Then she turned back to Aura and whispered directly in her ear half joking, half with passion.

"That's your man. I know. On his reproductive organ he has a birth-mark in the shape of a five-pointed star. And so you call his thing the 'Soviet Missile.' Right?" She laughed again and sprang back to continue her dance.

Aura went cold. They really did call Juan's member the Short-Range Soviet Missile or the Surface-to-Air Missile. Aura was sure that those intimate jokes had stayed between the two of them. Could it be that Juan was this woman's lover and had betrayed their secret language? It seemed impossible—for the last year Aura had hardly left Juan's side for more than a minute and the dancer was so young. When would they have had time? And where?

And all at once she knew where the dancer was from. The knowledge came from deep within—from the jungle, from the indigenous settlements nested in the blood of Aureliana Toledo. The young dancer was her own fugitive tongue. That explained the triumphant moistness, the contortions. Giralda winked at her from her dance.

Aura never doubted the power of *llaba*. Now she saw how *llaba* played out its spectacle. Aura downed a shot of rum and fitfully lit a cigarette. *Llaba* was power, and that ancient power suddenly stood in the way of her struggle. Before, she had emerged victorious from every skirmish, she had disentangled the most dangerous imbroglios. But she had never encountered *llaba* on her own before. She needed to win this battle. It was her duty to the Revolution.

Someone touched her on the shoulder. She turned. Behind her stood Don Guino, who beckoned her and Callo to follow.

They were put to bed in one of the rooms of that establishment—a room that appeared intended for the business of love, judging by the enormous red bed in the shape of a heart. Callo and Aura were so worn out that they fell asleep the moment their heads touched that heart's pillows. But an hour later Aura awoke—something roused her. She opened her eyes and saw Giralda's face above her. Her eyes shone in the darkness, her long hair flowed from her shoulders and reached to Aura's face. That tickling and fragrant touch had awoken her.

The dancer leaned over and her moist lips joined with Aura's—the strangeness of that kiss is difficult to describe. The two had a single tongue between them, and in the nocturnal delirium it was impossible to tell whose it was—it wandered around both their interlocked mouths, then Aura felt the touch of that tongue against her eyes. It ran down to her collarbones, shoulders, fluttered along her nipples, hard and dark. Giralda's naked body wound around hers in a single coil. Aura felt the young body as part of her own. She knew it on a micro level, and it seemed she had been breathing in the girl's sweet breath since before she was born, in a rounded and singing eternity. Giralda's hand spread the legs of the leader of the rebel detachment and the dancer's tongue tumbled down like an avalanche.

... *cette beauté va pencher tontá l'heure comme une avalanche*—this beauty will tumble down like an avalanche, Aura remembered someone's French phrase, unsure where she had heard or read it. The hot moist avalanche reached to her stomach, entered her navel and tumbled on, lower, to the dark spread legs of the leader. The tongue penetrated her, agile and tender, dancing and searching, living and crystal clear, like a wet flame. Aura had to bite her lip not to scream from pleasure. The orgasm shook her body and flung her spirit into some radiant sky, from the very heights of which she saw an endless and peaceful sea. "How long it's been since I've seen the sea ..." she thought with a gentle sadness (and how could such an out-of-body sadness come from the epicenter of an orgasm?) and on the horizon where the sea met the sky—she picked out a point of red. She aimed her vision at it like binoculars and saw that it was a tiny distant red flag, freely and joyfully unfurling over the sea.

At that moment Giralda's lips were once again at her ear and Aura heard her whisper. Tenderly mocking, with a strange, almost a prostitute's caress, the dancer whispered:

"You've always wanted to do that yourself . . . But you could never reach. And now you've reached . . ." She heard a quick laugh, and with that laugh Aura fell into sleep.

She awoke at daybreak—Don Guino shook her by the shoulder.

"Get up, Comandante. It's time to go to Corte Siesta."

Aura looked around. Giralda was nowhere near. Juan Callo slept soundly next to her. She did not wake him. Today he was to return to the detachment to take on its command. Let him sleep.

She quickly got up, put on her men's clothing and went to Don Guino's office. There on the mirror-top table several tidy rows of shining white cocaine were already laid out.

"Take some fortification," said Don Guino, indicating the cocaine with an inviting gesture. "You'll need your strength. The path ahead is not short. I found out what I could about *llaba-chochos*. The one who lived in Corte Siesta has died. But her pupil is there. I hear good things. Gather your strength. We'll leave soon. I'll take you. In such matters you should not waste time."

Aura nodded, took the plastic straw from Don Guino and inhaled the cocaine. In principle she despised drugs but today she really did need her strength. She remembered how the tip of her tongue used to go pleasantly numb from cocaine. Now only her upper lip felt numb and a light freeze passed across her front teeth.

The two of them left together in Don Guino's jeep.

The road to Corte Siesta was long. They were stopped several times by military patrols but Don Guino quickly settled with each of them. He had highly placed protectors in the military and in the government. They were let through. They drove through the night, the cocaine keeping them awake. Finally, they arrived and found the woman they sought. She was a native of about Aura's age with a somewhat harsh and closed-off face. She was left alone with this native woman in a small room with nothing but a hammock and a few woven chairs. The native woman had of course heard of the legendary Comandante Aura. She filled a clay bowl with water and drew her fingers along the water's surface, looking through to the bottom of the bowl. Then she sprinkled an amount of salt colored a bright orange. Again she touched the water as she sat with an implacable and unmoving face.

"This is not our *llaba*," she said, finally. "This kind of *llaba* is not found in these parts. I cannot break the curse. Listen, you fight against those who are supported by the gringo. In recent times, the gringo has crawled into every crack; he has dissolved into our air. He is not as simple as he seems. He is sly like the alligator. He fights not only with guns and money. He has learned the magic that we have received from our ancestors. He knows *llaba*. Have you heard of Don Carlos Castaneda? He was a gringo sent to learn about the *llaba* of Mexico. He was the first gringo to perform *llaba*. He wrote books about it for other gringos. Others followed him. They made their way to these parts. The *llaba* that has taken hold of you is a gringo *llaba*. That *llaba* is difficult to break. But there is no *llaba* without a *llaba-chocho*, a curse-breaker. You need a gringo *llaba-chocho*. I know one woman. She is very old. A gringa, a *llaba-chocho*. She's on our side. She'll help you. She'll break the gringo *llaba* if you can get to her. This woman, she lives in Lagon. Her name is Doña Dolores. Go there, and hurry. She is very old. Ask after her among the beggars on the steps of the Cathedral of Santa Maria Inmaculada of Lagon. They'll take you to her."

Aura left the sorceress and gave Don Guino a note. Reading the word "Lagon," he winced.

"Lagon is deep in the jungle and they say the *contras*, the right guerillas, control those parts," he said. "It's dangerous. But there's no other option. Let's go."

And again they rumbled along the jungle roads in Don Guino's jeep. At the approach to Lagon they were stopped by people with automatic weapons. These were not government forces. Don Guino tried to talk to them, but they tied his hands behind his back, blindfolded him, pushed him into a truck, and took him off somewhere.

When they took off Aura's blindfold she found herself on the porch of a wooden house. In front of her in a rocking chair sat a man in a colonel's uniform with a black mask covering his face. He was smoking a cigarette.

"Are you a woman?" he asked.

Aura nodded.

"What are you doing here in men's clothing?" the colonel asked.

Aura opened her mouth and gestured that she had no tongue. Then she again gestured for paper and pencil.

"I am the victim of *llaba*," she wrote. "My tongue disappeared. I'm from the capital, my name is Rosa Helen, I used to sing in a nightclub. I'm on my way to Lagon to find a *llaba-chocho* by the name of Doña Dolores."

"I know Doña Dolores," the colonel said. "She is a powerful *llaba-chocho*, but why do you need a tongue? You're a beautiful woman. Be my third wife. You'll bear me children. You won't need a tongue. I like quiet ones. You're lucky, there are few beautiful women here. It's a good offer."

"I'm married," Aura wrote.

"To that fat man? The one we arrested with you? He is no more."

"No, not to him," Aura wrote.

"None of that matters. You will be locked up while you think over my offer. Take as much time as you need. Let's go."

Two soldiers led her into the yard. The colonel followed. In the middle of the yard lay Don Guino, dead. The colonel turned over the fat corpse with the toe of his boot.

"There was no need for this man to keep living," he said. "He snorted too much cocaine. It's very bad for the brain. He became very stupid. He himself wanted to die. We simply helped."

Aura was locked in something like a shed. The dark days of her imprisonment dripped by. Several days later the colonel came in holding a newspaper. It was the communist paper illegally printed across the border. The colonel was without his mask. He turned out to be light haired and relatively young.

"Hello, Comandante Aura," he said, tossing her the paper. "Your male has forgotten you. A young beauty has taken your place."

On the front page a big color picture took up a whole column: Juan Callo and Giralda in camouflage, machine guns raised high. The headline announced: "New Victories in the Jungle: After the death of Comandante Aura, her detachment has been led by the fearless beauty Giralda Veño. She's given the detachment new life, reminiscent of the victories of the 1970s." Lower down was a small black-and-white photo of Aura in her beret with the caption: "She died for the Revolution."

The colonel laughed:

"Do you like this newspaper? Take it for yourself, as a long as you've already died for the Revolution! The uniform looks good on her. I could shoot you now or give you over to my soldiers. They miss their amorous amusements. Life here is harsh. But I won't do that quite yet. My offer still stands. Just don't think you can make a fool of me. If you try, you'll die a painful death. Think about it, Comandante."

He left. They fed her little but gave her plenty of narcotics. And she came to like them. From time to time the colonel would bring her a newspaper describing the victories of "Giralda's detachment." She would hear about them on the radio as well. Giralda became a nation-wide obsession. She became the flag of the Revolution. Aura was forgotten. But it no longer mattered to her. She sat in her hammock chewing *chimo*. She understood that she was deteriorating but it didn't bother her. She existed for the struggle, for the detachment, and the struggle seemed to be doing well without her—the detachment claimed victory after victory. So she could be forgotten, fade into her dreams. And she had incredible dreams, long, extended, magical dreams. She heard the voice of the jungle, that eternal gnawing punctuated with the cries of birds. An indigenous timelessness awoke within her—she dreamed of alligators and gigantic ants, and she tore off their heads and ate them like her ancestors had done, and she awoke with that hearty flour-and-oil taste on her lips.

After three weeks of darkness, stench, drugs, and dreams she agreed to become the third wife of Colonel Suarez, a middling commander of the *contras*, entrenched in that remote area surrounding godforsaken Lagon.

And another month later she was pregnant. She now lived in a spacious room, almost without walls and with three hammocks—hers and those of the colonel's other two wives. Though these two women (both natives) had their tongues, they were always silent, but they were kind enough to her. The colonel came at times and slept with her in their presence. She didn't care.

Once he came in a said:

"Doña Dolores has taken ill. They say she's dying. She somehow heard that you came here to see her. She asks that you be brought to her. Her word is law here—everyone reveres her, this old woman. I fear her myself. Put on something nice, comb your hair, and let's go."

Soon they entered Lagon in the colonel's jeep. Lagon turned out to be a small old town, barely big enough to contain its own cathedral, which was enormous and so sumptuous that it seemed the entire history of fruits, mermaids, animals, seashells, and monks played out on its walls. In the jeep, the colonel showed her the latest newspaper. On the front page was a photograph of Giralda smiling her languorous and enchanting smile. She was shaking the hand of a tall old man in a white tunic. "Breaking News:" the headline announced, "The Unappeasable Opposition Lays Down Its Arms. The leader of the ultra-left resistance, Giralda Veño, met with the president. In circles close to power, rumors circulate that the leader of the red guerillas was offered a post of minister in the future administration."

It was as if Aura suddenly woke up. Once again, meaning came back into her life. The newspaper smelled familiar; it smelled of betrayal. This would not stand. They drove up to the gates of an old house. Several dogs with glassy eyes circulated in the yard. Soon Aura entered the room in the old stone house where the old woman lay on her bed. Aura looked at her northern features: light-gray eyes shone from a face furrowed with wrinkles.

"Hello, Aureliana," said the old woman. "I know what's happened to you. I know whose *llaba* it was that nearly destroyed you. I will help you."

"Whose was it?" Aura wrote on a scrap of paper, as she sat down next to the old woman on her bed. "I want to find and kill that person."

Suddenly she felt love for that old and perhaps dying woman. In her ancient face remained traces of a past beauty, a sort of mysterious light-ness and transparency, something of a distant wintery sea. She smelled of the north. She had something that could not be found on the faces of old women in the south. Aura took the light hand of the old woman with its delicate, almost childlike fingers and, unexpectedly even for herself, pressed her lips against it. That fragile hand emanated a kind of cool power.

She wanted to scream, "Doña Dolores, don't die! Stay with me! I need your help. I need . . . I want to study with you. My people are in danger. Armed struggle alone will not save them. I must know *llaba*. How did you come to our dying region? What brought you here?"

The old woman smiled and carefully stroked Aura's black hair.

"You're pregnant, my child. You'll have a girl. That's good—boys like war too much. You do not like war. You do it for love. Name her in my honor—Lolita. That's what I was called as a girl. At times I will enter her soul, gently, as if in soft slippers. I will at times advise you through her lips. You will see me in her. But only until she turns twelve. Then I will abandon you both, leave for distant lands. Your thoughts ask me what brought me to your country. The story of my life—which is now coming to a close—is complex and mixed up. The beginning of my life was described by a virtuosic writer in a famous novel. It's a beautifully written book, but the events recounted are far from the truth. The book is narrated by my stepfather who, it says, corrupted me when I was twelve. He was supposed to have been in love with me, to have tormented me with his jealousy, and then to have lost his mind from grief when I ran away. After my mother's death I did indeed travel around the United States for some time with my stepfather but he never showed the slightest sexual interest in me. It was too bad even. I liked him. Then I fell in love with a famous filmmaker, lived with him, and acted in his experimental, semi-pornographic movies . . . I loved him with all my heart and would not have parted with him for anything in the world, but he was killed. In the novel, my stepfather commits the murder. But he had nothing to do with it. The murder came after our trip here, to Lagon. We made a movie here. My beloved at some point took an interest in *llaba*. Lagon is a very old and mysterious town and at that time it was famous for the people here who knew *llaba*. That's what we made our movie about. It was called *Rain* and it was in part about the rainy season, in part about sorcery, in part about the natives, in part about the spirits of the jungle and about sexual rituals, about magical sex and ritual orgies that people were supposed to perform in the forest here to placate the spirits and please the gods. The film followed an English boy and girl—adolescents around fifteen years old—raised in a prim and puritan spirit, who find themselves in this world. Their parents die and they get lost in the jungle. Naturally, in the course of the movie the children abandon all inhibition and become devoted followers of the sexual cults. I, of course, played the lead role, the English girl. I wasn't yet fourteen at the time, but I was always mature for my age. The orgies in streams of tropical rain, of course, were not filmed here but in the States in various greenhouses and botanical gardens . . . All the sexual rituals were entirely invented by Clare Quilty himself—that was the name of my beloved. He was a great inventor at times ingenious, at times—as these things go—completely mad. I'll never forget the elegant and touching verses he dedicated to me.

> *Officer, officer, there they go—*
> *In the rain, where that lighted store is!*
> *And her socks are white and I love her so,*
> *And her name is Haze, Dolores.*

> *Wanted, wanted: Dolores Haze.*
> *Hair: brown. Lips: scarlet.*
> *Age: Five thousand three hundred days.*
> *Profession: none, or "starlet."*

"Yes, I was a starlet in those blessed years. I was a happy child: I slept with my beloved genius, I readily dissolved in the flow of fantasies, we lived happily, wildly, and carefree—we did anything we wanted, took drugs, laughed, invented games . . .

"In fact we started the sexual revolution in the U.S. And then the psychedelic revolution ripened right afterwards. We were pioneers of those two revolutions, the first birds to fly their way to freedom.

"The movie *Rain* was conceived as an aesthete's erotic fantasy with the absolutely artificial flavor of the jungle. But Quilty wanted some truth about *llaba* to flash as if accidentally through that humid artificial paradise, a little bit of truth to blink along the sidelines of the film. And here, in Lagon we were able to shoot authentic scenes of real *llaba*. At that time several of the elders could still perform magic that no one any longer knows.

"Then we returned to the States. Quilty went into editing . . . And that's when he was killed. In the book I mentioned, it says that I was no longer with him at the time, that I had married a 'simple guy,' gotten pregnant, and soon died in childbirth. That's all lies and nonsense. I have never lived with any 'simple guy,' have never been pregnant. I have died many times—but in a completely different way. No one knew who killed Cue. Some suspected the C.I.A., others suspected religious sectarians, still others thought it was the parents of the girls in his films . . . I alone, the precocious child, understood that his death was connected to our trip to Lagon, connected to *llaba*.

"I made it my mission to investigate that murder, to find the killers and take revenge. For that I needed to understand *llaba*, to really learn it. So I started on the *llaba* path, which brought me here, to this room, where you kiss my old hands. I began to study magic, to travel to various wild regions, where ancient knowledge is still kept. Gradually, much became clear to me. I became a *llaba-chocho*. By that time I already knew who had killed Cue. I could have unleashed the most terrifying vengeance, but I did not. Lagon became my home. This town hypnotized me. I left many times. I lived in Iceland, in India . . . But I always returned to Lagon. And old age imperceptibly crept up on me.

"And now you can kill me if you like. It was me who has tormented you with *llaba*. Forgive me. I needed you to find me. And I needed you to come to me with child. I have long admired you, your voice and how you speak on the radio . . . You are courageous, you are the spirit of this country, and this is why I have chosen you to receive my knowledge of *llaba*. I will teach you through the lips of your daughter, whom you carry under your heart. You fight for the poor, but aside from the poor and the deceived there are many who are oppressed—they are invisible, they are not people, but they also deserve to be fought for. You can do this. Now I will die and your *llaba* will end—Giralda will disappear and your tongue will return to you . . . Farewell. Until we meet again."

Aura barely heard what the old woman said. At that moment she was not thinking about her tongue, about her child, or about the war. All of that seemed unimportant. To her surprise, to her horror, just now, in the thirty-sixth year of her life, she finally understood what love was. She continued to kiss the old woman's hand with unimaginable tenderness and passion, as if she were trying to hold her back, to warm her up, but Doña Dolores's voice no longer sounded and her hand was getting cold . . . Hot tears streamed down Aureliana's face and she still kissed the elderly childlike fingers as they cooled, and then something got in the way of her kisses—at first she didn't understand what it was, and only later understood—it was her tongue. Her tongue had returned. She got up sharply and went over to the mirror that hung in the corner. She opened her mouth and looked at her tongue. It was in its place, fresh and clean, like a child's, and at the very tip flashed a few golden sparkles.

Completed on February 5, 2005.
Translated by Bradley Gorski

Aleksandr Ilichevsky (b. 1970)

The Sparrow

A sparrow landed on the windowsill. It hopped, darted its eyes, moved its head around and pecked at the glass. Then it fluttered up—and got in. Kulyusha closed the sash, grabbed a towel, chased it, and knocked it down behind the bench.

Twisting its neck like a chicken's did not work.

So she tore its head off with two fingers, popped it off, like a flower from its stem.

Dark pains rushed from her ears, flooded her eyes.

Crawling on all fours from the pain, she lay down on her side and quieted into unconsciousness, to rest.

The headless sparrow still jerked a wing, tensed, gave up two more scarlet drops from the straws of its throat, and also went quiet, falling over on its side.

Ivan watched from the stove, completely still. Until dusk, without moving, he looked at his mother lying there, at the beak and the eye half covered by a grayish film. Like a bead that lay still, it gleamed in her bloodied palm. At times Ivan fell into the sparrow's eye—into its gray windy light, oscillating on a naked pliant branch; the pitching would make him sick, he would resurface—and again would see the room, flooded tall with light, his mother calmly lying there, a beam of light crawling across her cheek, the dusty window, the fence, the black street, the steppe beyond.

At sunset his mother awoke, sat up on the floor. She looked at her blackened hand, at the bird's head, and did not move.

The cold crimson steppe arched and, like a wing sinking into the sky behind the gulch, took within itself the long wind. The wind quieted and receded behind the horizon after the bloodied sun, like a cloak following after a murderous tsar.

Along the slopes of the glossy stubble fields flowed the gray of the first snow, prickly and fine. It had sprinkled down like dust on things, unnoticeable from the terrifying heights of the unmoving, bearded, waving clouds. These high sunset clouds resembled both ruddy dunes and the pattern of baked fish flesh split open along the steaming spine. Kulyusha had seen dunes on the way to Astrakhan where her husband used to take her in search of fish—the waves of sand steamed as the wind blew against their ridges. And last night she had had an unexpected vision of fish, though food had long since stopped coming to her in dreams.

For the first two months, however, food had tortured her dreams worse than an executioner. Sometimes her sisters would bring decorated cakes and meat pies for Easter. Other times she would make sugar puffs herself and sit the children next to her for a treat. They would wash them down with a dogwood compote.

And then, as if they were cut off, her dreams became empty, like a cleared field.

And that was what she dreamed of now. A horseman stood on the knoll, a black silhouette against the solar flare. The horse moved and shook its head, stepped this way and that—and the tip of the rays coming from beneath its head cast a scarlet blackness across its nose and then disappeared, relieved.

The stubble field prickled against her entire body. Falling, pulling Ivan with her, pushing him into the earth, she nearly poked her eye out. A short rigid stem bloodied her below the eye.

The desire to melt into the earth, to give herself over to its coldness entirely, was overwhelming; it blended with her grief for her husband. Her husband was her shelter, she could sense him there, far away, in the earth, like a divining rod senses water—cold, black, but her own, enormous and strong, like death itself.

She could not bury him, she fainted in the street. Since October they had been going house to house—and they took him. He was laid out for only a day, and she needed longer. The children crawled over him, played—tried to rouse their father, pulled him by the nose. They came, dragged him by the arms from the porch. She did not want to let them, but how was she to manage that? She clung to her husband. The Komsod[1] workers chased her

---

1   *Komsod* is an abbreviation of *Komissiia sodeistviia*, or Cooperative Commission, a general term for various volunteer brigades in the early Soviet Union.

off—the job was difficult enough as it was. They carried him through the yard, beyond the fence, and laid him in a neat row with the other corpses. She looked closely at the dead and recognized no one. She looked around painfully as she slunk down. The cart with the carved and painted beams was the same one that had brought Kopylov to them for the requisitioning. "There," she had whispered then, "here's bread for you! There you go, your requisition. What? Not what you were looking for?"

She sat down in the mud. The cart rattled away. But the driver said "whoa," turned and looked at her:

"Listen lady, maybe go lie with your husband, huh? No point in wearing yourself out here."

From under his palm the horseman looked out over the steppe; his whip fluttered against the top of his boot. He finally saw them. He approached at a heavy lumber. Now already very close, the footfalls resonated in the chest through the earth—but the horse is not stopping, it is coming right at them, crushing a hip, shoulder blade, head—and the head falls apart into fatty clumps of black soil.

She dreamed about fish that night because, for the third day already, at sunset, these mountainous waving clouds stood unmoving like the sands of dunes. She looked at them and it seemed she was walking with her husband along these orange hills toward Enotaevka. They would topple down, sinking with each step in waist-deep sand, and climb up long firm slopes, carrying Kalmyk sacks on their way to find fish; looking out when a village, a church, the wooded floodplains along the Volga would appear on the horizon . . . In the sacks they carried pieces of pressed millcake from the creamery for bait. When they arrived, on the very first day, Alyosha made his first catch with that millcake in a whirlpool, a twenty-pound carp that he reeled in for a whole hour, suffering in the heat. The line from the reel to the lure shuddered and cut the water in zigzags. Then he put his catch on a line, attaching it specially under the gills so it wouldn't suffocate—and from time to time he took it off the peg and walked it through the shallow waters like a foal. At the end he baked it in clay. Ah! What beauty shone around afterwards: across the sand and the water, scales as big as gold coins were scattered red in the sun. A big whiskered head lay in the sand with baked eyes and a powerful pinkish skeleton. Amazed, she raised the skeleton to her eyes. She turned the spine to the light like a spyglass, and the fish caught fire in front of her—it shone and swam unbearably strong, capacious, and shapely like the church at Grigorpolis . . .

And now she dreamed of a gigantic golden carp, stout as the hump-backed horse of fairytales, and with wavy ears, fins and tail—just like the golden fish from the children's book—it swam back and forth across the room, nudging her hands, ear, shoulders, kissing her cheeks, her eyes, like a slow moth in a dying lamp.

She showed the pictures from that book to her youngest when she carried him in her arms, saying goodbye. In the afternoon he suddenly went quiet, his little face smoothed over—and, understanding that he was dying, she took him in her arms, walked him back and forth, sung to him, showed him fairytales, babbled, laughed. Seryozha was already dead by evening, but she paced with him in her arms all night until she collapsed. Ivan woke her, came down from the stove, bit her hand—and she woke up, casting the cold effigy from her breast.

She and Ivan carried Seryozha out to the field and, having dug out the entrance to a bobak[2] hole, laid him inside. They covered him. They sat for longer, resting. Out of habit they looked around in case they saw a fatty gray stump across the field. Though they knew that the bobaks had left their fields back in October. And even if they saw one, they wouldn't have the strength to catch it.

Kopylov could be seen coming on horseback from the village. He approached indifferently. Without waiting for him, Ivan turned out his pockets. And closed his fist as if to say, no, we do not have any grain, see for yourself—there's nothing in the field at all. Mother awoke and also turned out the pockets on her tunic and straightened her hem. In October they had made their way here at night across the fields—they rooted around in mouse holes with their fingers, emptying them of any grain stored away for the winter; it happened sometimes that they had even gathered a handful. Now there was nothing at all—bare as dry bone.

The horse snorted, jerked its tail and, already walking, hooted and dropped out a smatter of steaming manure.

Kopylov disappeared behind the bare trees in the gulch.

The mother and son closed their eyes and long breathed in the thin stream, at times disappearing, of the warm hearty smell.

When they stood up, it seemed to them that they were full.

Kulyusha plucked and gutted the sparrow. She did not bother to cut off its legs. She singed it over the kindling, singed the head as well. She fed

---

2   *Bobak* is a local name for a groundhog.

the fire with straw—the dung cakes had gone when the cows had. She cut saltbush and goutweed into the pot, and put the sparrow inside, poured water over it, and salted it.

Ivan at first followed his mother with his eyes but then he was once again taken in by that unclear dark wind.

The soup seemed delicious to Ivan. He stood up a bit. The long stems of the goutweed made it hard to suck in the meat broth. Mother did not give up, drawing the spoon, strung with weeds, across his lips. But looking into the spoon, where the naked sparrow's head now lay, he took it into his mouth himself and sucked it apart carefully. Right away he also ate the half of the carcass that his mother had broken off. Having waited for her son to finish chewing, Kulyusha started eating, too. By the third spoonful she had tasted it and the fourth she gulped greedily, biting the edges of the spoon with her teeth.

Ivan called.

"Give me some more."

She raised her head. Ivan pointed his little hand at the second half of the sparrow: a few matchstick bones and threads of meat she had gathered into the spoon and held near her mouth.

"Oh, you're clever, Ivan, aren't you!" Kulyusha said, swallowing the spoonful and drinking down the rest.

That evening Ivan stayed in his cold breezy darkness longer than usual. He was rocked on a branch, jolted mercilessly, he barely had the strength in his legs to hold on. The wind ruffled right through his feathers. He hid his head first under one wing, then under the other, breathed into his skin to warm up, but he was so swayed on the branch that he had to throw his head back for balance. He wanted with all his might to wake up, to swim to the surface, to tear open his eyes on to Mother—it would be terrible without her. But all of a sudden a strong gust hit him in the back, his legs unclenched—and the icy abyss came over him and sucked him apart.

Kulyusha paced with Ivan in her arms, and trying to get through to him, she rocked him with all her strength. When she felt him getting cold, her eyes went dark and she fell, hitting her head against the bench.

In that winter of 1933, Kulyusha lost her husband, two children, her mother and two brothers.

She and three more sisters survived—Natalya, Arina, and Polya—there was a fifth, the youngest, Fenya, whose husband, as the godfather of the kolkhoz secretary's son, was able to hide away a heifer in a secret basement.

To stop it from bleating, he cut out its tongue and cut back its lips. And just then, at the beginning of December, it started to give milk.

By spring things got better. The ice melted from the stream. Kulyusha tied together a cross out of sticks, pulled a downy wrap across it and, barely able to move her swollen feet, went to the river beyond the garden. She netted a half jar of smelt and dried them in the oven. That was her first solid food.

In May when her awareness returned along with her strength, grief overcame her. At dawn she left the village and went out over the steppe, making her way slightly to the right, following the rising sun. She walked until she fell to the earth at dusk. She awoke, frightened—it was not the worst fright of her life: the sky, full of big stars, was inexorably falling onto her and there was nowhere to hide. The next night she heard wolves circling nearby, but then she thought to light a fire in the dried grasses around her. On the sixth day Kulyusha came across a salt cooperative on the steppe: a barracks and two sheds. A wolfhound jumped out from behind the buildings and she had to lie on the ground face down until evening when the workers came in from the steppe. The cooperative took her in. For several months she went into the salt marshes with them, gathered salt, carried it to the station, waited for the Astrakhan train and exchanged part of it—one to one by weight—for fish.

In fall she signed up for work in Arkhangelsk, but the employment office mixed up the paperwork and she ended up in Baku. She rode on the roof of a train car through Astrakhan, saw once again the Volga hills, the great watery plains, the bloodstream of the Russian lands, the islands, the wall of reeds, channels, the endless stretches of the seashore with a bevy of swans on them. To the right, on and on stretched the Streltsy sands, from the ridges of which the wind blew steaming swimming reddish tails, nimble as flames.

In Baku, Kulyusha found work on one of the building projects of the great five-year plan: the first synthetic India rubber factory in the country. When she signed up in the personnel office she said, "My husband died in the famine." The personnel manager went pale, sat back, hunched over and through his teeth told her, "Idiot. Stitch your mouth shut."

But she never stitched it shut. I loved listening to Kulyusha, her stories, as wide open as the steppe, about her childhood, about peasant work, about her widowed grandmother's pilgrimage to Jerusalem on foot, from which she never returned, how she wrote home a year later saying that she had married Rabbi Pinkhasa ben-Elisha and had become a Jew; listening to her witty, at first glance absurd, but often, as it happened, prophetic judgments about life—and even these terrifying and detailed stories about the famine. Now when I remember Kulyusha it's utterly clear to me why God created man out of earth: so that the soul could grow, even from a dead person, like a plant . . .

I especially loved to see myself in her stories, how I would walk with her through the salt marshes—through that sunny, absolute flatness, covered all the way to the horizon with milky bluish crystals, to see the circling of the fairytale Volga fish not far above—and sometimes to imagine myself as Ivan. Ivan who was always by Kulyusha's side. I've always been interested in how people live after they die. Interested in death as life's most widely known secret. And aside from that, it has always seemed to me that by thinking of Ivan, I was helping the inconsolable Kulyusha ask him for forgiveness.

Then I grew up. Kulyusha died. I grew up some more, forgot my childhood, its territories—the sea, the river, field, forest; the enormous circular space of happiness melted away like a rainbow—and I started to die from indifference and the calm of sorrow. Having understood too early and too well that life without childhood is so short that it is almost as if it is not there at all, I unwillingly fell into an anabiotic condition, as if the waters of Lethe started flowing from the faucet in my apartment . . . That continued for more than ten years, and would have continued on into the future, but by complete accident last year an event occurred that suddenly pulled me out of my torpor.

At that time, before finally quitting a very boring job, I got a curious monthly assignment. I was sent to conduct a final inventory of a warehouse before it was emptied. Our company had decided to discontinue selling computer monitors so they were getting rid of storage space. The warehouse was in the north of the capital, on Admiral Makarov Street, not far from the suburban railway tracks. It was an ancient brick barn—one of several dozen identical warehouses near the ruins of the freight station. On one end of each building white bricks spelled out an enormous NO SMOKING.

It was the middle of June, the work turned out to be nothing much, and I enjoyed the solitude. After counting up and marking in chalk the vertical cubic inventory, which was scattered around the warehouse in pyramids, I would sit down on a chair and enjoy a cigarette from the bottom of a chasm constructed out of cardboard boxes and pierced through with beams of sunlight that came out of the rafters through holes in the old slate roof. The plumes of smoke climbed up, widened out, quieted and hung in transparent silver sheets. Common swifts, emerging from the half-crown of the roof's ridge, sketched exclamatory zigzags in the light and at various heights stitched the triangular holes with mobile edges in the smoky slate. It was dry, warm, and quiet. With a cup of strong sweet tea in hand I read a book that I had gotten specially from the library about Admiral Makarov; about his genius for naval research, about his blunder at the Battle of Tsushima, about the Japanese napalm-type shells that helped sink Russian battleships and dreadnoughts. Around me, the whole warehouse district was busy with loading, unloading, bookkeeping. Occasionally, scandals over waste would flare up. Off in my own territory, I had already spent a week drinking up the tranquility.

When all of a sudden it was destroyed. A band of sparrows made a habit of coming down under the roof of my warehouse. With a hurricane of chirping and fluttering, they circled and lashed around above the complex cardboard landscape like Japanese kamikazes above the fleet at Pearl Harbor. For three days in a row there was no escape from the sparrows, and I had to undertake retaliatory measures. With a bicycle pump, a scrap of board, a rubber medical strap, petroleum jelly, and a piece of felt, I fashioned an air gun. I made the bullets from caulking that I picked out of the warehouse's doorjambs. To enhance the lethal force, I added pellets to the caulking. I spent a whole day calibrating the weapon. By evening the crates in my sector were sprinkled with my misfires. For the next two days, I lay in wait with the air rifle at the ready and didn't hit a single bird. It was in that position, gun in hand, that the warehouse custodian found me.

I explained myself. The old man heard me out sympathetically and added that sparrows are the bane of all the warehouses here. They drift from one warehouse to the next, they soil the goods, raise hell, and scare the loaders when they fly—a whole horde flies out of a corner right into someone's face . . . I learned that the sparrows were inherited from a distant past when this whole warehouse district, built at the very beginning of the 1930s, was still used to store Moscow's strategic grain reserves. Before, there was such an endless mass of sparrows here that they darkened the sky—but now, nothing but a pittance.

When the custodian left, I went around to the back of the warehouse and with the butt of my gun scraped up two handfuls of dusty soil. I went to the light and on a piece of cardboard sorted through the bits of litter that were mixed in with the dirt. Four black grains remained in my palm.

I held them up to my eyes and saw. Grain requisitions from Ladovskaia Gulch, Novoaleksandrovka, Grigorpolis, from all of Stavropol, from Kuban and Ukraine stretched out from the train stations, loaded onto freight trains. Some went abroad in exchange for gold and industrial equipment, some to Moscow—and the grain was unloaded right here, at this secret storehouse, under the abundant guard of the NKVD.

I folded the grains in a hundred-ruble note and tucked them beneath the cover of my passport.

When I quit that job, I took the grains with me to Velegozh and soaked them in a yeast solution. One sprouted—and last year in a pot filled with real black earth, acquired on a special trip to Michurinsk—it grew into a stalk of wheat.

And this year twenty-two stalks are ripening in my garden. And in a year I hope to treat Ivan to a piece of bread; a small one, no bigger than the Eucharist.

Translated by Bradley Gorski

Stanislav Lvovsky (b. 1972)

Roaming

I'm a beta tester. Being a beta tester means working for a Big Company, going to work every day except Saturday and Sunday, getting yelled at by Alexander Petrovich, and understanding technology. And not just technology, cell phones. Cell phones enhance our world, make it brighter, allow loving hearts to whisper sweet nothings from a distance and without taking a lunch break.

Cell phones are wonderful little things. Everyone loves them. We buy cases and stands for them, teach them to sing songs in angelic voices, give them as birthday gifts and hold them close to our hearts. Precisely in these words our Marketing Director explained the goal of his revolutionary tactic in the fight for consumers. He explained everything about The Competition that breathes fire and is ready to devour us, about The Recession that breathes ice and is ready to crush us. He spooked me with talk of a fall in stock prices. Then he put Mia on the table.

I looked at it and asked if he could give That to someone else from my department. I have entomophobia and I'm afraid of things with thin legs.

The Marketing Director said no, we can't, I'm the boss, it's a revolution, I have to test it. And then he turned That on. Mia opened her eyes, blinked, said "Hi," and turned to me.

I jumped up from my chair. Mia blinked at me and stopped. The Marketing Director giggled, looking satisfied, and asked what it was I was so scared of. I held out my hand to Mia. She quickly reached out her arms to me. I carefully picked her up with two fingers. The Marketing Director said the body is strong, the arms are made of a proprietary, flexible, but superstrong plastic, can't be broken, treat it like any other phone, battery lasts a day, less than a normal phone's, but she can run and jump! Carry on a conversation! I asked the Marketing Director if he was sure it was a girl. The Marketing Director said yes. It talks like a girl, thinks like a girl, is named Mia. It's a girl.

"Sounds good," I said.

"You have three weeks," the Marketing Director said.

And he walked out.

I was left with Mia.

That evening I sat at home, reading before bed. Mia sat in my shirt pocket. I had already somehow accepted the existence of her two pairs of arms, her bovine eyelashes and angelic voice. A telephone. Just a telephone. Then I felt that someone was lightly but insistently kicking me in the chest.

"You're getting a call," she said. "Masha is calling. +7 (095) 845-6789."

Masha is my . . . well, fiancée, sort of. Girlfriend. We go to the movies, go out to eat, take walks in the park. Masha has two main things: a long wiener dog and a short memory. Masha forgets everything. You can tell her the same jokes over and over. Sometimes I'm not sure if she remembers my face. Masha.

We agreed to go see a movie a couple of days later, a movie from a Hong Kong director about love and feelings. I put Mia on the table. She got up—sat up at first, then stood and came over to me.

"Tell me about Masha."

I told her about Masha for a long time—how we met, how we went for walks in the park and to the movies. And about other things, too. It was really strange because from time to time, I could see the scene from the outside. An adult, almost thirty years old, sitting alone in his kitchen and telling his cell phone about his girlfriend. Mia, by the way, at all the right moments threw up her hands, said, "Uh huh. Then what?" and generally acted like a pleasant and interested companion.

I mean, it was a great marketing coup. By the end of our conversation I had already forgotten that she was a cell phone. When I said it was time for bed, she turned her left cheek to me and I didn't immediately understand that she expected me not to kiss her good night, but to turn her off for the night. I even leaned over to her. But I caught myself in time (the display, I should say, had time to redden) and carefully, very carefully, slowly I pressed the power button.

Leaving Mia on the kitchen table somehow didn't seem right to me. I took her with me and put her next to me, only not on the pillow. Maybe that was a mistake.

The next day was all commotion because something with the latest model wasn't right, the phone rang too quietly, texts showed up encoded in UTF-8, and just everything was off. Pretty soon I got used to the fact that my phone didn't ring, but spoke in the business-like tone of a secretary just starting her new job: "It's Alexander Petrovich." The arms turned out to be a terribly convenient thing, because after each ring Mia would stretch out from the edge of my pocket and practically jump into my hand. It tickled a little, but that was fine. No big deal.

That evening I sat in the kitchen again. Drank kefir. When I was a kid my mom read me this poem.

> There was a lion, the lion was kind.
> He ate bread, bread with cheese rind.
> He drank kefir just before bed.
> His name was Leo, Leo Weatherhead.

Mia asked me if I had had other cell phones. She understood that I had, but what were they like?

"The usual," I answered. "Nokia, Samsung, Philips, Siemens. Phones. I don't remember all of them. I am a beta tester."

"And your very very first?"

"Oh! My first was a Nokia. I carried it in a little suitcase. It had an antenna like a satellite terminal. It was so heavy. Made of black plastic."

Mia fluttered her eyelashes, perplexed, and kept silent. She clearly didn't know what a satellite terminal was, but it seemed she was embarrassed to ask. And how did that work, in a little suitcase? I didn't really want to explain.

In the end I put her on my pillow. I really wanted to kiss her goodnight, but she was already asleep. I turned her off. And then—it's somehow strange, though. I don't know. Just strange.

The next day after work, Masha and I went to the movies. I always turn off my phone when the movie starts because if someone calls you at that Very Important Moment it's always unpleasant. Even if it's someone great, someone you love or just someone you like talking to. I told Mia that if someone calls, please tell them I'm not here, just remember who called and we'll deal with it afterwards. Mia promised to do everything as she was told, but asked me to pull back my jacket a little so she could see. I did. She somehow sat on the edge of my pocket and sat there for the whole film, watching without blinking.

When we left the theater, she insisted on telling me right away who called (who called, who called . . . Alexander Petrovich called. And my mom called). I had to take her out of my pocket. Masha immediately squealed, "Oh, it's so cute! Let me see!" She turned Mia over in her hands for a long time. Mia cringed. Masha touched Mia's arms and was completely delighted. Mia had the decency to say hello, but then went silent like she was holding a mouthful of water. When I put her back in my pocket I could feel that she was shaking. We walked Masha home and went back to our place.

Then we drank kefir in the kitchen. Mia first jumped up then sat back down on the table and asked me about my mom. And then about my dad. And then about my little sister who left for America a long time ago. Mia even knew a little bit about America, because of roaming. Before turning her off, I gave her a kiss. For that I had to put her on my palm and bring her up to my face. She took my nose in her arms and pressed herself to it. Mia.

During my lunch break, I sat at the table and ate a salad from a plastic bowl. It's a good lunch, salad and Japanese noodles and khachapuri from the bakery stand. Mia walked around the table, touching various things, swatting at pens, and from time to time getting stuck on the yellow block of post-it notes. When I finished, she came over to me and hugged my finger.

"What's that about?" I asked.

"Nothing. Just because."

"Just because," I mumbled, then stroked her across the keys and went to see the Marketing Director. He was really happy to see me and for a long time asked me how things were going. "Everything's good," I said. "It's a great idea you've had. Just great." The Marketing Director was glad. When I got back to my office Mia was sitting on the edge of the keyboard with her back turned toward me.

"Masha called."

"Where from? Her cell or her home phone?"

"Her cell."

I didn't have the heart to call her back. Later.

That evening I didn't call Masha back. And the next day I didn't call her back either. About five days later Mia stopped telling me about her calls. Or maybe she stopped calling. I don't know. Mia came to hug me by the finger more often. Sometimes, sitting in my pocket, she would press all her keys to me and quietly scratch me with her arms. At those moments I would somehow run out of air and my meetings would go a little awry. I would scold her afterwards. She would giggle. After a week of evening chats, I had told her everything—about me, about my family, about my girlfriends, about my cell phones.

She really wanted to try roaming. I told her that we'd definitely go to America to visit my little sister and we'd try everything there. We could because she had a dual-band antenna, and in America there's only GSM-1900, but there would be everything—Pacific Bell and AT&T.

Every time I kissed her goodnight she would hug me by the nose and tickle me with her eyelashes.

And then somehow the Marketing Director called. We talked for a long time about how everything was great and that this was the best telephone our Company had ever made and everything like that. That evening Mia was really pensive and kept asking questions somehow off-topic. And the next day at work I got a package. I knew that I hadn't ordered anything, but the delivery boy was insistent and said my secretary had called him at some point, and the bill was paid in some unknown way and, just take your phone, what, do you want me to take it back?

In the box was the latest Nokia model. Voice calling, color display, custom-recordable ringtones, color panels for the keyboard. I took it into my office.

"It was you who ordered this, right?"

"It was me."

"Nokia. And what am I going to do with this?"

"I don't know. Make calls. It'll be your phone. Completely yours, not for beta testing, just yours. For good. For you. They're taking me away soon, right? Well this is a Nokia. Like your first. I thought you'd like it."

I threw the box in the trash and walked out. I just managed to see how she covered her face with her hands.

The next day I went to the Marketing Director again. I wouldn't be long, I just, I asked him to let me keep her, and the Marketing Director didn't at all understand what I meant and explained that she costs a fortune and company policy wouldn't allow it and, really, you've lost your mind, it's a TELEPHONE. Telephone, yeah. I know.

At night I gave her a kiss and then turned her off. And she hugged me by the nose and rubbed me with her top keys. And everything was normal. But in the morning she didn't turn on. I charged the battery, pressing the power button the whole time, but nothing helped. At my lunch break I went to a repair shop I know. When the guy there saw Mia he whistled, but he took it apart, put it back together, and said everything looked good, he didn't understand, but it should turn on.

Nothing worked.

For two more weeks I raised hell with the Marketing Director, yelled at the Engineers, at the Vice President of the Company, broke into a Shareholders' meeting, screamed at the Shareholders' meeting. They didn't want to fire me because I'm a very good beta tester.

And so I quit on my own. Still she didn't turn on.

They never put them into mass production because the Marketing Director told the Shareholders that no one would ever buy new phones. They would buy only one, and even if it was really expensive—that's all, forever already. It was a mistake in the end, a marketing miscalculation. Because it was impossible. I know now that it was impossible because I'm a good beta tester.

Sometimes she calls from somewhere out there. The first time, I got spooked. The second time it unsettled me, and the third time, too. Then I got used to it. And now we often sit in the kitchen, I drink kefir, and she tells me this and that and then says now she's hugging me by the nose, it's time to sleep, we'll be in touch. I say till next time and that I'm giving her a kiss.

I'm a beta tester. A very good one. No one knows more about roaming than me and Mia.

Translated by Bradley Gorski

Valery Votrin (b. 1974)

Alkonost

News of Babanov's upcoming trip to India had the exact same effect on all of his friends: they would immediately fall over themselves to discourage him. They told him all about the bad water and strange food. They tried to scare him with stories of dirt and unsanitary conditions. They described illnesses that even modern medicine can't handle, or that are unknown to science altogether. It's fine for the Indians themselves, they're used to it. Like, they can scoop water right out of the Ganges and drink it—the same Ganges, by the way, that's teeming with all kinds of crap. What's it to them? They're used to it. Whereas you, Babanov, would cash out in seconds. Just one sip—and sayonara. "His loving memory will live on in their hearts."

It turned out that, to a Russian person, India might as well be the Second World War or Stalin's purges: not one family remained unaffected. People went there just to get sick. Babanov soon learned that, for Russian tourists, the most popular souvenirs from India included hepatitis, dysentery, and enteritis. No one, by the way, ever came back from India enlightened, having plumbed the hidden wisdom of the heavens. Those who returned left behind the lion's share of their health in the vast, enigmatic land of elephants and rajas. It got to the point where, if Babanov casually mentioned that he was about to take a work trip to India, people's faces would immediately grow somber. Their eyes seemed to say: "Accursed India! For how long will you take from us our fathers, our husbands, our brothers! Here's another good Russian man about to leave, never to return. Look how young he is—still just a boy! What could his bosses be thinking, sending a young man like that to his death!"

With his flight just a day away, he even had to fend off an onslaught from his wife at home. It so happened that Alla had her own story to tell. Someone she knew had been poisoned by some mysterious fruit, and now this same person, all yellow and doubled-over . . . I've heard that one before, said Babanov. But you didn't even let me finish! The rest doesn't matter, said Babanov.

There followed the usual reproaches: he was insensitive, and "you don't respect my opinion," and "you never take what I say seriously," and "I sit here all day long and just go crazy, you understand, crazy, there's no one to talk to, I can't even leave the house, you never let me see my friends, even though they're not half as stupid as you claim, and don't get me started on your phone calls, every five minutes: 'Hey, honey! How are things?' But how do you expect things to be if nothing has changed since you last called? It's just your way of checking up on me, and when you finally get home, you're so exhausted I can barely stand to look at you, what are you even doing all day in that office of yours, I can't figure it out, you get home, collapse, and fall dead asleep, and I'm left to stare at the TV until God knows when." Last year, Babanov reminded her, you and I went to Antalya together. Yeah, that was nice. But so what? Will you spend the rest of our lives reminding me about that trip to Antalya? We don't even go to the theater, even though your idiot friends sit there every night in the best seats, buried in their phones, making dumb faces like the show was in Chinese. Or Hindi, added Babanov. That's right, you're about to go to India, but what do you actually know about it? It's not like you read books, and you're not interested in movies. It's already saying a lot if you've seen *The Jungle Book*. You're gonna catch something over there. Igor, promise me that when you come back, we'll make some changes. Promise me that there'll be more variety in our lives. Please, promise me. What the hell am I supposed to do—get a parrot?!

Babanov promised. The next day, he flew to Calcutta, where he stayed without incident for three days, and because all the papers were signed on the very first day, and two similar contracts, each more profitable than the last, were already in the works, he didn't think even once about water or diseases, but only lamented being so busy that he couldn't survey all the local wonders. India wasn't nearly as scary as people would have him believe. At any rate, he didn't see any neighborhoods full of beggars dying of pandemics from the car window. The Indians turned out to be great guys and pretty good business partners. It's true that at first, he worried that some of them might be unable to sign on the dotted line; back in school, he'd been taught that Indians were largely illiterate, having been oppressed and humiliated by their English colonizers. It turned out, however, that some of his business partners had been educated abroad and held all kinds of degrees from foreign universities. They all spoke excellent English, and Babanov, who had barely finished school and spoke no foreign languages, quickly relaxed—everything was fine, everything was exactly as it should be. Listening benevolently to the translator, he would nod in agreement, feeling completely satisfied. It was only shortly before departure that he suddenly remembered. The successful progress of his business here had entirely blocked out thoughts of home, and Alla's final words about the parrot had, oddly enough, transformed in his mind into a request. Though it was high time to drive to the airport, he asked to be taken to the bazaar first—on the off chance that he'd snag something worthwhile over there. It was there, at the bazaar, that Babanov bought the Alkonost.

At the time, of course, he didn't know that this was what the bird was called. He didn't even suspect that anything like it existed. Only belatedly did it dawn on him that, as a parting gift, India was showing him a true wonder. And yet, with the impassivity of the consummate collector, he showed no sign that he was astonished to the depths of his soul. He asked the price. The price was right. One of his Indian companions, who spoke passable Russian, urged Babanov to haggle. But haggling felt unseemly. For a mere five hundred dollars, he was buying something way cooler than just some parrot. Alla's jaw will drop. That'll show her—"you don't go to the theater or read any books." Here, feast your eyes on this. Won't be bored much longer, I'll bet. I wonder how I can take it out of the country without running into trouble. But as he was counting out the money, he noticed that everyone around had stopped what they were doing and lowered their voices to whispers. It was then that he asked, without handing over the cash, "Does it sing at least?"

His question caused a stir. They looked at him with near-indignation—a righteous indignation, that much was clear. It wasn't enough that he was getting looks from his companions—four of them, all Indians—but now, from every corner of the bazaar, from every stall and shop, a crowd of curious, silent, and variegated people suddenly gathered round; porters, and merchants, and delivery boys, and children, and all sorts of loitering folk formed a tight ring around Babanov and just stared. Perhaps they'd understood his question and were feeling silently surprised, surprised in their hearts that he would dare to ask something like that. Or perhaps it was simply in their nature to gawk. Either way, they stared at Babanov without blinking. And, finding himself in that tide of unblinking gazes, which conveyed something greater than mere curiosity, with the attention of what seemed like most of Calcutta focused upon him, Babanov suddenly felt, or sensed—the way you pick out the regular ticking of a cuckoo clock through the roar of trams on the street—that someone out there was not, in fact, looking at him at all.

It was the bird who wasn't looking at Babanov, though it should have been—after all, Babanov was buying it. But it appeared indifferent. It was staring at the ground, gaze glued to a half-eaten ear of corn, face almost completely obscured. Babanov could only see that it was a woman's face totally unlike the faces of Indian women. He couldn't make out anything else because of the crush of people behind him, devouring the money in his hands with their eyes. Now and then, the bird would abruptly turn its head to keep its face from being seen.

As he accepted Babanov's money, the vendor, a thin, desiccated man in a turban, spoke a few words. He said, Babanov's companion immediately translated, that Sir has nothing to fear: Haruda won't fly away, for her wings have been clipped. Babanov glanced down. The bird's wings were enormous, with a metallic sheen. They certainly didn't look clipped. She is condemned, said the vendor. Perhaps she has already expiated her guilt— we do not know, for no one can fathom the will of the gods. But her wings are clipped. She cannot take to the skies. The wings will heal, said Babanov without conviction. "They will not heal on their own," said the vendor. "I see," said Babanov. For a split second, he thought: Are they trying to pawn her off on me? Then paid the money anyway.

When it was time to board his flight, he fought hard to take the strange creature into the cabin rather than putting it in the cargo hold. He worried there would be problems at customs, but there weren't any. The customs officers seemed only too happy to send the bird off with Babanov. That was the sense he got, anyway. As for the bird, it was indifferent to everything until take-off, when it huddled up in anguish, and Babanov saw that its wings were trembling.

But that quickly passed. The bird's eyes stayed closed: it had fallen asleep.

Now he could take a good look at her—except, he couldn't really. Her face repelled him somehow, he didn't even want to glance at it, much less examine it closely. Even in profile, its eyes closed and mouth firmly clamped shut, that face somehow forbade scrutiny, as though keeping some unspoken secret that only the elect may know. Babanov didn't think he was one of the elect. Or, to be more precise, he could tell that he was not considered one. And so, he observed only that her face was very pale and weather-beaten. And there was something else—oh, she wasn't wearing any makeup. He couldn't remember when he had last seen such an openly un-made-up woman. Except she's not a woman at all, he reminded himself. She's a bird. It's not like she can put on makeup in front of the mirror every morning. She doesn't use masks or creams. She's a bird. She flies around with the wind blowing in her face.

An empty space had long since formed around them: the more timorous passengers had moved to further-flung seats and were now shooting occasional, fearful looks their way. Only two people had remained in their original places: a pair of men from the Caucasus in the row behind Babanov's. Apparently, nothing could surprise those two. During boarding, as they were making their way to their seats, they had surveyed the bird in passing, then looked at each other. From that point on, they'd been engrossed in conversation, paying no mind to anyone except the flight attendants, who, for their part, avoided Babanov's row entirely. Only at the very beginning of the flight did one woman appear before Babanov. She handed him a glass of mineral water from a tray, glanced briefly at the bird, squealed, and rushed away.

So, she can't fly anymore, he thought, picking up where he'd left off. She used to fly, once, but then they clipped her wings—and off to the bazaar. I gotta ask, why'd they do her like that? Better to charge her with something formally, like, under the penal code. She used to fly around, enjoy herself, it's great on the outside and terrible on the inside—and now here she is on the inside, serving her sentence. Don't they have an endangered species list in India? Surely she's on it. She's a rare one. Sorrowful wrinkles marked the corners of her mouth, and a thin, deep groove lay between her eyebrows. She has a pretty face, Babanov decided, not as swarthy as those Indian ladies. Bombay, forget about it, OK! he heard from the row behind. They didn't even come pick me up. I call their office to say, I'm here, OK, why aren't you here to meet me? I can't, he says, take a taxi. What taxi, I say. Your head's gonna roll if you don't show up, your head, do you hear me?

The bird opened her eyes at precisely the moment when Babanov, having mastered his emotions, was attempting to give her a quick but thorough once-over. He looked away, knowing he couldn't take the bird's gaze, because he'd suddenly realized that her eyes weren't human. She blinked, and for a moment her eyes disappeared behind a thin, yellowish film; yes, those were the eyes of a bird, but the main thing was that they were completely expressionless. For some reason, he'd expected to see pain and despair and anguish there—the feelings of a cornered, caged animal behind bars. But they were expressionless. And it was with those eyes that the bird now looked at Babanov, who had turned away, looked at him from the side, carefully examining his profile, his cheek, his ear, his hair, trying to gauge whether he had penetrated her secret and if so, how far? Fear shot through him. I bought you, he told her in his mind. Forked over five hundred bucks for you. Turn away. He was afraid to look over and meet her gaze again. The bird turned away abruptly, losing interest in him. Babanov exhaled. A parrot would definitely have been better; parrots make people happy and aren't all that expensive.

But true regret awaited him at home. As it turned out, Alla didn't need any parrot. As it turned out, he had once again failed to understand her. You see, he had never truly understood her. As though she hadn't been the one to say to him—just bring me a parrot, would you! He had promised something or other to her in the heat of the moment right before his trip, and now she was starting in again about the theater and whatnot, getting all agitated. Babanov wanted to interrupt her, to say—look what I brought you. It's not a parrot at all. It's way cooler than that. Have a look! You'll never find anything like this anywhere, not even at the zoo. But she wouldn't listen. She had gone off the deep end and didn't even notice the bird, which was crouching in a corner. Babanov was in no hurry to extract her.

Igor, you didn't even call. You didn't even consider for a second what I might be feeling. What, would it have been that hard to call? Or did they turn off your phone? It would be one thing if you were somewhere in Europe, that would still be OK. But here, every time I turn on the TV, there's India, always India—another flood in India, another epidemic in India, another massacre in India! And on top of that you don't call. I can't live like this anymore, Igor. Look what I brought you, managed Babanov, uttering his prepared phrase, and pushed the bird forward. Clacking its curved, hook-like talons on the floor, folding its enormous wings behind its back, the bird moved into the center of the room, and then, pausing in an awkward, inverted pose, glanced up at Alla. Immediately, soundlessly, Alla collapsed on the floor in a dead faint.

Later that evening, candelabras cast muted light from the corners of the room; music played, the table was set, and there was even a bottle of Rheinwein—Babanov had decided to celebrate his return and hopefully make up for earlier. Alla was transformed, laughing, she also wanted to paper over what had happened as quickly as possible. She even had a good appetite that night. She talked nonstop; she'd been talking ever since Babanov had shoved the cork from the bottle of smelling salts under her nose. Or maybe Babanov was just imagining that she was talking so much. Maybe he'd just gotten out of the habit of hearing her talk, of her, full stop, of home, could things really happen so fast, it's only been three days, or was it the bird, was she the one who shook me up so I still don't feel like myself, it's good that I looked away—or maybe, it would have been worth it to look her right in the eye. Such were his thoughts, but he didn't say much, and meanwhile Alla kept on talking. I was so scared, she was saying. It was so unbelievable—we were talking, I was freaking out, and all of a sudden you were all—look what I brought—and out she comes. This bird. I thought it was a dummy, but then I saw her eyes. And then . . . I gave you smelling salts, said Babanov. Yes, smelling salts, what an awful smell. I thought it was all a dream, there's no such thing, after all, but now I know, she's over there in the kitchen.

I thought you'd be pleased. You're the one who wanted a parrot! For the last time, I didn't want a damn parrot! You're the one I need. But you just had to go off to India and bring me back that monstrosity. She's not a monstrosity. Look closer. She's a very sweet woman.

What do you see in her? She's got feathers instead of hair, and she smells like a chicken coop. And it wouldn't be the worst thing in the world if she consulted an esthetician. Alla, she's a bird. She flies around with the wind blowing in her face. You men, who can understand you. First you say she's a woman, and now . . . What rock did you find her under? For the last time, I bought her at a bazaar in Calcutta! That's crazy. You just went to the bazaar, got some money out of your pocket—isn't that where you keep it?—and bought. This mythological bird. Did you even know you were buying something out of a fairytale? No. But isn't it amazing? Pff. Suit yourself! Come on, Alla, let's have some wine. I've read about her somewhere, said Alla. About this bird. She does something or other. Come on, what can a bird do? By the way, maybe you should go check on her, in case she messes something up. She's not going to mess anything up. She isn't capable of messing anything up. She's special, can't you see that? No. Look, you know, it's like if one of your Kolyas or Tolyas or whatever bought himself a dragon. Tolya can't afford a dragon. C'mere. Igor! What is it now? Give Libush a call tomorrow. Who? Libush, remember Libush? He's some kind of myth expert. Maybe he can give us some advice. OK, fine, I'll call.

In the morning, for no reason at all, Babanov recalled the baffled faces of the Indians at the bazaar when he asked if the bird could sing. What was up with those guys, anyway? That was the last question he had time to ask himself before the iron bars of a new workweek slammed shut behind him with a clang, cutting him off from words and promises, and the burbling drain of the workday sucked him in greedily, spinning him in the whirlpool of priorities and urgent tasks.

Babanov would return from work utterly drained and always with a strong sense that he'd just lived through not one day, but two or even several. In the vestibule, a wave of belated regret would wash over him, for he knew that by this point Alla was already asleep, which meant that yet another day had passed pointlessly for her, full of sadness and aggravation; she was probably all aggravated, not knowing how to fill up the time, whereas he was in a position to fix it somehow, although how, he didn't know. By the time he made it to the door, Babanov was usually already suppressing his regret, plying it with blandishments and vows, which felt easy and familiar. Babanov had no trouble convincing himself of things.

He stepped into the living room and turned on the light. He had forgotten all about the bird, he was still reeling from the day's hassles, but suddenly he remembered her, remembered that she lived in his house—all because their eyes met again. For the first time, he was gazing into her eyes without looking away. And he realized that those eyes would never express anything. He understood that they couldn't see anything anyway, because there was in fact nothing *to* see. There was no light, no sea, and no one's spirit moved upon the face of the waters. But most importantly, there was no Babanov—only the vestiges of some dim memory. As they whizzed through space, the particles that had once been Babanov could only sorrowfully reminisce about how good it was to be him, how sweet to live and drink and eat—and sexy sauna parties, just make sure Alla doesn't find out, and it's so nice at Tolya's dacha, and so on, and jeez, I've really done it this time, and now I'm doomed to fly around here, at the dawn of time, and meanwhile Whoever is still just mulling it over: should I even create the world? Come on! screamed Babanov's particles. Come on, say the words! Go on, say them! And other particles screamed along, swirling around like fine dust nearby. There were so many of them, and they all wanted the same thing: to return and be embodied. And suddenly he felt so sad, so sad, because he understood that Whoever would never say the words, and he even clearly heard the thoughts of that Whoever: enough, forget it, you try so hard, work yourself to the bone, but do you get any thanks? No, just complaints. It's a lot of work for nothing, and a lot of responsibility, too. I'll do it later sometime, I'm tired. And a heavy, unbearable anguish Babanov had never felt before, a deathly, icy anguish pressed down on him, and he choked, and then he was back in his own house.

He was looking into Alla's eyes. She sat huddled in an armchair, cowering, clasping herself in her arms, and looked out at the world from that position, and he looked, too, and they looked at each other. She's been singing, Alla whispered. She sang all day while you were at work. Oh, how sad it was! You can't even imagine how sad it was, Igor. When she started singing, I tried to stop her, to prevent it, but suddenly I lost all my strength to resist. She sang, and I . . . I understood everything, everything, and you know, she convinced me, I completely agree with her now, I understood how she feels here, how hard it is for her, more and more was revealed to me, and I realized that she's the bird of sorrow, although there was a time when she was the bird of joy, an Alkonost, you know, but, when she got here, she lost the will to be joyful or to sing joy's praises, and became the bird of sorrow. Now she doesn't feel quite as bad because she no longer has any hope, because it turns out that it's easier with no hope, because it's liberating, because hope is just salt in your wound, because (so she sang) you can't survive here while you still have hope and faith, and one must abandon hope, for it is easier that way.

But we're reluctant to abandon hope, we don't want to admit to ourselves what our lives are really like, the truth about our habitat, what we've been reduced to, and we pretend there's hope. You understand? We pretend there's hope. And right before you came home I started to sing along with her, and it started to get easier. For the first time, it started to get easier, Igor, because I was singing together with the bird of sorrow, and it's like my eyes were opened—I understood that you can't change anything, and I can't change you, or our lives together. She was still talking when Babanov lifted her up in his arms and carried her to the bedroom. On the way there she fell silent and pressed herself against him. It was hard for him, harder still because it had been so long since he had held her in his arms—he'd lost the habit. Thought failed him, though he did manage to think one little thing, which was: I'm gonna waste that bird!

In the morning, he called Libush, whose number he just barely managed to find in his old address book. Alla was still asleep, and he didn't want her to hear their conversation. Just in case, he closed the bedroom door as he dialed.

Hello? Gena? Yes. Hey, it's Igor, Igor Babanov, remember, we went to school together. Igor, hey! How are you? We thought you'd disappeared. Naw, I'm still around. So here's the thing. Yeah, we're all around, myself included. We recently got together, we called you, but you changed your number. Didn't you move? Nothing's changed for me, I'm still working at the same place, the design institute, no pink slips yet. Well, I just had a daughter. Congratulations. Gena, listen, here's the thing. So I recently went to India. No kidding, India! That's amazing, I heard you're a baller now, makin' the big bucks. How's Alla doing? She's fine, thanks. So, anyway, Gena, I bought this bird while I was over there in India. What kind? A parrot? No, not a parrot. A bird. It's kind of hard to explain. Listen, Igor, I'm sorry, I'm real glad you called, but I have to run to work, you caught me walking out the door. Let's talk tonight, you can tell me all about India. I can't, Gena, I can't wait till then, I remember back in college you were super into different kinds of myths . . . see, there's this bird, she's not a bird at all, she has a human head, a woman's head, see, and her singing just turns your soul inside out. Alla nearly went insane yesterday, and me right along with her, like, I'd just come home from work. Hello? Gena? What was that? What's that noise? Agh, it's nothing. Nothing. I just dropped the phone. And nearly fell over myself. Are you OK, Igor? Where are you calling from? From home, Gena, from home. And I'm stone-cold sober. Look, it's all true. I bought this bird at a bazaar in Calcutta. And it turns out it can sing. Have you ever heard a bird like that sing? I haven't, but Alla, yesterday, she nearly went out of her mind, fell into a trance, saying all kinds of . . . Jesus! What? Igor, do you even understand who you brought back from India? You brought back a Sirin! No, Alla called it something else. Alka. Alko. Alkonost?

No, it can't be an Alkonost. The Alkonost is the bird of happiness. If it was an Alkonost, you two would be jumping for joy over there. No, it's a Sirin. Jesus, it would be better if you'd brought home a crocodile, like certain idiots I know. I'm pinching myself right now. Maybe I'm asleep? Remember Viktor Vasnetsov's painting—"Sirin and Alkonost"? No, I don't. No big surprise there. Listen. I'm coming over. I mean, this is a sensation, Igor. You have to tell the world. What's a Sirin, Libush? I told you, it's the bird of sorrow. She weeps for everyone, mourns for the world. Tell me your address, I'm writing it down. Babanov hung up.

He came home from work early. He simply couldn't work. He went into his building, slowly climbed the stairs to the third floor, opened the door with his key, and just stood in the entryway for a moment, straining his ears to hear what was happening inside. Then he started walking through the apartment. He paused in a doorway. Inside, Alla was reading poetry out loud. He had never heard her read poetry before. Who's that for? thought Babanov.

> Oh my deep-rooted song, do not fear!
> For where else can the two of us flee?
> Ah, the mortal adverbial: "here"—
> That they spurned when they shook on the tree.[1]

Her voice died away. Babanov walked into the room. They were sitting face to face—Alla and the Alkonost. In harmony, he thought. The bird jerked its head—it was turning to look at him, and he saw tears in its eyes. Suddenly, the phone rang. Babanov picked up. It was Libush. Without pausing to listen, Babanov pressed the "off" button. Igor, heaven really does exist, said Alla. Hell, too. Except hell isn't the place where people realize there's no hope; it's the place where they pretend that there *is*. She's been singing again, hasn't she, said Babanov affirmatively. Yes, said Alla. I'm leaving you, Igor. Babanov sank into a chair. I'll take her with me, said Alla. Well, yeah, said Babanov. I'm not sure yet how to move her, but I think that particular problem has a solution. Yes, said Babanov. I think so, too.

He waited for the door to slam shut, then picked up the phone and called his driver. Volodya, he said, do you know any good veterinary clinics? Where is that? Is it far away? Good. Go over there and bring me a vet, but pick the very best one, like a professor or something. Say we'll pay for a consultation.

The bird started, jumped down onto the floor and clacked past him into the hallway. He followed. Once in the front room, she jumped onto the table and fluffed up her feathers. Want a drink? asked Babanov. It came out mockingly, which was not his intention. He walked over to the bar and poured out two glasses of whisky, feeling terrible. It's a serious offer, he said to the bird. You don't have to say anything—just nod. The bird continued looking out the window. You're making me angry, said Babanov. Something like anger really was bubbling up inside him. He drank down his glass, but that failed to extinguish his anger. He remembered that whisky burns. He should have had some water. You just sit there, don't you, he said to the bird

---

1   Quoted from Pasternak, Boris. *My Sister Life and the Zhivago Poems*. Trans. James E. Falen. Evanston, IL: Northwestern University Press, 2012, 46.

contemptuously. Don't know your own worth. Why can't you sing joyful songs, make people happy? Why? Why did you stop singing good songs? Why are you so sad? Conscious of his growing agitation, he lunged at her and shouted into her face: What is it you know? They looked at each other, and Babanov saw that tears were once again filling her eyes. My heart, said Babanov, turning away. You're breaking my heart.

A short time later, the bell rang. Babanov moved uncertainly toward the door and, after a moment's hesitation, opened it. On the stoop stood an unflappable man in glasses. Volodya, the driver, was hovering around behind him. There, he said, pointing at the unflappable man. I brought the best one. Thank you, said the doctor and asked Babanov tersely, Where? Wait in the car, said Babanov to the driver, and, turning to the doctor: Over there, in the front room. On the table. The doctor went inside. Babanov waited for muffled cries and exclamations. But he heard nothing of the sort, and when he walked into the room, he saw the doctor skeptically examining the bird, which sat on the table exactly as before, paying no attention to anyone. All right, said the doctor. She looks perfectly healthy, though she's a little pale. What have you been feeding her? Poetry, said Babanov, remembering Alla. Hm, said the doctor. Man does not live by poems alone. Fair enough, said Babanov. What's her complaint, anyway? said the doctor. Her wings are clipped, said Babanov. The doctor examined a spread wing, careful and businesslike. The bird shifted slightly, but betrayed no sign of agitation. I see, said the doctor. People never do tire of mutilating animals! Could you make it so she can fly again? asked Babanov. It's not that I can't, said the doctor. Don't worry about the money, said Babanov. That's not what I mean, said the doctor. Money's the least of my worries. But can you imagine her flying around the city . . . She won't fly around the city, said Babanov. She's not . . . Not what? asked the doctor. She's not of this world, Babanov said firmly. None of us are of this world, said the doctor. They were silent for a moment—looking at the bird, which refused to look at them. Where did you even get her? asked the doctor. In India, said Babanov with sudden rage. The doctor sighed. Look, I get it, he said. A friend of mine recently went to Egypt. Came back all rested and refreshed. And also, coincidentally, bought himself a bird. A phoenix. Evidently it was already old, which is why they pushed it on him, he wasn't exactly up on the fine points of phoenixes, it's not like they tell you that kind of thing at the travel agency. So he brings it back, goes off to work, and the bird up and bursts into flames. And? Babanov prompted. The house burned down to the ground, said the doctor. They fell silent again. I'll meet you at the clinic tomorrow first thing, said the doctor. I'll try my best. It'll cost you. And don't tell anyone about her.

Right after the surgery, Babanov took the bird away to his dacha. Alla's calls pursued him right up to the door, but he didn't answer. On the third day, it was time to take off the bandages, and he and the doctor observed in stunned silence the complete absence of postoperative scarring. She needs some practice, said the doctor. There's time yet, said Babanov. They were drinking tea on the terrace. The bird perched on the railing some distance away, grasping it so hard with her enormous talons that it seemed ready to crumble under the pressure. And how are you feeling? asked the doctor. Because India, as you know . . . People bring all kinds of stuff back. Eh, I feel fine, said Babanov. It's just the bird. Sure, sure, sighed the doctor, standing up. Well, see you the day after tomorrow. I'll walk you out, said Babanov, also standing up.

But he and the doctor didn't see each other again after all, because when he came out onto the terrace the following morning, Babanov didn't find the bird in her usual place on the railing. As he rounded the corner of the house, he heard rustling overhead and saw her sitting up on the roof like a gigantic rooster. You'll fall, he said to her. But she had no intention of falling, and he understood that today was the day she'd fly away. Don't go! he said suddenly. There's hope. There's always hope. All at once, he saw her gaze soften, a hint of tenderness appearing in her eye. She looked tenderly down at Babanov, and he suddenly felt released from some burden. He grew embarrassed. He had thought that now, at last, the Alkonost inside her would overcome the Sirin, and that she would finally burst into lovely, enthralling song. But it turned out that the all-forgiving glance from above meant incomparably more to him. Fine then, he said. Fly away. But when you feel like coming back, don't land in India. They'll catch you again and drag you to the bazaar. Next time come to us. Come as an Alkonost.

All day he waited for her to take off. But only near evening, after he'd gone back inside, did he hear the powerful sound of her wings. He went outside to look. The bird was gone. He called Alla and heard her agitated voice. It's over, he said. Everything is fine. Please come back.

There was still the matter of the keyed-up and obstinate Libush. By the time that insistent man finally sniffed out Babanov's address and showed up at his door with a photojournalist friend in tow, it was already Sunday; Alla was off visiting some friend, and Babanov was home alone. He opened the door, and an excited Libush burst in, overwhelming him with immoderate emotions and inquiries. The photojournalist friend was right behind him, examining every corner with the piercing eye of a photographic Pinkerton, and they repeated in unison: Well, where's that bird of yours? Where is it? And Babanov said, as though suddenly remembering: Oh, right, the bird! He led the men, high on the near prospect of success, breathing hard, through the rooms of his apartment—and then he opened a door. They stood there, looking at the bird, and the bird looked back at them: a large green parrot, perching in a cage with an enormous metal dome, gazed at them mockingly with its one open eye.

Translated by Maya Vinokour

Linor Goralik (b. 1975)

A Little Stick

It had turned out to be an ugly business; he was going there, as he told himself, to ask for advice, but really—well, why does anyone go to houses like that? To ease the soul, to cleanse oneself, to repent, to be absolved, to be bathed in all that . . . all that stuff. He brought with him something appropriate (something expensive-ish and modest at the same time)—waffle cookies that are not waffles in the ordinary human sense, but in the German, alpine, gooey sense. And they gave him tea in a glass-holder pitted with ancestral memory, and Mashenka woke up ("Oh look, Mashenka's hatched!")—Mashenka woke up and ran into the kitchen on her unsteady, fat little legs in white tights—clever head like a little pumpkin, skin translucently bluish, eyes black with sleep. Oh, it was really an ugly business; he waits to speak, everyone already knows about this ugly business, which smells of blackmail—intelligentsia blackmail, maybe, "for everything good against everything bad," but blackmail all the same, ordinary blackmail with money and all that. Everyone knows everything, there's already a consensus: now he'll start talking, repent—and be forgiven, consoled; at the end of the day, it was his right—but surely not in front of Mashenka?

No, a couple more minutes. Mashenka, what can I get you? The nice man has tea, do you want tea? Mashenka wants "juice with a little stick." Mashenka's mother, the impossible, nineteenth-century part in her hair glittering (in Moscow apartments like this one, parts never ceased to glitter, not even in the gray, lice-infested, communal years), raises her darling, aristocratic eyebrows as if to say, just look at her! A tall glass is placed between Mashenka's two little paws, tomato juice pours out in heavy glugs, then salt, then a slice of lemon, then a dash of black pepper—and a little stick of celery. Wow! Wow, and several other interjections. Mashenka licks the celery, Mashenka, go play the piano—that's a family joke, the obligatory piano has long since gone stiff, it lives in the half-dead room next door, Masha plays on the black-covered keyboard with her red-and-yellow pull-apart robots. He's never seen this piano—this pianette, this pianella—but suddenly he does see it through the wall separating the dead room from the eternally living kitchen: there's something sentimental, though ironic, on top of it like always; what is it? He sees teacups, a Soviet china set with large dots consigned—he sees—to eternal reserve. Very charming, charming and witty. Cups right on the saucers, and he sees the off-center tea-pot, and the teacups, of course, have charming, charming trash inside—a pinecone, a twig, a pinewood slingshot spontaneously generated in Gorky Park, a ballpoint, snallpoint, thingamabob. Mashenka has run off behind the piano, and now he's about ready to talk—but what does he have to say? To explain himself; it was his idea, his scientific baby, they promised, and now—they've leaked it, they could have paid him at least—"But why do I still feel like such an asshole?" "Pasha, my dear, that's just because" (here the unnecessary words he came here for, why he came crawling, why he brought an offering of sticky waffle cookies). ". . . And, certainly, what you did for them . . ." (more, more—and here somewhere is where he'll start to mellow out). "And it's only thanks to you that they . . . And you had every right . . . But they . . . But you . . ." "But why, why do I feel like such an ass-hole?" "My dear, it's because it's just because that's how we all are, we're all incapable of . . ." (after this comes something that does mellow him out: we're good people, everyone else is bad, some petting, scratching, mutual caressing). "I don't even know." "Oh, but we do know." They know, they know—so let them say it. Five minutes, and that's it. Oh please, let's just start already. He's already readied himself, sucked in his belly: "Listen, can I just vent for a second . . ." Mashenka runs in, Mashenka is carrying a half-empty glass, her translucent face covered in meaty juice: "Mama, I want to play a word game!" "In Russian or in English?"

And at that moment he up and said very calmly and very, very loudly:

"Ablarblarblabarblablabla. Burbalblablablablabla. Purbulbal bow wow brawrarawrawraw. Suburbarubula. Bow wow wow rawrawrawraraw-rawaburpburpupruprpr bla."

And then came a split second where it felt like something sticky, neat, and waffley snapped and came unglued inside his chest. He even wanted to silently open his mouth wide, like the mouth of a fountain—so that "blarg-blurl blurburblurbluarlblarg" would pour out of there in a thick, black, even stream. Or bark. Barking would be even better. He even opened his mouth wide, and something did come barking out—did it ever; and it was as if even this charming, charming, cotton-soft kitchen of ours exploded into black, clean, cold streams that crashed into its walls. But the part in the hair blazed gently, the great-grandmother's teaspoon clinked against the great-grandfather's teacup, merry Mashenka shouted, "That's not English! I know, I know, that's not English!"

Oh, Pasha, Pasha, Pasha. Oh, Pasha, Pasha, Pasha. Oh, Pasha.

1:38 A.M.

The only reasonable mirror was in the hallway: when she came out of the bathroom, her gaze would catch in the mirror and she would get stuck. With the years she had grown used to looking at herself as if through a narrow slit: she had a good belly and bad thick thighs. That morning she had calculated that she'd need about an hour and a half all told, with a little leeway just in case. At five she turned on the water in the tub and spent a little while worrying about her nails: she could remove the polish now, but then they'd soften in the tub and it would be harder to paint them. She could do the bath first, and then the polish (there was no way to do a full-on manicure, she'd have had to leave work at three), but then it would smudge during the rest of it. She could paint them right now, sit there, nails drying, and worry about the clock's incessant ticking. She could write him to come a half hour later. She turned off the water in the tub and started rooting through the bag of polishes. Obviously, the smartest thing would be to do everything else first, and then quickly cut the nails short and apply a single layer of clear polish. She really didn't want to do that, but there didn't seem to be a better option. She turned the water on again, stuck her pajamas in the hamper and turned it around so its maw would face the wall. She had cleaned her place the day before. The eternal question of stockings hadn't been decided and couldn't be: she firmly believed that they were absolutely essential, but with her thighs they looked really iffy, even the ones with the wide thick elastic on top. On the other hand, the edges of the black robe would come down on either side, and besides, during the main event none of that would matter anyway. She dug through a drawer, drawing out by a single strap a black lace garter belt whose hour had finally arrived: although the stockings were held up by silicone, she had always thought that stockings looked cheap without a belt. The bathwater turned out to be too hot, and she sensed that sitting there too long would give her a headache. So she pushed back washing her hair and began by shaving her mons and bikini line under running water (here the thought of his bare hand touching that bare mons unleashed a wave of anticipatory arousal she decided not to suppress, letting herself slowly float on the acute, tense feeling of expectation). Her hair had to be washed and dried because the steam had made her hairdo fall apart, and of course she had to use fast-drying product and now she couldn't shake the disgusting feeling that if he grabbed her by the hair, strands of it would stick out stiffly above her crown—but in the dark, again, this wouldn't matter. After the bath her skin felt tight, she began to spread a strongly scented citrus moisturizer on her legs, but then suddenly felt embarrassed by its brazen, provocative smell, quickly toweled off her one leg and selected a different moisturizer, a vanilla one (which immediately seemed too girly, she got angry at herself and finished spreading it on the rest of her body, and her back, as always, turned out to be wet, the cream slid around unpleasantly on the skin). About forty minutes were left—and the nails. The nails had to be done after everything, after makeup, and she very much wanted to avoid foundation, because since her youth she had been hounded by the silly notion that leaving traces of foundation on the pillow (like for example when you're face down, and again the heat of anticipation poured over her) is shameful, although if it's traces of eye shadow (mascara, of course, has become waterproof since those times, thank God), then for some reason it's not shameful. Also, as always, she didn't want to put on the corset until the last second because the lavender one (the black one seemed to her today not unlike the citrus moisturizer, no, impossible) was, to be honest, too small, and to wait in it for twenty minutes (if he's not late, of course)—leaving aside that it's a little hard to breathe, her back would get sweaty again. For a few seconds she stood over her laid-out things: she could pull on the stockings now, attach the garter belt over the silicone (over the silicone isn't so easy, by the way), put on the satin robe, and then, at the last second, once the intercom sounded, get herself into the corset. But then she might smudge her nails and that wouldn't do, that wouldn't do at all. Once in the corset, she breathed in and out for a few seconds, shifed her shoulder blades, bent down a few times so that the cold clasps would arrange themselves properly on her damp back. Here it occurred to her that she could paint her nails standing up—it's super easy with the clear polish, and sitting in the corset is not exactly pleasant. All that was left was lipstick and shoes. She hoped very much that today was not one of those days when the lipstick, for reasons totally defying understanding, refuses to behave properly at the corners of the mouth, has to be wiped off over and over, the lips swelling, their contour growing imperceptible, and everything becoming some kind of unshakeable nightmare (about three minutes left now). The lipstick adhered properly; all she had to do was correct the always-rough edge of her upper lip with lipliner. The shoes she had been planning to wear slipped off these particular stockings (she had forgotten), and the only ones that didn't slip off looked too chunky with the robe. She took off her glasses and looked into the mirror again. The shoes looked fine. The robe and corset looked fine. The woman in the mirror, plumpish and not very young, though quite well groomed, looked fine. The intercom squawked. She went to the living room, stood for a moment, perusing the glasses, bottle, fruit, and then, carefully squatting in her high heels, raised the edges of her robe and lay down on the rug, her head almost butting up against a bed leg. The intercom squawked again, perplexed. She closed her eyes, thrust her arms out to the sides, and told herself honestly that, really, the most important part had already happened.

No Such Thing

"Or maaaaaaybe," she said in a mysterious voice, "she's hiiiiiding . . . under the bed?!"

Here she abruptly yanked the bedspread and looked down, but Nastya wasn't under the bed, either.

"Or maaaaaaybe," she said (the Bugs Bunny clock said five till six, in five minutes she should go to the kitchen to check the oven), "she's hiiiiiding . . . behind the curtain?"

Nastya wasn't behind the curtain, either: if there's one thing her Little Bitty was great at, it was hide-and-go-seek. She closed the window—in general, Bitty wasn't allowed to open it without permission; someone's going to get it today.

"Or maaaaaaybe," she said in the voice of a person visited by an ingenious thought, "maaaaaaybe she's sitting behind the toybox??"

Behind the toybox was the stuffed hippo that had disappeared three days before, and no one else, but a very faint giggling came from somewhere close by. Here she remembered that, oven aside, she still had to call Alyona to tell her to bring along the big salad bowl. It was time to finish the game. She sat down on the edge of the bed.

"OK," she said sadly, "I give up. Where's my Little Bitty?"

And we should really give this room a good once-over before they arrive, she thought, surveying the trampled drawing pad spread out on the floor.

"Maybe my Little Bitty ran away to Africa?"

The room was very quiet, not a rustle, not a single sound.

"Maybe," she said, "my Little Bitty has gone on a trip around the world?"

Silence.

"Maybe," she said, gradually losing her patience, "fairies have taken my Little Bitty away?"

And then she saw on the floor, right under the windowsill, a tiny, pinkie-sized, pointy leather shoe, and screamed so loud that Nastya tumbled out of the closet with a crash and also began to stare in deep bafflement at that little doll shoe, and then looked at her mom, and then at the fat doll Cecilia, hastily undressed the night before, and then back at her mom.

Come On, It's Funny

They weren't drinking a lot, it was just that the windows were open and outside everything looked blue and smelled like something that made everything seem funny, and he was glad that they were all there, and he loved them all. Someone was talking about how he got scared to death one time when a chick fell behind his collar—he bellowed and leapt around, lost his voice (they jumped in with stupid references to Hitchcock right away and kept on laughing until they cried). The girl Pasha had brought said that when she was a kid, she'd been afraid of Boyarsky in the role of Matvei the cat—she would run away to the kitchen and once even tried to hide in the fridge. "But there was a penguin in there!" said Pasha abruptly, everyone cracked up, Marina groaned, "People, come on . . . Stop it . . . my belly hurts . . ." "That's nothing," he said and laughed. "Listen to this: when I was something like four, my mom sits me on her lap and goes, 'I'm not

Mom, I'm a wolf who's turned into Mom!' I didn't believe her, she goes, 'No, really! I'm a wolf who's turned into Mom! I'm going to eat you up!' Like five times, I'm like: 'No, come on!' And she's all: 'Yes, yes!'—and all of a sudden I believed her. Boy, that was terror. Serious terror, for real. I fell for it so hard, you know how terrifying it was? Man!" He laughed again and waved his plastic cup—but nothing happened, and he marveled how from up here, on the fifteenth floor, you could suddenly hear the plodding of the slow night trolley down in the street.

The Foundling

They were so sorrowful, so calm. Afraid of nothing, concerned with nothing. They knew how to live, how to earn their daily bread, and how to stick together. He walked up and lay down among them in the walkway between the Mendeleevskaya and Novoslobodskaya stations—palms to cheek, knees to stomach—but then he looked closer: no, that's not how they were lying; he put his elbow under his head, and immediately felt comfortable. They didn't protest and didn't chase him away—someone stuck a warm snout under the hem of his shearling coat, someone slapped their tail against his knee—and against the background of the monotonous scraping of human footsteps they fell asleep, the whole pack.

We Can't Even Imagine Heights Like That

All day he walked around with a mysterious look and got on everyone's nerves so much with his enigmatic hints that during the last break Big Marina pressed him against the map closet and began to tickle him. He yelped, writhed, breathless with shrieking laughter, but didn't crack, and after school they had to tail him to the vacant lot. He dragged them past the bottles, paper scraps, past the broken-off mannequin arms that instantly attracted everyone's attention, past all sorts of off-color trash to a ginormous rock about his own size. He said it was a meteorite.

"Imagine," he said, "just imagine how high up this meteorite must have been when it fell! We can't even imagine heights like that."

He told us that according to his scientific calculations, this meteorite fell to earth literally yesterday.

"If the meteorite fell to earth yesterday, then why has it already grown into the ground?" Big Marina asked caustically. She was a fat, strapping girl forced to live by her wits. Then he said that when a meteorite falls, time around it goes faster. A day is like a month, or maybe even a year. Or three. He said that science doesn't have the most exact data yet.

That night he returned to the vacant lot, spread his jacket out on the ground, hugged the meteorite and lay there right up until morning. He got very cold, but those seven years were worth it.

Cyst

She decided to tell Katrina everything the next morning at breakfast. Then she decided she would tell her on Monday before sending her off to school, so the girl would have something to distract her. Then she decided not to tell her at all—just to pretend everything was OK and tell her the truth in a month or two, when there wouldn't be any choice. That was the decision she settled on. She opened the apartment door extra slowly, holding her breath, so it wouldn't creak, but Katrina wasn't asleep anyway, she rose from the couch to meet her, the TV remote plopped on the ground. She smiled with all her might.

"Sorry I didn't call," she said. "Some mother! But I thought you were out somewhere."

"No," said Katrina. "No, I'm here."

"Great," she said. "Everything is great. Everything is great, can you believe it? It was just a calcium deposit, a cyst."

"A cyst," said Katrina.

"A cyst," she said. "Just a calcium deposit. I was so happy I just went off to the movies, if you can believe it."

"What'd you see?" asked Katrina, squatting down for the remote but not taking her eyes off her. She almost growled through the bared teeth of her joyful smile.

"Some people," she said sternly, "are up way past their bedtime. I won't be able to get those people out of bed tomorrow at seven-fifteen, not even by force. What do those people think about that?"

"Listen," said Katrina. "Will you give me that skirt for tomorrow?"

"You won't sit on the grass?" she asked with feigned mistrust.

"When would I?" said Katrina dolefully. "Seven classes and a presentation."

Then she clambered out of the skirt, stuffed it into her daughter's hands, awkwardly pressed the girl to her—hard, with her whole body, as though she were still five or six—and quickly went to her bedroom. And while she struggled to quell the biter chill, lying under her icy blanket in the blind darkness that pressed on her from above, in the next room her daughter was staring at the fringe knit along the whole front of the skirt in crooked, jerky, tangled knots, and didn't want to understand—and already understood completely.

Translated by Maya Vinokour

Alexey Tsvetkov Jr. (b. 1975)

Priceart

1.

That day the Goods Manager, who had departed for Egypt, left the Salesperson with lots of work, namely, to manually stick some two hundred price tags onto newly arrived books. And the Salesperson was deftly stamping away, removing the titles from the tape with his fingers. From the boxes he fished out erotic photo albums, albums of the masterpieces of the avant-garde, the old masters, and Japanese comic books. Sometimes he absent-mindedly made an error and glued the wrong price tag onto a book, so, for example, a fat album entitled *Paris, Paris* . . . boasted a completely different title, *History of the Tattoo*, on the barcode. Occasionally the result was amusing—the history of the tattoo started with the Eiffel Tower. But the Salesperson, having caught himself, frowned with annoyance, squeezed his eyebrows to the bridge of his nose and relabeled the product. And here a wave of illumination enveloped him. A squall of genius hit him in the face. The Salesperson froze on the spot, the price tag on his thumb not quite making it to the cover of a fashionable magazine. In that particular magazine, on the first page—he had time to peek inside—it was affirmed half in jest that in the upcoming season an exchange of goods would be replaced by donation, or more simply put, lots of all kinds of things would become unconditionally free of charge. The reason for such magic was simple—overproduction of goods and slumping demand.

It's not that our Salesperson had not thought about such like before or had not read about similar things. Of course he had read and thought about them, and even had asked witty questions from the audience at public lectures. These were the kinds of questions at which everyone starts nodding and smiling, not having listened all the way through. But here suddenly every piece fell together, fitting into a brilliant and at the same time elementary solution.

2.

The very next day, the excited Salesperson, smiling to himself with knowledge still unknown to others, sat in the Editor's reception room of said fashionable magazine. He had had to ring up a dozen of his acquaintances to get the meeting.

The Editor smiled at him in a most genial, almost tender manner and reminded him that in five minutes he had to leave for an urgent meeting. The Salesperson nodded, indicating that he would not detain him.

"I liked your editorial a lot. To be honest, I did not expect something like that. And once I'd read it, my hands reached for the cardboard and keyboard of their own accord, and here is what came out."

The Salesperson pulled out from an opaque packet a piece of cardboard with big letters FREE. They were assembled from real price tags—each of them bore an authentic barcode and the word FREE instead of a product name, and a blank space where the price would be. The Salesperson assured the Editor that the price tags were genuine, they scan on the shop's cash register. The Editor listened, amiable and benevolent. He waited for this "nutcase" to leave, and when he did so, the Editor turned the cardboard over in his hands. "On behalf of and authorized by the work team" was written in marker on the reverse. At that time the Salesperson did not quite realize his uniqueness and dared not sign the piece "I" instead of "we." Chuckling wisely, the Editor hung the cardboard with the FREE tag up on the wall, between diplomas and framed covers of the best magazine issues. "For a couple of days to amuse acquaintances,"—he thought to himself. But he never took it down.

3.

A week later in the center of the capital, right on the boulevard where the fashionable magazine was hosting a celebration, there took place a "giveaway" or an "American Indian ritual of a potlatch"—a funny promotion where everyone could give anything to someone (s)he happened to like. The Salesperson played a central part here—he put "FREE" price tags on the things to be given away: everyone found it much more fun to give and receive in this manner. Price: 0000 . . . How many zeros would fit on a price tag? But if asked persistently, he could also stamp an item with some absurd price—one ruble or conversely one million rubles. And instead of the name of the product, next to the barcode, he could input any words: "Fucking Amazing," "Unique," "A Long-Awaited Thing," "A Keepsake from Grey," or "Not for sale." To do this required a laptop with an accounting program and a small crackling printer from which the requisite pieces of paper crawled out.

4.

Soon the magazine ordered a photo session. A girl photographer followed the Salesperson, and together they pointed fingers at everything and, laughing, searched for/checked whether they had such a thing in their long rolled tape of price tags. And they stuck a tag on the things that happened to be present. Here is "Bench"—a price tag left on the back of a bench. "Stick"— the price tag stuck to a stick protruding from a garbage bin. "Brick"—all the seemingly identical bricks in the wall of a house had different prices— from three to three thousand rubles. They playfully fingered the long paper snake of price tags. Despite the wet autumn weather, the Salesperson was having fun with the Photogirl. She followed him, clicking away in a series of flashes, her laughter ringing with his, nodded, and, by the end of their stroll, she was already sticking on some price tags herself . . . A week later all of this ran in a glossy magazine and was all over the Internet. Later they purposefully went out again, he stuck on price tags as she took pictures, and they both were filmed by an acquaintance, to be uploaded on YouTube.

It somehow happened of its own accord that when they turned to the outskirts of town, and he kissed her surprised lips, their acquaintance continued to film. And he found a price tag with the greatest possible number and glued it just above the bridge of her nose where Buddhists have a third eye. Then on YouTube their friend set all this romantic stuff to perfect music. The girl said that price tags with barcodes look particularly good on birch bark. After their first adult kiss he moved her slightly away from himself to look over her shoulder into the distance. The naked forest stood far away like a drawn barcode and watched the lovers. The air was visible through the woods.

He started seeing the Photogirl often. After all, he was no longer a mere Salesperson, but the founder of a new trend, a "Price Artist," who was becoming popular, with certain fame ahead.

5.

For his first exhibition, the Photogirl helped him set out cave images made of price tags on a wall: half of a zebra—a giraffe—a hunter with a bow and arrow—the footprint of a stranger. If one approached and closely examined these figures, one discovered prices in rubles, and it would become clear how important a particular hoof, a tip of an arrow, a finger or just a strip were in the eyes of the artist. Moreover, the importance of these details was expressed in the language of economics, in maximally concrete monetary terms: this one at 120 rubles, and this other at 1,090.

6.

"But it was not just the importance of specific monetary units—the artist confided in interviews,—"the image made from price tags is a painting made from signatures, like those of the Conceptualists. In vain did we not think before what a price tag is, to what extent it is an object that is philosophical and ideal for art! The price tag is a sign that the ephemeral ghost of the commodity has already entered the thing and invisibly inhabits it. Before us there is the sign of an invisible transition from the physical body to the market unit, not a mere piece of paper. Price tags are spots, the most important spots of commerce, the dotted chromosomes of capitalism. "To think" means "to 'price' things"—the artist choked on his truth in front of the journalists, his forehead flashing with perspiration of delight.

A peculiar strain of Marxism was trendy in the circles of art critics. He had learned that much quickly.

7.

"Price Art" continued to perfect itself, and now fans and opponents frequently referred to it with an English neologism, Priceart, to appeal to foreign audiences. On weekends children gathered in the "Priceart Studio." Before them on the wall hung an enlarged sample of a price tag, and they painstakingly redrew it, some with crayons, some with colors, markers, pencils, copying the barcode, and peering at the sample for a long time. And every child wrote his word—"bunny" or "boat" or "spider-man"—on the tag and put its price below. And then they took them to their parents to show them off. Typically, these were the names of things the child wanted to receive, or, on the contrary, wanted to get rid of, to sell. The studio was located in a huge gallery, a former garage. Parents left their children there for a couple of hours to take a quiet look at the "adult" works of the Price Artist.

He was happy to tell children and parents alike how it all started. The first thing he did on that memorable day in the bookstore was assemble the letter E on a blank sheet taken from the printer. It consisted of a chance collection of price tags, "pencils." "As if drawn by pencil,"—joked the artist, showing this priceless relic. The Salesperson then put the letter E on the shelf, laying it over a photo album of portraits of American celebrities, stepped back three steps, looked at the result and saw that it was a stroke of genius. That's how he found himself in life and in art.

8.

Before long, an extra-parliamentary opposition summoned the artist, and he could not refuse. In their headquarters he exhibited nine hundred price tags with last names—set to the layout of the State Duma. It was debated for a long time whether each delegate should be given a different price, i.e., unique as a name, and what it should depend on, the politician's reputation, the faction (s)he belonged to, or on the attitude of the client. However, the Priceartist decided and insisted that he would do without individualizing the delegates' images, and typed again: 000000 on each, giving each the same price. Art should not be too politically aware, it needs to maintain a level of abstraction. This "parliament" of course caused a scandal, especially when it was shown at the Venice Biennale. But the scandal turned out to provide precisely the resonance needed to cultivate success.

9.

The Priceartist continued to deal with politics. He made the American White House and our Kremlin from price tags, as well as the hammer and the sickle, a swastika, and the flags of different countries. Entering the gallery, the viewer would be perplexed at seeing on the wall a mere rectangle filled with some gray dotted lines, but, approaching it, and reading the word "red" on the lower price tags, "blue" in the middle, and "white" on the top tags, the viewer became convinced that what (s)he beheld was indeed the Russian flag. Certain people advised tinting the price tags with spray paint, but this, of course, proceeded from a less than perfect understanding of the concept. The Priceartist executed the names of gods and mosaic portraits of celebrities who could be recognized only from afar, when the price tags blended into a familiar image in the viewer's eye. Nor did he steer clear of accusations of pornography, having laid out a vagina and a penis made of price tags on black glossy photo paper. And what exactly was written there on each price tag?—one had to guess for oneself. It was an erotic exhibition to which children and teenagers were not admitted.

10.

On City Day he arranged a special exhibition. Everyone who so desired could say any word, name, or action, and put any price under it. "Any price for any thing!" proclaimed the banner made of price tags. People came up with the strangest ideas: someone used the last name of his ex-wife, while someone else requested a certain phone number instead of a name. Many wanted the artist to autograph the price tag. "Having received a genuine store price tag with a barcode, your chosen word, and the sum you assigned, you may make use of it at your discretion—glue it onto the named thing or keep it for yourself, as a souvenir of your gesture of creative price-forma-tion. There are no moral, political, or commercial restrictions in the choice of words and prices,"—so the Artist explained to a well-known writer who came to see who values what and how much. The Priceartist had read his books and for some time had tried very hard to insert himself into one of them.

He often recalled now how once, as a destitute student, he walked along the street looking for work, and heard a song flying out of a car's window: "Life is a theater, Shakespeare said, and we are all actors in it." He did not hear the next part, the car had left, but, with nothing to do, he made up the rest: "But there are also spectators as well as directors. There is the cloakroom attendant with a hanger and the lighting designer. And also the one who determines the price of a ticket."

It was precisely as a lighting designer that he was not hired on that day, though not at a theater but at an open-air stage of a children's festival.

Now he considered this to be a prophetic incident. "The one who assigns prices"—this described him perfectly. He could not know at that time who he would become, but somehow this idea had penetrated from the future, seeping from his triumphant maturity back into his luckless loser youth.

It came back to him, after the theater incident, how he saw a price tag for the first time in his life. Still a schoolboy, in some journal translated from Czech, he read an article about what a useful thing a barcode is, how much information about the product it contains. But he did not see barcodes on any goods in his Soviet childhood, no matter how much he examined them. At that time the price was deeply imprinted into the surface of books and cooking pans as a permanent brand. And the boy dreamed that one day they would appear, that barcodes would sit on things like patterned nocturnal moths, and then the future would arrive. And he rejoiced when they appeared, although he was no longer a child. He loved to talk about this at interviews which he now gave every day.

People tried to imitate him, but no one wanted to take the price tags of others, of epigones, everyone wanted to have the authentic price tags of the auteur, the one who had invented it all, preferably autographed.

11.

In his workshop, devices were continuously rattling, ribbons with ready-made price tags streamed out of them. Assistants typed out the required words, taking phone orders, bringing him individual price tags and finished mosaics for signature. His wife who had long ceased being a Photogirl—she had no time for amusement—now managed it all. She responded to calls, signed contracts, set up meetings with the press.

"I myself!"—the Price Artist never tired of the daily dive into euphoria, squeezing his wife, or not necessarily his wife, in his arms.—"I myself decide which price a word, thing, or creature has. I myself stick price tags onto them. God dictates figures to me and shows me the items the way he showed Adam all the creatures of the earth to assign them names."

12.

That's how the former Salesperson who had become a real artist made nothing more in life other than price tags with barcodes. At the peak of his career, having hired hundreds of workers, he pasted price tags all over the

German Reichstag and the Pompidou Center in France, to remain there for three days. Of course the fad for Priceart eventually calmed down, but the line of customers to the studio did not run out until the very last day. And so that last day arrived.

In the hospital the famous old man stuck with his shaky hands the last price tag onto a matryoshka sent to him by some girl, not for money but just because one needs to do good. At his funeral there gathered a crowd of young and not so young people wearing T-shirts emblazoned with enlarged copies of his best price tags. Flags with barcodes soared above their heads. On the wall of the cathedral, like a laser epitaph, the price tag with the last name of the deceased, and created by him, trembled sorrowfully in the twilight to his favorite music. The tombstone was a glittering marble that sparkled like sugar. It had the black stripes of a barcode, the first name, the last name, and two dates instead of a price. It was superfluous to explain who lay there under the tombstone. True, he was far from the first to lie under a barcode-tombstone. He himself more than once made sketches for others' gravestones.

13.

But this is not the end of the story. After the funeral of the great Priceartist, after the funeral repast and condolences, at first in a half whisper, and then in a full voice, the question was raised and repeated everywhere: Who will make price tags for us now? To whom did he delegate this right? Heirs from different lines of kinship brought a lawsuit, but no one had sufficient evidence, everyone relied on unverified oral testimony.

Besides, nobody really wanted to buy from the relatives. Who were they, after all? The price of the artist's tags constantly grew, everyone wanted to buy them, but nobody wanted to sell because no one doubted that in a few years these sticky, slightly rubbed out little bits of paper, no matter what the price indicated on them, would equal the value of platinum and diamonds. Over the years the barcodes grew opaque, evaporated, and no longer scanned at the cash register, but precisely this made them truly antique, expensive. They were placed under glass in the guarded halls of museums and private collections. They were frozen in repositories. The Priceartist was no longer with us. Without him the world grew empty. And people decided that genius has no heirs. Price tags with barcodes became again what they had been before the illumination experienced by the Salesperson in the store. They returned to the state of being ordinary labels, convenient machine messages.

The priceless pricetags of the master. Their number will remain forever limited. Individual madmen from the list of the richest people in the world have made it their mission to gather them all, no matter the cost. Their agents have negotiated, outbid each other for the rarities; the rich have gone bankrupt in despair, but no one in the world has had enough money to buy all the artist's barcodes. Besides, there is no guarantee that suddenly some person would not put up for sale some new, previously undisclosed tags that could be authenticated by an autograph.

More than a few forgeries appeared. What was needed was the signature of the master on the tag. But this, in fact, had been forged. Or, instead of a signature, at least five witnesses who closely knew the Priceartist were required to confirm authenticity, but they could be bribed. Being a friend of the deceased became a most profitable business. A hundred friends formed an influential club that no one else was allowed to join, any other "friends" were written in quotes and not recognized by the market.

Nobody ever again was able to, nobody had the right to turn a price tag or a barcode into something more than just a price tag and a barcode. In memory of the deceased, out of respect for art, out of consideration for market stability—and in general. And this is the real end of our story.

Translated by Sofya Khagi

Lara Vapnyar (b. 1976)

Salad Olivier

My mother has always removed her shoes under the table, placed her feet on top of them, and entertained herself by curling and uncurling her toes. Aunt Masha liked to scratch her ankles with her stiletto heels. Uncle Boris stomped his right foot when he argued. "I insist!" he would say, and his hard leather heel went boom! against the linoleum floor. My father's feet weren't particularly funny, except when he wore mismatched socks, as he often did.

We, my cousin Violetta and I, liked to spend holiday meals under the table. From there, hidden behind three layers of tablecloth, we watched the secret life of the adult feet and listened to adult conversations.

"Mm, mm," they said, above our heads. "The salad is good today! Not bad, is it? Not bad at all!"

They champed, they crunched, they jingled their forks, they clinked glasses.

"In Paris they serve Olivier without meat," Uncle Boris said.

"Come on!"

"They do!"—angry boom of Uncle Boris's right shoe—"I read it in *A Moveable Feast*."

"Olivier can't possibly be made without meat!" My mother's toes curled. "It's even worse than Olivier with bologna."

"Olivier with bologna is plebeian." Aunt Masha's stiletto heels agreed.

If I giggled, Cousin Violetta covered my mouth with her cupped hand. She had rough fingers, hardened by piano lessons. Her mother also took her to drawing and figure skating lessons. She said that her figure-skating teacher liked to bend the kids' backs to the point where their vertebrae were about to break loose and scatter onto the rink. Poor Cousin Violetta. I didn't have to take any lessons because my father was the genius of the family. "The Mikhail Lanzman," people said about him. He used up piles of paper, covering it with formulas; he often froze with a perplexed expression during meals and conversations, and he did every simple chore slowly and zealously. When we all prepared Salad Olivier and my father sliced potatoes, he did exactly four cuts across and six lengthwise.

At that time I tried to copy him. My mother put a sofa cushion on my chair, so I could reach the table, and gave me a bowl of peeled eggs—a safer ingredient that wouldn't soil my holiday clothes. I didn't mind, even though Cousin Violetta had been trusted with sour pickles. I liked eggs. They were soft, smooth, and easy to slice.

I held an egg between my thumb and index finger, carefully counted the cuts. My father, who sat across from me, nodded approvingly. From time to time his reading glasses would slide to the tip of his nose, and it was my job to push them up because I had the cleanest hands. "Puppy Tail!" he would call, and I would slip off my pillow and rush to his end of the table, push the glasses to the bridge of his nose, and command, "Stay there!" But invariably the glasses slid down again, often as soon as I made it back to my place and resumed counting.

By the time I could reach the table without the pillow, my slicing zeal had cooled off. Strangely enough, it coincided with a vague suspicion that my father was an ordinary man after all. Ordinary, and maybe even boring. The puppy tail stopped wagging.

By the time we moved to America my cutting zeal had perished altogether.

"Slice, don't chop!" my mother says in our Brooklyn kitchen. I remove the large potato chunks that I'd just put into the crystal bowl and slice them some more.

It's June 14, our first American anniversary. We'll celebrate it alone, the three of us, consuming a bowl of Olivier and a bottle of sickly sweet wine that rests on top of the refrigerator. We are not happy. In my mother's opinion, it's my fault.

"You can't say that you don't meet men. You work with men, don't you?" My mother rips sinew out of the chunks of boiled pork.

I raise my eyes. I work in a urologist's office and my mother knows it.

"Mother, the men I meet are either impotent or carry sexually transmitted diseases." This isn't completely true. The urologist also has two or three incontinence cases and a few prostate cancers, which I neglect to mention.

She purses her lips and starts knocking with her knife against the cutting board. She works fast when she is angry. The bits of meat fly from under her knife all over the table. I pick the bits up and throw them into the garbage, seeing a corner of the living room with my father's small figure sprawled on the couch. His feet, clad in perfectly matched gray socks, are placed on top of the armrest. His feet are the first thing I see on entering the apartment. Sometimes he taps with them rhythmically as if listening to a sad, slow tune; at other times they just stay perched there like two lost birds.

His feet were the first thing I saw yesterday, having returned from a date that had started with my mother's phone hunt for a "suitable boy" and ended with the "suitable boy" telling me I could be certain that he would never ever ask me out again.

"He's not our kind, Ma. I'm sure that in his family they put bologna in the salad," I said, trying to console her. She didn't buy it.

"The fact is, Marochka, that Tanya does have suitors," she says on the phone. "Wonderful men. But Americans! You understand me, don't you? There are differences that can't be resolved, different cultures and such. We want a Russian boy for her."

I listen from the kitchen, while scraping the salad remains off the sides of the bowl.

As the call progresses, CUNY becomes NYU, the linguistic department becomes medical school, and my receptionist service at the urologist's becomes my medical work. When she sees me look over at her, my mother throws me a defiant look.

I know, I agree. If I were worthier, she wouldn't have had to lie.

She ends the call, with "I see," followed by "Yes, please, if you hear anything." The receiver falls onto the base with a helpless clunk.

Then she walks into the kitchen and pours herself a glass of currant juice. Don't pity me, she seems to be saying, while slurping the red liquid. It's not me who has just been rejected, it's you. I dated enough in my time. I found a man to marry. Her black mascara melts together with tears and runs in tiny twisted streams down her cheeks.

At times I want to shrink so I can hug my mother's knees, press my face against her warm thighs, and cry with her, wetting the saucer-size daisies and poppies on her skirt.

At other times (increasingly often lately) I want to walk up and shove her, making her spill the juice all over her sweaty neck and her stupid flowery dress.

Instead, I rise from my chair, dump the bowl into the sink, and leave the kitchen.

A boyfriend had been prescribed by a psychologist we consulted after my father's first few months on the couch.

"There is a pattern," Aunt Masha told my mother shortly before that. "They lose their jobs, then they take to spending their days on the couch, and then a woman turns up. How? When? You ask yourself. He barely even left the couch!"

It was my uncle Boris who'd first suggested the idea of emigrating. "A scientist of Mikhail's stature will never be properly appreciated in Russia," he said.

I wanted to ask if Cousin Violetta had learned how to ski. The last I heard about her was that she had moved to Aspen and was living with a ski instructor. "The snow in Aspen is as soft as a feather bed and as sweet as cotton candy," she wrote me once. She hadn't written or answered my calls since then.

"Your husband and father can't handle the pressure," the psychologist explained. He spoke to my mother and me because my father had stormed out of his office, refusing to be treated like a madman.

"He yearns to be relieved, but in a subtle, not humiliating, way. It usually works better if he is relieved by a male child, but sometimes it helps when a daughter marries, thus finding a man who will figuratively replace her father."

The idea filled my mother with almost religious fervor. "When Tanya finds a boyfriend," she would start frequently, often out of nowhere. "When Tanya finds a boyfriend" signified a wonderful future, when all wishes would come true and all problems dissolve before they even developed. Not only would the boyfriend "relieve" my father, he would also explain to us all the mysterious letters we got from banks, doctors, and gas and electric companies. He would help us move to a bigger, nicer place. "Closer to a subway stop. On the other hand, no. It's too noisy if you live near the subway." The boyfriend, who would of course own a quiet, roomy car like the one we used to have in Russia, would take us upstate to pick mushrooms and blueberries. "Do you think he'll like my mushroom dumplings?" my mother would ask, seeing a shadow of concern on my face.

The only problem was that the wonderful future refused to come.

By the end of our first year in America I'd met only four men who were willing to date me—one at school, the others on the subway—none of them Russian, and none of them even remotely close to the idea of an omnipotent boyfriend. I'd slept with one of them, an Armenian dancer with lips the color of plums and equally firm and smooth. I didn't mention that to my mother.

Around June 1, my mother fished her notebook out of the drawer and planted herself by the telephone. She'd decided to take the business into her own hands.

The phone calls from potential boyfriends were rare but consistent. Some weird intuition helped me to distinguish them from other calls by the sharp mocking sound the telephone made.

The receiver felt damp and warm, vibrating with the voice of a strange man trapped inside. The voice is wrong—either too squeaky, too nasal, or too coarse. It is the voice of a man who doesn't want me, who called me because he wanted somebody, anybody—though not me—or simply because his mother made him do it.

Later, on the date, the man casually looked at his toes, but at the same time he discreetly scrutinized me, estimating the size of my breasts, the shape of the legs concealed by my slacks, trying to guess what I would and wouldn't do, trying to guess what was wrong with me (I'd agreed to a blind date, there must be something wrong), searching for flaws, finding them, finding the ones I'd been afraid that he'd find, finding ones I hadn't even known about.

"What is your car's make?" I asked him repeatedly, because I couldn't think of anything else to say.

It's not true that I was not trying, as my mother said. I was trying. I arched my back, I tossed my hair, I licked my lips and crossed my legs in a modest yet seducing way. I nodded sympathetically when he talked, I laughed when he told a joke, I smiled when his shoulders brushed against mine. It didn't help. From the very beginning I knew that eventually I'd fail. Sooner or later the disgust, the humiliation would erupt, and I would end up saying something insulting or indecent, or simply laughing like crazy, kicking with my knees and wiping the tears from my eyes, as I did when my date burped during our dinner.

"You think you're something, don't you?" he had hissed, before adding that he'd never ever ask me out again. "You think you're something!"

I wish I thought that.

And then, all of a sudden, I found a boyfriend. By myself. On a subway train.

It happened on a rainy day at the end of October. A man squeezed into the crowded subway car and brushed against my shoulder with his wet umbrella. I shivered. He said, "Excuse me," walked across the car to the opposite door, and pulled a book out of his shoulder bag.

His clothes were baggy and poorly matched. He looked about six foot two, with a broad body that swayed awkwardly when the train was moving. He kept looking at me from above his book. He liked me for no apparent reason.

After 23rd Street, he stepped forward and grasped a handle above my head. "Do you speak Russian?" he asked.

I said that I did.

He smiled.

That was it.

It's December and it's snowing outside. I open the door, shaking specks of snow off my knitted hat. He is here. There are his heavy boots, drying on the newspaper in the corner. He visits often. Sometimes he comes before me, sometimes he even comes while I'm at work, and then it's not his shoes but only his wet dark-brown footprints that mark the newspaper on the floor.

"Vadim apologized that he didn't wait for you. He had some errands," my mother yells from the kitchen. Not only has Vadim acquired his own mug and his own chair, there is Vadim's place at the table (by the refrigerator).

The psychologist's prescription has worked. My father's constant lying position became a sitting one—sitting at the computer, after Vadim introduced him to the Internet. He is sending e-mails to mathematicians all over the world, exchanging problems, questions, and even some obscure mathematician jokes.

It is his slouched back that I see now upon coming home. "I've got thirteen e-mails today!" he announces, half turning from his desk and pushing up his glasses. He reads and welcomes everything that comes to his mailbox, from breast-enlargement ads to tax-deduction advice.

"Marochka (Verochka/Genechka), guess who this is?" my mother sings into the receiver every night. She methodically repeats the calling circle of the previous months, making sure she doesn't miss any woman she had begged to find a boyfriend for me.

"By the way, did I mention our Tanya's new boyfriend? . . . Yes, he is Russian . . . A computer programmer. He's not a Bill Gates, but he is very talented. And nice, too. Very nice."

Sometimes he slips and calls my parents Ma and Pa.

"Vadim misses his parents," my mother notes approvingly. His parents had to stay in Moscow because of Vadim's grandfather, who's been bedridden for years. Vadim sends them money, adult diapers for his grandfather, and sugar-free candies for his diabetic grandmother. I know this not from Vadim but from my mother's phone conversations.

"We're pleased. We have nothing to complain about," my mother tells her friends.

I have nothing to complain about either. Even the sex is good—ample and satisfying, like a hearty dinner.

I don't know why seeing Vadim's shoes in the corner makes me recoil.

Animated voices invade the apartment. My father's laughter, my mother's murmur, and Vadim's soft baritone buzz against a background of rhythmic knocking and banging. Have they got together to play New Age music?

I make a few steps toward the kitchen and stop, half hidden, in the niche.

They sit at the table with knives and cutting boards around the crystal bowl. They are making Salad Olivier.

"No, Pa, I'm afraid you're wrong." Vadim says. "It's a different salad in *A Moveable Feast*, not Olivier."

"You see! You see!" my mother charges. "What I've been telling you! Olivier can't possibly be without meat."

"Okay, but I still insist that Olivier's name was Jacques."

They take turns emptying their cutting boards into the bowl, then the rhythmic knocking resumes. The mechanism is working. They don't need me. I am free to go.

I tiptoe out of the kitchen and put on my hat, still wet from the snow. The door opens with a screech; I wait a few seconds to make sure that nobody heard me. A peal of laughter reaches me from the kitchen. I throw a parting look at the warped headline under Vadim's shoes: good news for the diaspora!

The snow-covered street is cold and soft. I slowly take it in, the powdered cars, the timid light of the lampposts, the naked twigs of the cherry trees. The weak and helpless snow melts on contact with my feet. It doesn't crunch the way it did in Russia.

I shiver as the cold gets to my toes.

Without me their perfectly tuned mechanism will stop. The gears will slow down and halt. The elements will fall apart.

They need me after all, if only as a link holding them together. I take a handful of the soft feeble snow and knead it in my palms. It melts before I am able to form a shape.

"I'm here," I say, on entering the kitchen. I walk to the table, push my chair closer, and pick up an egg.

Polina Barskova (b. 1976)

Reaper of Leaves

Where will the starlings make their nests, the ones without a nesting box?

I want to see all the way through him, as though he were a frozen January frog or a newborn eel, and reacquaint us with him, though we'll hardly welcome the renewed acquaintance. I mean to peer inside that machinery of word-production, the machinery which goes by the name "Bianci," and glimpse what has never been seen before. Influenced, perhaps, by his belief that hidden, invisible life is always more enthralling, more impressive, more elaborate than what submits to the indifferent eye or hasty conclusion, I find it comforting to think that nature is not what we imagine—nature not in the lofty sense of the great and lofty poet but in the plain sense of the poet who never developed, the clumsy poet.

It turns out that while we're floundering in snow and finding ice everywhere, underneath, far under, spring not only has quickened but is gathering-growing in earnest. Down in the burrows, in darkness and stench, a new harvest's offspring are crawling, water is pooling, dead plants begin to stir and roots spread to clutch at a new spring.

But where do we look for him, this observer of nature? And how will we recognize him when we meet him? The man who is my subject today did everything he could to cover his tracks, to draw predators and hunters away from his lair—both those who surrounded him back then and those who came later. The first predators and hunters were the kind who by means of flattery, cajoling, torture and forceful personal example pressured and seduced suppliers of words to assimilate, to change their nature for the sake of the things of this world—publishing and publicity, material comfort and a peaceful corner. Although the corners these lower-echelon wordsmiths got were fairly dank, the ceiling dripping into a saucer, drops splashing onto the cat's nose—he fastidiously shaking them off his whiskers, twitching his ears.

Whereas today's predators and hunters—from afar—are we, his readers, vigilant dividers of the wheat from the chaff (the hawk's pursuit, from up high) trying to consign to oblivion, to thoroughly douse in Lethe's sterile, uncreative solution, to judge and separate out the second-rate, the third-rate, the writers hopelessly trying to light a fire under the word. But the task of those writers was simply to stay alive and, if they succeeded, to preserve some small part of their real selves. Whatever that mirage meant to them—"realness"—this real part was hidden in a desk drawer, pickled in alcohol or—and this was the most effective approach—openly displayed at the hunting grounds to deflect the interest of hounds and predators by its very availability, as though this real part were "carrion":

> One of our forest correspondents reports from the Tver region: yesterday while digging he turned up, along with the dirt, some kind of beast. Its front paws have claws, on its back are some kind of knobs instead of wings, its body is covered with dark-yellow hairs like thick, short fur. It looks like both a wasp and a mole—insect or beast, what is it? The editorial view: It is a remarkable insect that looks like a beast called a mole-cricket. Whoever wants to find a mole-cricket should pour water on the ground and cover the area with pieces of bark. At night mole-crickets will seek out the damp spot, the dirt under the bark. That's where we'll find him.

Let's take a peek at the dirt under the bark—and see what there is to see.

Dueling Storytellers

Vitaly Valentinovich Bianci lived for work and drink, and toward the end of his life his voice reached its zenith, became almost a squeak, a mosquito falsetto, while he himself grew heavy and legless, but still he could not stop himself and kept tapping out his tracks on the typewriter with one finger. Contemporaries recall his Bunyanesque strength along with Bunyanesque slowness, the fading aristocratic charm of his gradually swelling face, looking like he'd been attacked by midges. Of these contemporaries, the one most inclined to observation wrote,

> Bianci grabbed me by the legs, turned me upside down and held me like that, laughing, not letting me go. Such an insult! It took me a long time to get over it. I wasn't physically weak but this I couldn't handle. Humiliating! The worst thing was his strength seemed rough and way beyond mine. A useless feeling that wasn't quite envy and wasn't quite jealousy consumed me. Eventually it passed. Bianci was simple and decent. But the devil had done his work . . .

But the devil had done his work.

The ethnographer of *belles lettres* repeats the phrase several times; it seems she likes it, it helps her diagnose the decline of her subject—a strong and benign creature warped by his own interpretation of affairs. Enter Evgeny Lvovich Shvarts, a dwarflike man with a head the shape of an egg, hands shaking from Parkinson's (sometimes he would leave the telegraph office with nothing accomplished, his hands shook so much that tracing a caterpillar of letters with the capricious rusty nib turned out to be impossible, with the line of people behind him simmering, irritable-resentful). A dwarf who utterly lacked the gift of forgiving and forgetting, of looking the other way, probably the most perceptive and fastidious member of a generation covered in spiritual sores. (And that's a sanitary way of putting it. When I try to imagine that generation's spiritual condition taking visible-palpable form—oh, what it would look like! . . .) Shvarts was venomous (from a monstrous capacity to feel wounded) and recklessly brave—he was one of those rare "valued persons" who refused in the fall of 1941 to be airlifted from Dystrophy City (the name is one of Bianci's later witticisms). By the time winter arrived, they had to drag him out of there, psychotic, demented from hunger.

Photographs of him, and especially photographs of him in the company of women, stand out sharply in the general current of the time—the angular, mocking, delicate faces glow like seashells lit from within. Evgeny Shvarts was painfully large-spirited: in the "inventory" of his notebooks, he does not name the friends who made denunciations, scandalmongered, went into hysterics, blackened reputations. When you look at the minutes of official meetings where his friends acted the fool, attacking him as a talentless saboteur, and compare them to Shvarts's memoirs about these same people, you stop short in amazement—did he actually forgive them? Or did he cut off all feeling for them?

Like all the jokesters who in those golden years made careers rhyming, crowing, meowing and bleating for "The Siskin" and "The Hedgehog,"

Shvarts was a libertine; he took his own and his companions' sins allegorically. Hence his choice of genre—after all, we're talking about fairy tales and fabulists. Hence also the refrain: the devil had done his work. Shvarts was interested—and following him, so are we—by the allegory of the human soul's duel with the devil of the times, the pitiful stratagems used by those who inhabited those times as they tried both to placate and to hide from the devil. Bianci, soon after his second stroke, said to Shvarts, "If you want to know what it's like when it hits you, just put on those glasses." On the table was a pair of black glasses, the lenses made the world look dim. Black light enveloped the fabulist Bianci toward the end. The fabulist Shvarts witnessed and grimly confirmed this.

How to Translate White

Bianci's grandfather, an opera singer, had the last name Weiss. This gentleman, at his impresario's request, translated himself from German into Italian to go on tour in Italy—the sound, the tune, changed, but the color remained. The sound was now weightless, lofting upward like a bubble—a bubble floating over a white, white field with just the tracks of small, tired paws along the edge: Take a guess, children, who can it be?

A young boy, darting up and down, passes dioramas of mounted animals—under the silver hoof of an agitated, dead-eyed deer with flared nostrils (if they really shoot it up, does it make the taxidermist's job harder?) sprouts a dead mushroom. For some reason these little glass mushrooms are pinned all around the animals' legs—so we won't have any doubts, just recognize these forms of non-life with a guilty tenderness. Above the deer's head they nailed a woodpecker stuffed with shavings. Observe how the bird's eye knows no fear—it is open to the world and keenly focused.

The mounted animals were hideous, the aging Bianci recalls near the end of his story. "How can we bring them back to life?" old man Bianci asks in his child's voice. What you need are some good, strong words. "What you need is poetry": that unwieldy, cardboard word he carried around all his life, to no avail.

Before he discovered ornithology, the young boy was driven on another sort of hunt—soccer. He played for the storied clubs "Petrovsky," "Neva," "Unitas." He was the winner, incidentally, of the Saint Petersburg season trophy for 1913. The season trophy—in April the wind from the Neva fills with the scent of dun-colored, crumbling ice. Rostral beauties raise to the wind their buoyant, erect nipples.

Tall for his age, wearing gaiters, with a sweaty forehead and gritty, salty hair, the adolescent Bianci pursues the ball: his breathing grows sharp, with the occasional pleasurable ache.

His father, a famous ornithologist, the very one after whom the young boy trotted along the large-windowed, empty halls of the museum, did not approve of soccer—he wanted to see in his son a replica of himself, naturally. His son obediently enrolled in the natural sciences section of the Department of Physics and Mathematics at Petrograd University, but he never finished, since things finished of their own accord.

Cold-blooded?

Almost a graduate, almost a poet, almost a scholar. "People touched by fire are sensitive, fragile." Those touched by fire, Shvarts observed, not wanting to observe anything, and those abandoned on the ice.

Now what should/shall I do? Stop dead? Go quiet

Encased in ice, shall I pretend to be ice? Take the form of the coming winter? Freeze over, like a frozen dream: in the white-pink night the river Fontanka flows like tomato juice from a broken jar into a puddle, when actually it's your hands covered in blood. And I, who up to this moment have accompanied you at a delicately maintained distance and with res-PECT-ful aloofness, bow down to lick those idiotic bloody smashed huge fingers. Fighting off drunken surprise, you sternly say, "That doesn't give you the right to act familiar."

Yes—I think I'll pretend to be ice.

Bianci himself, by the way, writes magical (that is, good and strong and useful) words about turning to ice. He spits on the end of his stubby pencil and writes not poetry but the diary of a naturalist. The onset of autumn's chill he depicts either as torture or as the act of love, there's no distinguishing:

The winds—reapers of leaves—tear the last rags from the forest. Having accomplished its first task—undressing the forest—autumn sets about its second task: making the water colder and colder. Fish crowd into deep crannies to winter where the water won't turn to ice. Cold blood freezes even on dry land. Insects, mice, spiders, centipedes hide themselves away. Snakes crawl into dry holes, wind around each other and go still. Frogs push into the mud, lizards hide under the last bark left on the tree stumps and enter a trance. Outside there are seven kinds of weather: it tosses, blows, shatters, blinds, howls, pours and sweeps down from the sky.

To become a motionless snake curling up against other motionless snakes, to hibernate—that is my task today. The leaf-reaping season is one you can survive, can overcome, only by metamorphosis: by changing your nature so you become part of the background, be it snow, dirt or night.

A Tunnel and a Certain Someone

How can you make out white against white? Bianci hoped he could see it, while hoping others couldn't see him. Now for perhaps his most terrifying story.

Mr. Fox and Mousie
Mousie-mouse, why is your nose so black?
I was digging in the dirt.
Why were you digging in the dirt?
I made myself a burrow.
Why did you make yourself a burrow?
To hide, Mr. Fox, from you!
Mousie-mouse, I'll keep watch at your door!
Oh, I've a soft bed in my burrow.
You'll have to eat—then out you'll sneak!
Oh, I've a big cupboard in my burrow.
Mousie-mouse, I'll dig up your burrow!
Oh, I'll run down a little tunnel—
And off he goes!

It's likely Bianci was arrested by organs of the Soviet secret police more often than most of his literary colleagues—a total of five (5) times. Five (5) times in a row he repeated the drill: the awful wait for the inevitable, the awful relief when the awful event itself begins, the humiliation, the hopelessness, the hope, the despair, the weeks and months of paralysis, the miracle.

A local historian who got access to the archives reports:

While digging around in the files of the former archive of the regional committee of the Soviet Communist Party, I came across an interesting document completely by accident—a summary of charges written up on February 23, 1925 by the Altai office of the State Political Directorate to bring to trial a group of Socialist Revolutionaries living in Barnaul and Biisk. (All of them had arrived "from Russia," as they said back then.) It included several references to Vitaly Bianci. They are: "In November 1918, there arrived in Biisk one Belianin-Bianci Vitaly Valentinovich, an SR and writer for the SR newspaper *The People*, who was active in the Committee on Education and who around that time, fearing Kolchak's reprisals, changed his real name from Bianci to Belianin. The said Belianin-Bianci, upon arriving in Biisk with his wife Zinaida Alexandrovna Zakharovich, stayed at the apartment of local SR and member of the Constituent Assembly, Liubimov Nikolai Mikhailovich. It was through him that Belianin-Bianci began to make contact with the local SR organization . . . He entered the employ of the Biisk Agricultural Board as a clerk of the second class . . ."

In 1921 the Cheka in Biisk arrested him twice. In addition, he was imprisoned as a hostage for three weeks.

In September 1922 V. Bianci received word of pending arrest and, on the pretext of a business trip, left for Petrograd with his family.

At the end of 1925 Bianci was again arrested and sentenced to three years exile in Uralsk for belonging to a nonexistent underground organization. In 1928 (thanks to constant petitioning by, among others, Gorky, who approached Cheka chief Genrikh Yagoda) he received permission to move to Novgorod, and then to Leningrad. In November 1932 came another arrest. After three-and-a-half weeks he was released "for lack of evidence." In March 1935 Bianci, as "the son of a non-hereditary nobleman, a former SR, an active participant in armed resistance to Soviet power," was again arrested and sentenced to exile for five years in the Aktiubinsk region. It was only thanks to E. P. Peshkova's intervention that his sentence was commuted and Bianci was freed.

The bulk of his fairy tales are about the hunt and the chase, about deadly danger and struggle.

But what's most striking is his tone: not a trace of sentimentality, no sympathy for the preyed-upon or the fallen. Each death, each act of cruelty, belongs to the natural order.

If you kill a bird with a metal ring on its leg, remove the ring and send it to a tagging center. If you catch a bird with a ring, write down the letters and numbers stamped on the ring. If not you but a hunter or birdcatcher you know kills or captures such a bird, tell him what he needs to do. No pity for anyone; the hunter is always justified in his desire to master and seize and sacrifice a life—and to turn it into a mounted specimen. Every victim gets his chance to escape, says Bianci, and it's a sorry fool who doesn't see it and grab it.

"A Gust of Wind"

At first all of these words and shadows of birds and fish, and the giant with the voice of a munchkin, were indistinct forms inside me, and when they first took hold, they looked like this (autumn had just begun, and in the Amherst dusk you could hear all around the moaning of owls arrived *en masse* from god knows where):

The massive-awesome Bacchus Bianci
Thrusts fat fingers into suspicious cracks in the
Frozen earth, and from there (from where)
He harvests miracle-solace-refuse-sense;
Tipsy sober timid bombastic, he knows each
Root-tangle, and he writes, he almost pounces.
The stilling forest thrusts the wind's damp shag
Down his throat—the black box of
Night sky on the verge of winter.

Ready for first frost are you now yourself?
Ready for first frost are you now an owl?
Ready for first frost are you now a widow?

Here the author dozes off, and the owls, too. The author dreams of the other author's poem:

The wind roared up the riverbank,
Drove waves upon the shore—
Its furious whistle gave a scare
To a red-throated loon.

It knocked the magpie from the grove,
Whirled and dropped into the waves—

There it took a giant gulp
And choked, and down it dove.

The thing he did best was tracking birds.

Notes of an Ornithologist

Why Vitaly Bianci went to Leningrad during the blockade, how he ended up there—the explanations we have don't make sense. Either he went to bring food to his Leningrad friends, or he was trying to get food from his Leningrad friends (both versions astonish), or he went just to have a look, or to make an appearance, or to punish himself. When he returned, he lay down and did not get up.

That is what his diary entries show:

April 6: Stayed in bed.
April 7: Stayed in bed.
April 8: Stayed in bed.

Nevertheless, everything he had heard/seen he well described and well (meaning, up to the day of his death) concealed. I am prepared to state that among those who visited during the blockade, the naturalist-dilettante Bianci turned out to be the most well-qualified, perceptive and methodical: what was impossible to look at, he examined and categorized. Nevertheless, his notebooks—fully published now—have not, of course, found their reader.

They've winged past us like yet another repulsive salvo from 1941—one today's readers try to duck as frantically as their unfortunate predecessors tried to duck bombs on Leningrad's streets, so visible and familiar to the German pilot.

Bianci—an unsuccessful/unrealized scholar, but a scholar nonetheless—organized his impressions under phenomenological rubrics: blockade style, blockade humor, blockade consciousness, blockade smile, blockade language, blockade cityscape, blockade femininity, blockade Jews. This is to say that in two weeks he understood what we have yet to formulate for ourselves: that the blockade was a unique civilization with the characteristic features of all human societies.

This is how they smile here.
This is how they barter here.
This how they fear, and no longer fear.

This is how they joke here, and it is this subject—which is curious and handy for our script—which brings them together: Bianci quotes Shvarts as one of the best blockade humorists. Since we know that Shvarts left the city in December, we may conclude that his jokes lingered in the city into spring—they didn't melt (in general, nothing in that city melted).

Yes, here they meet—two utterly different fabulists of the Leningrad scene, two magic wizards and didacts. The one had a bear and a dragon, the other had fireflies, titmice, shrews—all metaphors for blockade life. The writers themselves were transformed by the era into clowning tall-tale-tellers forced to camouflage their brutal and piquant observations about human nature.

Shvarts the blockade comic eventually produced the most important book we have on the phenomenon of "Leningrad literature of the mid-Soviet period"—his "phone book" (variously, his "inventory"), a *Kunstkamera* of spiritual deformities and disasters. Among the era's victims is a cardiologist listed under the letter "D," a man with hideously burned hands. His patient Shvarts, seeing those two pink, tender, shining hands, reflects: "During an experiment an oxygen tank exploded, the door was jammed, and he forced open the burning panels with his bare hands. They were so badly burned that he almost lost them. He was considered one of the best cardiologists in the city. He was beaten to death for reasons far removed from science, but whether there were parts of his soul as deformed as the skin on his hands—I could not discern." That's precisely what he wanted to do—to discern, to see inside.

It turns out the blockade was the main event of Shvarts's life in Leningrad—though the whole time he meant, he prepared, to speak about the Terror, his main conscious task. He kept being swept toward the blockade winter that followed the Terror—he could not control himself, couldn't help speaking about it. For him that winter illuminated and explained everything and everyone, whereas the recent purges had made everything confused and unclear. Almost every topic, every figure, every character in his "phone book" reminds him of that winter, drags him back there. He remembers roofs, bombs, bomb shelters, the faces and conversations of his neighbors in the dark and, most of all, his failed intention to write about it, right then and there, in the wake of words just spoken—his failed play, in which he tried to render his strongest impression, the endless blockade night: "We descended to the bottom of the cage-like staircase and stood in a corner like a coven of witches, while the planes and their mechanical-animal whine would not relent, they circled and circled and with every pass dropped bombs. Then anti-aircraft fire—and when it hits its mark, there's a dry pop, and the smooth tin bird flaps its tin wings." Only in this avian metaphor will their visions of the blockade coincide: Bianci calls his blockade notes "City Abandoned by Birds." For him that's a euphemism, dialect for a curse, his "no" to hope.

Shvarts's notebook was a lamentation for his play that never quite appeared. But through the notebook's scattered, roughly stitched-together human plots the blockade emerges as the true home for the soul of the Leningrad intellectual who lived through the '30s. In other words, it was hell, the only vale where the coward-soul, slave-soul, traitor-soul, the soul in constant pain, never and nowhere not in pain, might abide—those Leningrad writer-survivors who, in front of the witnessing Shvarts, go out of their minds (then later, reluctantly, taking their time, come back into their minds), faint noiselessly as leaves on exiting the torture chamber of Party hearings, and continually hone their skill at slander. Shvarts buried, escorted off and lost one by one all his titans, his cherished enemies (nothing matches the white heat of his elegiac and erotic hatred-passion for Oleinikov). All he saw around him now were Voevodins, Rysses and Azarovs and other small fry wiped out by the century: these characters were relieved to find themselves in the blockade—in what he called, narrowing his eyes, a *benign* calamity, the kind that kills you without implicating you.

Can we say that for Bianci, too, the blockade was a benign calamity?

Apparently there is a phenomenon called "precipitous birth"—the infant bursts into the world through a mother who has had no time to get accustomed to that degree of pain.

The precipitous blockade of someone who visits the city suddenly and briefly is the precipitous birth of knowledge. He sees everything—not accustomed to the situation, not fused with it, he does not experience the slow, daily disappearance of meaning and God. On the wings of an airplane (which he immediately compared to a bird, Bianci was incapable of doing otherwise), he is transported to a place of blank, universal desolation—until then, he had only heard of it from the pitiful, apologetic letters of his dying Leningrad friends.

Shvarts's interest in the blockade was people, preferably the extras (the big stars for the most part nimbly made tracks to the east during the warm months of the year): children, old ladies, custodians, luckless local officials and spies, almost none of whom would live until spring.

But Bianci, hounded from childhood by the word "poetry," is interested in metaphors, namely, hybrid monsters: birds and fish fused with planes, fireflies joined with phosphorous metal in the night sky. How do fragments of blockade existence camouflage themselves, what forms do they assume? Here the blockade becomes a natural phenomenon; here emerges a kind of *Naturphilosophie* of the blockade world. From the very start everything looks unnatural; the plane's wings, unlike those of Bianci's bluethroats and starlings, are rigid—and the plane isn't even a bird but a fish, an *aerial fish*. Monstrous specimen!

All this he tries to discern in the blockade city—and can't find the direct words for (for which reason, most likely, he subsequently falls ill), so he reconstitutes it metaphorically. The dead city revives, acts like it's animate—like a museum diorama: *The city spreads out around us farther and farther. Slowly, as in a slow motion film, slowly people wander. Not people: monkeys with noses. Especially the women: boney faces, caverns for cheeks— unbelievably sharp, elongated noses . . .*

As it was with that childhood diorama, it's impossible to make out what's dead and what's alive, what is a monkey with a nose and what a deformed blockade soul caricatured by dystrophy.

On returning from the dead city, he wrote down a terrible little poem; as often happened with him in moments of agitation, the words spilled out:

Unbearable: the cold like a wolf,
A growing list of deprivations,
A hammer going in my temples:
There people are dying, dying in vain!

Wagtails. The Language of Birds

On returning from the dead city, he slept as long as he could, scribbled something in his secret diary and again took to walking deep into the forest and just standing there—his eyes sometimes open, sometimes shut, listening hard, sniffing, studying. The world Bianci inhabited is alien; his words are obscure and hence alluring, and they unsettle us even as they speak to us:

> Bluethroats and brightly colored stonechats are appearing in the wet bushes, and golden wagtails in the swamps. Pink-chested fiscals (shrikes) are here, with fluffy collars of ruff feathers, and the landrail, the corncrake, the blue-green roller have returned from distant parts.

So tell me—what are all these creatures? What do we picture as we follow the phrase "the pink-breasted shrikes," what sort of impossible, absurd marvel? It is perfectly obvious—perfect and obvious—that the author invented them all. Displayed before us is some other planet born from the imagination of a man who could not come up with a persuasive reason to inhabit his own.

Wagtails? What do you mean, wagtails? No, you're wrong, Bianci insists, that's us living on our planet, in our swamp—alien, blind, speechless, bereft.

We (meaning I) are not familiar with the bluethroat (bird of the thrush family, sparrow *genus*. Depending on classificatory approach, may, along with all varieties of nightingale, be ascribed to the family of flycatchers. In size somewhat smaller than the domestic sparrow. Body length about 15 cm. Weight of male is 15–23 grams, female 13–21 grams. Spine light brown or gray-brown, tail feathers reddish. Throat and crop blue with reddish spot in the center; the spot may also be white or bordered with white. The blue color below is edged first with black, then with red half-circles across the breast. Tail red with black sheen, middle pair of tail feathers light brown. Throat whitish, bordered by a brown half-circle. Bill black, legs black-brown.)

Whatever the throat and crop look like, when you descend into this prose, you descend into an invented, crafted world. The further you proceed into that crow-blue and green-azure language, the less you hear the waves striking University Embankment, and the farther all the hysteria-hypocrisy of the city—with its *literati* stinging one other and raising glasses of poison, and its ultra-literary sidewalks—fades into the distance. Bianci remains, only Bianci, stepping into the slush of the frozen swamp, listening with his whole being—here you have the voices of birds, you have the voices of fish. That very same fairytale dunce who, scrambling to hide from the tsar, ran into a grove and suddenly understood the language of the forest. "I hope to create an explanatory dictionary of the language of local worlds." A language not of this world! In periodic self-imposed exile in the village of Mikheevo in the Moshensky region, where he ended up-holed up during that first winter of the war, he does not stop collecting the magical words that protect him: a hidden, invisible language, a collection of real words—his article of faith.

A Happy Ending

Our forest correspondents cracked the ice at the bottom of a local pond and dug up the silt. In the silt there were a number of frogs who had gathered there in heaps for the winter. When they pulled them out, they looked like pure glass. Their bodies had grown extremely brittle. Their tiny legs would snap from the slightest, faintest touch, and when they did they made a light ringing sound. Our forest correspondents took several of the frogs home with them. They carefully warmed up the frozen juvenile frogs in their heated rooms. The frogs came to life bit by bit and began hopping across the floor.

And off they go!

Translated by Catherine Ciepiela

Arkady Babchenko (b. 1977)

Argun

We halt for the fourth day at the canning factory in Argun. It's the best place so far during our deployment and we feel completely safe inside the fence that skirts the perimeter.

The trouble with this war is that there are no rear positions and no base where you can be withdrawn for rest and recuperation—we are in a permanent state of encirclement and can expect a shot in the back at any moment. But here we are sheltered.

Two automatic mounted grenade launchers are positioned in the administration block and cover the whole street from the direction of the gates. There are two more launchers on the roof of the factory's meatpacking section and a machine-gun nest on the second floor of the entrance block. This way we completely control the surrounding area and feel relatively secure. We relax.

April has arrived and the sun is already beating down. We walk around practically naked, wearing just shorts made from cut-off long johns and army boots, and we are alike as brothers. And brothers we are, for there's no one in the world closer than emaciated soldiers with lice-bitten armpits and sun-browned necks on the rest of their white, putrefying skin.

The battalion commanders leave us in peace to get our fill of food and sleep. Yesterday they even fixed up a steam bath for us in the old sauna room in the guardhouse and we sweated away there for almost an hour. They issued us with fresh underwear into the bargain, so now we can enjoy two or three blissful lice-free days.

Fixa and I sit on the grass by the fence and wait for two Chechen kids to appear. Our bare bellies upturned to the sky, we bask in long-forgotten sensations of cleanliness and warmth. Our boots stand in a row and we wiggle our bare toes and smoke.

"Bet you five cigarettes I can stub out this butt on my heel," he says.

"Think you'll wow me with that one, do you?" I reply. "I'll do the same trick but for two cigarettes."

The skin on my soles has grown as hard as a rhino's from the boots. I once drove a needle into my heel for a bet and it went in more than a centimeter before it hurt.

"You know, I reckon the brass is being too wasteful in handing over our guys' bodies to the families," Fixa muses. "They could put us to far better use after we're killed, like make a belt sling from a soldier's hide. Or you could knock out a pretty good flak jacket from the heels of a platoon."

"Uh-huh. And you could make a bunch of them from the guys who died up in the hills. Why don't you tell the supply officer, maybe he'll give you leave for the smart idea?" I suggest.

"No, I can't tell him, he'll just sell the idea to the Chechens and start trading in corpses."

A gentle breeze plays over our bodies and we laze ecstatically as we wait for the kids to show up.

The knot of nervous tension inside just won't loosen up after the mountains and fear keeps churning away somewhere below my stomach. We need to unwind. Two signal flares are stuffed into the tops of Fixa's boots that we'll swap for marihuana. We already gave three flares to the Chechen kids as an advance and we're waiting for them to come back with the promised matchbox of weed.

There's a small gap in the fence at this corner and a small market has sprung up. The kids sit all day on the other side and soldiers come up on ours and offer their wares: tinned meat, diesel, bullets. Half an hour ago the battalion cook stuffed a whole box of butter through the gap. Fixa wonders if we should give him a beating but we can't be bothered to get up.

We get an unexpected treat of meat. The infantry caught and shot a guard dog, roasted it over a fire and gave us two ribs. It turns out some of them are from Fixa's home region. It's a fine thing to have common roots with guys in your unit. Only when you are far from home do you realize what a bond you have with someone who wandered the same streets and breathed the same air as a child. You may never have met before and are unlikely to meet again later but right now you are like brothers, ready to give up everything for the other, a Russian trait through and through.

We chew the tough meat and bitter-tasting fat runs down our fingers. Delicious.

"Spring onion would be good now, I love meat with greens," says Fixa. "But most of all I love pork fried with potato and onion. My wife cooks it just how I like it. First she fries the crackling until the edges curl upwards and the fat oozes out. It has to be well fried or the fat will be stewed like snot and not tasty. And when the fat starts to sizzle in the pan she adds thinly sliced potato, fries it lightly on one side and then the first time she stirs it she adds salt and onion. The onion has to go in after the potato or else it burns. And then . . ."

"Shut up, Fixa." I suddenly have a craving for fried pork and potatoes and can't listen to his gastronomic revelations any more.

"There's no pork here, they're Moslems and don't eat it."

"Just noticed, have you? You won't find pork here in a month of Sundays. How are they supposed to have pork fat if they can't even wipe their backsides with paper like human beings, I ask you?"

This aspect of local Chechen culture engenders particular hostility in Fixa and the rest of us, too. Quite apart from anything else, our soldiers resent the Chechens because they wash themselves after doing their business, rather than using paper.

In each house there are special jugs made from some silvery metal with a long spout inscribed with ornate Arabic script. At first our boys couldn't figure out their purpose and used them for making tea. When someone finally told them they freaked out. The first thing they do now when they occupy a house is kick these jugs outside or fish them out with sticks.

Actual faith doesn't matter one bit to us, be it Allah, Jesus or whoever, since we ourselves are all a godless lot from birth. But to us these jugs embody the difference between our cultures. It seems to me the political officer could distribute them instead of propaganda leaflets and we'd rip Chechnya to shreds in a couple of days.

"My cousin served in Tajikistan and told me the Tajiks use flat stones after the toilet," I say as I inspect the dog rib in my hand. "It's still the Stone Age there, they don't know about toilet paper or even newspaper. They gather pebbles from the river and use those. Each outdoor bog has a pile of stones beside it like a grave."

"So what's it like in Tajikistan then? Bound to be better than here. What else does your cousin say about it?" asks Fixa.

"Nothing. He's dead."

My cousin died just two days before he was due to be demobilized. He volunteered for a raid at the border. The patrol was made up of greenhorn conscripts who still didn't know anything and so my cousin stood in for some young kid. He was a machine-gunner and when the shooting started he covered the group as they pulled back.

A sniper put a round into his temple, a rose shot, as we call it: When the bullet hits the head at close range the skull opens up like a flower and there's no putting it together again. They had to bind up my cousin's head for the funeral or it would have fallen apart right there in the coffin.

"Yeah," says Fixa. "It's all just one war, that's what I think. And you know what else, Chechnya is just for starters, the big war is still to come, you'll see."

"You think so?"

"Yes. And I also think I'm going to make it through this one."

"Me too," I say. "Maybe since my cousin was killed I believe I'm going to survive. Two Babchenkos can't die in battle."

We finish the ribs. We've gnawed off all the gristle and soft tissue and all that's left in our fingers is five centimeters of hard bone that we can't chew down any further. We put the stumps in our cheeks like lollipops and, lying on our backs, suck out the last traces of fat. Our chomping is the only noise for the next fifteen minutes. Finally even this pleasure ends, the ribs are empty.

Fixa wipes his hands on his shorts and gets out a notebook and pen that he brought along specially.

"Right, tell me where we've been then. I just can't remember the names of these villages."

"OK. You joined us at Gikalovsky, right? So, Gikalovsky, then Khalkiloi, Sanoi, Aslambek, Sheripovo, Shatoi, and . . ." I pause for a moment, trying to get my tongue round the next one. ". . . Sharo-Argun."

"That's right, Sharo-Argun. I remember that all right," Fixa mutters.

"You don't forget something like that in a hurry."

"We'll draw a gallows beside Sharo-Argun," he says, sketching awkwardly in the notebook. His fingers are not comfortable with a pen, he's more used to handling steel. Before the war he wielded a trowel and spade as a builder, now a rifle and grenade launcher.

I lean over and look at the crooked gibbet and the figure hanging from it. Sharo-Argun. What a dreadful name. We lost twenty men there: Igor, Pashka, Four-Eyes the platoon commander, Vaseline, the list goes on.

There are lots of places like that in Chechnya: Shali, Vedeno, Duba-Yurt, Itum-Kale, all names of death. There's something shamanistic about them, strange names, strange villages. Some of my comrades died in each one and the earth is drenched in our blood. All we have left now are these odd, un-Russian words, we live within them, in the past, and these combinations of sounds that mean nothing to anyone else signify an entire lifetime to us.

We take our bearings from them like from a map. Bamut is an open plain, a place of unsuccessful winter assaults, a place of cold, of frozen earth and a crust of bloodstained ice. Samashki—foothills, burning cars, heat, dust and bloated corpses heaped up by the hundred in three days. And Achkhoi-Martan, where I had my baptism of fire, where the first tracer rounds flew at me and where I first tasted fear.

And not forgetting Grozny, where we lost Fly, Koksharov, Yakovlev, and Kisel before them. This land is steeped in our blood, they drove us to our deaths here as they will continue to do for a long time yet.

"You should draw an arse instead of a gallows," I tell Fixa. "If you imagine the Earth as an arse, then we are right in the hole."

I shut my eyes, lay on my back and put my hands behind my head. The sun shines through my eyelids and the world is tinged orange. Hell, I don't even want to think about it, the mountains, the snow, Igor's body. I'll get to it later but for now everything has stopped, for a while at least. Right now we are alive, our stomachs filled with dog meat, and nothing else matters. I can lie in the sun without fearing a bullet in the head and it's wonderful. I suddenly recall the face of the sniper who was gunning for me in Goiti. For some reason I wasn't afraid then.

Then I remember the photo of the little Chechen boy we found near Shatoi. He's only about seven but he's showing off with a rifle in his hands while mum stands alongside, beaming at her grown-up son. How proud she is of him, so full of joy for the holy warrior who already knows how to hold a rifle.

There will be even greater pride in her eyes when he severs the head of his first Russian prisoner at the age of seventeen. At twenty he'll attack a column and kill more people, and at twenty-two he'll run his own slave camp. Then at twenty-five they will hunt him down from a helicopter like a wolf, flush him into the open and fire rockets at him as he darts between shell craters, splattering his guts all over the place. Then he'll lie in a puddle and stare at the sky with half-open, lifeless eyes, now just an object of disgust as lice crawl in his beard.

We've seen warriors like this, grown up from such boys, into wolves from cubs. And to think, my mother would have flayed the skin from my back with a belt if I'd ever thought to pose with a weapon when I was a kid.

Enough, no sense in dwelling on this now. Later. Everything later.

Fixa and I lie in the grass in silence, neither feels like talking. The sun has tired us out and we daydream, maybe doze off for a while, it's hard to say—our hearing stays as sharp in sleep as when we're awake and registers every sound, from the twittering of the birds to soldiers' voices, stray gunshots and the chugging of the generator. All harmless noises.

We don't rouse until the sun sinks beneath the horizon. It gets chilly and the ground is still damp. I'm covered in goose bumps and I want to get under cover. My cold stomach aches, I get up and pee where I stand. The stream of urine quickly wanes but I get no relief, my belly still hurts. I'll have to go to the medic.

The Chechen kids never showed up. We wait another half an hour but they still don't come. Evidently our signal flares went to the fighters' beneficiary fund free of charge.

"Some businessmen we are, Fixa," I say. "We should have got the grass first and then paid. We've been had, come on, let's go."

"We should have brought our rifles, that's what, held one of them at gunpoint while the others went for the weed," he says.

"They still wouldn't have showed up! They're not fools, they know we won't do anything to them. Would you shoot a boy over a box of grass?"

"Of course not."

We follow the fence back toward our tent, brick debris and shrapnel scrunching under our boots. There had been fighting here at some time, probably in the 1994–96 war. Since then no one had worked at the factory or tried to reconstruct it. These ruined buildings had only been used for keeping slaves.

I suddenly remember Dima Lebedev, a guy I transported coffins with in Moscow. His armored car ran over a mine by Bamut and the whole unit except Dima died instantly. He said he saw his platoon commander fly up like a cannon ball as the shock wave tore off his arms and legs and dumped his trunk on the ground, still in the flak jacket.

Dima was heavily concussed and lay there for almost a day. The Chechens that emerged from the undergrowth after the blast thought he was dead and didn't bother to put a bullet in him. He came round at night and ran straight into another group of fighters who took him with them into the mountains and kept him at a cottage with six other conscripts.

Their captors would beat them, cut off their fingers and starve them to get them to convert to Islam. Some did, others like Dima refused. Then they stopped feeding him altogether and he had to eat grass and worms for two weeks.

Each day the prisoners were taken into the mountains to dig defensive positions and finally Dima was able to escape. An old Chechen took him in and hid him in his home where Dima lived with the family like a servant, tending the cattle, cutting the grass and doing chores. They treated him well and when Dima wanted to go home they gave him money and a ticket and took him out of Chechnya to the garrison town of Mozdok, moving him at night in the boot of a car so the fighters didn't get them.

He made it home alive and later corresponded with his old master, who even came and stayed with him a couple of times. That's what Dima called him, master, just like a slave. He was scarred forever by captivity. He had submissive, fearful eyes and was always ready to cover his head with his hands and squat down, shielding his stomach. He spoke quietly and never rose to insult.

Later his master's nephew came to his home, knocked his mother around, abducted his sister and demanded a ransom for her release. Maybe he even kept her here in the basement of this factory with dozens of other prisoners, I wonder.

"Tell me, would you really have finished off that wounded guy back in the mountains?" Fixa suddenly asks. We stop walking. Fixa looks me in the eyes and waits for an answer.

I know why this is so important to him. He doesn't say so, but he's thinking: "So would you finish me off then if it came to it?"

"I don't know. You remember what it was like, it was snowing, the transport couldn't get through for the wounded and he was going to die anyway. He would just have screamed—remember how he screamed, how awful it was? I just don't know . . ."

We stand facing one another. I suddenly feel like hugging this skinny, unshaven man with the big Adam's apple and bony legs sticking out of his boots.

"I wouldn't have shot anyone, Fixa, you know that, and you knew that then in the mountains. Life is too precious and we would have fought for it to the very last, even if that lad had puked up all his intestines. We still had bandages and painkillers and maybe by morning we could have evacuated him. You know I wouldn't have killed him, even if we had known then for sure that he would die anyway."

I want to tell him all of this but don't manage to. Suddenly there's a single shot and a short burst of rifle fire immediately followed by a powerful explosion. A cloud of smoke and dust envelops the road by the entrance block, right where our tents are pitched.

My first thought is that Chechens have blown up the gate.

"Get down!" I shout and we dive face down onto the asphalt. We freeze for a moment and then hurl ourselves over to the wall of the transformer box where we lie motionless.

Dammit, no rifle, idiot that I am I left it in the tent, now of all times. I'm never without my weapon! Fixa is also unarmed. We completely dropped out guard at the factory, thought we could take it easy and go a hundred meters from our position without rifles.

Fixa's eyes dart around, his face pale and mouth agape. I can't look much better myself.

"What do we do now, eh, what do we do?" he whispers in my ear, clutching my arm.

"The flares, give them here," I whisper back, petrified with fear. Without a weapon I am no longer a soldier but a helpless animal, a herbivore with no fangs or claws. Now they'll pour through the breach, take us right here in nothing on but our shorts and butcher us, pin our heads down with a boot and slit our throats. And there's no one else around, we are alone on this road by the fence. They'll get us first and kill us before the battalion comes to its senses and returns fire. Dumb holidaymakers we are.

I look round. We'll have to make a run for it behind the warehouses where the vehicles are parked and where there are people.

Fixa pulls the flares from his boots and hands me one. I tear open the protective membrane and free the pin. We hold them out in front us, ready to fire them at the first thing that appears on the road and we freeze, holding the pull-strings.

It's quiet. The shooting has stopped. Then we hear voices and laughter from the direction of the entrance block. They are speaking in Russian, no accent. We wait a little longer and then get up, dust ourselves off and go round to find the battalion commander, supply officer, chief of staff and some other officers milling around, all half drunk. They've dragged a safe out of the admin block, fixed a stick of dynamite to the door and blown it in half. It's empty. One officer suggests blowing up a second safe in the building in case there's anything in it, but the battalion commander is against the idea.

"Morons," Fixa growls as we pass by. "Haven't they had enough shooting yet?"

Our own damage is not so bad. I tore up my knee slightly on a piece of brick when I threw myself down and Fixa has a long scratch on his cheek. What bothers us more is that we are filthy again and the steam bath has been a waste of time. We go into our tent and bed down.

That night we come under fire. A grenade flies over the fence near the transformer box where Fixa and I had prepared to defend ourselves. A second grenade explodes, then tracer rounds illuminate the sky. A few bursts pass over our heads and the bullets whine in the air. It's not heavy fire, maybe two or three weapons. The sentries on the roofs open up in reply and a small exchange ensues.

Three signal rockets rise from the other side of the fence, one red and two green. In the flickering light we see the figures of soldiers running from tents and clambering up to the tops of the buildings. While the flares hang in the air the fire in our direction intensifies and we hear a couple of rifle grenades being launched.

We crouch by our tents and watch the sky. No one panics, as it's clear that the only danger from this chaotic night shooting is a random hit. The fence shelters us and there are no tall buildings near the factory, and since our attackers can only fire from ground level the bullets just go overhead. Our tents are in a safe place so we don't run anywhere. We can only be hit by shrapnel from the rifle grenades but they explode far away.

The fighters could inflict far more damage if they fired through the gates but they either didn't think of this or they don't want to risk it. Our lookout post is in the admin block where the two grenade launchers and a machine-gun are set up, and it would be hard to get close on that side.

We sit watching the light show as green streams of tracer fire course across the sky. Then the guns fall quiet as suddenly as they started up. Our machine-guns on the roofs pour down fire in all directions for another five minutes and then they also cease. It's now silent apart from the background chugging of the generator.

We have a smoke. It's great outside and no one wants to go back inside the stuffy tents where the kerosine lamps are burning. We are almost grateful to the Chechens for getting us out. The moon is full, it's night time, quiet. Garik comes down sleepy-eyed from the roof of the meatpacking shop where our grenade launcher is mounted. He slept right through the shooting, the silly sod. Pincha was on duty with him but he stays up top, afraid that Arkasha will give him a thrashing.

"Why weren't you shooting?" I ask Garik.

"What was I supposed to shoot at, you can't see anything beyond the fence. And we didn't want to drop any grenades, we might have hit you."

He knows it sounds unconvincing but he also knows we won't do anything to him, none of us were wounded so there's nothing to get worked up about.

"Enough of your stories," says Arkasha, the oldest and most authoritative among the privates in our platoon. "Do you want to spend two whole days up there? I can arrange that for you, no sweat."

Garik says nothing, knowing he can land himself in hot water. Arkady can indeed see to it that they spend two more days on the roof.

Fixa nudges me. "Those were our flares, did you notice? One red and two green, just like I gave the boy. Definitely ours. Return to sender, you could say."

"I'd have preferred if they'd just tossed the matchbox to us," I mope.

The commanders step up the guard for the rest of the night and we sit like cats up on the roof. Fixa, Oleg, and I join Garik and Pincha, while Arkasha, Lyekha, and Murky head over to the admin block.

I know they'll just crash out to sleep as soon as they get there. We also have no intention of peering into the steppe all night and we take our sleeping bags up to the roof and bed down between two ventilation shafts.

The generator chugs away below us. In Argun lights glimmer at a few windows, seems they already hooked the place up to the electricity. All is quiet out in the steppe, not a single person is to be seen, no movement. Chechnya dies at night, everyone locks themselves into their homes and prays that no one comes for them, that no one kills or robs them or drags them off to the Russian military detention center at Chernorechye. Death rules the nighttime here.

On the horizon the mountains stand out as a dark mass. We only just came from there. That's where Igor was killed. I fall asleep.

Replacements arrive, about 150 crumpled-looking guys who are trucked in to our battalion from Gudermes. They stand huddled in a crowd on the square in front of the entrance block that we dubbed the parade ground. They carry only half-empty kitbags: all the things they had with them had been bartered for drink on the way.

This lot are no use as soldiers, there isn't a single bold or cocky one among them, or even one who is physically strong. Each new batch of replacements is worse than the last in quality. Russia has clearly run out of romantics and adventurers and all that's left is this worthless muck that has nowhere to go apart from the army or prison. This lot on the parade ground have darting, lost eyes set into swollen, unshaven faces, and seem to blend into one monotonous, gray mass. And they stink.

We stand by the tents and bluntly survey the new recruits. It's a dismal sight.

"Where the hell do they get them from," says Arkasha. "We've no bloody use for this sort here, all they can do is guzzle vodka and pee in their pants. We have to talk to the commander so he doesn't take on any of them—warriors like these we can do without."

"What do you want then, for them to send us linguists and lawyers?" replies Oleg. "That kind are not very keen to come here. All the smart, good-looking ones managed to wriggle out of this war, but since the draft board has to meet its quotas they just shunt whatever's left this way."

We're short of people in the platoon but Arkasha is right, there's no place for this rabble, we'll manage somehow without them.

Two are assigned to us anyway, slovenly specimens of an indeterminable age, rat-like, unreliable. They immediately dump their kitbags in the tent and make themselves scarce, mumbling something about vodka. We don't hold them up.

"Maybe they'll get chopped to bits at the market, it'll be less hassle for all of us," says Pincha, digging dirt from between his fingers with his bayonet.

Arkasha has the idea of breaking into the trailer wagon that the supply officer tows with him all round Chechnya behind a Ural truck. It's constantly guarded by cooks and what they keep in it is anyone's guess, but you can be sure it's not state bank bonds.

To effect the burglary we plan a full-scale military operation. Arkasha's plan is simple. It came to him at night while we were being bombarded and in this instance, the arrival of the replacements will only be to our advantage.

When it gets dark we emerge from our tents, turn left along the fence, make our way to the fence opposite the vehicle park and jump into one of the useless sentry trenches the cooks dug for themselves there.

In front of each trench a firing slit had been cut in the fence and the embrasure lined with turf. Judging from the fortifications they are preparing to defend the stocks of canned meat to the bitter end.

Lyekha and I get two hand grenades and pull the pins while Arkasha wraps his rifle in three ground sheets and aims it into the bottom corner of the trench.

"Ready?" he whispers.

"Ready."

"Now!"

We toss the grenades over the fence and they explode with a deafening clap in the night silence, or maybe it just seems that loud, such is the tension. Arkasha loses a few bursts into the ground.

The muzzle flash is invisible inside the ground sheets and the sound seems to come from the earth. It's impossible to tell where the firing is from, it seems like it's coming from all sides at once.

Lyekha and I throw two more grenades and I fire a signal flare.

The overall effect is extremely realistic.

"That'll do!" says Arkasha. "Let's get out of here before they wake up!"

We manage to run about ten meters when the machine-gun on the roof comes to life. I'm suddenly afraid that in his stupor the gunner will take us for attacking Chechens and cut us down in the wink of an eye.

Meanwhile, cooks emerge from every nook and cranny and lay down a withering barrage of fire. We also fire a few bursts in the air, our faces hidden in the crook of our arms and averted from the illuminating muzzle flashes.

No one pays us any attention. The whole battalion is now dashing round in disarray and within a minute firing issues from all corners of the factory grounds.

The new recruits stoke the confusion, shouting "Chechens, Chechens!" as they run toward the fence with their rifles and indiscriminately spray bullets from the waist and generally behave like children. To make matters worse, they are firing tracer rounds, which ricochet and whiz all over the place, perfectly creating the impression that we are being attacked.

We freeze for a moment, dumbstruck. Little did we suspect that four grenades and a couple of rifle bursts could stir up such pandemonium. It must be said, a battalion is a force to be reckoned with.

We make our way amid the chaos to the wagon. There's no guard. Arkasha breaks the lock.

It's pitch black inside and we hastily grope around the shelves, chancing upon tins and small sacks and packages that we sweep into an open ground sheet. I come across a heavy, bulky object wrapped in paper. I stuff it inside my tunic and fill my pockets with more tins, spilling something in my haste, sugar maybe. Speed is of the essence.

"Give me a hand, lads, I've got something here," says Arkasha. I feel my way over to him. He is holding something by two handles, big and heavy, covered with a tarpaulin.

"It's butter," exclaims Lyekha. "Just look how much that bastard has stolen."

"Right, let's get out of here," Arkasha orders. It's almost as dark outside and only small sections of the roof are lit up by muzzle flashes. There's still a fair bit of shooting but the commotion is gradually dying down.

Someone is approaching the wagon, panting his way toward us with a stench of onions on his breath. Looks like some sneaky character also decided to take advantage of the melee. Arkasha lashes out blindly in the dark with his boot and the man yelps and falls.

"Leg it!" I hiss and we bound and stumble our way back. The wooden chest with the butter is unbelievably heavy, it painfully thumps my ankle-bones and slips from my fingers but we're not leaving it behind. It's impossibly awkward to run with all this stuff—apart from the chest we have those tins bouncing around in our pockets and I have to hold the package inside my tunic with my spare hand to stop it falling out.

We reach the warehouses and find a small ditch that we dug earlier and lined with ground sheets. We dump the chest in with our tins and packages and cover it all with more ground sheets that we brought with us. Finally, we scatter chunks of brick and lay a sheet of metal over the top. Then we hasten back up to the roof.

The shooting has almost died down. We race across the roof toward the entrance block, jump down to ground level by the meatpacking shop and wander leisurely back to our tents. I jab Arkasha with my elbow and he bumps me back with his shoulder. We grin at one another.

The next morning they fall in the whole battalion on the parade ground. The commander tells us how last night, while the battalion was repelling an attack, some swine broke into the transport park's store wagon and stole food from his comrades. There is to be a search of all personal property and vehicles while we remain on the square.

"Like hell it was from our own comrades," says Arkasha. "Our comrades would never have seen this butter. We should regard ourselves as battalion delegates for sampling food products intended for us. Later we'll tell the guys how delicious the food is that we are supposed to get."

They keep us standing there while the supply officer personally shakes down every tent and armored car, throwing everything out onto the ground as he overturns bunk beds and knocks over cooking stoves.

His lower lip is swollen and he is in a foul temper. He's the one Arkasha kicked, right in the face. We were damned lucky that he didn't grab his leg and pull off his boot. They'd have beaten us half to death for this, but now it's impossible lo identify us.

We gawp impudently at the contorted face of the supply officer and smile among ourselves. The stolen goods are well hidden in the ditch and there is no evidence.

The search continues for six hours and we grow thirsty—the sun beats down. I read somewhere that the Germans used to force concentration camp inmates to stand in the sun half the day for fun, much like this.

But we're in good spirits nonetheless. Covered in ground sheets in that ditch by the warehouses awaits a chest full of butter and we'd happily stand on the square a whole week for that.

"OK, lads, I invite you all for tea," says Arkasha. "I promise each of you a butter sandwich that weighs a kilo. Pincha even gets a double portion."

"Wow," says Pincha. "But where's the butter from?"

"Let's just say there's no more left where that came from," grins Arkasha, winking at Lyekha and me.

Eventually they fall us out. As was to be expected, the supply officer didn't find a thing. Nor did he expect to—any fool knew that no one would keep the stolen stuff in his tent. He just wanted to get his own back for the split lip.

The rest of the day we wander idly around the factory but stay away from the hole. That night we are all put on guard duty again. Toward morning we leave our positions and make our way to the warehouses. Arkasha shines his torch in the ditch as Lyekha and I retrieve the booty.

Our raid yielded eighteen cans of various foodstuffs, bags of sugar, four sets of dry rations, a hefty chunk of pork fat that must weigh about three kilos—the package that was in my tunic—two loaves of bread, six blocks of cigarettes and . . . a generator! The exact same one we looted near Shatoi, a beautiful, plastic-cased Yamaha, complete with that crack in the housing. It stands in the ditch, covered with ground sheets as if this was its rightful home.

"It's butter, it's butter!" Arkasha says, angrily mimicking Lyekha. "Can't you tell the difference between butter and engine oil?"

"Actually, I can't, I've been pretty much unable to tell the difference between any smells recently. My nose is probably bunged up with soot. And anyway, it was in a case and doesn't smell too much of anything."

He's right, the supply officer has kept the generator in good condition, clean and dry and not one new dent in it.

"Never mind, we can sell it," I say. "The Chechens would give their arm for something like that and still think it was a bargain. For them a generator is like manna from heaven, and this one will power up twenty homes. Have you seen how they mount a Lada engine on a stand and turn it into a dynamo? And this is a factory-made generator and a diesel one at that."

"Risky," says Arkasha. "We can't get it past the fence and it won't go through the gap. We'll leave it here for the moment, maybe we'll think of something."

Until dawn we carry some of the stolen goods to our tent and stash the rest in a personnel carrier driven by a mate of ours. We put two tins in our armpits at a time and walk through the yard with a bored air, yawning as if we were just out for a stroll and a breath of air. We carry the pork fat and cigarettes inside our tunics.

Later we divide the spoils equally. We also give Pincha a tin of condensed milk to make up for the lost butter. It's his birthday in a week and he stashes the tin away, almost swooning with happiness—it's the best present he's ever had in his life. He says he won't open it before five a.m. Friday, the time he came into this world. He's lying of course, he'll wolf it down tonight, unable to wait.

That evening we have a feast for our stomachs and no one goes to the vehicle park for the usual gruel. Pincha eats his fill of pilfered canned meat and noisily stinks the tent out all night.

The *kombat* (battalion commander) has caught two recruits from the anti-tank platoon up to no good. It turns out they had passed some boxes of cartridges through the fence to the Chechen kids, then drunk a bottle of vodka and fallen asleep by the gap.

Half an hour later the *kombat* chanced upon them and gave them a beating before keeping them overnight in a large pit in the ground. Today their punishment is to be continued and they fall us in again on the parade ground. We know too well what will happen now.

At the edge of the square they dug an improvised torture rack into the ground, a thick water pipe that has been bent into the shape of a gibbet. At the *kombat*'s orders, the platoon made it during the night by placing the pipe against two concrete piles and using an armored car to bend it in the middle. Two ropes now dangle from it.

The anti-tank gunners are lead out, hands bound behind their backs with telephone cable and dressed in ragged greatcoats and long johns. Their faces are already swollen and purple from beating and there are huge black hematomas where their eyes should be, oozing pus and tears from the corners. Their split lips can no longer close and pink foam bubbles from their mouths and drips onto their dirty, bare feet. It's a depressing sight. After all, these are not tramps but soldiers, ordinary soldiers, half of the army is like these two.

They stand the soldiers on the square. They raise their heads and look through the gaps in the swelling at the ropes swinging in the wind.

The *kombat* grabs one by the throat with his left hand and hits him hard in the nose. The soldier's head snaps back to his shoulder blades and emits a cracking noise. Blood spurts. The commander kicks the second one in the groin and he falls to the ground without a sound. The beating begins.

"Who did you sell the bullets to?" screams the *kombat*, grabbing the soldiers by the hair and holding up their swollen faces, which quiver like jelly from the blows. He traps their heads in turn between his knees and lashes them with blows from top to bottom.

"Well, who? The Chechens? Have you killed a single fighter yet, you piece of shit, have you earned the right to sell them bullets? Well? Have you even seen one? Have you ever had to write a letter of condolence to a dead soldier's mother? Look over there, those are soldiers, eighteen-year-old lads who have already seen death, looked it in the face, while you scum sell the Chechens bullets? Why should you live and guzzle vodka while these puppies died instead of you in the mountains, eh? I'll shoot the fucking pair of you!"

We don't watch the beating. We had been beaten ourselves and it long ceased to be of any interest. Nor do we feel particularly sorry for the gunners. They shouldn't have got caught. The *kombat* is right, they have seen too little of the war to sell bullets, we're the ones entitled to do that. We know death, we've heard it whistling over our heads and seen how it mangles bodies, and we have the right to bring it upon others. These two haven't yet. What's more, these new recruits are strangers in our battalion, not yet soldiers, not one of us. But most of all we are upset that we can no longer use the gap in the fence.

"Cretins," spits Arkasha. "They put the gap out of bounds, got themselves caught and ruined it for all of us. So much for selling the generator."

He is more bothered than any of us. Now he'll have to go to the local market to satisfy his passion for trading. We don't like it at the market, too dangerous. You never know if you'll come back alive. You can only buy stuff from the Chechens at the side of the road, when one of you jumps down from the armored car and approaches them while the platoon trains their rifles on them and the gunner readies his heavy-caliber machine-gun.

The market is enemy territory. Too many people, too little room to move. They shoot our guys in the back of the head there, take their weapons and dump their bodies in the road. You can only walk around freely if you take the pin out of a grenade and hold it up in your fist. It was a whole lot more pleasant to trade through the fence on our own ground. We were the ones who could shoot people in the back of the head if need be.

"Yeah," says Lyekha, "Shame about the gap. And the generator."

The *kombat* works himself into an even greater rage. There's something not right with his head after the mountains and he is on the verge of beating these two to death.

He lays into the wheezing bodies with his feet and the soldiers squirm like maggots, trying to protect their bellies and kidneys, a vain hope with their hands tied behind their backs. The blows rain down one after another.

The *kombat* kicks one of them in the throat and the soldier gags, unable to breathe. His feet kick convulsively and he fights to gulp in some air, eyes now bulging through the swelling.

The rest of the officers sit in the shade of a canvas awning near the entrance block, watching the punishment as they take a hair of the dog from a bottle of vodka on a table in front of them. Their faces are also swollen, but from three days of continual drinking.

Our political education officer Lisitsyn gets up from the table and joins the *kombat*. For a while they flail in silence at the gunners with their boots and the only sound is their puffing from the exertion.

We understood long ago that any beating is better than a hole in the head. There had been too many deaths for us to care much about trivia like ruptured kidneys or a broken jaw. But all the same, they were thrashing these two way too hard. We all thieved! And every one of us could have wound up in their place.

Thieving is both the foundation of the war and its reason for continuing. The soldiers sell cartridges, the drivers sell diesel oil, the cooks sell canned meat. Battalion commanders steal the soldiers' food by the crate— that is our canned meat on the table that they snack on now between shots of vodka. Regimental commanders truck away vehicle loads of gear, while the generals steal the actual vehicles themselves.

There was one well-known case when someone sold the Chechens brand new armored cars, fresh from the production line and still in the factory grease. Military vehicles are still riding round in Chechnya that were sold back in the first war and written off as lost in battle.

Quartermasters dispatch whole columns of vehicles to Mozdok packed with stolen goods, carpets, televisions, building materials, furniture. Wooden houses are dismantled and shipped out piece by piece, cargo planes are filled to bursting with stolen clutter that leaves no room for the wounded. Who cares about two or three boxes of cartridges in this war where everything is stolen, sold and bought from beginning to end?

And we have all been sold, too, guts and all, me, Arkasha, Pincha, the *kombat* and these two he is beating now, sold and written off as battle losses. Our lives were traded long ago to pay for the generals' luxurious houses springing up in the elite suburbs of Moscow.

The blows eventually cease. Those two jackals step back from the gunners, who lie gasping face down on the asphalt, spitting out blood and struggling to roll over. Then the armaments officer steps forward and helps Lisitsyn lift one up, raise his arms and tie his wrists in the noose. They tighten the rope until his feet dangle a few centimeters above the ground, suspending him like a sack, and string up the second guy the same way. They do it themselves as they know that none of us will obey an order to do it.

"Fall out," the *kombat* shouts, and the battalion disperses to its tents.

"Bastards," says Arkasha. It's not clear who he means, the gunners or the *kombat* and Lisitsyn.

"Pricks," whispers Fixa.

The soldiers hang there all day and half the night. They are opposite our tents and through the doorway we can see them swaying on the rack. Their shoulders are pressed up to their ears, their heads slumped forward onto their chests. At first they tried to raise their bodies up on the rope, change their position and get a little more comfortable. But now they are either asleep or unconscious and don't move. A pool of urine glistens in the moonlight beneath one of them.

There is a hubbub inside the command post as our commanders down more vodka. At two in the morning they consume another load and all tumble out onto the square to administer a further round of beatings to the dangling gunners, who are lit up in the moonlight.

The officers place two Tapik (TA-57) field telephones under the men and wire them up by the toes. The units contain a small generator and to make a call you wind a handle, which produces a charge and sends a signal down the line.

"So, do you still feel like selling bullets?" Lisitsyn asks and winds the handle of the first phone.

The soldier on the rack starts to jerk and cry in pain as cramps seize him.

"What are you yelling for, you piece of shit?" Lisitsyn screams and kicks him in the shins. He then rewinds the Tapik and the soldier howls. Again Lisitsyn lashes at his shins. And so on for maybe half an hour or more.

The officers of our battalion have turned into an organized gang that exists separately from the soldiers. They truly are like jackals and so that's what we call them, us contract soldiers, who in turn are called "contras," or sometimes "vouchers," as we are there to be spent. And the two camps hate each other for good reason.

They hate us because we drink, sell cartridges and shoot them in the back in battle, because every last one of us yearns to get discharged from this lousy army. And since we want nothing more from it than the money it pays us for each tour of duty, we don't give a damn about the officers and will screw them over as the opportunity arises. They also hate us for their own poverty, their underfed children and their eternal sense of hopelessness. And they hate the conscripts because they die like flies and the officers have to write letters informing the mothers.

What else can you expect of the officers if they themselves grew up in barracks? They also used to get beaten as cadets and they still get beaten at their units. Every other colonel of ours is capable of little more than screaming and punching, reducing a lieutenant, captain or major into a moaning, disheveled wretch in front of junior ranks. And the generals too no longer bother meting out penalties to the colonels but simply hit them.

Ours is an army of workers and peasants, reduced to desperation by constant underfunding, half-crazed with hunger and lack of accommodation, flogged and beaten by all, regardless of the consequences, regardless of badges of rank, stripped of all rights. This is not an army but a herd drawn from the dregs of the criminal masses, lawless apart from the dictate of the jackals that run it.

Why should you care about soldiers when you can't even provide for your own children? Competent, conscientious officers don't stay long and the only ones left are those with nowhere else to live, who cling on to empty assurances that they will be allocated an apartment some day. Or those who cannot string two words together and know only how to smash in the teeth of some young kid! They make their way up the career ladder not because they are the best but because there is no one else. Accustomed from the very bottom rung to beating and being beaten, they beat and are beaten right to the top, teaching others to follow suit. We learned the ropes long ago, the ways of the gutter are the universal language in this army.

Lisitsyn gets bored of winding the Tapik. He puts a flak jacket on one of the gunners and shoots him in the chest with his pistol. The round doesn't pierce the jacket but the impact rocks the body on the rope. The soldier contorts and gasps, his lungs so close to collapse that he is unable to draw breath. Lisitsyn is about to fire again but the *kombat* averts his arm, worried that in his state of drunkenness he will miss and hit the wretch in the belly or the head.

We don't sleep during all of this. It's impossible to doze off to these screams. Not that they instill fear in us, they simply keep us awake.

I sit up in my sleeping bag and have a smoke. It was much the same in Mozdok. Someone would get a beating on the runway and I would sleep with a blanket over my head to keep out the light and muffle the cries and I'd think, great, it wasn't me today. Four years have passed since then and nothing changed in this army. You could wait another four years and forty more after that and it would still be the same.

The yelling on the parade ground stops and the officers go back to the command post. The only sound now is the moaning of the gunners. The one who was shot at wheezes heavily and coughs as he tries to force some air into his chest.

"I'm sick of their whining," says the platoon commander from his sleeping bag. "Hey, shitheads, if you don't settle down I'll come and stuff socks in your gobs," he shouts.

It goes quiet on the square and the platoon commander falls asleep. I pour some water in a flask and go outside. Arkasha tosses a pack of cigarettes after me.

"Give them a smoke."

I light two and poke them between their tattered lips. They smoke in silence, no one speaks. What is there to say?

An illumination flare rises in the sky over the police post near the grain elevator, then a red signal flare. A firefight starts. Short, chattering bursts of rifle fire echo across the steppe and then a machine-gun on the roof of the elevator opens up. Our eighth company is holed up on the 22nd floor and from there they can cover half the town. The fighters have no hope of dislodging the police after one of our guys, Khodakovsky, mined the stairs for them.

The machine-gunner has spotted some fighters and looses off short, targeted bursts. After a while the exchange peters out and the police troops send up a green flare to give the all-clear.

The cigarettes burn down. I stub them out and give the gunners a drink of water. They gulp it greedily. I remember that we still have some rusks in our rations—they'll have to suck them now like babies as they probably have no teeth left. The battalion sleeps.

At the morning parade the two gunners are beaten again but not so viciously as yesterday. They no longer squirm and just hang there, moaning quietly. Afterwards the armaments officer unties the ropes and they fall to the ground like sacks of flour. They can't stand or lift their swollen arms. Their hands have gone black and their fingers are twisted. The *kombat* kicks them a few more times then takes their military ID cards and tears them into shreds.

"If I catch one more son of a bitch with cartridges I'll shoot him without trial. That means every last one of you, old and new. Is that clear?"

No one replies.

"Throw this refuse out of the gate," he orders, nodding to the two prostrate forms. "Don't give them money or travel documents, they don't deserve it. They can find their own way home. I don't need shit like that in the battalion."

The gunners are carried out and dumped on the street. They turn their heads and look up at us as the gates close behind them. They have no idea where to go or what to do. There's no way they'll make it to Mozdok. The fighters will probably get them right here in Argun. If I were them I'd try to reach the police block-post and ask the guys there to put them on a convoy to Khankala, the main base outside Grozny.

The police troops won't refuse since our guys helped them last night. But even then they'll be unable to fly out of Khankala and they'll be left to wander around until they get taken prisoner. We stand in silence. The *kombat* turns and goes back to the command post.

The gunners sit at the gates like abandoned dogs until night falls. At dawn I take up my lookout shift in the admin block and the first thing I do is glance onto the street. They're gone.

One morning the battalion gets a visit from the top brass. We've just got up and are washing ourselves from hollow support blocks, knee-high piers for propping up the metal walls of the unfinished meatpacking shop. Each one holds about five liters of greenish water from melted snow, no good for drinking but fine for a rinse.

A captured Mitsubishi off-roader belonging to the regiment commander Colonel Verter drives in with two armored personnel carriers loaded with humanitarian aid packages.

Colonel Verter steps down from the silver jeep and the battalion is hastily ordered to fall in as if the alarm had been sounded. We come running, still dressing.

"I wonder what's up?" says Pincha, leaning on Garik as he wraps a puttee around his leg. The cloth is black with filth and stinks to high hell. Used to all manner of stench as we are, we wrinkle our noses, unable to fathom how he managed to foul his puttee so badly. We'd only recently had a steam bath and all this time we did nothing except sunbathe half-naked. Then again, Pincha always walks around in several layers of clothing and boots and his feet are usually so dirty you could plant potatoes between his toes. Arkasha tells him he should scrape off the dirt from his feet for blacking his boots and just sell his polish. We never fail to laugh at that one.

It's forty-five minutes before morning parade time and no one knows why we have been fallen in. We stand for a while, guessing what might have happened, then a rumor spreads along the ranks that the regiment commander has brought medals and will decorate those who have distinguished themselves.

Medals are good news and we brighten visibly. We don't say as much but we all hope to get one and return to our homes in full splendor. We didn't give a damn about this in Grozny or up in the mountains where the only thing we wanted was to survive. But now peace is within reach and we want to go back to Civvy Street as heroes.

I nudge Lyekha and wink. He'll certainly be able to hang a "For Bravery" gong on his chest today after being twice commended by the platoon commander before we had even left Grozny. He grins back.

They carry a table covered with a red cloth onto the center of the parade ground and arrange lots of little boxes and award certificates on it. The medals cover almost half the surface, enough, it seems, for all of us to get one.

It starts to drizzle. A few drops spatter on the covers of the booklets and smudge them. Two soldiers pick up the table and move it up to the wall for shelter, placing it next to the torture rack. We are to be decorated with a gallows as a backdrop!

Pincha thinks our first award ceremony might have offered a little more pomp and ceremony and that the colonel could have arranged a military band.

"I've seen medal presentations on TV and there's always a band playing a brass fanfare," he says. "Otherwise there's no sense in awarding the medals. The whole point is that you get them to a fanfare."

"Yeah, right," I scoff. "And maybe you'd also like the president to kiss your butt while they give it to you?"

"That's not a bad idea," says Pincha, a thoughtful look appearing in his eyes. "I reckon every last one here should be able to pin a medal on his chest. Ever been in Chechnya? Well then, dear private, please accept this 'Merit in Battle' medal. Were you there during the storming of Grozny? Then have 'For Bravery' too. What, you even served in the mountains? Then you must also have the 'Order of Courage.'"

"You know they only give 'Courage' to those who were wounded or killed. The most you can hope for is 'Merit in Battle, First Class.'"

"Well, that's not bad either," Pincha concedes. "But in that case I expect a fanfare with it."

"D'you know how many regiments there are in just our army group?" Garik asks. "No band could attend all those medal presentations. And how do you know they even have a band?"

We then argue whether the army group has a full military band. Pincha and Fixa are adamant that such a large formation must have one, or at the very least a small company of musicians. How else could they have celebrated the February 23 Defenders of the Fatherland Day in Khankala? There was bound to have been a parade of some kind and you don't have a parade without a brass band.

Garik and Lyekha don't think there is a band in Chechnya. But either way, everyone agrees with Pincha that some extra sense of occasion is appropriate today.

Still the question arises: If there's no band, how do they give generals a proper send off if one of them gets killed?

"Generals don't get killed," says Oleg. "Have you ever heard of even one of them dying here? No, they all sit tight in Moscow."

"What about General Shamanov?" objects Pincha. "He's down here and drives around the front line. He could easily get blown up on a mine. And Bulgakov, he was up in the mountains with us, wasn't he?"

"Shaman won't get blown up," I chip in. "I've seen how he travels. He has two armored personnel carriers riding with him and two choppers buzzing round overhead all the time. And even though he rides in only a jeep you can be sure the sappers have swept the road ahead. No, Pincha, it's not so easy to blow up an army group commander. Colonels, sure, they get whacked. I've seen a dead colonel with my own eyes and even heard about colonels being taken prisoner. But generals are another matter."

"But they come down from Moscow for inspections here, don't they?" persists Lyekha. "Some generals or other from GHQ fly in and bunches of them get flown around in choppers. They could easily get shot down in the mountains."

"I somehow don't recall a single inspection by generals in the mountains," I say. "Seems to me they just come down in order to collect their warzone per diem, and even then no further than Khankala or Severny, those places also count as forward positions."

"How is Khankala a forward position?" asks Pincha, confused. "It's well in the rear."

"It might be the rear for you but in the generals' expense claims it's the front line all right. Each day they spend there counts as two, and then they get the presidential bonus of 1,500 roubles a day in wartime, and extra leave. Three trips to Chechnya and they get another 'Courage' for their chest."

"I stopped in Severny on my way back from hospital," Lyekha tells us. "It's great there now, not like a couple of months ago. Nice and peaceful, green grass, white-painted kerbs, straight roads. They hooked it up to the electricity recently and now Severny lights up like a Christmas tree in the evening. They even have women there, officers get posted there with their wives. Just imagine, in the evening couples wander round the lanes under streetlights, just like back home. The soldiers there don't carry weapons with them and they get hot food three times a day and a steam bath once a week. They don't even have lice—I asked while I was there. They built a modem barracks there, you know, just like in the American movies. They even have porcelain toilets with seats, white ones, I kid you not! I went specially to use them. And lads, you won't believe me, but they even have a hotel for the generals' inspections we were talking about. Televisions with five channels, hot water, showers, double-glazed windows . . ."

We listen, mouths gaping, spellbound by Lyekha's description of the Severny base and airport on Grozny's outskirts, as if we were hearing a fairy tale. White porcelain toilets, mess halls, double glazing. It seems fantastic that Grozny can have a hotel. We saw this city when it was dead, when the only residents were rabid dogs that fed on corpses in the cellars. And now it has a hotel—that surely can't be true?

Severny is only a stone's throw from Grozny's Minutka Square, where the heaviest fighting took place, and from that cross-shaped hospital where we lost hordes of guys. This is a city of death, and as far as we are concerned there should never be any luxury there so that what happened is never forgotten. Otherwise this whole war amounts to nothing but a cynical slaughter of thousands of people. It's not right to build new life on their bones.

We just returned from the mountains where our battalion took fifty per cent losses, you couldn't even raise your head without being shot at. Up there they are still killing and shooting down helicopters while in Grozny our commanders are supposedly taking hot showers and watching TV. We are willing to believe in white porcelain toilets but a hotel for the generals is going too far.

"You're making it up," says Murky. "It can't be true."

"Oh yes it can, I saw it myself."

"Saw it yourself, did you? You, the same person who tells us that herds of generals prance around in the mountains like antelopes? Well that at least can't be true, they'd never leave the hotel."

"I still want to know what happens when they bump off a general," Pincha says, returning to the topic. Lyekha's account has made no impression on him, he took it all for a fairy tale and nothing else.

"If a general dies, do they pay his widow an allowance or not? And how do they pay it, do they bring it round to her home or does she stand in line with the rest of us at the cashier's office at the bases and write letters to the newspapers saying 'please help me, my husband was killed and the state has forgotten me.' There were lots of women like that back at my regiment, struggling through all the red tape after their men got killed."

Pincha's right. When we signed our contract to serve in Chechnya we also saw such women. We got an advance before we moved out and we stood in the same line as them for money. We always let them go ahead in this queue for the state's attention, to receive some elementary compassion and sympathy, out of respect for a mother who gave up her most precious possession for her country, the life of her son. And who got nothing in return, not even money for his funeral.

These women always got brushed off everywhere by the bureaucrats. Now the mothers of Fly and Yakovlev and the others are probably also fighting their way through red tape to get some basic rights.

"Of course they don't stand in the same queue. You can be sure a general's widow gets her payments in full and straight away," says Fixa.

"After all, we're talking about a general, not some worthless Pincha, the like of which they can heap up a hundred a day and not care. But we don't have that many generals. They have to be bred, trained in the academy, educated. I dare say the president himself knows them all by name. Yes, I bet he does." Fixa pauses to consider his latest revelation. "Hmm, I wonder what it's like when the president shakes your hand in greeting . . ."

Arkasha finally puts an end to the discussion.

"It doesn't matter if you are a general or a colonel," he says. "What's important is the position you hold. To be the widow of the chief of the military accommodation authorities and the widow of a general in command of some military district deep in Siberia are quite different, even though the district commander is higher in rank. And like hell does the president know them all by name, we have countless numbers of generals. Up there in the Defence Ministry they wander round like orderlies and clean the latrines—since there are no ordinary soldiers there the generals have to get on their knees with rags and mess up their dress trousers. I heard this from a colonel who asked us to help file a complaint on his behalf. A general beat him up and broke his tooth so he grassed on him, told them how the general was using stolen materials to build himself a house and had soldiers sweating away for him on the building site. They have their own system of hazing in the ranks, you can rest assured."

I don't believe him, it seems unlikely that they have violent hazing even in the ministry. Then again, why not? Generals are not made from pastry, they were once lieutenants themselves. A couple more wars like this and our *kombat* will also become a general, get promoted and cudgel us all from up there instead. And what's so special about it?

At last regimental commander Verier comes out onto the parade ground accompanied by the *kombat*. We fall silent.

"Greetings, comrades!" he shouts, as if addressing a parade on Red Square and not some depleted battalion in Argun.

"Greetings, sir," we reply half-heartedly.

"At ease," he tells us, even though it hadn't occurred to anyone to stand to attention.

The colonel talks to us about drunkenness. He calls us bastards and pissheads and threatens to string us all up by our feet from the rack so ingeniously devised by our *kombat*. He fully approves of this innovation and will advise commanders of other battalions to draw from our experience. And just let any soldiers dare complain to him about nonregulation treatment, for he intends to fight drunkenness and theft in the ranks!

After this he goes on at length about the duty we have fulfilled in the mountains and how the Motherland will not forget its fallen heroes, and such nonsense. He strides up and down on stiff legs, his beer belly thrust forward, and tells us what fine fellows we are.

"Calls us crap, then sucks up to us," Murky comments.

"You know what?" says Arkasha, narrowing his eyes. "He's on his way up. He just got appointed deputy division commander and that means he'll be a general. And for a successful anti-terrorist operation in Chechnya, Colonel Verter has been put forward for the 'Hero of Russia' medal. A guy I know in the GHQ saw the letter of recommendation."

"No way!" exclaims Oleg. "He's a coward! He's only been to the front once. Got half the battalion killed for some lousy hillock and he still didn't manage to take it. His sort should be shot, no way can he become a general and get 'Hero of Russia' to boot."

"Sure he can. It may be a lousy hillock to you but in his reports it's a strategically important height, defended by superior enemy forces. And we didn't throw ourselves at them head on for three days, we executed a tactical maneuver as a result of which the enemy were forced to abandon their positions. It's all a matter of presentation.

Don't be so naive. The war isn't fought here but in Moscow. What they say goes—don't you agree that you are a hero? I suppose you'll refuse a medal now?"

No, no one intends to turn down any medals. If each of us helps heave a handful of colonels and generals up the career ladder then let them give us something for our trouble in return.

"I wonder what Verter will do with his Mitsubishi after the war?" Pincha says.

"Don't worry your pretty head about it, he's not going to give it to you," replies Arkasha.

"Now that would be a fine thing. I wonder how he'll get it out of here, on a transport plane probably."

After the colonel's address the awards begin. He stands at the table below the rack and in a wooden voice starts to read out the decoration order of the army group commander.

We wait impatiently, who will be first? Who does the Motherland see as the best and worthiest among us? Maybe Khodakovsky, he never got a scratch but was one of the first to reach Minutka Square during the assault on Grozny. And he fought like a true warrior in the mountains. Or Emil, our Daghestani sniper who crawled fifteen meters one night to the enemy trenches and fired on them at point-blank range. He killed thirteen and came out unscathed, earning himself a commendation for "Hero of Russia" from the *kombat*. Or maybe one of the mortar-men, they heaped up more dead than all of us?

After he reads the order, the colonel takes two steps back and lets the *kombat* forward to the table to hand out the decorations. He takes the first box, opens up the medal certificate and draws a deep breath. We freeze in anticipation, who will it be?

"Private Kotov, step forward!" he announces loudly and solemnly.

At first I don't have a clue who this private Kotov is. Only when he passes through the ranks and trots up to the table with an embarrassed smile and raises a clumsy salute do I realize it's Kot, the cook from the officers' mess. He cooks for the *kombat*, lays the table and serves up the dishes.

The *kombat* probably just happened upon his medal first by chance. He might have shown a bit more care, the first person in the battalion to get decorated should be the best soldier or officer.

The next medal goes to the staff clerk, then the transport chief, and then someone from the repair company. We lose all interest and ignore the ceremony, it's clear enough what this is all about.

"Everyone who was in this stinking war should get a medal," says Lyekha. "Cooks, drivers, clerks, everyone, just for being here. Every last one of us has earned that much."

"Right enough," says Arkasha. "And Kot above all."

Standing beneath the gibbet, the *kombat* awards the next medal to the next "outstanding" soldier. It suddenly strikes me that he perfectly embodies our state, a gibbet behind his back and medals in his hand for lackeys. For he is the highest authority on this strip of land inside the fence. For us he is judge, jury, prosecutor and parliament rolled into one. Here and now, he is the state. And so it turns out that the state has screwed us over yet again, heaping favors on those who are closest to it and who sucked up to it best.

Khodakovsky and Kot now both wear the same "For Bravery" medal, although the first could have been killed a hundred times in the mountains and the second risked only dying from overeating.

The only one in our platoon to get even "Merit in Battle, Second Class" is Garik, and then only because he worked as a clerk for a month in the headquarters. After he is decorated he resumes his place beside us, shifting with embarrassment.

He wants to take off the medal but we don't let him, he earned his gong.

We no longer believe in these decorations, to us they are now just worthless metal. We are far more likely to receive a smack in the mouth from our country than an award that actually means something.

"Hey, Fixa," I say, elbowing him. "It's a right shitty country we live in, isn't it?"

"Yep, it's shitty all right," he answers, picking a blister on his palm.

After the decoration ceremony we are addressed by a representative of the Soldiers' Mothers Committee. A feisty, cigarette-puffing woman of about forty she is bubbly, big-framed and still pretty. She has a command-ing, chain-smoker's voice and can hold her own with us swearing.

We take to her at once and smile as she tells us simple things like how this war has ravaged all of us but how peace is not far away, how we must hold on just a little longer, and how folk back home are thinking of us and waiting. And as proof of this, she says, she's brought us presents. She then distributes to every one of us a cardboard box with lemonade, biscuits, sweets and socks. It's a grand haul.

Later they prepare a sauna for the regimental commander, the officers and the female guest. They steam away a long time before the procession finally troops out and the half-naked officers sit in the shade beneath the tarpaulin and start on the vodka. A sheet periodically falls from the repre-sentative of the mothers' committee, giving us a flash of her ample white body. She's not in the least bit shy and soon we forget our own shyness.

Even Arkasha refrains from joking. We like her and no one dares to cast judgment on this woman who came to war bearing gifts for the boys. She is the only person in months who has spoken to us like people and we unconditionally forgive her for the things we'd never forgive the regimental commander: the half-naked fraternization with the officers, the drunken-ness, the box with aid intended for us that stands on their table. After all, she could sit tight in Moscow and not risk taking a bullet here. Yet she chose to rattle her way down here in a convoy from Mozdok without expecting anything from us in return.

Before she leaves she gathers phone numbers and addresses, offering to call home or write for us and tell everyone we're alive and well.

She calls us all boys and even "sonny." Arkasha's pockmarked face creases in a smile and he gives her his phone number, tells her they might even meet after the war.

I also come up to her and give her my home number. When she hears I'm from Moscow she snaps off a quick photo of me, hugs a dozen nearest soldiers and then leaps nimbly into an armored vehicle as the convoy pulls out.

A cloud of dust swirls for a while beyond the fence and settles and we stand like orphaned children by the gates as they close. It really does feel like our mother has left, our common mother, and we soldiers, her chil-dren, have been left behind.

"Fine woman," says Arkasha. "Marina's her name. Her son is somewhere here and she's driving round different units looking for him. I feel sorry for her."

The regimental commander is still here and they put us on the roofs on reinforced guard—the brass must see that we are carrying out our duty properly.

We clamber up onto the meatpacking shop, kick away rusty shell fragments that have lain here since some barrage and seat ourselves on black tarred roofing sheets that are baking hot from the sun. We have four of the aid boxes with us and spread the grub out on jackets.

"In the name of the Russian Federation the flesh of private Fixa is hereby decorated with the Order of the Stoop, Second Class with lifelong entitlement to dig near electricity lines, stand under crane booms and cross the road when the light is red," Arkasha announces ceremonially, and presses a biscuit onto Fixa's chest.

Lyekha sings a fanfare, wipes a tear from his eye and gives the grinning Fixa a fatherly clap on the back as we salute in unison. Then we get stuck into the food, scooping condensed milk into our mouths with biscuits and washing it down with lemonade. Our fingers get sticky and we wipe them on our sweaty bellies, munching away with smiles on our faces. Emaciated, unwashed soldiers in huge boots and ragged trousers, we sit on the roof and gorge ourselves. We've never had it so good.

"Enjoying that?" Fixa asks me.

"Not half. Are you?"

"Couldn't be better."

Two tins of condensed milk, a bag of biscuits, a dozen caramel sweets and a bottle of lemonade. That's our sum reward for the mountains, for Grozny, for four months of war and sixty-eight of our guys killed. And it didn't even come from the state but from mothers like our own, who scrimp and save the kopeks from their miserable village pensions that the state still whittles away to raise funds for the war.

Well to hell with the state, we're contract soldiers, mercenaries who fight for money and need nothing more from it. We'll go into battle right now if need be and they can pin their medals onto their backsides to jangle like baubles on a Christmas tree.

Fixa wipes his milk-smeared hand on Pincha's britches and daintily takes a postcard from one of the boxes. It bears the Russian tricolor and the gold-printed words "Glory to the Defenders of the Fatherland!" Afraid to smear it, he holds it in two fingers and reads aloud:

"Dear Defenders of the Fatherland! Dear Boys! We, the pupils and teachers of sixth class B of school 411, Moscow Eastern District, extend our heartiest congratulations to you on the Defenders of the Fatherland holiday. Your noble feat fills our hearts with pain and pride. Pain, because you are exposed to danger every minute. Pride, because Russia has such courageous and strong people. Thanks to you we may study in peace and our parents may work in peace. Look after yourselves and be vigilant. May God protect you. Come home soon, we await your victorious return. Glory be yours!"

"Are we supposed to be the strong ones here?" Pincha asks, spraying crumbs from his mouth.

"Yes mate, it's about you," answers Garik.

"Good postcard," says Fixa.

"Bad one, it's on glossy paper," I disagree.

"I mean it's well written, you fool."

There is a slight tremble in Fixa's voice and his eyes are misty. What's up with him, surely he's not touched with emotion? Can it be that this tough guy from Voronezh, who usually has no time for frilly sentiment and understands only the most basic things like bread, cigarettes, and sleep, things that are as simple as he is, has been moved by a postcard from some children. Well, I'll be damned.

I take the card from him and look at it. It's nothing like those despicable cards they sent us before the presidential elections in 1996. For a while they stopped calling us bastards and sons of bitches and started to refer to us as "dear Russian soldier" and "respected voter." These were the first elections in our life and for three of us in my unit they were the last ones. They didn't get to cast their ballots and died in the first Chechen war before they could fulfill their civic duty.

"This school is in the east of the city, not far from where I live. If you like, after the war I'll drop by there and thank them," I tell Fixa to make him happy.

"We'll go there together," he says. "We'll go to the school together. We have to, don't you see? They remembered us, collected money, sent us aid packages. What for? Who are we to them?" He pauses. "It's a shame Khariton is gone, I shouldn't have driven him on at the hill, shouted at him.

Nor should you," he tells Arkasha. "What did you hit him for? He was just a kid. Why did you hit him, eh?"

Arkasha doesn't reply. We sit in silence. Fixa is crying. I fold the postcard in half and put it in my inside pocket. At that moment I really believe I will visit that school after the war.

After the glut of sweet food we suffer a fresh epidemic of dysentery in the battalion. Our stomachs were unaccustomed to normal food and we are stricken twice as hard as last time. The inspection pits in the garage are full to brimming and black clouds of flies circle above them.

Oleg says this outbreak is our bodies reacting now that the danger has passed, we relaxed and sickness is now kicking in.

"The same thing awaits us at home," he says. "You'll see, we'll come home from the war decrepit wrecks with the A to Z of illnesses."

I think there's another reason. The battalion is squeezed into a small area and those same flies buzzing over the pit settle on our mess tins when we eat.

We crouch half-naked in the meatpacking shop, the only place left we can still use. We sit this like half the day, there's no point in putting on our trousers since dysentery sends you running continuously. Sometimes you can't force anything out, other times you jet blood.

"False alarms are a symptom of acute infectious dysentery," says Murky, flipping through a medical encyclopedia he found in Grozny and carried with him across Chechnya, establishing erroneously that we have symptoms of typhoid, foot and mouth disease, cholera, and plague. Now the encyclopedia itself befalls a terrible fate, being made of soft pages like newspaper, and within two days only the binding is left. Dysentery is the last disease that this fine medical reference book diagnosed in its time.

"Remember how they made us crap on paper?" Garik asks with a grin.

"Oh God, yes," Oleg laughs back.

Before we were sent to Chechnya, the regiment would file out of the barracks twice a week and, company by company, drop its pants after placing a piece of paper on the ground. While a pretty young woman medic walked through the ranks they made us defecate and hand her our excrement to be analyzed for dysentery. The cattle must go to the slaughter in good health and our shame at this act bothered nobody.

Now no one shows us such concern. All they do is give us some kind of yellow tablets, one pill between three of us. We take them in turns but this treatment has no effect whatsoever.

"Heavy caliber, take cover!" warns Fixa before loosing off a deafening burst in the pit. Arkasha responds with a smaller caliber, Murky fires single shots. But Pincha outguns us all, straining long and hard before producing a report that would shatter all the windowpanes in the area if any had still been intact.

"Tactical nuclear warhead with enriched uranium, explosive power equivalent to five tons of TNT," he says, smirking.

"That's prohibited weaponry, Pincha," protests Arkasha with a belly laugh.

At night the battalion resounds to deep rumbling and moaning. The sentries do their business straight off the rooftops, it's too exhausting to run down twenty times a night.

The night sky is illuminated by bright stars and gleaming white soldiers' backsides. Walking under the roofs is hazardous.

My bleeding starts again and my long johns are permanently encrusted with blood. We all have it. Your rectum swells up and protrudes several centimeters. Half your backside hangs out and you sit resplendent like a scarlet flower. Where are we supposed to find wiping material? We strip the remaining scraps of wallpaper from the storerooms and rasp at our poor backsides, inflicting further harm on ourselves, sending blood gushing from our trousers.

War is not just attacks, trenches, firefights and grenades. It's also blood and feces running down your rotting legs. It's starvation, lice and drunken madness. It's swearing and human debasement. It's an inhuman stench and clouds of flies circling over our battalion. Some of the guys try to heal themselves with herbal folk remedies that end up making many of them only sicker.

"This is our reward from the Almighty," Arkasha says. "The whole battalion has flowers springing from their arses, that's our springtime!"

"What did we do to deserve this?" moans Pincha.

I find a roll of kitchen towel in the admin block and hide it in a pile of rubbish, using it only when there is no one else around. It wouldn't last the platoon even half a day but this way I'm OK for a while at least.

In a bid to fight the dysentery the battalion commander imposes a strict regime of mess tin cleaning. Now after each meal a duty soldier washes the platoon's mess tins. There's no water here and we wash them in the same water we wash ourselves in each morning. Flakes of soap and grease float in the green water with mosquito grubs and we have to scoop away the flora and fauna with our hands to gather enough water for tea.

People start pilfering water again amid the shortage and our position by the gates gives us a strategic advantage. As soon as the water truck drives in we block its path until we have filled every container we have.

Arkasha and Fixa found an old bathtub somewhere and we also use that. The supply officer threatens to have us shot but we still carry out the tub every morning as we go water collecting.

In the recesses of the unfinished meatpacking shop we find more concrete support piers with dips full of murky water. We keep the find secret but people cotton on and we have to mount a guard. It comes to blows as we jealously protect our source.

"It would be better if we were fighting again," says Fixa. "At least there's no problem with supplies then."

That's true enough. The commanders only think about the soldiers when we are being killed by the hundred. After each storming operation they fall us in and tell us what heroes we are and give us normal food and water rations for two or three days. Then once again we get half-cooked gruel for breakfast and a smack in the mouth for lunch.

"But these lulls are still good," says the platoon commander, washing his feet with "dry-fruit water" they call "compote" that we are supposed to drink.

"Warm, dry and nowhere to go. Not even for washing water—look at this brew, it isn't even sticky because it's peacetime."

Peacetime compote is indeed different from the stuff they serve during the fighting. What they give us now during this slack period can be used for anything. You can drink it, wash in it or soak your underwear because it doesn't contain a single gram of sugar or dried fruit, the supply officer traded both commodities for vodka. He does the same during combat phases but not so often, the conscientious fellow.

One day a jeep carrying police officers is shot up near the village of Mesker-Yurt. We are alerted and set off in two armored personnel carriers, a platoon of infantry and our three gun teams.

The first vehicle churns up great clouds of dust behind it, making it impossible to breathe or open our eyes. The dust grates on our teeth, blocks our noses and coats our eyelashes, eyebrows and hair in a gray film. We cover our faces with bandanas but they don't help and we still can hardly breathe. Bloody weather, impenetrable mud in winter and vile summer dust that turns into dough when it rains.

The jeep stands on a road between fields and has been almost completely destroyed. The fighters waited in the undergrowth and hit it with a rocket launcher. One side has been blown apart; mangled metal and a seat hang out with a pair of dangling legs and some other lumps of flesh. The four guys inside were torn to pieces. The attackers evidently raked the jeep with several rifles after the explosion and the other side is peppered with holes where bullets and shrapnel exited.

The local police arrive and there is nothing for us to do except guard the investigators. We leave after a couple of hours.

That evening we are sent again in the direction of Mesker-Yurt. A paramilitary police unit has located the same rebel group that killed the officers earlier. They holed up in the village after the attack and were waiting to ambush us but we never came.

I can't mount my grenade launcher on the personnel carrier, my hands don't respond and the bedplate won't go onto the bolts. My body is like cotton wool, my fingers can hardly feel the nuts and I fumble to tighten them. I look at them and can't focus properly. I sense that I must not go to Mesker-Yurt today. I'm scared.

Fear fills me gradually, rising in my body like a wave and leaving an empty space behind it. This is not the hot, rushing fear you feel when you suddenly come under fire, this is different, a cold, slow-moving fear that just doesn't recede. Today, near Mesker-Yurt, I will be killed.

"Go and get two cases of grenades," the platoon commander orders.

I nod and go to the tent. The cases weight fifteen kilos each and I can't carry two at once, they are slippery and there's nothing to hold them by. I empty my knapsack and stuff one case inside and put the second under my arm and run out of the tent to see the column already driving out of the gate. The platoon commander motions me to stay behind.

I watch them disappear toward Mesker-Yurt and suddenly I am seized by furious trembling. I feel chilled to the bone, my arms are weak, my knees give way and I sit down sharply on the ground. Blackness clouds my sight, I see and hear nothing and sit uncomprehendingly, on the verge of vomiting. I haven't felt such terror in ages.

Fixa is standing near the gate.

"How come you didn't go?" I ask.

"I got scared, you know?" he replies.

"Yes, I know."

He gets his cigarettes out. My hand is trembling so hard I can't even strike a match. What the hell is the matter with me, nothing like this ever happened before? I have to get a grip. The column left while Fixa and I stayed behind and are out of danger.

Our guys come back at night. Mesker-Yurt was taken but our battalion was deployed in the second security cordon around the village and didn't take part in the fighting. The police paramilitaries did all the work and lost ten men.

We didn't take any casualties that night but I still feel that it would have been my last. I want to go home.

I live with fear constantly now. It began that day and doesn't abate. I am scared all the time. The fear alternately turns slowly like a worm somewhere below my stomach and floods through me with a hot flush of sweat. This is not the tension I experienced in the mountains but pure, animal fear.

One night I beat up Pincha for leaving the lookout post before he was relieved and then did the same to two new guys. They didn't hit it off with our platoon and sleep separately in the cook's armored car. Then the pricks go and brew tea right on the windowsill of the lookout post. Their fire flickers away for all to see and is visible for several kilometers, giving away the position and maybe drawing the attention of snipers. And I'm the one who has to relieve them.

I can no longer sleep these days. I don't trust the sentries and spend most nights in the admin block or on the parade ground. I always wear my webbing yoke stuffed with loaded magazines that I traded for food and cigarettes. I have about twenty-five magazines and it still seems too few. I also empty a few clips of bullets into my pockets and hang about a dozen grenades from my belt. It's still not enough. If they storm us I want to be fully armed.

One night I relieve the guys on the lookout. I stay away from the window and stand in the room round the corner, motionless for four hours, freezing at the slightest sound outside.

It seems I am alone and that while I am skulking in the admin block the Chechens have silently butchered the whole battalion and are coming up the stairs for me. I hate the generator as it drowns out every other sound. I try not to breathe and strain to hear what's going on in the building.

Sure enough, they're already inside. Brick chunks grate under foot as someone makes his way up the stairs. The Chechen turns on the stairwell and puts his foot on the last flight. Nine more steps and he'll reach my floor. My heart stops beating. I don't want to shoot because I'll give away my position. I may take one of them out but the rest will know I'm here and will get me with grenades. I won't be able to run away or hide anywhere, they are all around.

"I want to go home," I say out loud and draw my bayonet from the top of my boot. The blade gives out a dull gleam in the moonlight. I clutch the weapon with both hands in front of my face and tiptoe slowly to the stairs, keeping my back close to the wall, trying to step in time with the Chechen.

He's now on the second step. I also take a step. We move our feet simultaneously. Third step, fourth, fifth. He has four more steps to go, three, two . . . I leap forward and lash out wildly with the bayonet round the comer, striking a deep gash in the wall and scattering crumbs to the floor. A chip bounces down the stairs and hits an empty tin with a clink. There's no one there. I take several deep breaths.

The stairwell is deserted. The Chechens are of course already in the room. While I was fighting ghosts in the stairwell they occupied my position, climbed up the heap of rubbish outside and swung themselves stealthily through the window. Now they are fanning out to the comers. I can't hide any more and so I unsling my rifle, slip off the safety catch and tramp my way noisily toward the room. I kick a brick and it flies off to one side with a deafening crash. My footsteps are probably audible from the street. I give a sharp shout.

My plan is simple. They will hear me coming along the corridor and run out of the room one by one only to be picked off by me. But then I beat them to it, burst in, squat down and circle round like a wolf, training my rifle ahead of me. No one. I'm still alive, thank God!

I stand in the corner again and listen into the night. I can't see anything from here but snipers can't see me either. And in this corner I have a better chance of surviving if a grenade comes through the window. I crouch down, cover my head with my jacket and switch on the light on my watch. Thirteen minutes of my shift have passed. Another three hours and forty-seven minutes at the lookout.

I hear footsteps on the stairs and freeze. Five more steps. I draw the bayonet from my boot.

I stop talking to people altogether. I don't laugh or smile any more. I am afraid. The desire to go home has become an obsession. That's all I want and I can think of nothing else.

"I want to go home," I say as we have supper in the tent.

"Shut up," says Arkasha.

He gets more wound up than the others by the mention of home. He is not due for demobilization, he has no medals, and in any case if he goes home they'll likely lock him up because of an old bribery charge against him from his civilian days.

We've been halted in Argun for too long and the tension is now being displaced by fear. This spell of rest and recuperation can't last forever, something has to happen. They'll either send us home or back into the mountains.

"I don't want to go back into the mountains," I say. "I want to go home."

"They can't send us back into the mountains," Fixa assures me. "We've done our stint. There are so many different units and so they just send new brigades up there. No, we won't go into the mountains any more. And we can annul our contract any time we like, don't forget."

"I want to go home." I repeat.

Arkasha throws an empty tin at me. I don't react.

We wait.

I pay my daily visit to the medics to get the ulcers on my thigh dressed. They refuse to heal and continue to grow, having now reached the size of a baby's palm. Smaller ones dot my arms.

There are two new nurses at the first-aid point, Rita and Olga.

Rita is a redheaded broad, well built and with a drink-toughened voice that was made for firing off her earthy barrack-room jokes. She's one of us and the lads go crazy over her. But I like Olga more.

Olga is small, quiet and over thirty but her figure is still good. She hasn't had an easy time here—women like her have no place among drunken contract soldiers. She's a real lady and remains one even in the midst of war. She hasn't started smoking or swearing and doesn't sleep with the officers. The little white socks she wears under her shoes never fail to fascinate me, femininely dainty and always clean. God only knows where she manages to wash them.

I visit her every day for treatment. She removes the old bandages and inspects the wounds, bending down over my thigh. I stand naked in front of her but it doesn't bother either of us. She's seen countless unwashed guys encrusted in blood and I am in no condition to flirt with a woman anyway.

But it's still pleasant when her cool fingers touch my thigh and her breath stirs my body hair, bringing me out in goosebumps. I close my eyes and listen to her tapping gently on the skin and I will my leg to rot further so she will have to care for me a little longer. Olga's tender touch is so much like peacetime and her palm is so like the palm of the girl I left behind in the pre-war past.

"Why don't you wear underwear?" she asks one day.

"They don't issue us any," I lie. In fact, I am simply ashamed of my lice-ridden long johns and before each visit I remove them and hide them in a corner of the tent.

She sprinkles streptocide on my festering thigh ulcers and spreads pork fat on my arms to contain the others. Two weeks later they start to heal.

We hear a three-round burst of fire. Someone screams over at the infantry personnel carriers.

"Rifles on safety!" I hear Oldie shout. We run over.

It turns out some drunken driver forgot to put his rifle on safety and accidentally pressed the trigger. All three rounds hit home. One ripped off a contract soldier's jaw. He sits on the ground, blood streaming from his smashed mouth into a large, fatty pool on the earth. He doesn't make a sound, just sits there and looks at us, arms hanging limply before him. The pain hasn't set in yet and he doesn't know what to do.

The staff commander tends to him, injects him with painkiller and tries to bandage what's left of the jaw. Jagged splinters of bone tear the gauze as he binds the wound. The soldier starts to jerk so Oleg grabs him by one arm and pins him to the ground while Murky holds the other.

The other two bullets did far more damage, hitting Shepel in both kidneys. He lies on top of the armored car while Oldie bandages him.

The soldier's breathing is labored and uneven but he is conscious. Even in the light of the moon his face look deathly pale.

"Pity," he gasps. "Pity it ended like this, I almost made it home."

"Nothing has ended, Shepel," Oldie tells his friend. "Do you hear me, nothing has ended! We'll get you to hospital now and everything will be OK. Come on, mate, you'll see."

He applies bandage after bandage, several packets, but he can't stop the bleeding. The blood flows thickly, almost black in color. It's bad. Shepel no longer speaks. He lays with closed eyes and breathes heavily.

"I'll kill that son of a bitch," Oldie screams.

The personnel carrier leaves for Khankala with the injured men and Oldie goes with them.

"That's the most goddamned unfair death of this whole war," Arkasha says as he watches the vehicle disappear into the darkness. "To go through so much and die here, in the rear, from a stray bullet."

His fists clench and unclench and the muscles in his cheeks twitch.

"What an unfair death," he whispers into the darkness. "So unfair."

They don't let the carrier through at the checkpoint into Khankala. Shepel lies on the top dying while some duty lieutenant demands the password, saying he can't open the swing-gate otherwise. This rear-unit rat who spent the whole war in this field wants the password and couldn't care less that our comrade is critically wounded.

He is afraid to let them through, afraid that the brass will find out and that there will be consequences for him. They are all afraid that for any screw-up they will get sent to the front line. And then they will be the ones bleeding to death on top of a carrier while someone else bars the way to the hospital.

Oldie doesn't know the password and starts shooting in the air in fury, sending tracer rounds over this safe, snug Khankala with its cable television and double-glazing. He fires and screams and begs Shepel to hold on a little longer. They get through the checkpoint and to the hospital but Shepel dies a few hours later. We had failed to stem the bleeding.

They don't let Oldie out of Khankala and would surely have thrown him in one of the infamous "zindan" pits in the ground that captives are often kept in. But there aren't any pits in Khankala because there are plenty of journalists here and they consider it an inadmissible form of torment to keep soldiers in pits, although torment in my opinion is something quite different.

So to avoid antagonizing civilians the command has generously allocated some wheeled wagons as detention cells. There are lots of these wagons here, a few for holding our soldiers and the others for captured Chechen fighters.

One of the Chechen ones was dubbed 'the Messerschmidt' after some bright spark painted a white swastika on the side. At night harrowing screams rise from the Messerschmidt as our interrogators extract confessions.

Oldie has landed himself in an unenviable situation. Shooting in Khankala is a serious blunder. The rear commanders were scared witless when he unloaded tracer rounds over their heads and now they want to avenge their embarrassing display by pinning a drunken rampage charge on him.

We manage to visit him in Khankala after talking our way onto a transport run with sick cases. While our medic delivers them to hospital we look for the wagon where Oldie is locked up.

This place is completely different to how we remember. Khankala has grown to an incredible size. It's no longer a military base but a town with a population of several thousand, if not tens of thousands. There are untold numbers of units here, each with its own perimeter fence, and you can get lost here if you don't know your way around. But it's remarkably quiet, as if you are on a farm. The soldiers wander round without weapons and standing upright, now rid of the habit of stooping like they do at the front. Maybe this lot never even heard a shot, their eyes betray neither tension nor fear, they are probably not hungry and have no lice. This really is the rear.

It's a cozy little world, segregated from the war by a concrete wall. This is the way the army should be, ideal, astounding order. And it's just how Lyekha had described Severny to us, although we didn't believe him at the time. Straight, tarmac roads, green grass and white-painted curbs, long parades of new one-story barrack houses, a metal Western-style mess hall with a gleaming semi-circular corrugated roof, clubs, toilet blocks and saunas. Everything neatly swept and sprinkled with sand, a few posters here and there and portraits of the president gazing down at you every other step.

And streetlamps that work, casting light onto officers as they stroll with their wives. Lyekha was right, they actually bring them down here to live.

"I'm off to work, dear, be a love and hand me my bayonet," of a morning. And in the evening: "Have a good day, darling?" wife asks. "Yes, dear, excellent, I killed two Chechens." Some of them even have children with them, and they grow up here in Grozny.

We walk around Khankala, calling out Oldie's name. People stare at us, we are superfluous here in this place in the rear, where everything is subordinate to strong army order. The neatness of it all infuriates me. We walk around like plague victims and survey these well-fed soldiers with hatred. Let just one of them say a single word or try to stop or arrest us and we'll kill the lot of them.

"This place is a goddamned rats' lair," spits Fixa. "Pity we don't have a grenade launcher, we could stroll around and take care of this lot with a few bursts. Oldieee!"

"Oldieee!" I follow.

Finally Oldie's unshaven face appears in a tiny barred window. Fixa gives the sentry some cigarettes and we have a few minutes to talk. We can only see half of his face. We smile at one another and light up. I climb up on the wheel and pass him a smoke and the three of us puff away in silence.

We don't know what to say, loathe to ask how it is in there and what they feed him. What does that matter now, it has to be better than in the mountains.

As it happens, it's quite bearable in there. There are a few mattresses on the floor, he has a roof over his head, it's warm and dry, what else do you need? They don't even beat them here because of the journalists. They should have brought a few journalists into the mountains or to us in Argun when Lisitsyn shot at the soldier on the rack—that would be a hoot. Then they would know what real torment is. But with them it's all zindan this and zindan that. I think they just like the word.

"It's a resort here," Oldie says with a grim smile as he tells us of his existence. "Mountain air, three meals a day. Pincha would love it. No oat gruel here, they give us proper food from the officers' mess hall. Today, for example, I had meatballs and pasta for lunch."

"Oh really, nice set-up you have here then," says Fixa.

"Can't complain."

I look at his face through the bars and smile. I don't have any particular thoughts, I'm just happy to be here with him and that we are together again. I can't imagine being demobilized without him, or how I will live later without all of them, Oldie, Fixa, poor Igor.

"Shepel died," Fixa tells him.

"I know. I'll find the guy who did it."

"We'll find out who it was, Oldie, I promise."

"No, I'll find him myself. I have to do it, don't you see? If I don't find him, then the deaths of Shepel, Igor, Khariton, Four-Eyes, all of them, will cease to have any meaning? Then they've simply died for nothing, do you see? All of them could just as easily have been killed by some drunk with no retribution, no one bearing any responsibility. If I don't find him then all these deaths are some kind of dreadful crime, plain murder, slaughter of gray soldier cattle, do you understand?"

He is absolutely calm as he says all of this, his expression hasn't changed and retains the same good humor as if he were still telling us about the meatballs he had for lunch. But I know this is not just talk. He will find and kill this guy and *he* is fully entitled to do so.

The value of a human life is not absolute and Shepel's life in our eyes is far more valuable than the life of some drunken driver who never had a single shot fired at him, was never pinned down by sniper fire, never used his hands to staunch flowing blood, and who never saved anyone's life. So why should he live if Shepel died? How could it be that this person who never experienced the horrors Shepel did was able to go and kill him in a drunken stupor and stay alive himself?

It doesn't seem right. There is no other punishment apart from death because anything less is still life, and so it's no punishment. To shoot a swine of an officer in the back is in our eyes not a wicked deed but simple retribution. Swines shouldn't live when decent people die.

Oldie and Shepel were good mates, they immediately hit it off though they weren't from he same town.

"I understand. We won't touch him," I tell him.

"Did you come here with the medic?" he asks.

"Yes."

"Have we got many wounded?"

"None, just sick. The war is coming to an end now."

"Too bad, I really wanted to go home," Oldie says.

"We won't leave you behind. If need be we'll tear this shitty Khankala to pieces, but we won't leave you. You're coming home with us."

Oldie makes a tired gesture. He has let himself go since he's been here. Maybe Shepel's death broke him somehow or maybe he's just worn out by it all.

"To hell with the lot of them," he says. "It doesn't matter any more. The main thing is that we are alive. I don't care about anything else. After all, a few years behind bars is still a few years of life, isn't it?"

"They can send you down for seven years on these charges, you know."

"So what . . . It doesn't matter any more."

We smoke another cigarette and then it's time to go. We push a few packs of smokes through the window and head back to the hospital where the transport is waiting for us. Fixa and I turn and see Oldie watching from the window.

We won't leave him behind.

The battalion leaves for Kalinovskya where we are to be discharged. For us, the war is over.

It starts to rain. The tyres of the vehicles squeal on the wet asphalt and rainbows glimmer in spray thrown up by the wheels. I open the hatch and stick my face out under the rain. Large drops fall straight and evenly on my skin. The sun hangs heavily on the horizon and our column casts long shadows in its rays.

And that's it. Peace. This warm, damp day is the last day of our war. Shepel's dead. And Igor, Khariton, Four-Eyes, Pashka, Vaseline, Fly, Yakovlev, Kisel, Sanya Lyubinsky, Kolyan, Andrey . . . Many of them, a great many.

I remember all of my comrades; I remember their faces, their names. At last we have peace, lads, we waited for it so long, didn't we? We so wanted to meet it together, go home together and not part company until the whole platoon has been to everyone else's home. And even after that we should stay together, live as one community, always close, always there for each other.

What will I do without you? You're my brothers, given to me by the war, and we shouldn't be separated. But we'll always be together. We still have our whole lives ahead of us. I stand up to my waist in the hatch. Large raindrops roll down my cheeks and mix with tears. For the first time in the war I cry.

Hey, Kisel, Vovka! How's it going, Igor, Shepel? Hi, guys.

I close my eyes and cry.

The runway is deserted. Warm rain falls.

Translated by Nicholas Allen

Denis Osokin (b. 1977)

Ludo Logar, or Duck Throat

1.

At the end of my wits on a December evening, when it was already dark, I asked my Mari friends to find me the phone number of a person who could "stop a duck's throat"—and when I got the number, I called. Her name was Dina—she lived in Paranga—in the district capital two hundred and fifty kilometers from Kazan. Her voice was like a bell—although they told me that Dina was many years old. I know well these voices that sound younger with years—I heard them more than once during my expeditions—in the homes of those able to assist others. Dina, too, seemed to have recognized me—she exclaimed, surprised, wondering where she knew me from?—and she said: Come, of course! Come now! You will spend the night at my house. We'll start right away! I help those who are kind. And you are kind.

2.

At the time of this conversation, my house twinkled with alcohol like a Christmas tree with the most enchanting garland, shaped by the most skillful hand. I saw something before my eyes—something forgotten ever since the time when those close to me were nearby—and had not hidden themselves from me, far away and silent. But I knew that I would find them when I set out to look. For example, under the mattress in the child's bed, there is definitely a certain something—of the necessary flat shape. Behind the icons in every case—aha!—it would be there, only there were no icon cases in my house. Behind photographs in family albums. In a box for wedding rings. In new shoes—bought for that Australian film ceremony not long ago, where, blinded with joy and spotlights on stage, I clutched my statuette and bouquet, wished everyone a long life together with our loved ones, as the translator gently scowled and translated. In addition, that afternoon I had called a couple of alcoholic-sexual emergency services. And this is not the kind of emergencies that put you on an I.V. drip and give you a sleeping pill—rather, vice versa. They chided me, they were through with work, there was the evening traffic jam, but nevertheless they were already on the way. And I dream of placing a monument to them in some beloved alley of the city as a sign of my respect and affection. If need be, I will be their most ardent defender in the world to come. But at the same time, if we were to meet right now—as usual, I would plunge myself into moral hell for at least several years. A dove landed on my balcony to die. In the kitchen and the bathroom, little mosquitoes danced—I tried to put off for later the question of how they came to be in my house at the beginning of winter and simply drove them away from the food. All the pillows were already on the beds, like dead old men and children. The darkness was already swaying and was just about to sing. The corridors of silence had already opened and lay in all directions—I saw their inhabitants crowding around my temples. The doggish odor under my nose—a sure sign of trouble—could not be washed away by any soap. Sometimes it flowed into the smell of shit—and then back. Thus smells an army of demons that closely surrounded me—I know them well. And jackdaws—gray, black, and a few big white ones—flapped and sobbed around my windows for a long time.

3.

Gyorgiy came to me before anyone else. I dialed him immediately after the call to Dina and found the words to convince him to set everything aside and go with me to Paranga—to have a friendly shoulder nearby—because alone I could not stand the displacement. We ran out of the entrance, went to a neighbor's yard at my suggestion, and called a taxi there. When emergency services arrive for me and can't get into the apartment—they will decide that I'm asleep and will be less disappointed than if I had canceled my request. Being asleep and not hearing a knock at the door or the phone ringing—that's acceptable, because that's how things go. They curse me at the door—they pound on it—and go off somewhere—smiling and wishing me a long sleep, an early escape to dry land of health and strength—especially since they have the best food and drink on earth in their bags, which will not abandon them like I just did. We drove down the street to my parents—they came out of the foyer—gave us money and hugged me. My mother gave me a blessing, my father smoked. In the tundra they use the verb "to stretch" correctly with the meaning of "to go." So here we are—stretching toward Dina. We still have a long time to disentangle ourselves from the loops of the city's winter sweater—until we get to the northern bypass road and speed up. And then we spend three hours on dark slippery roads of the four kingdoms—their capitals on a high mountain, in a Greater Atna, in Morki and in Paranga. To my great joy, the driver was silent. Just the sound of the road and the radio.

4.

"Ludo logar"—what does this mean? When a person on his journey starts to drink—and continues up until the last thread that connects him to life—and does not stop until even this one starts to break—and often there is, along with that, a sea of activity, all sorts of love and wonderful plans for the future—the Mari believe that someone unkind has poured something through the throat of a duck. In a direct physical sense poured—through a cut in the duck's windpipe. From the bottle through the windpipe into the glass—and somehow caused him to drink. And while pouring made a wish: just as the duck cannot do without water—so this person now cannot do without drink. And the duck is the creator of the world, the duck is beauty and good. To be compelled to turn her into a curse—there's nothing more terrible. And furthermore, the person who has become "ludo logar"—with the duck's throat—begins to chase away his life—often in the shortest possible time. Unless someone stronger plugs up that duck's throat. I did not at all think that this would be my case. It's somehow a sin to put the responsibility on the duck's throat. But I thought: I'll meet with Dina—and we'll get to the bottom of this. The main thing is to do something. After all, I had behind me all the drug and alcohol rehabs our city and republic possessed. Rehab and I, we have long been ugly lovers—those who do not so much love each other as they torment each other, suffer, await a dirty trick, have no trust, and are angry. Traces of our questionable relationship covered my entire body. We were silent. Gyorgiy sometimes tapped my foot and said: how are you, buddy? I answered him: fine, thanks.

5.

Dina was talking in a kind of stew made of the Mari, Tatar, and Russian languages—that is, made from the Finno-Ugric, Turkic, and Slavic universes, cooked in a Parangian pot, perfect for this business. Above all, I believed in it—in my beloved land. And I asked for her help. And in Dina I expected to discover a sensitive guide, connected to this land. So it was. She was so happy when we came in. Red eyebrows—white kerchief. She said to me: while you were driving here—I remembered who you are! You are a good person, many Mari people know you, I've read about you in the newspaper. You wander around a lot, this is why you found the Demon. And she bowed deeply to Gyorgiy with these words: if only there were more people on earth like you. I will not take money from you: I have a daughter in Kazan studying in the medical school—and I do not take money from Kazan people. We had supper. Then she and Gyorgiy set up a sofa in the guest room. He stayed there to read the householder's *Ivanhoe*—and I went back to the kitchen with Dina. All night until dawn she burned juniper in a small frying pan on the stove. We worked like this—for twenty minutes Dina read aloud and silently over me, touching and not touching me with her hands and stomach, while I was sitting barefoot on a stool. Then forty minutes of rest on the beds. I got into bed carefully, so as not to wake Gyorgiy. Then another twenty minutes in the kitchen. Time flew, I saw how the hands of the clock on the side table moved. We finished about seven in the morning. Then we lay down and slept almost until noon. We ate breakfast and smiled. Me, Gyorgiy and Dina. Gyorgiy was telling us something about his teaching work. I don't remember at all what we ate. Although I do remember something—tea, mackerel, honey. I asked—with what words should I leave, what should I remember most of all? Dina said: the most beautiful thing in the world is the word spoken in time. I liked that very much. I thanked her. Just after eating I suddenly had a tremendous need to sleep—as if hands as strong and brown as an alder tree had broken out from the ground through the floor, grabbed my head and pulled it in. Dina said: this is the best I could have expected. You will recover. Lie down right here—where it pulls you. That night, Dina began to address me with the familiar "you." I slid from the table to the floor—I remember it stood there on its four friendly feet—and immediately disappeared for an hour and a half. It was something like rebooting a computer after it had been infected with a virus. Later

Dina told me—it meant that many Demons died. But you must take care of yourself.

6.

We left Paranga from the bus station—on the regular bus, which was small, white, and long, for which we waited a long time. I was fragile and terrific. I don't know what to compare myself with. With a tractor made of mica? A bicycle made of feathers and parakeet bones? A bridge over the Kama river in the steep mountains—made of ice as thin as a spider web? But these are all rough comparisons. Gyorgiy was nearby. I said to him: Buddy! Thank you! I very much hope that this trip will not end up as just another interesting ethnographic expedition. Gyorgiy replied: I hope so, too. And the bus went on and on. Stopping sometimes in roadside villages to take on and let off people. There were lots of empty seats. And behind us a very young woman fed a huge boy from her two huge breasts. The bus shook on the asphalt potholes and on big slabs of ice—and the boy lost his hold on the breasts and screamed. She calmed him down in a mix of Tatar and Udmurt. Gyorgiy slept—and I did not sleep and was happy. And I remembered all the words of gratitude that I knew in all the languages of the middle Volga. I felt melancholy. But this melancholy was the bitter taste of almonds. I felt sorry for myself and for people. But that pity was made of dry fragrant juniper—it inspired the heart, and did not sink into it with a paralyzing guilty taste.

7.

Two girls came on the bus—they took seats right in front of us, slightly to the left. Eighteen years. High cheekbones, with tinted hair. They took off their hats, unwrapped their scarves, each stuck one white ear bud in an ear from a shared source, took out a horrible pinkish gin and tonic drink in a one-and-a-half-liter bottle, which they'd already been drinking before they got to the bus. They sipped and babbled about their studies in the school in Atna, about their room in the dorm, using male and female names— Rezedushka, Alfiyushka, Azatik, Genka, Ruslan . . . they got drunk very quickly, began to fall asleep one after another, dropped their headphones, their hats, gloves, bags, on the floor, and the almost empty bottle which rolled in my direction, but then rolled forward. Several times I picked up their cellphones with pendants in the form of turtles and dotted with multicolored decals of a treble clef, and put them on one of them, the one who sat closer to me, on her knees, I put them into a hat, so they wouldn't fall again, not right away, but they kept falling, because the bus kept shaking. They were local beauties—maybe not for the covers of fashion magazines—but the desire for such as they are is raised up to the sky by the world tree depicted by Kazan artists and personally by me, they were the absolute Mari ducks to whom I had always prayed. I truly admired them!

8.

I looked at them intently and imagined that after a few well-known turns off the road, Greater Atna and its tall red mosque would appear—and they would get off and I imagined what would happen to them in the evening. They'll keep falling down, but they'll reach their destinations, fall asleep while sitting on the toilet, and collapse without wiping, then they will invite guests, then lie down with them or with each other, their bodies will shine out to all our Middle Volga-Vyatka emirates—and all our flags will be excited by them. Or everything will happen differently—but even more tragically. I saw them straight on and loved their bodies. I wildly wanted them. And I thought I could get off with them—and for a time ride on their wave. And we'd survive—taking care of each other—all that they were ready for, like apples ready to fall into the grinder and become pudding. Especially if they aren't ready for anything at all, but on the contrary—they would greatly wish to avoid it—now or later. They were darling and strong—no less than Dina. Only they were a different color. I quickly came up with a name for them—the black agates. Are black stones uglier than yellow or white? Even thinking that way was ridiculous. Black agate. Black jade. Black obsidian . . . I thought I could wear only these. So then, these sleeping girls of the Ilet River, smelling of booze—they are those precious jewels that I would choose for my body. Because all of this is what is most visible to me, smoke of my earth. Because all of this—the very same springtime slope cut by ravines and beloved to the point of bouncing higher than any mosque. The same wet arable land. And black structures in the graveyards. From all this, my heart flies over all the world, released from its black slingshot. And united with a black slingshot and gray smoke it gives birth gives birth! Because my heart is honey yellow, with green veins. I was like thawing water in the hollows now to them—to these fellow passengers. And they slept, drooling, dropped their telephones, and slid from their seats.

9.

All this is wonderful. But my banners! Like cleaning the glass, washing away the traces of a long rain knocking on the windows as the lime tree blossoms—the girls from Ilet dissolved Dina. Dissolved Dina's juniper, stomach and words, and our great saving night without sleep, in which everyone who loves me believes. In which I also believe. My kind great white god. There is not any protection. Except in lone human defenselessness. And that is the only reason one can hope to save oneself. Human life is only five or six or seven times longer than the trip, by bus, from Paranga to Kazan. And who will protect the defenseless?—no one. Which means that one simply cannot allow oneself to fall into the abyss. Only complete defenselessness ultimately turns into a fortress. Only the defenseless are truly protected. Because how can it be otherwise?—it absolutely cannot be otherwise. Dina is no stronger than the black agates—nor any weaker. I love them equally. They are beloved, to me and to each other. Besides, they are not black agate—just girls from the village of Ilet in the Paranga district of the Republic of Mari El, students from the district center of Greater Atna in the Republic of Tatarstan—Lena and Lyuda.

10.

My agates woke up in time. Somehow they collected all the stuff they had with them—and went off to Atninskaya Square—and they rocked and clung to each other like seaweed. We moved on. But from outside the windows came a wounded cry from one of them. This woke Gyorgiy. Through the rear window I saw one agate waving her arms—signaling the bus to stop, as the other covered her mouth. The driver saw—thought that they had forgotten something—and slowed down. The girls climbed back on. One crying, the other apparently scolding her. But taken together all this didn't sound like speech. The fact is that they had changed their minds and decided for some reason to go on to Kazan. They paid the driver. However, they didn't sit in their old seats, but right by the door.

*

Me ilena

Bez ale isen

Epir purnatpar-kha

Mi ulepes'.

Min' eriit'.

Min' shisotama.

Ma zhivoi ylyna.

My zhivy.

We are alive.[1]

**

Who will celebrate with me
a new book?

Kazan—2012, Kolomna—2013
Translated by Simon Schuchat

The New Shoes

1.

kapiton-kugyza, grandpa kapiton or uncle, an old man, more than seventy years old in a red sweater with a torn neck—a black hat—a black sheepskin coat. under the hat, blunt ears—and a stick in hand. he lives in shinsha, a sort of large village, near the paranga–morki road[2]—with his wife and daughter. he has five children—all long time on their own. his son mikhail is here in shinsha—his son vassily in nearby shurga—a daughter lily in the

---

1   The phrase is repeated in eight native languages of the Middle Volga—Field Mari, Tatar, Chuvash, Udmurt, Erzya, Moksha, Mountain Mari, and Russian.

2   Paranga and Morki are towns in the Mari El Republic in the Russian Federation. Osokin writes about life among the Mari people, one of the minority nationalities in Russia, who follow a pre-Christian, pagan religion.

capital yoshkar-ola—natalya in volgograd. the youngest, sashuk, has been very sick since childhood—never went anywhere or visited anyone. and kapiton's wife, alena, has been almost blind for five years. on saturday—the ninth of april—at seven twenty in the morning, kapiton went up to the road—got on the paranga bus—and went to morki to buy shoes.

kapiton is the eldest priest in shinsha. in the groves where the shinsha people pray, he is the most important. all the other priests obey him. kapiton would put on well-pressed trousers, a white shirt, a white felt cap. he would stand under the trees with the younger ones, set bonfires, put the people's offerings under birch and linden trees. set out honey and pancakes on the earth, hang new towels and scarves on the branches. goose and mutton in pots, about to be cooked. kapiton has been a *kugu onaeng*—an elder priest, not just in the shinsha groves, but the entire area. twelve years ago, in morki, during the summer festival, the *peledish-pairem*, the thirty-six morki priests voted—made him their elder.

kapiton certainly knows best about everything—about rituals and sacrifices and the prayers—with what words to feed the fire with honeyed-water, with what thoughts to pour water from the bucket onto the goose. Still alive, to be given to the gods, and what to whisper to cut off its head, before the women pluck the carcass. but the great prayers happen only twice a year. and apart from these two days, none of this is visible in kapiton—he lives and works around the house. now the bus was just getting packed—and the doors slammed shut.

kapiton squints, happy it is april. in the fields there is only a little snow left but it still fills the ravines. this bus, which now is carrying everyone, is so mud-splattered. both the bottom, and the glass. but nobody thinks badly of the driver, there's no need to wipe away the spring mud yet—there will be time. opposite kapiton sits lyudmilla, from sapunji, she's a bit cross-eyed, he feels sorry for the girl. kapiton remembers, as teenager, lying in the hospital in zvenigovo a cross-eyed girl loved him there—from the women's ward. she would try to catch him on different floors and he would run away from her. they are all very kind—the cross-eyed, thinks kapiton, and smiles to lyudmilla. and lyudmilla smiles back to him.

about an hour to go to morki, maybe a little less. bus jumps on the broken asphalt. a *kurgania*[3] runs behind the bus on the wet roadway, but kapiton doesn't see it. on great friday—in motley old clothes—the *kurgania*

---

3   This is the principal god of the Mari.

is the most restless and curious of the gods in the shinsha village grove. neither man nor woman. always different, at least different. for *kurgania*-friday, it's very important that kapiton go the district center and buy some nice, comfortable, inexpensive shoes. and return to shinsha, by three o'clock.

2.

there's something about this saturday—about this april. kapiton rides on to morki—and in shinsha it's as if everybody woke up on the wrong side of the bed—of their beds, to be more precise. everyone is unfocused, slow, and thinking about kapiton and his shoes, as if these shoes were the most important thing in their lives. some saw kapiton as he walked to the bus in the morning—others heard from somebody. the sun might be especially warm, pouring onto the head like the flavor of spring?—or does the sky have a fragrance?—connecting with the smell of the earth, it pulls at the heart—with something common to everyone? the shinsha people are surprised themselves, they laugh at themselves. they do various household tasks—play with the kids, or run after the kids, or drink or kiss. and racing through the heads in every shinsha house, spinning and spinning: elder kapiton went off to buy shoes. okay, so then what?

the wife of tolya, club director, works in the store—not the one close to the highway, but the other, opposite the village council. even before lunch, she suddenly locked up the store, ran home, and said to her husband: tolya, yesterday we got a weeder from morki. go look at it—maybe we need to buy one? he eats his soup and looks at his wife. elder kapiton is in morki, he's looking for shoes, he says, and then eats, smears bread with totally dried up adjika.[4] what sort of weeder is it? he finally asks.—well, like this, with a handle, a narrow iron head on a long handle.—and how much is it?—thirty-five rubles.—well, if you need it, buy it. it's not expensive. why should i go get it.—well, let's go together—it's better together.—well, let's go. they put on their shoes, out they go, they walk down the street. both speaking russian, "weeder." just try to say that in the mari language.

elder leonid—leonid ageyevich is also an *onaeng*, also a priest, also an elder, but junior to kapiton. he's sitting, sitting at home, drinking tea with a salad. and a little bit more of that "peasant" stuff—that is, moonshine. suddenly he puts on a white prayer shirt, trimmed with red, pins on a white

---

4   A spicy Georgian dip.

priest's cap, looks around the room, takes a bunch of pancakes, puts them in a bag, takes a piece of meat out of the soup, thinks that this one is too small, puts it back, for some reason grabs wooden abacus from the table, and sticks all this into the same bag. switches on the radio, a crackling sound. turns off the radio, goes out. mud in the courtyard, dog's chicken's and people's tracks—everything sparkles in the sun. thinks to catch the chicken, bring it along, but changes his mind, it's all right. leonid, a package in his hand, really wants to get up and go off on his hunting skis, but there is almost no snow, in some spots it's dirty in others it's dry—but after all its earth. leonid ageyevich is blinking—he almost cries. but then he comes down, very decisively, off the porch—he puts on his skis in the shed—and strides around the village toward the shinsha sacred grove. his house is on the outer edge of shinsha, the grove is right by the road, and no one will see him. he goes—unbuttoned, breathing, chooses the drier side of the road. kapiton went to get shoes, kapiton went to get shoes. whispering.

veniamin was watching tv at home, some comedy program. he and his wife laughed hard at it, as did their high school daughters. veniamin was going to heat the bathhouse, so he and his wife could both wash. he thought to finish the show and start the bath. but instead, he says to his wife: i'll be right back. and he gets up from the chair.—yes, just wait 'til it ends, the wife said, and burst into laughter. veniamin came out of the yard and went off fast. he went all the way through shinsha, up to the road, and walked toward morki. before that he bought a bottle of spirits in the store—the sweet kind that he never drank. veniamin was a physical education teacher in the shinsha school. the comedy program had been over for a long time, and veniamin's wife went out to the courtyard, then came back, and said to her youngest daughter: well, go to uncle kapiton's and look for your father.—but uncle kapiton went to morki, the daughter answered.—yes, yes, you're right. so, go heat the bath, then.

kapiton's eldest son—mikhail—the one who lives in shinsha—his wife was cleaning fresh fish by hand, now she had started to make fish soup. she finished the fish, sprinkled on dry spices and herbs, and left the kitchen. mikhail came in from the hallway, and sniffed—it turned out well. hey, wife, he says, bring me my hat.—white or gray? asks the wife from the other room.—and where are you going?—bring the gray. although, no, go get me the white—the one which i wear in the grove. mikhail's wife went back into the kitchen, past the kitchen doorstep. mikhail was standing on the threshold—already wearing shoes, holding a pot of fish soup in both hands. he tilted his balding head toward his wife and said: put it on.—where are you taking the soup? planning to eat it?—the wife wants to ask, but she hesitates, because her mikhail is also a priest, who knows why he needs her fish soup. so she just opens the door for her husband, then the gate. she took out a cigarette from his jacket—put it in the corner of his mouth—took out matches—lit it, and now mikhail smokes. she asks anxiously: so your father is coming today? mikhail, already on the street, turns to her and smiling his toothless smile, says, valenka, don't be afraid. i'll make you some more of your little fish soup.

today is a day off—and vitaly semyonovich—who is also a priest by the way and works at the mill—first thing in the morning, when he heard about kapiton going off for shoes—he went to the mill, changed into his flour spattered work clothes—and started up the mill. such a roar inside. vitaly runs out onto the street and sniffs the air. then back, listens to how the machine's croaking. he ran like that, then sang the beautiful song "avai"—(it means "mommy")—then took off his cap—(the kind of cap which construction workers wear under their hard hats in winter)—knelt and walked around the mill three times on his knees, kissed the ground, kissed the cap, kissed the wall, too—and said with tears in his voice: a white, white, white swan—a white sun—white, white mill-engine—let my family laugh along with me for a long time—and kapiton will return from morki with new shoes. hatless, vitaly stands on the ground. all shinsha can be seen easily from the mill—transparent light pours down on top of it—shinsha signals to him with its saturday bath smoke.

if you look into any house in shinsha—or take anyone in the street—you'll see a similar, absurd caress.

3.

kapiton jumped off the bus in morki like a schoolboy. he limps—but goes quickly to the market. he walks among the rows of stalls and looks around. greets someone with a handshake. and unexpectedly he thinks to himself: scary, somehow to buy shoes. very very scary. it would be good to wear them for a long time—you wouldn't have to die in them. in which world, this or that one, will i have to run in them? new shoes—you can't imagine anything more serious. buying new shoes—it's like flipping a coin. it would be better if it were not spring—it would be better to come to the market in winter to look for shoes. these were the thoughts he found. but in fact one needs spring shoes. new shoes are the heart. it's kapiton's heart—in a white box lying somewhere nearby—probably with some more rubbish written on the box. the *kurgania* is somewhere nearby—it drags its stilts along behind it—can't walk on stilts through the market—but it stood up all the same—it bites its lip and looks at kapiton alarmingly. kapiton walks slower and slower.

what are these thoughts why this alarming?—kapiton is surprised.—or is it only during the strange days of spring that buying shoes causes so much anxiety? and there will be joy, too? but the april sun warms up all of the morki market—and kapiton as well, who has pulled his cap off his head—and stands between the rows swaying like a waterlogged horse-tail—he looks around—twists the button of his sheepskin coat—twists and turns—until, broken, it falls off. kapiton suddenly saw, more clearly than ever, how he will lie in a red russian coffin in his dark-blue suit in a winter fur hat (as is the custom among the mari) with a bunch of rosehip flowers in his fist, in these new shoes that he hasn't yet bought. and kapiton began to cry. on a saturday morning there are a lot of people in the market—jostling against kapiton—so he doesn't stand there—he breaks away and begins to swim along the rows of stalls. kapiton walks along the market howling—elder kapiton—senior priest of shinsha and the whole morki district. swimming along, looking at new shoes.

kapiton was lost—lost his way—doesn't know—but guesses—that the reason for everything might this certain fineness—which takes possession of the world on some mornings and evenings on the edge of march into april. when the sky disappears—and having disappeared penetrates completely into the head—when the earth tenses and pulls at you especially strongly. not everywhere and not always—but in morki it's more or less like that. kapiton doesn't yet know what is going on in shinsha. someone takes kapiton by the elbow. he looks back—everything in front of his eyes is sparkling—his blood pressure is rising: lyudmila. she is taller than him. elder kapiton, she says, what's the matter with you?—help me buy shoes, liuda.—and what are you looking for?

kurgania turned away—so as not so much to worry so much about kapiton and lyudmilla—so as not to watch directly. it left—warily carrying its stilts. at the exit from the market it bought itself a mug of instant coffee—and a pig in blanket sausage. it will wait for them here.

4.

leonid ageyevich strode along the snowless earth in his hunting skis for a long while, although the grove was right here. what he really wanted was to feel the spring and slowness. sometimes on a pile of snow he would purposely turn—would stand—would sink—and mist would rise from the snow and from the earth—and from leonid ageyevich himself. the shinsha grove stood on a small hillock. at the hillock leonid-elder took off his skis—left them at the bottom—and bowing he began to ascend. here they are—all the elder trees. here are four tall legs-linden trees—that's the fifth big leg—a birch. here's a board at one of the lindens—on the board is written "mother of life. leonid petrov, *onaeng*"—this is the linden of the shochin ava, the mother of life—she who had a previous elder leonid. and here's kapiton's personal tree—a very old fir. two towels hang on its wet green branches. leonid put pancakes beneath her—loudly said a prayer—he asked all the various different spirits of the grove that kapiton would bring shoes to shinsha, and would wear them as long as he could. he took the wooden abacus from his package and looked at it with great love. he calculated—played on its bones how long he had been coming to this grove. a thousand—nine hundred—forty—six—(clicks): he first came here at the age of fifteen to give his first gifts to the gods. one thousand—nine hundred—sixty-six: he is already an assistant to the priest-*onaeng*. one thousand—nine hundred—ninety—two: since then he has been *onaeng* himself—before the senior mother-linden. so, elder leonid, having clicked this abacus—which he had from his parents—left it too on the warm holy ground—under kapiton's fir—next to the pancakes. a bird shrilled loudly, amusedly, not frightened. leonid's eyes were wet. forgive me, grove, for i had nip of moonshine—this morning i didn't know that i would come here. thinks. he scurried off—went back from kapiton's tree, following the same path that he came on. on his way he strokes the bark of the trees—touches wet hummocks of earth and thawing decaying leaves—sniffs his palms cautiously. passing by the linden tree of which he is the elder—he looks—under the board with his name lies something blue and shiny. he bent down—it is a folding shovel—brand-new—still with a store sticker. a blue shovel—handle unpainted. leonid took it in his hands—admiring it—and gently folded and unfolded it again. is it for me?—asking as he lifted his head. his head spun.

mikhail kapitonovich—elder mikhail—went out to the morki road with a pot—to the place from which kapiton had departed in the morning.

it's good that the fish soup had not cooled yet. he removed the lid. he bowed to the asphalt road in the direction of morki—and in the other direction, toward paranga. he bowed to shinsha—to the right. and to the left—toward the far-off field sloping slowly upwards with its lonely distant tree. then— squinting—he bowed to the sun. the sun is already seated high up—so it turned out he did not bow but nodded the back of his head—that's also permissible. altogether only five times. poured some soup on both sides of the road—in both directions—and a little bit, a thin little line, across the road. he turned over the empty saucepan—sat at the edge of the road—lit a cigarette and began to wait for his father. at three there should be a bus from morki. still a long time. but mikhail is in no hurry. but even if he were in a hurry, he would spit on everything. nothing now is more important than sitting here and waiting—looking toward morki.

if mikhail's eyes could follow the road around all the turns—he would see, six kilometers toward morki, how venya is moving—veniamin the phys ed teacher—his dear friend and his wife's close relative. yes, and veniamin, if he looked around and just looked back—he would see his brother-in-law misha in a priest's white cap sitting on the saucepan—and also be surprised. but mikhail does not know that veniamin decided to dedicate to his father's new shoes his own long walk from shinsha to morki. and veniamin doesn't know that for the very same reason mikhail poured his sister's own tasty soup on the road.

and the mill is nearby—it's also beside the road. mikhail thinks: what's that buzzing?—today is saturday. vitaly semyonovich, in honor of kapiton's new shoes, is working hard—he tops off the bags of grain, he stitches sacks of flour on the floor. and animal fodder and bran. it's awkward alone—it's a job for two—and he runs up the iron staircase from the foundation— upwards. mikhail took off his boots—he took off his boots—and his socks. he sits on the very edge between the dirt and the asphalt. sometimes he gets up—he touches the ground with a very white bare foot—he rubs the warm asphalt.

tolya's wife—also a lyudmilla—quickly opened and removed the lock from the shop door—put the long latch down on the step—they both went in. this is an ordinary country store—in which on one side of the cash register there's vegetable oil, canned tomato paste and noodles—on the other side are nightgowns notebooks knives tops soft toys and here if you please for example the weeder. here it is—lyudmilla almost cried to her husband— she ran to the counter—and from there she handed it to tolya.—well, what do you say? tolya is looking carefully at the weeder—he doesn't know what to say. but what is there to say—well, let it be. the screw that holds the knife onto the handle is not completely screwed in—well, we'll tighten it at home. he looks at his wife—and behind the counter his wife is so happy before him. tolya smiled—it's all right, take it. lyudmilla replies: what do you mean take it? you buy it from me. tolya laughs: but i have no money. lyudmilla hands him hers—here you go. tolya says: give me, please, the weeder. lyudmilla says: pay me thirty-five rubles. tolya holds out the money: take it. lyudmilla stretched out her hand and he grabbed it. very slowly sunlight flows into the store—all the windows are uncovered—someone is knocking loudly on the porch—shaking off the clods of april mud from their boots. tolya left the store—and goes off—carrying the weeder under his arm— with which now he will never part. thinks: when i die—i'll ask for it to be stuck in my grave. god, how sweet it is. suddenly he wrinkles his brow— he thinks he may need to give it to kapiton—since he is the elder in the grove—he would always have it in his hands instead of a rowan-wood staff. he stopped: no i can't—maybe i'll lendit to him sometimes. he moves on— reaches the house—steeped in serious doubt.

5.

at the same time at the market in morki lyudmilla from sapunzha is hold-ing kapiton's arm—asks a cheerful young woman—whose kerchief has slipped down over her shoulders—unveiling a head of red hair: how much for shoes?—which ones do you want?—brown or black? kapiton nods.— black? kapiton shakes his head.—brown? kapiton nods again. the woman takes brown shoes with velcro ties and says, here, try them on uncle kap-iton—velcro is more convenient after all. don't you remember me? i'm lyuba, from lower yuplan. you hung my towel in the kuzhersky grove. take them—they're good—worth five hundred rubles. try them on!

she puts down two layers of cardboard for kapiton to stand on while he changes shoes—it's very dirty everywhere. kapiton can't bend over— his sheepskin coat is in the way. lyudmilla unbuttons his coat—takes it off—and holds it. in his red sweater the thin little kapiton takes off his boots—puts on the shoes—fastens them—stands up straight. lyuba asks so are they okay? kapiton says: yes, i think so. lyudmilla nods, they're very beautiful. kapiton leaned forward. velcro goes chik chik—he unfastens them. chik chik—he fastens the velcro. he says—we'll take them. lyuba was delighted and said, i still need to give you free polish and a shoehorn. she pulled a dazzlingly white empty box out from under the counter. she got out the polish—with a foam sponge in the lid. a small yellow plastic shoehorn. kapiton said: well, thank you. behind the market, the *kurgania*, after drinking a fifth cup of coffee, throws the empty container into the trash bin.

what time is it? almost twelve. and the bus to shinsha from morki is at two. you can certainly go out on the road—flag down a car—everyone always does that. but probably kapiton doesn't want to leave. he stepped out onto the street from the market. and lyudmilla was with him. she also traveled to the market—for a blouse. which she looked for but didn't find. she only bought a bar of soap—and some kind of detergent powder. sapun-zha is right after shinsha—so they can take the same bus. lyudmilla is not in a hurry either. so she and kapiton start to walk around morki. they walk and walk. they look in all the stores, agricultural supplies, the pharmacy— and the photographer's shop—where lyudmilla buys some "konica" film. they get some coffee to drink from the stalls on the street—something to eat—probably also something doughy. in one hand elder kapiton holds his stick—in the other a box fastened with twine. the *kurgania*, on stilts, walks behind them, sometimes without stilts. kapiton put his sheepskin coat back on—didn't zip it up. lyudmilla has on a red down jacket—with spattered bottom—beautiful shoes—and woolen tights—a hat she took off in the market—lyudmilla's hair is light red, too—like lyuba's—a sparkling zipper bag on her shoulder—in her hand a black bag with solid handles. kapiton thinks, if not for lyudmilla, how would i have survived this market?—and if i survived—would i have found the road back to shinsha?—or would some-one have had to take me back like a baby? lyudmilla squints.

it is unclear how it happened, but they missed their bus. obviously, they liked morki on a warm saturday, with two and even five-story build-ings here and there, flags on the buildings of the district administration and the district court, the schools and the twenty-fourth college, the kiosks and gas stations. having become more cheerful, kapiton likes to think that although he doesn't have his office here—he is also an elder—and here is his capital—and that the morki people love him. it is pleasant to smile at thememory of how he was standing in the grove, ten years ago in the med-ical white coat given to him by a paramedic relative—the younger priests were wearing them, too—at the time there were no sacred white garments edged with rowan tree lines. and his blind wife alena, who now as always sits on the couch behind the stove curtain and watches without seeing the white oven, kapiton laughs at the memory: her hearing was healthy—like a bear.—he thinks of his wife like that, for some reason, in russian, and sees a photo of alena as a bride, in heavy breastplates with the family silver—and heavily ornamented legs, dressed up for the wedding. so they walked along; sat on benches on plastic bags. they arrived at the bus station—the bus was already gone. next one at seven in the evening. that's okay—they stayed a little while at the bus station—and went to the road. right away, they caught a "breadloaf" minibus going to parangu. they got in and took off. kapiton was in front with the driver—lyudmilla sat behind them. ten minutes later they passed veniamin—almost running to morki. kapiton was surprised— but did not ask the driver to slow down or signal.

an hour earlier on the road near the village of chinga veniamin saw the bus from morkov to shinsha—on which he thought kapiton would be rid- ing, with the shoes. immediately he waved his hands—the bus slowed—he called to kapiton—no kapiton. the driver said he hadn't seen kapiton—and the shinsha guys on the bus also confirmed that he had not ridden back. veniamin would expect that kapiton went home long ago—found a ride. but he was so concerned—he said "oy, god forbid," and ran to the market in morki. past morki—to the cigarette and beer kiosk. at the kiosk—on great friday—the *kurgania*. hey, venya!—it shouts.—don't run—kapiton bought the shoes, and left on a minibus to parangu.

6.

kapiton stands on the asphalt—on a side street off the main street and roof- tops of shinsha—with a blindingly white box—in which the shoes knock. it's a very loud and sharp knock—because after all it's his heart. kapiton is not sure whether it belongs to him alone. brown shoes with velcro—they are his exactly. and his heart may be shared, it may belong to shinsha—or the entire morki district—since he's here as *kugu onaeng*—senior priest. but who knows? he squints again—eyes follow the "breadloaf" minivan with lyudmilla from sapunzha. mikhail stands up from his saucepan. he does not say anything to his father. but he sees. nearby, vitaly semenovich shuts down the mill.

a man with new shoes in a box: undiluted horror with undiluted joy: but the living try not to think about what's bad. out of this living struggle horror and joy melt into each other—and the heart is born. we need another april—as a necessary laboratory. but not its every day. neither every one— nor only one. but this second saturday in april this year in shinsha was this way. and other similar days must have been like it and will be. kapiton puts his hand in his jacket pocket. there is a bar of soap—in morki, for some reason, lyudmilla went and put it in there. on the soap was written: "absolute." kapiton shuddered—and came down from the asphalt paved road.

7.

new shoes with shoe polish and shoehorn—a blue folding shovel—a weed-er—a long way at a half run along spring asphalt—fish soup poured out on the road—the mill working on saturday—the friday god on stilts—"abso-lute" soap—a wooden abacus left under the fir—the eyes of lyudmilla from sapunzha . if there is no connection, and—set aside the "shoes" for now and re-read this list between march and april. morning or evening? the connecting figure will emerge in a flaming burst. a figure typical of spring, now clear, now melting away.

8.

all evening until nightfall people from morki called kapiton, everyone who didn't see him themselves with the box—everyone it seemed called. even from krasny steklovar, mashnur, maskanur—and pamashol.[5] did uncle kap-iton buy shoes?—yes, yes.—did uncle kapiton buy shoes?—yes, yes—and they gave me shoe polish and a shoehorn.

much later—almost eleven—a dog barked at kapiton in the yard— there was someone knocking at the window of his house. kapiton sleepily looked out—then he stepped outside. tolya stands with a weeder and a huge pie. a fish-pie with canned mackerel. he had no time to catch fresh fish. besides, some of these canned fish—mackerel or sardines—are, by the way, delicious. kapiton-elder—do not be angry with me—i told you i can't give you the root extractor. please don't be angry—please take this pie from me and lyudmilla.

---

5   All towns in the Mari El Republic.

9.

and veniamin came home from somewhere around the same time. his clean and flushed wife and daughter were watching tv. there was laughter again. his wife says: go wash up—there's a towel there for you. walking across the yard from the porch to the bath venya hears a strange and often quite strong crackling—somewhere very close to his head. he thinks the sky over shinsha is splitting open—everyone is very tired from today. venya even pulled the cigarette out of his mouth—lifted his head—listening. but it's no longer there—the crackling is heard no longer. then venya realized—this was the crackle of his cigarette—the paper was burning each time he inhaled. how quiet it is here.—thinks venya.—after morki.

Morki, 2005

Translated by Simon Scuchat

Maria Boteva (b. 1980)

Where the Truth Is

Of course, I was never pulled off a freight train, I lied about that, but the others believed me for some reason, even though I'd never done anything like it. It's funny, you can make up all sorts of things, and people will believe you, like when Legs lied to Zoika about his fatal illness so she'd think he wouldn't get drafted. She believed him and, as a result, fell in love with him with all her soul without being afraid that they'd soon be separated, though it was obvious, if it was a fatal illness, that they'd be separated anyway soon enough. The fact that she was so calm made no sense at all. Maybe she just wanted to think they'd never be separated, and so she kept thinking it. What'd she see in Legs anyway? Marty was much better, I mean, if you compare them, Legs didn't make any sense. And then the draft card came, the order to appear for a medical examination, and he came back completely drunk and the next morning lay motionless for half the day. And it was only later that everyone found out why he got so loaded: the committee confirmed his illness, he got the exemption, it was true; they conducted a bunch of tests, and after every test or procedure he'd come home trashed, and, with his illness, this was absolutely forbidden. In the end they put him in the hospital for testing, but after a while the doctors themselves got tired of it, because Legs made a terrible patient: it wasn't just that he didn't fit on the bed, he was always walking back and forth through the hallway all day long, smoking on the sly, arguing with the nurses, all because of nerves. What's more, Zoika started coming and standing under his windows every day. It was November, and she'd be there in a jean jacket and a short skirt without a hat. The doctors would chase her away, tell her to go home, and she'd leave to warm herself in the deli for a half an hour and then be standing there again. They had to let her into Legs' hospital room, otherwise they'd be stuck treating her kidneys, too, like they needed that. Here, everyone in the entire city gets treated at this hospital, there was nowhere else to go, the doctors already know everyone, and so they knew Zoika wet the bed until she was five, when they cured her kidneys, so they knew that if she stood around in the wind in November it'd be the same shameful spectacle again. Then the school started sending for Zoika. It was no joke: here it was, ninth grade, graduation, and she was loitering around the hospital. Legs' old homeroom teacher even came out to convince him to chase her away. But what was it to him? He's sick, he loves Zoika, she loves him, and that's all there is to it. They both suddenly realized that they didn't have much time left together, and so they were soaking up every last minute. None of us outside the hospital believed it, that Legs didn't have much time left. People'd say: uh huh, he's made all sorts of trouble, and now he's kicking the bucket just to get out of it, what if everyone did that? But he came back from the hospital after the testing and showed everyone his test results saying that he didn't have long to live, so everyone had to believe him. And they had to forgive him, and forgive him for a lot, because he had made a whole bunch of trouble. Legs himself went from house to house with his test results asking for forgiveness. And if he couldn't come see someone right away he'd send Zoika to feel them out, and she'd start in a roundabout way: you should know, they say Legs is sick, the poor thing. The people she was visiting would say: yeah, poor thing. And Zoika says: as much dirt as he's done, well, now he's sorry, but the things he did are still there, after all, those things don't go away. And the people she's visiting say to her: come on, we've almost forgotten, really. Zoika says: maybe you could say that to him, yeah? They'd say: really, what's there to say? And the next day or even the same evening Legs would come with beer or port wine, and that was it, everything would be taken care of. Everyone would forgive Legs: even grandma Niura, who he shot with little pieces of wire with a slingshot and who didn't leave her house for two weeks because of the bruises, she forgave him, too. To tell the truth, Legs was a real monster before his illness.

But now everything changed. He even came to me to ask for my forgiveness, not right away, it's true. He dragged it out to the very end, though no one ever ended up seeing his end, his final minutes: he kept living and living, only he was always getting some treatment or other. Marty and I kept wondering whether he would come or not, or, rather, my brother did, he kept thinking about it. I didn't care, I had already forgotten that Legs was guilty because of what he did to me, even more than with anybody else, I mean, I hadn't forgotten, but somehow I didn't really dwell on it. If you're always thinking about people who screwed you over, you won't have time for anything else. By the way, Legs could have come to us a long time ago. He'd already figured out a long time ago that no one was going to press charges, he even came to see me with chocolate right after that incident, but Marty didn't even let him in the gate. He would have beaten him up, but Legs fell down after the first blow, then got up on his knees and almost fell over. He was bleeding. Marty turned away, he felt really terrible, later he said that he'd almost puked his guts out. And Legs just kept standing there for all to see, the chocolate in his hand, bawling like a baby: he really didn't want to go to prison. My brother kept looking and looking at him. He wanted to beat him up, but I kept shouting down from the window, telling him not to. He got tired of it and left, but Legs kept standing there for about five minutes before leaving, with a kind of funny walk: his legs had gone numb and were all tingly inside. And I never did press charges, although Marty kept grumbling about it for a long time. If it had been anything else he would have yelled about it, but not in this case, and I had nothing to wear all winter long: my coat had gotten so covered in creosote and something else that I burnt it right away. True, Marty sold his computer and bought me a new pink coat, a real pretty one. It's still hanging in the closet: my brother won't agree to sell it back, he thinks I'll wear it, but there's no way. Ever since, I've forgotten about coats, skirts, and pretty white blouses—I don't wear them any more. Sometimes at home I pull on the coat—after all, it really suits me—but I never go outside in it. And in general I try not to go out when it's dark outside. Marty picks me up in the evenings: we agree ahead of time about what streets we'll take, we have cell phones, after all. But I'm still afraid to dress up in something really feminine or to pierce my ears, let alone wear a skirt in the evening. Legs knocked that desire out of my head back then, when we ran into each other on the railroad tracks. Really, it would have been different, much better if I had cried out, but the thing was that I lost my voice in a single second, and all I could do was turn around and give him a little punch in the nose. It was a weak blow, it's true, because it was so unexpected: none of us had ever heard of something so low, attacking a girl from behind, touching her from behind. Nothing like that had ever happened. But back then Legs had only just moved to our railroad station. None of his relatives were railroad workers, none of them were from honest, working-class stock, and that's why he was always such a low-life. That's what everyone said, and that's how it was. But nobody knew just how much of a low-life he was. I was the first to realize it when I turned around to punch my attacker and saw that it was Legs. He also realized then who he had attacked, and that's why he threw me to the ground, I mean, onto the railroad ties (we ran into each other at the dead end at the station, where I was looking for my mom). He probably wanted to beat me to death so I couldn't tell anyone about him, and I wanted to yell at him, but my voice had disappeared and wasn't working. It was hot in my throat and all that came out was some sort of hoarse sound, and it was too bad, because there were some workers just a little ways off. He started to hit me and strangle me. I didn't really understand, but I was afraid, and I couldn't cry out or even raise a hand against him, although he wasn't holding my hands down or anything else, and now I think: maybe he was really only standing nearby? Somehow I can't remember very well. I couldn't kick him either: I walked into that dead end before the school dance, all dressed up in my long skirt. Who knew that kicking would come in handy? I needed to give Mom back her house key, because I had just lost mine and was walking around with Mom's. Legs kept choking me and choking me and suddenly he jumped up and ran away. Someone chased after him, but he managed to get away. Some men from Mom's work ran up to me, picked me up, asked me who it was, but I started to wail and didn't say anything to them. They let Mom off work early, and we left together. I kept wailing on the way home, but when I got home I suddenly wanted to cut off all my hair—it smelled real badly like the oil from the railroad ties—and I cut it off with Mom's little sewing scissors, really short, but it smelled anyway. I stuffed my coat into the stove piece by piece. Mama didn't yell at me, she helped. Small Fry helped, too. He was sad, too, and wanted to burn his coat, too, but Mom didn't let him. I wailed, and he hugged me from time to time and kept peeking into the stove to watch the flames burning the scraps. Marty came home in the evening, found out about everything and yelled real loud, howled, the walls even shook, and the tub on the stove, too: who was it?! But I didn't want to answer him, and besides, I lost my voice again. The same thing would repeat itself again later, whenever I remembered that encounter, I'd lose it. Now it's not so bad, now I just have dreams sometimes, I don't remember what they're about, but I feel like my voice is gone. But otherwise it's not so bad, it's all behind me, and my hair has grown out, too, but that evening Marty shaved my head with his razor. Really, he'd bought it for himself, his first one, but I really couldn't stand to look at my noggin, so I asked him to shave me. I burnt my coat anyway, so I didn't have anything to go outside in, and by March my head already looked like a light-brown dandelion, because I have light-brown hair. Everyone in my family has light-brown hair, and none of us have any special features, so they would have had to look for me for a long time if I really had run away back then. But I didn't run away, because, first of all, I felt like Marty was right and I was really guilty, so I didn't go anywhere. And this time it was Legs who didn't give me away for lying right to Marty's face, and Marty didn't object that Legs had just lied to everyone about how he was about to die. And after I told him that I had forgiven him, as soon as I told him that, he said: well, now I can die. And so everyone was waiting for him to die any day now from his illness after this forgiveness of mine and what he said. Zoika was as pale as a ghost. But then something else entirely happened. Marty went to look for me, I didn't hear them talking, he told me this later, when she left. Maybe she was telling him something about Legs, but probably not, but maybe he figured it out by himself: this strategy of sending Zoika was well known, but maybe nothing like that actually happened. I don't know, Marty always told me very little about himself. Only when she left did I climb out of the closet and ask what she wanted. He answered, in a very sad voice, that I shouldn't have bothered sitting in the closet, but I only wanted to do what was best! He was thinking that she'd come into the house and stay for a little bit while I talked to her about homework. But I wanted them to be together, just the two of them, alone, for a while. To be honest, I don't have anything against Zoika, it would have been good if she had abandoned her views on Marty. All the more so, by the way, because it was her who had called him that, because he played chess better than everyone else at the tournament. She said it just like that: she said, well aren't you're a smarty! That's where the nickname Marty came from. That's how it all started, she said it not for no particular reason but with a kind of ecstasy, and why wouldn't she, he beat absolutely everyone! And then he looked at her, and that's how it all started with him. And that's why I thought that nothing bad would come of it if I hid in the closet and they had a relaxed talk, who knows, what if after Legs she started running around with my brother? But they didn't talk then or in the future. She stayed so faithful to Legs that she couldn't even say the littlest thing to someone on the side. It all ended with her coming up to me during the break before phys ed. and saying straight up: Legs wants to come see you. I said: let him. And they came to see me that very same day, literally right after class. Marty didn't show up until right before they left, they had just started to put their things on, we had just reached a truce, though I regretted that Zoika was still looking at Legs with the same devotion. She had already walked out onto the porch when Marty walked right up to Legs, raised his hand, and scratched his head lightly. What're you doin', we have truce,—Legs said to him and sniffled—a truce? A truce, a truce,—I said and realized what it meant. And that's when Legs announced that now he could die, but by then Zoika had gotten tired of waiting on the porch and started to peek back through the door into the house.

They left. But we stayed there, and I felt bad and uneasy, Marty, too, but just then Mom and Small Fry came back from the garden, and so we went to go on living somehow. We had to make dinner, our stepfather, Small Fry's dad, was returning from a flight in the evening. That evening, before going to sleep, Marty asked me: so this means you forgive him? And he went to his own room, I didn't even have time to answer him. And again, for the second time that day, I felt guilty toward him. And, for some reason, when I was talking to Legs I thought that I should also apologize to him, although there was no reason to. Or rather, I barely said anything and only listened to his apologies and words of repentance, but sometimes I said: well, come on, don't worry about it and on and on like that, especially when he got down on his knees and I picked him up. It's a good thing my brother didn't see that.

But what could I have done, you can't run up to Legs and say: you know, I thought about it and no, I don't forgive you, you shouldn't have bothered getting down on your knees, and your Zoika, well, your Zoika's a little idiot. And of course none of that's true. But Marty was offended. All the more so, because he had to see Zoika and Legs together again.

That's how it all happened. I was also offended that Marty didn't try to understand me. If it wasn't for that, I would have answered our stepfather some other way and no one would have gotten into any trouble. The next day I came right home from school without waiting for Marty. On Wednesday we get out of class at the same time, and I go by his school, wait five minutes, and we head off home together. But in the morning he didn't say hello to me, nothing, he only said: I'll prove to you that he's lying, put his mug with his unfinished tea on the table and went running off. I'd almost left, but just then our stepfather came in in his undershirt, he really doesn't like it when someone doesn't finish their tea and leaves it in their mug. He asked: who was it who didn't finish drinking their tea? Well it wasn't me, I said. And I left for school. I shouldn't have done that, I should have just taken the mug and washed it, I'd done it before, but not this time, because I was mad at my brother for not waiting for me and for not wanting to make up. After all, even if Legs lied that I had forgiven him, he solemnly promised that he wouldn't allow himself to do what he had done to any other girl, even if by some miracle he gets better, then especially he wouldn't do it. And Zoika will never be with Marty, only with Legs: she opened up to me when they came by. True, I didn't ask what would happen after, how could you ask that?

It continued in the evening, I mean, after school I went into my room and realized that my stepfather had been there. Sometimes he does that, comes into our rooms and looks to see if they are tidy. If he's unhappy about the table being a mess he'll go and knock everything off the table onto the floor, my alarm clock got ruined that way once. And this time my notebooks, books and unfinished scarf and knitting needles were lying on the floor, the ball of yarn unwound all over the floor. He didn't like that my clothes were hanging on the back of my chair, so he threw them on the floor and knocked the chair over, too. I quickly picked everything up, went to Marty's room, it was the same thing there, I wanted to tidy up his room, but just then my stepfather walked in and sent me to shovel snow around the porch and clear a path to the fence. When I was shoveling the path Marty came home, I wanted to tell him what was going on in his room and that our stepfather was mad, but I didn't have time: he started to tell me about Legs' forged medical papers. But I could care less, I was telling him: wait! Shut up a second! Shut up a second! But he kept talking and talking. I got mad and told him that I would run away if he couldn't understand anything, and then finally he was silent. I started telling him about his room and our stepfather, but my brother was silent and was looking at me with big eyes. That evening he would look at me that same way, but that was later, now it turned out that our stepfather was standing behind my back and heard everything, and that's why Marty was trying to find a way to get me stop to stop talking. Our stepfather ordered us to go inside, both of us, while he went to the garden to get Small Fry. We couldn't tell if this was good or bad. But anyway we were already in an idiotic mood, we started to argue and even got in a fight. I kept telling my brother that I would run away from home, that I really didn't need to take all this lecturing, and that I had done the right thing by not cleaning his room or washing his mug. After that I got dressed and left.

Where could I go? For starters, the lamp on our street hadn't worked for years, and there was snow on the ground. But there was nowhere to get lost: there were only two directions, there and back. And you never get lost if you walk along the river. There were fish and water in the river, you won't die of hunger. But it would be pointless to make it to the river, because it was far away, it was dark outside, and, anyway, I don't have a fishing rod or an axe to chop holes in the ice to fish. If you go along railroad tracks you'll never get lost, either. It's light there, you can get on some train there. That's why I headed that way. There was a freight train on the far tracks, I just had to walk past the engine without being noticed. But this was, so to speak, a well-trodden path, a lot of people bring coal here for the train furnaces, even though they sell it cheap to the railroad workers. It did in fact turn out to be a train with coal, headed south, so I was lucky, but only sort of, because I'd be sure to get dirty. Thankfully, the train had cars with heavy machinery, only who knows why they need heavy machinery down south. The earth is soft there, you can move it around with shovels. And coal is even more useless, it's warm even without it. True, I didn't even manage to climb into the shovel of the nearest backhoe: it was so strange, Legs was already asleep in it. I wanted to tell him to move over, after all, it'd be warmer with two people, but I was afraid that he had died of his illness, since he said that now he could die in peace, and that he came here out of pride so that no one would see his final minutes. Maybe I should have just left, I don't know, but I decided to stay and feel his pulse. He literally leapt up in the shovel! Completely, with his whole body! He looked at me with a wild gaze. It turned out he was alive. I asked why he was lying there, what, did you come here to die? But he just kept lying there and staring at me silently. He didn't say anything, why he was lying there, where Zoika was, where he was planning to go, he was kind of strange, all his life. Suddenly he started bawling, bawling genuine tears, lying there in the shovel. I started to drag him out of there, out of the shovel, but very gently, I was really afraid to break him. Who knows, maybe his bones had all but disintegrated. I was pulling on him, and he was bawling, that's how I found it all out, he told me everything. About the forged medical papers and how he drank with Violetta, the one who gives out medical papers at the hospital. It wasn't that he didn't want to join the army, he just didn't want to be separated from Zoika, and that was it, that was the answer. And now he was planning to run so that Zoika would always have a high opinion of him, but now, whatever may come, they would never be parted, because, first of all, they really did find something in him, nothing fatal, but, this is not surprising when one keeps lying in excavator shovels in the winter. Gradually he calmed down, and we walked toward our fate. Walking along the coal path we saw Marty, he was following my footsteps. When he was still far off, my brother started yelling at Legs to get away from me. But I lied to him that Legs had pulled me off the freight train because I was planning to run away. Zoika ran up and immediately hugged her dear one. Now she would never get away from him, there was no doubt about it.

Marty was silent the whole way home, and only at the gate did ask me, pretty much in the same tone, was it really true that Legs had pulled me off freight train. And I lied again that it was true, or else my brother would never have forgiven me for the medical papers and the incident at the dead end. Really nobody pulled off anything. But what I told is the truth, that's where the truth is. So be it.

Translated by Jason Cieply

Marianna Geide (b. 1980)

Ivan Grigoryev

Ivan Grigoryev, my classmate and a big bastard, shoved my face into the grating of the locker room, so for a few seconds I stared at all the clothes dropped by hasty fellow classmates into the hands of the disgruntled gym workers. There were blue and gray fluffy objects there, and frequently birght-pink and lemon-colored things, and very seldom-hung strong-smelling leather jackets, and on the right a red knitted glove plaintively threw five fingers into the air.

Ivan Grigoryev did not like me because I was a swindler—from his point of view all kikes were swindlers, from his point of view I was a kike, and last, from his point of view, I was a swindler. Ivan Grigoryev looked at me from these three points of view, as a stern three-faced god, and chose how to punish me—whether I should be beaten in the face with an iron grill, or with some book across my weak head, or just to be utterly despised me for my threefold wretchedness. I could not boast of such a striking argument. I just did not like Ivan Grigoryev, but all my memory protested against my dislike and did not want to part with the outlines of Ivan Grigoryev's face, because I wanted to step on it, like a stone staircase carved into a cliff. I still remember that face, in a black-and-white photograph with a chewed-up right bottom edge, for which I nearly strangled my cat and spared it only because Ivan Grigoryev remained undestroyed, hanging over a white velvety abyss, beneath which the absence of an edge began.

Ivan Grigoryev did not consider me a swindler without reason, but through an understanding of the matter: all the cards were like cards, all alike, the same ones, with the failing reflections of long-nosed figures, and mine were all invisibly marked, on which I, with an ease he found distasteful, determined what was beautiful, and what—regarding this person and everything connected with him—had no place in my mind. With his unexpected beating, he educated my memory, so if you woke me up at night and asked who I was and what I wanted, I'd answer: I'm a swindler, I'm a kike, I'd like to step just once on Ivan Grigoryev's face and see whether it is made of stone or just looks that way.

Once I was hungry and I got in the queue at the canteen, which wasn't so long, but it had Ivan Grigoryev in the middle. For some reason, he noticed me and suggested—miraculously—that I come stand near him. The miracle was that he wanted to hit me, but he came up with a way that was not quite ordinary for someone in line for cherry pie. He asked me: so you say there's a God, so explain to me—what does it mean that "God created humans in his image and likeness" if he "created humans, man and woman." Did this mean that Ivan Grigoryev was wondering whether God is both a man and a woman? And when I began to answer this idiotic question, Ivan Grigoryev bought three cherry pies, put one in his mouth and thus, pie in mouth, departed.

I was gripped by despair, because I did not have the strength to hold my enemy back and ask: Who is man? Who is woman? Who are the Jews and why are they swindlers? What does it mean—created? I had to be born anew, and Ivan Grigoryev needed to be born again, so that we could talk and I broke the five-ruble coin in my hand in despair that I couldn't just as easily break his neck—it seemed to me then that the whole line was looking at me, saying: Swindler! Counterfeiter! You stand among us with this crappy little thing in your hands and you think you can get a glass of tea, at least, for it, but Ivan Grigoryev was just here, who got three pies, and could have gotten more. The whole line consisted of men and women, grown a meter or two in height, and each, depending on their size, could either head butt me in the stomach or pour a bowl of hot soup over me. I could not stand it and walked away, I was tired of their breathing, mixed with laurel leaf smell.

My hands, my body, my whole figure was always smothered with dirt. It seemed that dirt had also tattooed onto my skin, because, no matter how much I scrubbed my poor hands over the sink in the school bathroom, they still seemed to be covered in smoke. A pitiful little piece of soap looked like the fatty heart of a small animal, and it was disgusting to take it into my hands. I stood and scrubbed, scrubbed one hand against the other, and did not know what to do with them.

At the age of fifteen, I started smoking for some reason, maybe wanting to make my life a bit harder. I wanted to spit yellow mucus and choke with a constant cough, as if I was being pounded from the inside with an iron pestle. Back then we all coughed, one by one, drowning out the teacher's voice and at different pitches. My cough was like someone was hitting the toe of a boot in an inflated paper bag. Ivan Grigoryev's cough was more impressive, like banging a shoe in a bag full of water. I wanted to see how Ivan Grigoryev, after another coughing fit, would breathe his last breath and dissipate over the carved and cut desktop, and I, in order not to look cold, could also cough, and could also eventually die. I felt more sorry for him than for myself, because my death was marked out with the roughness of a marked card, like everything I tried to touch, and his was totally smooth and smelled like any death, like everything I tried to avoid—so I did not want him to die, for him to die now would mean that the question of how God managed to create a man, a man and a woman, in his own image and likeness would forever remain unanswered. In my bold dreams I answered Ivan Grigoryev: what's more interesting is that God managed to create not a man and a woman, but me and you, Ivan Grigoryev. But he contemptuously told me: "really, you're a swindler and a kike—huh?" and immediately dissolved in my traitorous dreams.

At the age of fifteen, I not only started smoking, but also—how to say this?—I myself dissolved. I have long ceased being tortured—by Ivan Grigoryev because he left school for some more suitable part of the world, by the others because they got used to my agony before I did myself. But the torture continued, and now it carried itself out by that part of my being that was pinned against—was pinned rather than struck against—to the locker room's iron grate, so that I could ignore it, not notice it, completely not notice it, like I don't notice the road signs—and I've already gotten used to this pain, which tore at my right cheek for several years in a row, and I took my pain lightly—even more lightly than drunkenness that could end in a headache, or than insomnia, which also could end at the most inopportune moment. I used to walk around with my eyes closed all day, and strange figures and faces grew out of the numbers in my notebook, and only pain remained in my face, in my childish cheeks, in each finger and even in each ballpoint pen with its leaky, chewed cap. I took things too seriously to let them out of my field of vision, whether they got closer or more distant. I lost interest in any particular thing, whether small or large and transparent, only when I accepted it, understood it in my own way, and let it go. A thing too close to me remained that way, having split my memory into pieces, my conscience—for how many mental murders, mental suicides did I have on my conscience now! If I had at least created as many imaginary characters as I killed, I could compete with "War and Peace" in the size of my cast of characters. Alas, every second I committed a small mortal sin in my head, and my whole life turned into a protracted Judgment Day. Sometimes it seemed to me that I was already dead and watching my own sins from some remote place, which was still occupied by my body. I was not scared. To look at a woman with lust then was easier for me than drinking a glass of water. To drink a glass of wine was easier than to drop asleep after a long, long day. It seemed that all beauty purposely climbed out onto God's light so that I could read it like a blind man with a braille book, here and there, so that I was not so scared in my death.

Along the street passed blue-sided rectangular trolley buses, cut through by lilac bushes. Suddenly their antennae fell from the cable above onto their backs, like dying insects, and then everyone went out into the street and walked on foot to the next stop, and I took the opportunity to walk to complete exhaustion. My incipient bronchitis was not enough for me; I wanted to spit something more significant and less tangible on the ground, something that would shake not only my weak, crooked body, but also the earth. In spring, it's hard to surprise the earth with anything— it's almost entirely covered with the black crust of previous snows and the chocolate smear of canine excrement. Something more had to remain of me, more even than my whole body, which had not grown since then. And something, undoubtedly, uglier than my body—because I was not small enough, I was simply not tall, that is, almost tall but not quite. No one called me swindler or a kike, they already asked me about insignificant things and waited for my answer. They waited persistently, as if they were going to be rewarded with something afterwards. All my classmates were busy, very busy. It always seemed to me that they were paying for my brief exist- ence with their attention, that then, when I would cease to exist and would starts a slow hellish cycle through my lived life, they would be more than compensated for their attention. Even their beauty occasionally stopped worrying me, as if I were handed beautiful objects to hold for a while, and I trembled out of fear of breaking them.

My school seemed to me an enchanted place—I could be there, I could speak and know that it would end. The disappearance of Ivan Grigoryev only reinforced and permeated my conviction. After all, it was only two years earlier that he had left for that part of the world, which would never again cross with mine. He became a hundred times more unreachable for me because now, not only could I not answer his question, he would never be able to ask me that question again. That had now become what is called "childhood"—some golden age in which each of us held a treasure worth a sealed vessel of wine, and only the most reckless were already drunk with it. I was one of those, one of the reckless, who since then no longer need events, no need even bodies in order to live. I have been forced to nourish myself with this forbidden liquid for the rest of my life, which no one could share with me. Submissively, I accepted into my memory a hundred people who were with me, who aged with me, and who had names that were sweet or hateful to my ears. It is useless to try to look away now, pretending that I remember who was this one and who was that. Maybe that could be my answer to Ivan Grigoryev: he, God, remembers equally the faces and names of women and men, and all the old age that will manifest in their faces, all he has to do is breathe on them and wipe them with his sleeve. With only one difference: that instead of love, my memory pulled in hostility and horror, and with equal parts of hostility and horror fixed their elusive features within me. If I possessed any inherent kindness, even to a small extent, then the differences contained in thoughts and memories would cease to be significant for me, and I would cease to know who are women and who are men, and finally, who is Ivan Grigoryev, but it turned out that the blade that cut the space between these differences had sliced too deep and had dismembered my very soul along with my memories. And my soul was disgusted with all destruction, all death, which meant another beauty I did not love. It hurt my soul to associate human faces, human hands with that invisible wall, against which they break, leaving behind a hiero-glyphic mark, perfect and useless. Any object is stronger than a dead body, and I liked to look at such things—glass, marble, iron, silk embroidered or handwritten. In them was an inexorable firmness that erosion could overcome, but they did not fall apart on their own, or from within. Those who remained in my memory, it seemed to me, fell apart on their own and went off, unconnected, freed from any further obligation to live. I imagined that to remember them and to fear their deaths was the only way to some-how maintain their existence, and I most strongly kept in existence those I did not love, who did not love me—as if I was paying some cruel trib-ute for my dislike and for their dislike. Therefore, at the most unexpected moments—when listening to music, when hearing wise and well-formed words addressed to me, I would suddenly recall some Ivan Grigoryev, and I would enthusiastically pounce on his memory, as if I were hungry and hadn't seen a living human being for a month, and only having slaked my memory, I would be surprised to find I remember his name and his face. Then suddenly I'm thrown back many years, and suffer from unflagging pity for this poor, strong, creature of stone, and I want to be strong, I want to crush stone, I want to be born again—all alone, in a completely different place, bigger than my body, greater than my memory, because I'm weak, still weak, still capable of killing. Perhaps what Ivan Grigoryev meant by his "kikes," "swindlers" and other things was just an unrecognized attempt to say: "You are a murderer, a potential murderer, which is even worse." You make beauty from me, my own weak, crooked beauty, which eyes cannot see. You give me no peace—and you will give me no peace for ten years, for this I do not love you. You should have been strangled in the cradle, and your memory divided among the needy." If it's how it was, if that's true, then I don't dare argue with him.

When we finished school, when we drank a fragile, acidic liquid, which made the tongue drunk, but not the head, my classmate said: Ivan fell in love with him—and pointed at me—one could say, at first sight. I was flattered to hear this. I would like, if it were possible, to be loved by stones, trees, the moon, every living and non-living thing. And I knew it was a lie, a pathetic attempt by my classmate to say something paradoxical. Because if it is true that a stone, a tree, an Ivan Grigoryev can be in love, then they must be in love not with me. I am a stone, a tree, the dirt in their path. They go their own way, and I remain motionless in my circular hell. In vain I give up my memories of them for love, being in no condition to devise another path to salvation. Since that very time, as I've said infinite times, since that very time.

Translated by Simon Schuchat

About the Authors

ARKADY BABCHENKO
(b. 1977, Moscow)

Arkady Babchenko is a journalist and prose writer. Since 1995, Babchenko has served in the communication corps in the North Caucasus. He participated in the First Chechen War and later volunteered for six months during the Second Chechen War. After leaving the army in 2000, he worked as a war correspondent for more than a decade. In 2006, his novella "Argun" was published in *Novyi mir*. This story initially appeared in the anthology *War & Peace: Contemporary Russian Prose* (*Glas: New Russian Writing* 40) and later in Babchenko's collection *One Soldier's War* (London: Portobello, 2008; New York: Grove, 2009) in English. Since 2017, he has lived in Kiiv and worked as a journalist for the TV channel ATR. In May 2018, the Ukrainian Security Agency faked Babchenko's assassination in order to expose Moscow's plan to assassinate him.

NIKOLAI BAITOV
(b. 1951, Moscow)

A poet and prose writer, Nikolai Baitov (this is his pen name, derivative of the word *byte*) graduated from the Moscow Institute of Electronic Machines. During Perestroika, he published an almanac of independent literature titled *Epsilon-Salon* (together with Aleksandr Barash), and later organized numerous literary events in Moscow. His prose includes two volumes of short stories and an epistolary novel, *Mura's Love*. In 2011, he received one of the most respected Russian literary prizes—the Andrei Bely Prize—for his prose. The two stories in this volume are taken from his 2014 collection *The Beast Is Breathing* (Novoe Literaturnoe Obozrenie). He lives in Moscow.

POLINA BARSKOVA
(b. 1976, Leningrad)

Polina Barskova began publishing her poetry at the age of nine. Her first collection came out in 1991, and in 2000 she was a finalist for the Debut Prize. In 1998, Barskova moved from her native St. Petersburg to the United States. She graduated from the School of Philology at the Saint Petersburg State University (BA) and the Department of Slavic Languages and Literatures at the University of California, Berkeley (PhD). To date, Barskova has published eleven books of poetry, including three collections in English translation. Her book of prose, *Tableaux vivants* (2014), won the Andrei Bely Prize. Among other works, it includes the text in this volume. Barskova is an associate professor of Russian literature at Hampshire College. She is the author of a study of Leningrad under the siege (1941–1944) entitled *Besieged Leningrad: Aesthetic Responses to Urban Disaster* (2017). She lives in Amherst, Massachusetts.

MARIA BOTEVA
(b. 1980, Kirov)

Maria Boteva graduated from the School of Journalism at the Ural State University, as well as the Ekaterinburg Theatre Institute, where she studied as a playwright in Nikolay Koliada's seminar. She has published six books of poetry and prose. Her first book of short prose, *The Light ABC. Two Sisters, Two Winds*, won the Triumph Prize for young writers (2005); her 2013 book *Ice Cream in Waffle Cones* was shortlisted for the

Andrei Bely Prize. The story in this volume first appeared in *Oktiabr'* in 2009. Boteva lives in Vyatka and works as a journalist.

ELENA DOLGOPIAT
(b. 1963, Murom)

Elena Dolgopiat graduated from the Moscow Institute of Railroad Transport with a degree in applied mathematics. In 1989, she entered, and in 1993 successfully graduated from, the Institute of Cinematography as a screenwriter. Four of her scripts have been produced as films. Since 1994, she has worked at the Moscow Museum of Cinema. She has published her short stories in major literary journals of Russia. She has authored several collections of short stories and novellas. Her short story in this volume was first published by *Novyi mir* in 2005.

MARIANNA GEIDE
(b. 1980, Moscow)

Marianna Geide graduated from the School of Philosophy at the Russian State University for the Humanities in Moscow. She has authored a number of scholarly articles on Thomas Aquinas, as well as three books of poetry and two collections of short prose. Geide's poetry received the 2003 Debut Prize. She is also the laureate of the Triumph Prize for young authors (2005) and the Andrei Bely Prize for her 2010 short story collection. "Ivan Grigoriev" appeared in the magazine *Vestnik novoi literatury* in 2002. Geide lives in Moscow.

LINOR GORALIK
(b. 1975, Dnepropetrovsk, Ukraine, USSR)

Between 1989 and 2000, Linor Goralik lived in Israel. She graduated from Ben Gurion University in Ber Sheva with a degree in computer science. In 2001, she moved to Moscow. Goralik has worked as a columnist for a number of online and print publications, including *Grani, OpenSpace, Russkii zhurnal, Snob, Teoriia mody, Novoe literaturnoe obozrenie, Vedomosti, Voszdukh,* and others. She is also a popular blogger. Goralik works in multiple genres: short prose, poetry, essays, interviews with contemporary Russian poets, fairy tales, and comic books. She has also written two novels: *N.E.T.* (2004, with Sergei Kuznetsov) and *Half of the Sky* (2004, with Stanislav Lvovsky). In 2018, she completed a new novel, *Anyone Able to Breathe the Breathing.* Her collection *Found Life: Poems, Stories, Comics, a Play, and an Interview* was published in English by Columbia University Press as part of their Russian Library series. The stories in this volume are taken from this collection. Currently, Goralik lives in Moscow and Israel.

ALEKSANDR ILICHEVSKY
(b. 1970, Sumgait, Ázerbájdžán, USSR).

Aleksander Ilichevsky is a prose writer and poet. He graduated from the Moscow Institute of Physics and Technology, and he later worked in Israel and the United States. He returned to Moscow in 1998. Ilichevsky has authored three poetry books, eight novels, and six collections of short prose and nonfiction. His novel *Matisse* (2006) won the Russian Booker Prize, and his novel *The Persian* received the Big Book Prize in 2010. "The Sparrow," published in *Novyi mir* in 2005, also won the Yuri Kazakov Prize for the best short story of the year. Since 2014, he has lived in Israel.

MARGARITA KHEMLIN
(b. 1960, Chernigov, Ukraine, USSR)

Margarita Khemlin graduated from the Moscow Literary Institute in 1985. She started publishing in 1991. Khemlin became famous for her short stories and three novels about Ukrainian and Russian Jews. Her books have won nominations for the Big Book Prize and the Russian Booker Prize. Her novel *The Investigator* was translated into English in 2015. The story in this volume appeared first in the Moscow magazine *Znamia* in 2005.

KIRILL KOBRIN
(b. 1964, Gorky)

Kirill Kobrin is a writer, literary and art critic, historian, and journalist. He graduated from Gorky State University in 1986 and later earned his PhD in medieval Welsh history in 1993. In the middle of the 1980s, Kobrin was involved in a local rock scene and co-founded the rock band Cronop and several zines. Between 1986 and 2000, he taught European history at Nizhny Novgorod Pedagogical University. Since 1994, he has contributed to Radio Free Europe/Radio Liberty (Russian Service) as a freelancer; in 2000, Kobrin moved to Prague and started working at the RFE/RL headquarters (in 2009–2012, he was the acting managing editor). Since 2006, he has co-edited the intellectual magazine *Neprikosnovennyi zapas.* Kobrin is the co-founder and co-editor of the online art-literary project *post(non)fiction*. He is the author of more than twenty books in various genres and numerous publications in many Russian and European presses. His prose has been translated into English, Latvian, Ukrainian, German, French, Italian, Turkish, and Chinese. The volume *Best European Fiction* (2013) includes Kobrin's short story "Last Year in Marienbad." His book *Eleven Prague Corpses*, from which we borrowed the story for this collection, was published by Dalkey Archive in 2016. Kirill Kobrin currently lives in Riga and London.

NIKOLAI KONONOV
(b. 1958, Saratov)

A poet, prose writer, critic, and publisher, Nikolai Kononov is the author of two dozen books in different genres. He graduated from the School of Physics at Saratov University in 1980 and from the graduate program of the Department of Philosophy at Leningrad State University. He has previously worked as a math teacher and, later, in the 1990s, as an editor of intellectual presses in St. Petersburg. He has authored four novels, including *Flaneur* (2011), a seminal work of queer literature. His first novel, *Grasshopper's Funeral*, won the Andrei Bely Prize in 2000; his book of poetry *Pilot* won the prize of the Russian Academy of literary criticism (2009). His short story "Evgenia's Genius" appeared in the online literary magazine *TextOnly* in 2000. He lives in St. Petersburg.

LEONID KOSTIUKOV
(b. 1959, Moscow)

A poet, prose writer, and literary critic, Leonid Kostiukov graduated from the School of Mathematics at Moscow State University and later from the Literary Institute. He has worked as a math and literature teacher and as an instructor at the School of Philology at Moscow State University. His prose, poetry, and critical articles have appeared in the major literary journals of Russia. He is the author of two novels and four books of fiction. His short story "Verkhovsky and Son" first appeared in 2000, in the literary magazine *Druzhba narodov*. Kostiukov currently lives in Moscow.

STANISLAV LVOVSKY
(b. 1972, Moscow)

Stanislav Lvovsky graduated from the School of Chemistry at Moscow State University. After obtaining his degree, he moved into advertising and journalism. Lvovsky has published six poetry collections; a collection of short stories, *A Word on Flowers and Dogs* (2003); and a novel, *Half of the Sky* (co-authored with Linor Goralik in 2004). He has also authored a number of translations from English (Vytautas Pliura, Charles Bukowsky, Leonard Cohen, Diane Thiel, and others). The Moscow-based company Theatre.doc staged his play "Sixplays," written together with Linor Goralik. He has received numerous literary honors, including awards from the Moscow Free Verse Festival (1993) and Teneta Internet Literary Contest (1998), as well as the prize for best new poetry of the year in 2003. He was shortlisted twice for the Andrei Bely Prize (2005 and 2009). His poetry has been translated into English, French, Chinese, Italian, Georgian, and other languages. His story "Roaming" first appeared in the collection of fantastic prose *Russkie inorodnye skazki, vol. 1* (2003) compiled by Max Frai. Currently, Lvovsky is completing a doctorate in Russian Studies at Oxford University.

DENIS OSOKIN
(b. 1977, Kazan)

Denis Osokin studied at the Department of Psychology of Warsaw University (1994–96) and graduated from the School of Philology of Kazan University (2002). He has produced a TV documentary about the traditional cultures of the people of the Volga region. He is also the director of the Center of Russian Folklore in Kazan. His first publication, *Angels and Revolution*, received the 2001 Debut Prize. He has published three books of prose. Aleksei Fedorchenko based his three films—*Buntings/Silent Souls* (2010), *Celestial Wives of the Field Mari* (2012), and *Angels and the Revolution* (2014)—on Osokin's prose. Osokin's scripts for Fedorchenko's films received several national and international film awards. His book

Celestial Wives of the Field Mari (2013) won the Andrei Bely Prize. Osokin's short stories in this collection were published in 2005 ("The New Shoes") and 2013 ("Lugo Lagar, or Duck Throat") —both in the journal *Oktiabr'*. He currently lives in Kazan.

PAVEL PEPPERSHTEIN
(b. 1966, Moscow)

An artist and writer, Pavel Peppershtein studied at the Academy of Fine Arts in Prague. He was a founding member of the Medical Hermeneutics Inspection Group. He wrote a psychedelic/ mythopoetic novel, *Mythogenic Love of Casts* (vol. 1, 1999; vol. 2, 2001), with the artist Sergei Anufiev. Peppershtein has authored three books of short stories. "The Tongue" was included in his 2006 collection *War Stories*.

EVGENY SHKLOVSKY
(b. 1954, Moscow)

Evgeny Shklovsky graduated from the School of Philology at Moscow State University and earned his PhD in literary criticism at the same university. He has worked at such publications as *Literaturnaia gazeta* and *Literaturnoe obozrenie*. He has worked as an editor at *Novoe Literaturnoe Obozrenie* since its foundation in 1991. He has been writing prose since the late 1980s, and his works have appeared in the leading literary magazines of Russia. Six collections of Shklovsky's short stories and novellas have come out since 1990. His story "The Street" first appeared in *Novyi mir* in 2001. He currently lives in Moscow.

SERGEI SOLOUKH
(b. 1959, Leninsk-Kuznetsk).

While educated as a mining engineer, Sergei Soloukh has also worked as a researcher, IT specialist, and the manager of a transnational company. Publishing since 1982—and from the 1990s onwards in Russia's major literary journals—he has authored four collections of short stories, six novels, and several books of nonfiction, including a detailed commentary on Jaroslav Hašek's *The Good Soldier Svejk*. Soloukh's work has been shortlisted for every Russian literary award, including three nominations for the prestigious Yuri Kazakov Prize for the best short story of the year. "A Search" was first published in *Novyi mir* in 2006.

VLADIMIR SOROKIN
(b. 1955, Bykovo, Moscow Region)

Born into a professor's family, Vladimir Sorokin graduated from the Moscow Institute of Gas and Oil, but has worked mainly as a graphic designer. In the 1980s, his literary texts, which developed the ideas of Conceptualism, began to be known in nonconformist circles and circulated in *samizdat*. Later they were published abroad, mainly in Germany. His first short-story collections appeared in Russia in 1992 and produced a shock effect. His novel *Four Stout Hearts* (1992) was short-listed for the first Russian Booker Prize in 1992. In the early 2000s, Sorokin and his novel *Blue Lard* were targeted by the pro-government youth group Moving Together, which led a campaign to persecute the author on the grounds of distributing pornography. Since 1999, and ironically following Moving Together's campaign, Sorokin's work has gained broad popularity. Along with several novels, numerous short stories, and plays, Sorokin has written the screenplays for such feature films as *The Kopeck* (dir. Ivan Dykhovichnyi), *4* and *Dau* (dir. Ilya Khrzhanovsky), and *Moscow* and *The Target* (dir. Aleksandr Zeldovich).

In 2006, Sorokin published the novel *Day of the Oprichnik*, in which—in an allusion to the neo-traditionalism of the Putin era—the monarchy and *oprichnina* (the tsar's death squads from the time of Ivan the Terrible) are restored. He has twice received the NOS Prize for New Writing for his novel *Blizzard* (*Metel'*) in 2010 and for *Manaraga* in 2017. His novel *Telluria* (2013) offers a panorama of post-apocalyptic Eurasia divided into fifty microstates, each with its own language and culture. Sorokin is a master of short stories. His first samizdat collection, *The First Subbotnik* (1979–1984), included textual "bombs" (in his own words), exploding conventional discourses. In 2008, he published a collection of short stories titled *Sugar Kremlin* as a sequel to *The Day of the Oprichnik*. A story in this volume first appeared in Sorokin's 2010 collection *Monoclone*. In 2018 a collection of Sorokin's new short stories, *The White Square*, with strong overtones of political critique, appeared. His novels *Queue*, *The Ice Trilogy*, *The Day of the Oprichnik*, and *Blizzard*, as well as several of his stories, have been translated into English. Sorokin currently lives in Moscow and Berlin.

ALEXEY TSVETKOV, JR.
(b. 1975, Nizhnevartovsk)

A prose writer, journalist, and left activist, Alexey Tsvetkov graduated from the Moscow Literary Institute in 1998. He has authored more than twenty books of fiction and nonfiction. His collection of short prose, *The King of the Drowned* (2014), which includes "Price-Art", won two major literary prizes—the NOS (New Russian literature) and Andrei Bely Prizes. Tsvetkov currently lives in Moscow.

LARA VAPNYAR
(b. 1976, Moscow)

Lara Vapnyar spent the first twenty years of her life in Moscow, where she earned a degree in Russian Language and Literature. In 1999, she moved to the United States with her husband. In the United States, Vapnyar began to write stories in English. Her first publication appeared in 2002. In 2011, Vapnyar received a Guggenheim Fellowship. Vapnyar has published three novels and two collections of short stories. Her work has also appeared in *The New Yorker, Harper's Magazine, Open City*, and *Zoetrope: All Story*. "Salad Olivier" first appeared in Vapnyar's collection *Broccoli and Other Tales of Food and Love* (2008). She currently lives in New York.

VALERY VOTRIN
(b. 1974, Tashkent, Uzbekistan, USSR)

Valery Votrin graduated from the Department of Romance and Germanic Languages at the Department of Germanic and Romance Studies at Tashkent State University. In 2000, he moved to Belgium, where he received his MSc in Human Ecology and PhD in Environmental Science from the Free University of Brussels. He has worked as an environmental consultant specializing in environmental due diligence auditing. Votrin has been publishing short stories and novels since 1995. In 2009, his novel *The Last Magog* was shortlisted for the Andrei Bely Prize. Another novel, *The Speech Therapist*, was nominated for a string of literary awards, including the Russian Booker Prize, the Big Book Prize, and the Alexander Piatigorsky Prize. He has translated and published short stories by Flann O'Brien, T. F. Powys, and Eric Stenbock, as well as numerous poems by English and Scottish poets from the seventeenth to twentieth centuries. "Alkonost" first appeared in his collection of short stories *Zhalitvoslov* (2007). Currently, Votrin lives in Bath (UK).

Translators

Nick Allen is a British journalist who lived in Russia, where he covered the conflict in Chechnya and worked for *The Moscow Times*. He has also worked for *The Daily Telegraph* and the German Press Agency (DPA). He went on to work for DPA in Pakistan and Afghanistan, where he completed a two-year book project on the conflict there. He has translated for the literary journal *Glas: New Russian Writing*. He is also the translator of Arkady Babchenko's book *One Soldier's War* (London: Portobello, 2008; New York: Grove, 2009).

Catherine Ciepiela is the Howard M. and Martha P. Mitchell Professor of Russian at Amherst College. She is a scholar and translator of Russian. Ciepiela is the author of *The Same Solitude* (Cornell 2006), a study of Marina Tsvetaeva's epistolary romance with Boris Pasternak; co-editor, with Honor Moore, of *The Stray Dog Cabaret* (NYRB 2007), an anthology of poems by the Russian modernists in Paul Schmidt's translations; and editor of *Relocations: Three Contemporary Russian Women Poets* (Zephyr 2013). She is currently translating a book of Polina Barskova's poetic prose, from which we took the piece for this collection.

Jason Cieply is a scholar of early Soviet and contemporary Russian culture and an occasional translator of Russian literature, literary criticism, and philosophy. He is an Assistant Professor of Russian at Hamilton College. Cieply has published on Dostoevsky, Bakhtin, and silence in the polyphonic novel and is currently at work on a monograph on revolutionary affect and interclass imitation in narrative fiction from the early Soviet years.

Bradley Gorski is Assistant Professor of Russian and East European Studies at Vanderbilt University, where he teaches Russian literature and culture of the twentieth and twenty-first centuries. He has published on contemporary Russian literature, subcultures in the postwar Soviet Union, and medieval festivals in today's Russia. He is currently working on a monograph on the post-Soviet literary field and its encounter with capitalist markets.

Sofya Khagi is Associate Professor of Russian Literature at the Department of Slavic Languages and Literatures at the University of Michigan. Her first book, *Silence and the Rest: Verbal Skepticism in Russian Poetry*, has been published by Northwestern University Press (2013). Her other publications include articles on nineteenth- and twentieth-century Russian poetry (Tyutchev, Baratynsky, Brodsky, Kibirov), post-Soviet literature (Victor Pelevin, Dmitry Bykov, Alexander Ilichevsky, Garros-Evdokimov), science fiction and film, and Baltic literatures and cultures. She is currently finishing a manuscript on Victor Pelevin, entitled *Terabytes of Unfreedom: Victor Pelevin's Poetics, Politics, Metaphysics*.

Veronika Lakotová is a translator (of English, Russian, and Slovak) who is currently living in Bratislava, Slovakia.

Simon Schuchat is a retired American diplomat with over twenty-five years of experience, including service in Moscow, Beijing, and Tokyo. Originally trained as a Sinologist, he did graduate work at Yale and Harvard, as well as the National Defense University. His translations of Chinese and Russian prose and poetry have appeared in various anthologies and magazines. His own poetry has been published in four collections. His translations of Moscow conceptualist poet Dmitri Prigov will appear in 2019 from Ugly Duckling Presse.

Margarita Vaysman is Assistant Professor of Russian Studies at the University of St Andrews. Originally from Russia, she has her undergraduate and *kandidat filologicheskikh nauk* degrees from Perm State University, as well as her MPhil and PhD from Oxford University. Her research focuses on nineteenth-century Russian literature, intellectual history, narratology, and gender studies. Over the years, she has written on a variety of topics, from *sots-art* and Russian Gothic to digital humanities and fictionalized biographies. Her first monograph *Self-Consciousness and The Novel: Nineteenth-Century Russian Metafiction* is forthcoming with Legenda.

Maya Vinokour is Assistant Professor in the Department of Russian and Slavic Studies at New York University. She is the co-translator and co-editor (with Ainsley Morse and Maria Vassileva) of Linor Goralik's *Found Life: Poems, Stories, Comics, a Play, and an Interview* (Columbia University Press, 2017). Her translations have also appeared in *The New Yorker*, *Columbia Journal*, *Fence*, and *Inventory*.

CPSIA information can be obtained
at www.ICGtesting.com
Printed in the USA
BVHW041045080120
568938BV00016B/816/P

9 781644 690550